MARC E. FITCH

DEAD ENDS

This is a **FLAME TREE PRESS** book

Text copyright © 2023 Marc E. Fitch

FLAME TREE PRESS
6 Melbray Mews, London, SW6 3NS, UK
flametreepress.com

US sales, distribution and warehouse:
Simon & Schuster
simonandschuster.biz

UK distribution and warehouse:
Hachette UK Distribution
hukdcustomerservice@hachette.co.uk

Publisher's Note: This is a work of fiction. Names, characters, places, and incidents are a product of the author's imagination. Locales and public names are sometimes used for atmospheric purposes. Any resemblance to actual people, living or dead, or to businesses, companies, events, institutions, or locales is completely coincidental.

Thanks to the Flame Tree Press team.
The cover is created by Flame Tree Studio and with thanks to Shutterstock.com. The font families used are Avenir and Bembo.

Flame Tree Press is an imprint of Flame Tree Publishing Ltd
flametreepublishing.com

A copy of the CIP data for this book is available from the British Library and the Library of Congress.

1 3 5 7 9 8 6 4 2

PB ISBN: 978-1-78758-848-6
ebook ISBN: 978-1-78758-850-9

Printed and bound in Great Britain by Clays Ltd, Elcograf S.p.A.

MARC E. FITCH

DEAD ENDS

FLAME TREE PRESS
London & New York

'Is it just me, or is it getting crazier out there?'
Joker, 2019

'The way I see it, the world is divided into the watchers and the watchees, and there's more and more of the audience and less and less to see. People who actually do anything are a goddamned endangered species.'
We Need to Talk About Kevin, 2003

PROLOGUE

Lucas had watched the house across the street since he was a boy and now, when he was sixteen, it spoke to him. It was a strange language. It came from the dark windows and the hollow inside, from the grass that grew tall like a prairie, stalks rubbing together in the warm summer breeze that moved through his small neighborhood. The house was an outcast, just like him. It was despised by the neighbors, just like him. It was owned by insanity, just like him.

He found his way, finally, inside and walked through the rooms that rotted with mold and mildew, where old things, forgotten things, were left piled high, scattered without thought or consideration, abandoned to history. In the garage was a car, rust red, its gasoline long since evaporated, its oil now sludge. The carpet was worn, pea green faded in old footsteps. The smell overwhelmed him. A sofa, a broken table, chairs overturned or left to dust. He moved through the house and saw himself in the patina of an ancient mirror. He saw through himself to something else. He was both possessed and possessor, pale and tall and lanky.

The house was haunted and he searched for the ghost.

His parents hated the house. They spoke about it in whispers sometimes, as if it held some shameful secret. Everyone wanted the house either sold or torn down, but still it sat, quiet, empty and sagging under the weight of whatever secret his parents feared.

They hated him in much the same way. They did not hate him in the way most people hate, with anger and malice. They hated him the way people hate time. He withered them, left their eyes encircled with dark, their faces with deep lines, their bodies shriveling, their hearts filled with fear of what he would do next. They did not understand him. No one did, because they could not hear the voices that spoke to him. They did not see the world as it really was, so they labored in fear.

He had watched the house for so long, fascinated with it. He would sometimes leave his yard, walk across the street, and climb the tree that arched out over the house. He would sit on the roof in the evening sun and the neighbors would pass by and see him on their way home from their jobs. All these plumbers, teachers, nurses and dental hygienists. People who wore name tags to work because they didn't know who they were. They would see him sitting like a statue in the setting sun atop the roof of this abandoned house they all feared and hated. He watched their heads turn in horror as they drove by.

His parents, growing more faded and see-through each day, told him to stay away from the house. They pleaded with him to behave the right way, to stop talking to the voices. The therapist told him to speak of feelings. The doctors gave him pills to swallow. The teachers and principal monitored his every action, every word, because they lived in fear of him. In this way he was a god.

The bus driver logged when the god set foot onto the bus for school and when he stepped off. They all took copious notes: the god seemed pleased today; the god was angry; the god would not respond to any questions; the god displayed a 'detached affect'.

The god was quiet, biding his time.

They gave him things to please him, things to do, and he accepted or rejected their offerings. The police would occasionally speak to him and also take copious notes. The neighbors all whispered and tried to keep their children away.

His parents pleaded with him. His father raged at times, his mother cried, but it did not touch him. Rage was inconsequential, tears incomprehensible. It made no sense and did not matter.

He would ride his bike through the small, insular neighborhood shaped like a cancerous liver, tracing its line of pavement from the main road where cars sped to unknown places, up Woodland Drive, dip down fast till the end and then turn left onto Beechwood where it split with Oakwood, and then circle back toward his house on Ridgewood Drive.

The streets all had leafy names. Ridgewood Drive was a dead end with a cul-de-sac.

The neighborhood was filled with trees, surrounded by woods that bled into backyards. He would walk through the woods and stare at the backs of houses. He would smoke marijuana and drink liquor from his father's cabinet and watch them all. Sometimes he would see their lives, like watching ants move to the rhythm of the queen. At night, when the lights were on inside like yellow eyes, he watched them go about cooking and cleaning, their televisions flashing bright colors and shadows, and he thought how easily they could be crushed. He thought of how small they were in these tiny boxes. Those boxes were rotting away, and they strived to keep those boxes upright, to keep the grass from growing high, to keep their offspring in their school buses and keep their little lives spinning like wheels on driverless cars.

He saw all of this and heard the whispers and turned to look upon the house, with its strange, oversized chimney tower and dark windows of nothingness, and he wanted to see inside.

Now he walked its bowels. The broken glass of a rear window lay in shards on the floor. From the outside, the house was small. None of the houses in the neighborhood were big, just small houses made for small people trying to hide in obscurity. But now that he was inside, it seemed vast. The wallpaper peeled away in strips. Its dull colored stripes seemed to blend, move, shift and open up to new space. There were symbols and markings painted on the walls. Some things he recognized from school books, others he couldn't place but somehow seemed familiar. And there were eyes. Eyes everywhere. He looked deep into them and they looked back through him. The walls watched him, the low ceilings giving way to a labyrinth, space not measured in length or width, but by time and intent. Picture frames hung crooked from walls, the faces in them etched back through time, through lives. He felt it all converging. There was a boy in a picture, shaggy and lanky and pale like him, and he wondered if this was always his home, some past life come to be. *This is me.*

Cabinet doors were open. Scraps of old life: old plastic containers, scraps of cardboard cereal boxes that had faded into nothingness, cans, expired. There was no water, no electricity, no heat. The toilet water was stained black, the air infused with particles and spoors. The mattress in the bedroom was mildewed. He lay on it for a time and stared at the ceiling fan above with its blades like the petals of a flower. It grew dark outside and he slept. In his dreams he did not exist and he moved into people and through them.

He woke in the morning with summer light pouring through window blinds. He did not know where he was at first. He sat up on the bed and remembered the house spoke to him in a dream. It called to him for relief. He felt the weight of the world on this place and it longed to die. He walked to the windows and peered out. The neighborhood was quiet and still in the morning heat. He looked at his old house and it was silent and steady. He had been gone all night but no one searched for him because he was without mooring. His parents' cars were not in the driveway. The mouth of the mailbox left gaping. The garage door closed. The basketball hoop stood straight and stark.

He relieved himself in the cesspool of toilet water. A big black fly buzzed in the bathroom, large as a hummingbird. He shut the door and waited for it. It flew and buzzed and bounced off walls with audible knocks. He took a small roach from his pocket, lit the tip, and inhaled and watched the fly. It bounced on the tile and he crushed it underfoot. *That is how you kill it.*

The house was frustrated and exhausted. It buckled under the weight of its history. He heard its voice like the buzzing of a big black fly. His head swam with it. He stepped out of life and looked in on it from afar. *We are all trapped in boxes.*

In a small, cramped anteroom at the back of the house were stacks of thick, heavy cans of paint, paint thinner and kerosene. The walls were half-painted and the paint was old and chipped. The ceiling sagged from water damage. In the corner were old gasoline containers. The floor here was rotted wood and it creaked and groaned and the voice spoke to him. He sat cross-legged among the ruins. Chemicals suffused the air, and he lit the last of his joint. The air was stifling in here. He heard voices of neighbors, distant. He heard their comings and goings. He flicked the flame of his lighter into existence and then out again.

Then the ghost appeared to him in that room and looked upon him and he upon it. It stared at him with hollow eyes and gaping mouth, but it had no form. It was a big, dark stain, a history that had been wiped through with a bare hand. It was full of rage but he was not frightened. It spoke to him.

There, in that place, something burst like a flame into existence. Something that could move through walls and houses and neighborhoods and cities. It rose from chemical wasteland, like a phoenix. It sparkled and shimmered and danced and breathed until it could breathe no more. Then it grew in strength and breached the walls and windows and danced on the roof where he had sat like a statue for the gaping onlookers. Lucas was one with it, and he walked out the front door and into the world. He did not return home but rather walked down the road in an everyday, boring neighborhood, surrounded by trees and bleak of future. Nothing but a young man walking down the street. There was nothing extraordinary about it.

CHAPTER ONE

John Ballard did his penance. Four tons of gravel were delivered and piled onto the driveway Saturday afternoon, and now John had shoveled and moved half of it to the backyard where he had dug out the grass, dirt and stones and leveled an area for a patio. He piled the stones he dug from the ground to form a small, unsteady wall where he had dug into the slope of the backyard. Now he plunged his shovel into the gravel, loaded it into a wheelbarrow with a flat tire and pushed it around the house to fill in the patio base. Beside the patio clearing were stacks of slate which he would fit into place in the gravel like puzzle pieces. His wife, Jessica, had wanted the patio since the house was built five years ago. As a family, John, Jessica, their daughter Caitlin and son James had marveled at the new life they would have in a brand-new house after years of striving and living with Jessica's parents in an in-law attachment while they saved for the down payment.

Like anything, the promise was not what it seemed. The builder had skirted town zoning rules that declared the property wetlands by building a wall of massive rocks that encircled the lowest part of the backyard and separated it from the woods and marshland. But during heavy rains, it flooded and the water would creep back up into the basement with a worm-like trickle that seeped beneath the basement door. It was never more than a quick mop could solve, but it was there and it bothered him. Water in a house was never a good thing, and the house was brand new so everything should be perfect. That slight trickle of water, only during the heaviest summer rains, wriggled in John's mind, distracted him at times, frightened him at others.

Jessica's solution had been to build a patio. The idea was kicked around between them for two years and, like most home improvement ideas, perpetually put off. There wasn't the time or the money, or it was winter and the ground was too hard, or it was spring and the ground was too muddy. Most times, it was that he'd just spent fifty hours that week laying asphalt on some highway or local road, standing in the sun or rain, feeling the cars shake the wind as they passed him and his crew while they filled potholes or repaired storm drains, and the last thing he wanted to do on the weekend was put another shovel in his hands, no matter how much that occasional trickle of water occupied his thoughts. Frankly, he didn't see a patio as a solution. The water would still be there. But now, he had little choice in the matter.

Three days after he'd been arrested for his second DUI – after the arguments, the looks on Jessica's face, the disappointment, the estimation of attorney's fees, sleeping on the couch, the repeated promises to quit drinking for good – he woke one morning and found Jessica in the backyard with a shovel, digging up the grass beside the big rock wall.

He walked onto the back porch and looked down at her trying to work the shovel around God knows how many rocks and said, "What are you doing?"

She stopped and looked up at him, eyes squinting in the morning light. "I'm building a patio."

He said nothing for a moment, simply rested his big forearms on the wood banister and felt the dawning heat of summer.

"I'm going to dig this all out, get a couple tons of gravel and slate stone and make a patio with a fire pit," she said. "I looked up how to do it online and I'm doing it."

"How big?" he said.

She traced a kidney-like outline with her finger that stretched from one end of the big rock barrier to the other.

"That will take four tons of gravel," he said. "A couple hundred dollars' worth of slate."

"I saved money for it," she said.

"Since when?"

"It's my money," she said. "It's my patio."

The lingering DUI meant he could only drive to work and back. That left Jessica with hauling the kids around, doing all the grocery shopping, driving the family anywhere they needed to go when she wasn't at the hospital, working as a nurse on the psychiatric floor, a brutal job that saw her insulted and occasionally assaulted and often leaving John with the desire to track down a couple of the patients and beat them to death. He felt bad in that moment. She shouldered heavy burdens and now shouldered the burden of his latest fuckup.

"I'll grab a shovel," he said.

After that, the project was his labor, his penance.

It was a Sunday going on eleven in the morning and already hot. He had his gloves and work boots on. He could shovel and dig all day if he had to. Most of his life, it seemed, was spent with shovel in hand, digging. It was something he was good at, and that bothered him as well. It required no thought or intelligence, it was not recognized or rewarded; no one would hear that he had spent the day digging out a ditch and marvel at his existence or abilities. He was just a strong back, dirty hands and sweat. His thoughts on any matter were to be discarded easily, shoveled aside. He told himself it was good work, honest work with honest pay. But that was what men told themselves when they knew their bodies were nothing but machinery and their brains were going to mush.

At his twenty-year high school reunion, John tried to gloss over the details of his life. He lived only forty-five minutes away from his hometown. He had never lit out for other states, other countries. When an old classmate would ask, "Where do you live now?" he felt embarrassed that he was thirty-eight years old and had never left the state. When they asked what he did for work, he mumbled quietly that he worked for the municipal Public Works Department, filling potholes, placing traffic cones, and inhaling hot asphalt. Dominic, always a goofy kid in high school, had earned so much as a chemical engineer for some biopharmaceutical company that he'd spent the last two years simply traveling the world. Keith, at one time the ratty high school quarterback with a love of LSD, was now a vice president at Goldman Sachs and had more money than he knew what to do with. "I thought he would be lying in a ditch somewhere stoned out of his mind by now," John had whispered to Jessica. She looked at him and saw it and said, "You have nothing to be ashamed of." But, at that moment, he knew the truth – that he had quickly become an anonymous nobody, someone not to be remembered, regarded or respected. It had gnawed at him for years like that small trickle of water beneath the basement door. No one marveled at the plight of the ditchdigger. His life was to be tossed into the trash bin of a small, personal history, and now Jessica even looked upon him as pathetic.

And that weighed on him more than four tons of gravel ever could. That night he spent in a jail cell at the state troopers' barracks two towns over was the final burial.

He pushed the wheelbarrow loaded with a million small stones around the side of the house and pulled back on it when he reached the small slope to the patio area. Jessica stood in the dirt, raking it flat, putting down canvas to keep the weeds from growing through. She looked bright and brilliant in the sunlight, triumphant and strong. She looked at him as he dumped the gravel into the pit and smiled as if she were smiling at a stranger on the street and then looked back down at her work. He watched her a moment. The night he was arrested, after she picked him up and drove him home from the police barracks at three in the morning, his truck towed to some impound lot somewhere, she had whispered, "When is this going to end?" more to herself than to him. But he was there and he heard it and now it was a massive rock wall between them and everything was gathering, flooding up before it. His daughter was ten years old, his son eight, and they played on the rock wall, jumped from boulder to boulder, their images cast bright against the darkness of the trees beyond.

Then there was a sound, vaguely familiar, like heavy machinery grinding to life – screeching gears and burning diesel fuel – and of glass breaking. He heard it and thought it was Anthony powering up his mini-backhoe. Anthony and Rachel Carter lived the next house over, separated by a small wooded area like every other home in the neighborhood. Each house its own small kingdom, a property separated by trees so they were isolated and private. He never could have lived in one of those sprawling, suburban enclaves where every house was the same and every yard bled into the other. Here, at least, there was privacy enforced by foliage. Anthony was a nurse and Rachel a school teacher and yet, somehow, they had amassed one of the nicest houses on the street and a variety of toys to go along with it – a boat, ATVs for both themselves and their two kids, three cars and a mini-backhoe that Anthony used to constantly rework the yard. They were almost too nice and neighborly, great parents and friends with everyone on the block, and John, although a much bigger man than Anthony, always felt small, incompetent and a failure beside him. Yet another reminder of all he wasn't.

The sound seemed to wane for a moment and then roar back to life, louder and more intense, and now it didn't sound like a diesel engine; John couldn't hear the strokes of the pistons and there was a metallic grinding and twisting. He looked at the neighbors' house and saw no movement, no sign of Anthony rolling around the yard in his backhoe. The sound grew more intense and glass shattered. Jessica heard it, too, and stared at him with a questioning look on her face. John left the wheelbarrow and walked to the front of the house where he could see down the street. As he turned the corner there was another burst of shattering glass and he saw orange flames and smoke pouring out the side window of the abandoned house two doors down. The old, forgotten Widner house – the conversation topic of many neighborhood gatherings, where everyone said its existence lowered their collective home values – creaked and groaned and twisted as fire curled onto the roof.

John yelled to Jessica to call 911 and then ran toward the fire. He didn't know why he ran toward it, but he had seen Lucas, the crazy neighbor kid who was a constant source of trouble, sitting atop the roof some evenings. Jessica ran around the side of the house with a phone in her hand talking to the dispatcher. John ran up Ridgewood past the Carters' home toward Leadmine Brook and stopped in front of the abandoned house. The fire was coming from a side room. It was loud and intense. Already the tall grass was wilting from the heat and John worried it might melt the siding of Anthony and Rachel's house, but there was nothing he could do. And he realized that in the moment, he was completely helpless. He could only stand and stare and watch as it burned and raged. 'Rage' seemed the most appropriate word, he thought. He'd never seen a fire like this, it was so all-consuming, as if it would burn down the whole world. He stood in the street, his stained and sweaty hat in his hand, and didn't know what to do. He turned and looked back at Jessica as she too stared into the flames.

Jessica was on the phone with the police. "I don't know the number of the house, it's just on Ridgewood Drive and it's the one on fire, I'm sure you'll see it."

Why had he run down here to stand helpless in front of a burning, abandoned house?

John thought for a moment, felt the heavy heat radiating outward, wobbling the air. It seemed to push against him. He ran to the Carters' front door to alert them, to get them out of their home in case the fire spread. He heard a voice beneath the roar. "They're on vacation, they're not home." Jessica was pointing toward her phone. "I already texted Rachel." He walked back to the street and watched. His son and daughter walked the street toward him and he waved them back. To Jessica he said, "Keep them back, we don't know what this thing is gonna do!" Jessica rolled her eyes and corralled the children with one hand, phone in the other.

John turned to look up and down the empty, quiet street. Slowly, others converged toward the fire as if entranced, the low, lumbering dead standing at the edges of their lawns to look upon it.

He could see the woman who lived in the corner house with the mahogany wood garage, the state representative whose name he could never remember but annoyed him all the same. She copied the look of that famous senator from Massachusetts, right down to the sandy-blonde hair cut short that women over fifty always thought looked smart but really just looked severe. Even on a Saturday morning she wore a pantsuit, as if it were a campaign appearance. She stood at the edge of her property, arms crossed, glasses glinting in the sun.

He saw Vernon Trimble, who still lived with his ailing mother just around the corner on Beechwood, walking softly and slowly toward him. Vernon didn't do shit, hadn't worked in years, holed up in that old house with peeling paint and a yard that needed serious care. Nothing happened in the neighborhood that didn't get his attention. It was almost like clockwork that he should appear, walking his delicate and chubby features down the street to relieve himself of an eternal boredom.

A maroon minivan turned from Leadmine onto Ridgewood and slowed as it passed the politician without stopping – no one had time for the Hillary wannabe – and then stopped when it came beside him. The window rolled down. Inside was Amber Locke, the pretty woman from three doors up with her two sons – one a foul-mouthed juvenile delinquent who palled around with Lucas Lovett, the other a sweet boy just into first grade that John's own son played with at times. "I hope the whole damn thing burns down," Amber said to him. "Nothing but a blight on our street."

The whole side of the Widner house was engulfed in flame and the four of them looked upon it as one would a backyard bonfire. There was another shattering screech of wood splitting and metal twisting and a fireball burst through the living room window, billowing smoke into the blue sky. The smoke rose. It swirled in the air and seemed, for a moment, to resemble a great winged creature, a phoenix or a dragon, or perhaps something more satanic. The smoke curled around into circles like two eyes, the fire took form and stared down at them for a moment and they back at it and then, just as quickly, dispersed into the air, nothing more than a black stain over their quiet, wooded place.

John could hear the sirens in the distance. They echoed over the valley, lonely in the deep sky, and reminding him of something long forgotten.

★   ★   ★

It was an event. It was something. Fire trucks filled with small-town volunteers of overweight middle-aged men and gawky high school kids who liked to wear fluorescents and mount sirens purchased from Best Buy in their late-model Pontiacs swarmed the street and the front lawn of the old Widner house. They hauled fire hoses over their shoulders like snake skins, they wore ill-fitting fire helmets and set up a small tent for shade over a folding table with bottles of water. An ambulance arrived; the resident state trooper called for backup. It was a great day for them all, perhaps the greatest day. An actual structure fire. Not the usual car accident where the fire engine merely blocks traffic while the paramedics get all the glory and police reconstruct the scene. They had trained for this, they loved this, they had all traveled into the city to help with actual, real fires but had always arrived too late, the real work left to the professional firehouses, and they, the lowly volunteers from a town of five thousand, relegated to directing street traffic or fetching water. Now, they were the first on the scene. This was their town; this was their fire and there was an overall sense of joviality in the extinguishing. The fire engine pumped water from its tank. They sprayed the house and yelled jokes and nicknames to each other over the burning and the spraying and the smoking and the sizzling of embers. The sun was hot. The fat men sweated.

The whole neighborhood seemed to be there, drawn out by the sudden and previously unknown presence of lights, sirens, authority in action. Paul Vecchio, the plumber from Beechwood Drive who collected classic cars, was there, seemingly always joined at the hip with Tom Fagan, who lived across the street from him. Every time John drove down Beechwood in the evening, the two of them and their wives would be seated in camping chairs, drinking beers in Tom's driveway. The bitch from 24 who complained when Caitlin and James rode their bikes onto her driveway made a brief, spinster-like appearance only to retreat back inside and watch from the window. Becky and Dale Atkins drove down from the cul-de-sac in their signature golf cart, always stocked with a cooler of beer and wine, and parked in front of John's house. Dale's prosthetic leg hung straight from the golf cart, his boisterous voice heard for miles; Becky's laugh like a woman who had grown up in seedy bars. Jim and Julie Katz joined them at their golf cart. They were all friends. They talked of moving to Maine together. Julie kept an irrigated garden. Jim would sit in his outdoor hot tub at night playing music from the eighties. The pretty, single mother with two young boys James played with made an appearance, another name he could never recall. Mark and Maryanne Keller from across the street stood at the end of their driveway. Mark, normally clad in hunting fatigues and loading or unloading rifles and tree stands from his pickup on the weekends, stood with his arms crossed. Maryanne, a bundle of nerves who talked rapidly with wide eyes even on normal days, turned in circles. John raised his hand slightly and nodded. Mark did the same. Even Nancy from next door rolled out to the end of her driveway with her walker, dragging an oxygen tank behind her, to assess the commotion. All the kids on the block came to watch on bicycles.

John knew them, but didn't know them. He knew their faces and some of their names. He had lived here five years. They were all strangers, yet somehow deeply entwined, brought together by the intimacy of this forgotten, mangled loop of pavement.

They gathered on John's front lawn. They gathered around the Atkinses' golf cart. They set up camping chairs in a circle to discuss and watch the fire. The tribal elders come to read the tea leaves in the subtle pouring of alcohol. This was the way of things.

"The town tried to force him to sell. He wouldn't. He hasn't set foot in that house for sixteen years."

"I hope they have to demolish. Maybe then he'll sell the property."

"He lives a few towns over. Smokes pot constantly. He once told me he set booby traps all over the yard to keep people off."

"Bullshit."

"Naturally. What do you expect from a weirdo?"

"I was inside once. Filled with old paint cans, paint thinner, kerosene. No wonder the place went up so quick."

"There are forensic techniques to determine the cause of the fire."

"There was no electricity to the place."

"Could have been anything."

"They can determine if there was an accelerant used, what kind, where it started. Fascinating really."

"Maybe you should have been a detective, Vern."

"There's a 1969 Jaguar in the garage. Maroon colored. Been sitting there since the eighties. I offered to buy it from him but he never got back to me. Damn shame. That car is gone."

"I used to tell the kids it was haunted. They believed it."

"You ever see that Lucas kid sitting on the roof?"

"He's trouble. Bet the cops will be hunting him down right-quick about this."

"You see him anywhere today?"

"Nope. Haven't seen his parents either."

"I had him in my ninth grade class. Scary kid. Very troubled."

"Damn shame about that car. All that shit in the garage probably burned hot as hell itself."

"You got one of those beers for me?"

"Nothing like a neighborhood fire to get everyone together."

"Booby traps. That guy is fucking nuts."

"Now he won't be able to sell the place for shit. Should have taken the offers when they came."

"You know how many blight complaints I've made to the town about that place?"

"How many?"

"I can't remember. A lot. Here, have another drink."

"You don't think that kid was in there, do you?"

"God only knows. Let's not talk about that."

"Someone better find his parents and figure out where he is."

"The cops already knocked on their door. No answer."

"The cops know him well enough, that's for sure. A blight on this neighborhood. Lowers property values."

"The kid or the Widner house?"

"Both."

The politician walked close to the encampment in John's yard, tenderly holding her arms, dressed immaculately, listening to the talk. Why couldn't he remember her name? It was posted on lawn signs all over town. It was on the tip of his tongue. She looked at them and turned away again.

"Think she'll win it again this time?"

"Not from this neighborhood."

"Signs everywhere in the city: Elect Elizabeth Tutt."

"Yeah, you don't see any of her signs around here, now do ya? She's got a challenger, for sure. I think we'll be seeing more of him soon. Wonder what the Almighty thinks of this."

"It's a judgment."

"Damn right."

Amber Locke walked down the street with her oldest son and approached a state trooper. The trooper took notes. They all watched. Her son talked with the officer. Amber pointed at John.

"That kid is always out there with Lucas."

"That kid is trouble, too."

"You hear he called the cops on Amber and Joe because she took away his cell phone?"

"Shut up."

"It's true. The cops showed up and gave him a talking to. Put the fear of God in him."

"Maybe not."

"Fucking kids these days. Technology is messing with their brains."

"Societal breakdown."

"Pass me another. Thank you."

Eventually, the trooper came to John with a notepad. John recognized him. It came slowly, as if remembering a dream; the knock on his driver's-side window, the shining of a flashlight, the orders to walk a straight line in the dead of night. Officer Brett Badgely – his actual, shit-you-not name. Almost a joke. For some reason he remembered Badgely's elbows. Really, all of Badgely's joints held a vivid place in John's memory of that night. He was thin, somewhat gaunt, but his joints seemed like those of a larger man, as if the bones were trying to break free of his skin. The trooper was almost as tall as John but lacked the forty pounds of workman bulk that hid his elbows and knees.

"You called in the fire?"

"My wife called it in. I just saw it first."

"Come with me so I can take your statement."

John saw the eyes of the neighborhood on him as he walked with Trooper First Class Badgely. He had run toward the fire. He had alerted authorities. He welcomed them to all sit in his yard and drink beer and wax poetic. His statement would matter in the investigation. He was younger and stronger than them all. He was a neighborhood hero.

The abandoned house was smoldering, skeletal, its bones black and open to the world, a husk of what once was. The firefighters soaked the ruins, kicked through the embers, pawed at the leftovers.

Badgely opened the passenger-side door of his cruiser. Deep leather seats, computers, guns, gizmos. "Here, you can sit in the front seat this time."

John thought of smashing Badgely's head against the driver's-side window. It would be so easy to do. His big, calloused hand on the side of Badgely's bony head and then putting it through the window. "I'm good with names and faces. Comes with the territory. Staying out of trouble?"

"Making it up to the wife by building a patio in the backyard."

"You have a permit for that?"

"C'mon."

"Fine. Why don't you tell me what happened?"

"I heard a noise that sounded like heavy machinery. It was loud. I heard glass break. I came around the house and saw fire shooting out of the windows on the side there and catching onto the roof."

"Did you see anyone around?"

"No one."

"Did you hear anything beforehand? Anything unusual?"

"No. Nothing."

"Then what did you do?"

"I told my wife to call 911 and I ran over here."

"Why did you run to it?"

"Well, occasionally the neighbor kid over there will sit on the roof and I was worried he was inside. Plus, I was worried it might spread to the next house."

"Did you go inside?"

"No."

"Why would you think he'd be in there?"

"He's always hanging around the place. Just occurred to me is all."

"But you didn't see anyone in the vicinity? Hear anyone?"

"You already asked me that."

"I'm asking again."

"No. Totally quiet until the fire."

John shut the door to the police cruiser and walked home. The volunteer firefighters were all smiles now, laughter, drinking bottled water under a small tent. Someone brought out sandwiches for them and they ate. A woman – couldn't be more than twenty-four – stood in the street talking with Elizabeth Tutt, a digital recorder in her hand, her beautiful face nodding slightly as Elizabeth spoke, her free arm tucked under the other, auburn hair brushed slightly to the side. John slowed to listen. Elizabeth was recounting her experience of the great fire and the young reporter listened intently. He waited until the cursory nod from Representative Tutt and the reporter walked away.

"What newspaper are you with?" he said.

She glanced up, a slight look of annoyance in her eye, as if he were interrupting an important phone call.

"I'm Meredith Skye with the *Register-Citizen*," she said. "Do you live here?"

"Right there," John said and pointed. "I'm a subscriber. Get the paper every day. I called in the fire. Do you want to interview me?"

"Oh, uh. Sure. That would be great."

She was so bright and pretty. John told her his story. She asked one question and then fumbled with her bag to put the recorder away. She asked for directions to get out of the neighborhood. He told her to take a right and then another right and then possibly a third right, depending on where she wanted to go. "Wouldn't that be a full circle?" she said. "Not around here," he said. She turned to leave in her car and John walked back to his yard. The tribal circle had grown. Everyone was having a fine time. It was nearly three in the afternoon and hotter now than it was at midday.

He sat down on a camping chair and someone offered him a beer. It had been over a month since his arrest and his promise to stop drinking. But this was different. There had been an event. He had stepped up. He wanted to see his name in the newspaper. He would cut out the article and save it. He opened a twist-top. The tribe welcomed him with open arms. Jessica glared at him from the driveway. She wouldn't understand. She never understood. The patio could wait.

It was always the same anyway. A never-ending loop. Work, kids, house, lawns, patios, bills, debt, neighbors, newspapers, internet. It was all too much and yet not nearly enough. There had been a fire. It was new and different. Even though it was over, it still burned somewhere, somehow. Maybe it burned beneath the grass, catching and spreading underground until it would reach up for them all. Maybe they sat atop a growing Hell. There were remnants of smoke in the sky, the smell of burned wood and paint in the air, a heat rising up from the ground.

CHAPTER TWO

She felt she had seen enough. Enough of the fire, enough of the volunteers the town depended on for just these rare emergencies, enough of the glares of the uneducated rabble gathering together in groups like this was some sort of block party. Elizabeth had made the rounds, she had done her part. It would get her name in the newspaper, she was sure. Any slight political angle on anything always made the papers and Elizabeth had been sure to get a campaign point in: "This just shows the need for our town and city to address the problem of blight. If something like this can happen in a small town, imagine what our most vulnerable, underprivileged urban residents must face." She knew Meredith Skye. There had been numerous interviews over the past two years during her tenure as state rep. It was the dawn of campaign season and the fight was coming quickly. Meredith had been kind enough to snap some pictures for the story: the burned-out house, the firefighters hauling hoses over their shoulder, sweating in the sun; Elizabeth shaking their hands, smiling, handing them water bottles. It was a wink and a nod. Meredith would make sure that picture made it into the paper. The young reporter knew how to get it done, knew how to retain access to someone she would need in the future. It was a symbiotic relationship with the press. Elizabeth had learned that quickly and efficiently. As she walked away, Elizabeth saw Meredith talking to that big lug just down the street, the one with the kids who were always riding their bikes screaming at the top of their lungs, and the wife who could barely contain her misery living with him. It was almost visible on the poor woman's skin. Elizabeth couldn't blame her; marriage could be like that.

There was a loud bark of laughter and Elizabeth looked over her shoulder to the gaggle of slack-jawed yokels who had been her neighbors for well on a year now. They spread their bulky, aged bodies in lawn chairs and tried to numb their brains so they could laugh. She hadn't been able to find one of them with an interesting thought. When she first moved to this neighborhood last year she attended the annual block party and was bored to tears. They stuffed their white bodies with sausages and hamburgers and beer; they played music from fifty years ago; they talked of weather and lawn care and hunting. Their takes on current events were blunt, racist and conspiratorial. Frankly, their conversations, their concerns, their prognostications sounded like the last gasps of a dying generation. They were two weeks away from sitting in rocking chairs on the front porch with shotguns, mumbling about 'those damn kids' and waiting for a stroke. They talked in apocalyptic tones of crime in the city – the same city that made up the bulk of her district – about how 'those people' don't work, don't want to work, and just collect welfare. There was a police officer who lived on the other side of the block, and who eyed her distrustfully, lowered his voice when she was near. He said how 'they' won't talk to the cops, even when there was gunfire. "They want to let their neighborhood be overrun with shootings? Fine, don't talk to us," he said. "It ain't my neighborhood that's getting shot up." Another piped in about a protest that had blocked traffic on the highway. Several hundred protesters had marched from city hall to the nearby highway and blocked traffic for an hour. He said he'd been late getting home from work after a long day. "Should have just run them over," he said and then gave a cursory look in her direction.

She had never felt more like an outsider. She was a blue candidate in a swing district and living in deep red territory. This was not her constituency; they would vote in her election, but these were not her people. She was alone here. A newly single woman, educated at Wesleyan, smart, ambitious, opinionated, and she was sure they resented her for that. She had arrived with no husband to talk with these goons about the intricacies of lawn care or block engines; she did not deign to wear a t-shirt and jeans; she didn't get drunk with them and laugh about inanities. She had left the block party early and walked down the street to her home alone. That was the last time she attended any neighborhood get-together. She felt eyes on her as she walked away. She trailed whispers.

Now there was this. The old abandoned house was an eyesore and she had given it a cursory glance and a shake of her head when she moved into the neighborhood, but, frankly, she didn't care much. If anything, she appreciated that there was one less neighbor or family on the street, fewer eyes looking at her. She had come here to escape, although not particularly of her own volition, and bought the finest house available. The previous owners at least had a bit of class. The interior of the house, including the garage, was mahogany and brick. Bright windows let in the sun and a carefully curated garden of fine shrubs and bushes blossomed in the spring and summer. And while it was all fine, this was not where she belonged, this was not where she wanted to be.

Her ex-husband had left her with nothing but a last name that was already being used against her in the upcoming election. 'Let's Kick Tutt!' The Republican candidate, Andrew Whitcomb, already had faintly misogynistic lawn signs popping up. There were even a few around the corner on Beechwood. When she drove by, her own name seemed foreign and strange and, then, embarrassing. She wondered at times why she had chosen to go into politics to begin with. It seemed a losing game; even if you won an election, you lost something else. She had been an associate professor of political science at Brass Mill Community College. Most of the students were from cities, from poor high schools with few prospects, trying to become nurses or get a degree – any kind of degree – to get them into some entry-level assistant position. Over the years, she saw how they dwindled, dropped out, failed out, just disappeared. Sometimes they re-enrolled, sometimes they were just gone. The college had a graduation rate below fifty percent. She tried to teach them about being politically engaged, about changing the world so they and their children – and many of them already had children – could be better off. She taught them about the institutional racism and bias that kept their high schools in poverty; she taught about the greed and corporate money that kept their families in low-wage work while billionaires made more money than they could ever spend; she taught them about the men and women who did make a difference, and those who stood in the way. She attempted to spur in her students a fervor, a righteous anger, a willingness to take to the streets, to the business world, to the halls of power, and demand change for the better. Most of her lectures were met with half-hearted shrugs and late term papers.

So two years ago, she launched her own campaign. She recruited her students to help door-knock, to show them how the political process works. She harbored few illusions about the campaign trail, based on her own studies, but the reality of local politics was much more divisive and personal than even that of national politics. She was called every name in the book online. Reading about herself in the third person, it felt like they were talking about someone else, but then it hit home and she felt vulnerable, opened up to the world for scrutiny and criticism. She never knew the thick skin she would have to build in order to get through the next two years.

Even now, the hurt of it lingered. She was hated and loved but, when she lay alone in bed at night, she felt, in a word, frightened. She couldn't say what exactly it was that frightened her. But she felt as if the weight of her own history were bearing down on her, all of it flashing through her mind in a kaleidoscopic moment. She was left in the darkness with the lone question: "How did I get here?" All the incidents, coincidences, decisions and lost opportunities seemed to crash like a wave, and she was suddenly very alone in this nice little house on the corner of Ridgewood and Leadmine Brook, surrounded by strangers.

Of course, part of her fear stemmed from her own incomprehensible actions. Maybe not incomprehensible to those used to reading such things, or experiencing such things, but incomprehensible to her. The campaign had meant late nights, stress and a public battle. She felt far away from home even when sleeping beside her husband at night. They barely spoke after twenty-three years of marriage. They barely saw each other. They had gone from a married couple without children to roommates who shared a bed. Her campaign manager was a man in whom she confided. She was only fifty-five, she wasn't dead. Locked in a closed environment with a shared goal, it was easy to become close with someone.

It was an indiscretion. Something she couldn't have foreseen but recognized now that it was something she wanted. She had been hurt deeply when he told her he would have nothing more to do with her after only three flings. It somehow hurt her more than anything she could remember at the time. At her age, it seemed the rest of the world, including her husband, was ready to write her off as sexually expired, but she was ready for no such thing. She didn't feel fifty-five. She was still a proud woman, one who was not writing herself or her desires off. She had life to live and she would not accept some male-defined standard of sexuality that rendered her little more than an autumn leaf waiting to fall from a twig. She was hurt by his rejection, but also invigorated by the newfound future, as if the clouds had parted and the sky suddenly opened up. It seemed she had the world in hand and convinced herself through rapid interior monologue and perhaps faulty logic that nothing more could touch her; she had won an underdog campaign, she had experienced another human being in the most intimate way, she had a career and now political power. She was light-years ahead of the rabble.

She also figured that after twenty-three years of marriage – and suspicions of his own indiscretions she had harbored for years – a fellow academic such as Allan Tutt would be willing to overlook it, chalk it up to a more cosmopolitan style of marriage. He didn't. He filed for divorce immediately after her election victory. It seemed he had been waiting for such an opportunity, poised and ready to pounce. He didn't even try to work things out and that hurt more than her beau's rejection. In her more paranoid, insomnia-riddled nights she wondered if it had all been a setup. They had no children to argue over and therefore no reason to keep the marriage together for the sake of the kids. His breath of relief at signing the divorce papers made her feel small and insignificant, as if she'd been little more than an old burden. It made the papers but Meredith Skye had been shrewd enough to leave out the details, even when Elizabeth secretly confided in her, woman to much younger woman. Elizabeth and Allan sold off their upscale townhouse, and she bought this home in the forgotten backwater edge of her jigsaw district. As much as she championed the lives of the underprivileged in her district, she had to admit, she didn't want to live there. It made her nervous. The city did have a high crime rate – the yokels were right about that. Waterbury was post-industrial, had been for sixty years, and it wasn't making a comeback any time soon. It was not the kind of city with burgeoning culture, expensive nightlife or an intellectual elite. One could probably put a dome over it and label it an asylum, but it presented an opportunity for her political ascent, to make it a place where someone like her could feel more at home, a place that would draw money and investment and raise the city – and herself – up from the ashes.

But this neighborhood was cut off. She hadn't realized the extent of it at the time she purchased the house. It was like a small, undiscovered tribe still lost in the forest at the edge of civilization. Sure, the people had jobs and cars and such, but they were a different breed altogether. They were their own micro-climate of political and social dissatisfaction. In some ways it was endearing to see block parties and bonfires and general camaraderie. But there was also a darkness to it, one that made her uncomfortable. They were cliquey, suspicious, well-armed as far as she could tell and, in a word, strange. She wondered at their lives, so different from her own experience of city life where one felt alone and surrounded by strangers, but part of a larger picture. On this forgotten block, they were alone among themselves and useless, like an organ that had lost its utility over eons of evolution; an appendix to society.

And now she was trapped by low housing prices and only a couple years in on the mortgage. It seemed she wouldn't be leaving any time soon. Despite the campaign season, despite seeing her name on signs, she felt forgotten as well. When she approached the cadre of drinking buddies down the street, it seemed they looked through her. She was weakened to the point of transparency.

There was nothing to do but move forward. There was work to be done and she girded herself for it. There could be no backing down. A loss of her seat would be devastating at this moment in her life. She led in the polls but feared defeat, nonetheless; she feared a loss of her new self.

Elizabeth took a last look at the smoldering skeleton of the abandoned house and the gaggle of neighbors gathered down the street, gossiping and drinking. She called Meghan Brooke, her new campaign manager, to give word of the interview.

"The article should be out in tomorrow's edition," she said. "It was Meredith, so we should get some good coverage. I think we should work the blight angle, absentee landlords, getting properties out from under them so people can have a decent place to live."

"How about a land bank?" Meghan said. "It would have to receive state funding, but it was done in other cities with some success."

"You think the other reps will hop on board?"

"You might have to give a little somewhere else."

"Let's get some flyers made up with the idea, start hitting the low-income areas."

"Internal polling is looking good, but he's making some gains. Mostly in your neck of the woods."

"Well, trust me, my neck of the woods is a lost cause," Elizabeth said. "Cities win elections."

"Good news on the artist front," Meghan said. "Shondra said she will do it. The museum is completely on board and excited. The work will be displayed outside but they're going to construct an outdoor shelter for it to keep it out of the rain and let the people have access."

"It will be up before November?"

"Absolutely," Meghan said. "They think it will be a big hit."

This was a cultural lynchpin for Elizabeth and the city, and it would come out right in the middle of the election season. Artist Shondra Waite had conceived a structure, a miniature house made of giant black pieces of glass that streamed online social media images built around a single sapling planted on the grassy lawn just outside the Amherst Museum of Modern Art. Viewers would be presented with two images, one of reality, the other of pseudo-reality. They would be surrounded by the black glass splashing digital images – social media, news stories, hate-filled online chat, videos of calamity and unrest – juxtaposed with the natural world, the sapling, in the center with sunlight shining down through an opening in the top of the structure. It was meant to refocus the mind, to talk about humanity and nature and what we've lost. It was something that could give Waterbury an extra bump in the right direction of culture and bring needed funds to the museum. Elizabeth had met Shondra at an exhibit in Boston and was fascinated by her. An artist who had grown up in the projects and worked her way into Yale. She was an inspiration for all the urban youth. Elizabeth contacted the museum to see about getting Shondra's work displayed and, after she reached out to the artist, Shondra pitched her next project. All they needed was funding and Elizabeth managed to secure $100,000 in the last state budget for tourism. This was her doing. This was her event. She would stand beside Shondra Waite at the opening, deliver a speech on the necessity of the arts, the need to invest in education, and mark the moment when the city began to turn a corner sixty years in the making.

"We'll need you for door-knocking next week," Meghan said. "You can sell them on the new art exhibit and start pushing the blight issue."

"I'll have to move some things around," Elizabeth said. It wasn't actually true, but she did hate going door to door begging for votes, trying to get people who should care to actually care. It was always a depressing experience, a lowering of oneself to beg at the doorways of men and women who would rather spit at her than listen to her ideas on how to improve their lives. Frankly, it was ungrateful, but the masses usually are. They lift you up and then tear you down. There are no friends in politics.

"It's absolutely necessary," Meghan said.

"I'll wear sneakers this time," Elizabeth said.

Elizabeth walked onto her front porch and felt the warmth of the afternoon sun, tinged with a cool breeze that smelled of smoke. She felt elated now, a sensation she knew would wear off as the evening progressed and she was left home at night with nothing but her thoughts and the quiet of the house surrounding her. The fling with her former campaign manager had ended as quickly as it had begun, and hopes of starting a new life with someone else faded as she lost herself in her role as a politician. Her life oscillated from far too busy to endless days of nothingness. Today was one of those nothingness days. In a way, the fire had been a gift and, for a moment, she recognized the desire of her neighbors to gather round, to discuss, to hypothesize, to gossip at this new thing on a street where nothing out of the ordinary ever happened. She envied them in a way. Part of the problem with humanity, she had found, was its need to be both together and apart. It was the basis of society, to live together but within little fiefdoms. Together and separate, connected and divided. It was unnatural and Elizabeth felt it. Perhaps that was why she was so enamored with Shondra's latest artistic undertaking. It spoke of these things, these vital contradictions, that doom us all to forget what should be, what could be.

The fire trucks had left now. The neighborhood kids had biked back to their homes. There were more police cars. Two officers stood in the yard next door, speaking with Tonya and Frank Lovett. Tonya looked beside herself; Frank looked broken with anger. They were asking about Tonya and Frank's son, Lucas, the boy who resembled the angelic Boston Marathon bomber when he graced the cover of *Rolling Stone*. The whole neighborhood suspected, the police suspected too. He had a history, like all the other troubled youth who went on shooting sprees, raging against an incomprehensible world. It was only a matter of time.

She stared at the blackened bones of the burned-out house and it seemed to stare back at her, to reach inside. It spoke to her in its own way.

CHAPTER THREE

In the growing dusk, Vernon Trimble walked home slightly drunk and elated with the possibilities. He had followed the fire marshal around the ruins looking for signs of arson. These were signs Vernon knew well. He offered the fire marshal pointers based on his deep knowledge of forensic science and crime scenes. The marshal was stern, with a mustache like steel bristles and deep lines in his face, a stark contrast to Vernon's soft, forgettable baby face. But it didn't matter. Looks didn't matter; he was just as capable. In due time, they would see his intellect was hidden. A man like the marshal – so dismissive and probably steeped in old-fashioned ideas of detective work – was a thing of the past. He may look stoic and reliable, but he would probably reach an indecisive conclusion because he was old and tired and didn't want to do his due diligence. Fires, in particular, could be difficult, but fires also told stories. Forget the witness statements, the rumors and innuendos spewed by his neighbors who hadn't educated themselves in the intricacies of forensic science. You have to follow the path of the fire. The part of the house most blackened and burned would show where the fire started; a sample of the burnt wood put through a gas spectrometer would show traces of whatever accelerant was used to start the burn. You have your accelerant, you have your suspect. It was as easy as that. It could be solved in a half hour.

Vernon had finally been escorted away from the scene by an officer. He offered his advice to the trooper as best he could and then decided he would return later that night with a flashlight, or perhaps the next day, and sift through the burnt rubble himself. Houses don't just spontaneously combust. It was a well-known fact in the neighborhood that there was no electricity running to the old Widner house; there were no natural gas or propane lines that could have leaked into the basement and built up enough pressure to combust – that would have been an explosion that leveled half the houses on the street. No. This was clearly intentionally set, maybe by the Lovett boy, maybe not. Everyone saw Amber Locke and her teenage son talking to the trooper. Everyone knew the implications.

But one mustn't jump to conclusions. One must follow the evidence. One must eliminate causes until there is only one path forward through the morass. Simple detective work; logic, reason and science.

The others were still drinking beer in John's yard but he had to get home to his mother. He'd had enough of the chitchat and they all talked over him anyway, disinterested in his ideas, in what he could explain to them about how to solve this mystery in the heart of their neighborhood.

Vernon's home, set back far from the street, partially hidden by overgrown trees, seemed to tilt to the right like a gravestone sinking into the earth. He hadn't mowed the lawn in a month, the shrubs and bushes lining the exterior had grown unwieldy and the brown paint over the shakes chipped and fell in flakes that nestled themselves in the long grass. He knew the neighbors valued his mother's house just slightly more than the one that had just burned. Perhaps they'd like to see it burn, too. Property values are very important and worth watching things burn regardless of how or why. He would get to the yard and the painting soon. It was near the end of August. Too hot for such work. And there was the matter of his back pain and his knee that would occasionally throb and ache when pushing the old mower across the yard. He wasn't a professional landscaper. He marveled at and pitied those who spent their weekends in their yards, trimming, preening, primping like it was prom night for their properties. He marveled at their capacity to work and maintain after what was surely a long workweek; he pitied their obsession with something so pointless. Vernon considered himself a bit more philosophical, unable to reconcile such trite habits with the overwhelming fear of life. A few semesters in college had taught him that.

His father had been much the same as the rest of the neighborhood until he keeled over dead three years ago from a heart attack while snow-blowing the driveway. He was a simple, stolid man. Content with the little things, like all the others. Vernon had found his father's body partially covered in the snow late that morning after he woke in his basement bedroom and glanced out the half window nestled between the bushes and saw the heap of jacket, gloves and hat lying in the driveway beside the snowblower. The man who had given him life was frozen stiff by the time Vernon walked out the door to find him. That had been a bad day, perhaps the worst of his life, and now just getting out of bed in the morning seemed a chore not worth completing. His mother had already forgotten all about it – as she had most other events over the past ten years – recalling now only memories from adolescence and childhood. It was as if she were receding back in time. Perhaps she was lucky in that respect. Perhaps time, as a function of consciousness, could, in fact, be altered. It was something to ponder.

It was hot inside. The green shag carpet in the entryway was nearly worn down to the backing. It was dim and there was a smell of old food left out. He looked for his mother and found her sitting beside her bedroom window gazing into the front yard, which was rife and dark with tall trees. For a moment she appeared dead, her thin, white hair hanging down like a shroud over her face and shoulders, her nightgown soiled twice over, the smell of bitter urine.

"Do you see them?" she said. She looked at Vernon and did not recognize him. "Who are you?"

"It's me, Mom. Vern, your son."

"I have no son," she said. He didn't bother to convince her anymore.

"Do you see them?"

"See what, Mom?"

"Those little things running around in the yard, up and down the trees, with their bushy tails. What are they?"

"Squirrels, Mom. Those are squirrels."

"Are they everywhere or just here in this part of the country?"

"They're everywhere, Mom."

"So fascinating," she said. He could see the reflection of her face in the window as darkness settled.

"C'mon, let's get you cleaned up," he said.

"I'm unclean!" she screamed out, a sudden wild fear in her eyes. "Unclean!"

"You're fine, Mom. Just a bath now."

She trembled as he helped her from the chair and led her by the elbow to the bathroom. He poured the bath water and helped her from her nightgown. He put on latex gloves, removed her adult diaper, heavy with saturation, and threw it in the garbage. His mother stood before him stark naked, a withered crone, innocent as a child. The image had long since lost its shock and shame for him. The body, like the mind, betrays its owner.

He lifted her body, withered away to maybe one hundred pounds, and placed her gently in the bathtub. He had hardly any muscle to speak of, and she was light as a feather. She sang an old song while he helped soap down her body and wash her thin hair that, when wet, showed her scalp like an old man's. In age, there is little difference, he thought. Vernon had never had to care for anything in his life like he had his mother. His father never had to do this and now, staring at his naked mother dripping and tiny in the water, he envied the old man. Despite feeling bad about it, the sight of his mother filled him with a certain disgust, left him feeling sexless, alone and desperate. He needed this to be over quickly. He needed to retreat to his room, hidden in the basement, his place of solitude and comfort that shielded him from the arcane realities and responsibilities of life – they could all wait for another day, another month, another lifetime.

He had moved back in with his parents five years ago after being laid off from a data entry job and his girlfriend's announcement that she was moving out of their shared apartment. Twenty-eight at the time, he had been considering a marriage proposal, somehow duped by his own mind into believing that she still loved him after two years together, when, in fact, she announced that for as long as he had been considering marriage, she had been considering ending it between them. The relationship was going nowhere, she said. More specifically, he was going nowhere. He had been content in their little life; she had not. Contentment and comfort were the goals of life, he believed. In some way, all people struggled for them. He believed at the time he had found them and needed nothing more. Claire was less content, however, and in the blink of an eye she was gone, as was his job that required only the associates degree he had earned in less than spectacular fashion. In a mere few days he had gone from perfectly content, willing to live out the rest of his days in a quiet, separate peace of late-night television watching, video games and take-out dinners with a partner, to being totally alone and rejected both professionally and personally. It was a moment that should have been devastating but instead was surreal. How quickly life changes, like flipping through channels on the television or a heart attack. There one minute and gone the next, never in control of your own destiny. Vernon was merely flotsam in the wake and he believed that was true of everyone, whether they liked to admit it or not. Think what you will of a thirty-three-year-old man living at home with his mother, there was little difference between the meaning of his life and that of anyone else who thought they somehow mattered. None of it truly mattered, it could all be taken away in an instant.

He lifted his mother from the bathtub and dried her. He dressed her in a new diaper and nightgown and took her to her bed.

"It's so dark," she kept saying. "The dark is everywhere."

"It's nighttime, Mom," he said. "You know there was a fire around the corner today? The old Widner place burned down."

"I can't see!"

"You can see, I'll leave a light on for you."

Vernon gave her pills to help her sleep, hiding them in pieces of cheese like one might feed heartworm medication to a dog. He had begged the doctor for the prescription. Otherwise, she would be awake through all hours of the night, wandering the house, standing over his bed screaming for him to get out, cursing him, her pale white face and hollow eyes a glaring nightmare that haunted him. At times she was merely gentle and forgetful; at other times she seemed a vengeful spirit, demanding he leave the premises so that she could remain at peace. She occasionally discovered the pills and spat them out. She was surprisingly clever and stubborn. He received counsel from a visiting nurse who, for a time, stopped in once a week to check on her, courtesy of the state. When he had problems handling his mother, he would call Stacy and she would come over and help put her at ease. For some reason, his mother was much more receptive to Stacy's gentle voice and pretty, youthful face. He liked it when Stacy arrived. They would talk of his mother's health, but Vernon continually tried to steer the conversation to other topics, normal topics. It was the closest thing he'd had to a date in five years. He had hoped, at one point, to ask her on an actual date until she not-so-casually mentioned a boyfriend. He was disappointed that day and quickly ushered her from the house to hide his embarrassment. He couldn't tell if Stacy had picked up on his cues. Perhaps she had. Women were perceptive like that. It was no matter. The nurse visits ceased shortly thereafter. He received a small stipend to tend to his mother, so it was, in effect, his job. His mother received social security. The house was fully paid for and his father had a life insurance policy they had been living off for the past few years, so the social security checks and his stipend were put away in a bank account, his own personal nest egg. When she died, he figured, he would sell everything and move away, someplace tropical and warm, maybe. Someplace where he could start over. At the very least, a new place to remain in comfortable contentment with the respect naturally granted anyone who could afford to live comfortably without work.

One could never truly become an adult until one's parents were dead.

His mother took the pills without incident tonight, which relieved him. The thought of her wandering the house or hovering over his bed ate at his nerves constantly. She had been violent once in the past, resisting his attempts to put her in bed with surprising strength that seemed impossible for such a small creature. But she was devoid of any hesitation or thought. She could be pure strength, using every muscle in her dwindling body to fight and run and scream and hit and claw. She was a like a madwoman that night, a woman possessed by the demons of her own demise. Stacy had warned that if it happened again, they might have to institutionalize her. Sundowning, Stacy had called it. The loss of light triggered the dementia, made it worse. As much as it would be a burden lifted from him, Vernon couldn't bring himself to commit her. The expenses and paperwork alone were too much. The costs for housing her would consume his nest egg within months, force him to sell the house to pay for her care and end any dream he had of escape. He could bear it a little bit longer. She had birthed him into life. In her passing, she would birth him twice. Love of her was no longer possible because she was not the woman he knew as his mother. She was something else entirely now. Now she was a responsibility. Perhaps, it was a different form of love. He just had to do his time in this dark, stuffy, crumbling house. He had his own means of escape for the time being.

The opening sequence, the narrator's deep, intriguing voice, soothed him in an odd way. The colors flashed across the screen of his television, bathed his basement room in shades of blue tinged with red blood droplets. The synthesizer music drew to a close and the opening narration began, telling the story of murder in a small forgotten town, a place where things of this sort never happen, where people leave their doors unlocked and neighbors all know each other by name. But they become fearful of their lives and the lives of their children when the news of a brutal and bloody killing reaches their doorsteps. It was small town America and it was trembling under the weight of violence and death.

There were hundreds of episodes on his streaming service and he had watched them all through and through so many times he could remember each one. The small town, the murder, the investigation and that one piece of forensic evidence – the autopsy, the latent fingerprint, the DNA taken from the root of a hair follicle – that led investigators to the killer and saw him put away forever in prison. He watched nothing else. Sometimes he spent days watching it on endless repeat. Vernon had watched them all: *Forensic Files, The First 48, Murder in the Heartland, Unusual Suspects, Swamp Murders, American Monster, Cold Hearted Killers, Most Evil, Disappeared, Homicide Hunter, Deadly Women, Killer Cases, The Devil You Know, Unsolved Mysteries, Texas True Crime, Wild Crime, Cold Case Files, Murder on the Internet* and the new techno-frenetic reboot of *America's Most Wanted*. It had come to the point that, to him, murder seemed the most normal and natural way to die.

Vernon took a joint from an eyeglass case he kept in his sock drawer and lay in bed smoking, letting the haze take his mind in new and different directions. It allowed him to step outside the bounds of his everyday worldview and think about things in a new and different way, and so often his thoughts drifted into the realm of his true crime shows. He imagined what it must feel like, truly feel like, to be one of the victims.

What must it feel like to be stabbed, he wondered. To feel the knife blade between your ribs, to see the familiar face of the person who held that knife and then briefly marvel at the realization that this person – a person you have known for so long, as is most often the case – is killing you before your very eyes.

Most people probably imagine they would feel intense fear and shock, but Vernon knew better. Murder was banal; the person familiar, the surroundings your own, the sharing of a moment between two people that is merely one step beyond normal experience. How many times had that man held a knife in the presence of his wife and she thought nothing of it? The only difference this time is that the knife was inside her. Perhaps there was a certain comfort in being killed by someone you know. Perhaps, murder is only shocking to the victim when it is a stranger, but then, there are so many strangers in the world; what's one more just because he is killing you?

He thought about the fire today. He imagined how the narrator would describe the incident. He could hear the voice: *Harington was a small town of five thousand people. A place where there was only one stop light and families, secluded away from the bustle and poverty of the nearby city, could rest easy at night knowing they were safe inside this leafy, rolling hamlet. But all that changed when a mysterious fire in an abandoned home revealed a sinister darkness in their midst....*

Then the forensic investigation into the mysterious fire would begin. Not like this lame and impotent walk-through conducted earlier today by a fire marshal who was three days from retirement and probably didn't care.

There was a sound from upstairs. The creaking of a floorboard. Perhaps it was his imagination. In the night, when he lay in his bed, high, mind reeling into new realms of understanding, all sound seemed amplified. Things so small seemed so large. His mind spiraled outward to the possibilities. Homes can be invaded, people murdered before they even realize what is happening. What must it be like to wake in the night to a figure standing over your bed and then shoving a piece of metal into your gut? Would you even be able to react at all? The volume on his television was turned low but he could hear it just fine. He was nestled in this place awaiting a doom that would seem so ordinary. He pondered death.

The floorboards above creaked again. The house seemed to shift and groan. He heard a shriek in the night. "The dark! The dark! I can't see!"

The sleeping pills didn't take. His mother was up again, wandering lost in the house. The darkness made her lose all trace of normal memory; the light switches, the rooms, the layout of the house itself would suddenly be lost to her. At any moment she could plunge down the stairs.

"The dark! Help!"

Sometimes in the night, when he went to guide her once again to bed, he swore she would glow in the dark, and in those moments she seemed so far away, something foreign to his world, an image from another dimension, another universe; and perhaps she was. Perhaps they were all just colliding universes, every life an entirely different universe unto itself. The world could only be experienced by the individual and yet there were so many of them, so many different views, experiences colliding into each other, trying to create the whole out of interwoven threads, none of them having any real idea what it looked like all together.

He rose from his bed, irritated and angry at this interruption from another world. She was so far away, so far gone, a stranger wandering above him.

"The dark! The dark! Someone help me!"

He would have to increase the dose of her sleeping medication. He felt himself on the verge of something large, a new becoming, while she wandered through a dark chasm of her own mind. He put on a t-shirt and left his room to retrieve her.

He went to the staircase and looked up. She stared down at him, pale white in the darkness, her mouth open with an inaudible scream, her finger pointed at him in horror. She did not know who he was. He was the stranger in her house, the murderer come to take her life. And in that moment, he was terrified both of her and of the nothingness he had become.

CHAPTER FOUR

The dogs. Always the goddamned dogs. They barked and howled at the door, jumping, scratching to get outside. Two big, gray Weimaraners that Amber's husband, Joe, just had to have at twenty-five hundred a pup, a bill on their credit card she was still paying off three years later. He had some strange affinity for this breed bequeathed to him by his uncle, who'd taught him to hunt and insisted that all his dogs be Weimaraners. So Joe's early childhood memories of time with his beloved uncle were tied up in the childhood joys of playing with these dogs, notoriously difficult to train, obsessed with hunting down and killing anything that reached their heightened sense of smell or sight, overly large and dumbly single-minded. He had purchased them as puppies, gave them two fine German names, Otto and Helmutt – the latter, she had to admit, a rather humorous play on words – and said he would use them for hunting, but he never actually trained them and the dogs grew big and bored and ached for something to chase. Every passerby – every jogger or family out for a walk, every kid on a bike or squirrel in the yard – caused them to erupt.

Amber was in the kitchen. The barks and whines seemed to shatter her eardrums. She hated the noise, and, it seemed, her life was suffused with noise that flowed from the ever-present chatter of her sons and their various electronic devices, the television that streamed talking heads blathering on about politics as Joe sat on the couch, beer in hand, belly in his lap, and the goddamned dogs, whose barks were like gunshots. It had already been a long day and she felt a weight upon her, the weight of her family.

Amber looked at the security camera screen mounted at the corner of the kitchen counter that showed the outside of the house in black-and-white night vision. Joe had installed the home security cameras after a series of car break-ins in the neighborhood by hoodlums from the city. They loved riding out here in the middle of the night and testing car doors to see if they were open and grabbing whatever they could. The neighborhood had been hit a couple years back. Amber and Joe were both awakened at five in the morning by a state trooper who had patrolled the area and saw her minivan door was left partially open. The trooper asked if she would look through the van to see if anything was missing, but, frankly, she had little worth stealing and if they had stolen that godforsaken Dodge she probably would have sent them a thank-you card. It seemed every other month it had some major breakdown requiring either Joe's undivided attention for an entire Saturday or another trip to the mechanic for a bill just shy of a thousand dollars, which they didn't have. But after the break-ins Joe insisted on installing the four-hundred-dollar camera system that looked out on the front porch, driveway and backyard. They were still making the credit card payments on that, as well.

The camera screens showed nothing; just the front porch, the cars, the backyard and beyond that, trees and darkness. But still the dogs barked and howled as if chasing down a fox. She looked back at her husband and two sons. It was like they didn't hear the dumb dogs at all, each lost in white noise.

"Nobody move, I've got it!" she said. No one even looked up. Family was a matter of infinite love and infinite hate and feelings could oscillate from one to the other several times a day. She opened the door and the dogs burst out into the night, constrained, she hoped, by electronic dog collars that kept them confined to the property. In the past, their rabid zeal had pushed them through the electric barrier and she and her sons – Vincent and Thomas – had spent the better part of an afternoon trying to wrangle them back to the house, apologizing to neighbors for letting loose the dogs of war. She tried to keep a bit of humor about it. The dogs were only three years old, ate eighty dollars' worth of food every month, and she would be stuck with them for at least another eight years unless one of them jumped in front of a car, which was a distinct possibility that she secretly desired.

She had wounded herself today. Taken her fifteen-year-old son, Vinnie, and walked him down to the site of the burning Widner house and forced him to talk with the state trooper. The whole neighborhood had seen it; the whole neighborhood knew that Vinnie and Lucas were often together, riding bikes through the street or walking in quiet conversation. She knew Lucas's history, his suspensions from school for marijuana, his violent outbursts toward his parents, his occasional disappearing acts. She tried to keep Vinnie away from him but it was all a matter of ability. Both she and Joe worked during the day and Vinnie and Thomas were left to their own devices during the summer.

Tommy was only seven years old, sweet, tender-eyed, loving. He was her prize, her reminder to herself that she had at least done something right with her life. The kid was an angel and everybody thought so, from school teachers to neighbors. And he looked the part too: big, brown eyes, soft round face and a mop of shaggy hair. Sometimes, she would pick him up and hold him in an embrace for as long as she could; she would stop herself from crying in those moments, marveling at his innocence, his goodness, and thinking to herself that everything she had sacrificed in her life for this family, leaving behind her youthful ambitions for fame – she had been attractive enough to garner interest from photographers and modeling agencies when she was only sixteen – was worth it for this one embrace. She selfishly hoped that he would remain young forever, if only to give her these moments. The boy seemed innately driven toward kindness and love, a stark and jarring juxtaposition with Vinnie.

She knew her oldest son was a bit of rotten fruit. As his mother, it was hard to admit, but it was true. He had grown into something else entirely, something foreign and indifferent to her or anything outside himself. Just this past year she punished him by taking away his cell phone. He used the house phone to call the police, who arrived at her front door, asked her humiliating questions trying to ascertain if he was an abused or neglected child. Then the officer took Vinnie outside and laid into him about phoning in a fake police report. Amber secretly hoped the officer would arrest him, put the fear of God into him, but afterward he appeared indifferent. She had the sneaking suspicion that he was nothing more than a burgeoning sociopath. The whole neighborhood saw the police car and word got around quickly. That night, Joe took Vinnie by the collar, put him against the living room wall and slapped him heavy-handed across the face. That scared the boy pretty good, and he had it coming. He was headed in the wrong direction and she felt powerless to stop it. Joe could wield a horrible temper with the boy, so she kept many of her concerns secret in order to keep some semblance of peace. But that meant bearing all the weight of it herself and today it seemed too much. Brute force was sometimes the only thing that could properly be understood.

Vinnie told the officer what she had instructed him to: that Lucas hung around the abandoned place often, that he had a predilection for fire, that he had been talking of ghosts and voices that spoke to him. She shuddered at the thought her own son might be connected somehow. She felt for Lucas's parents. In a way, she understood what they were experiencing right now in a less extreme degree: the feeling that somehow the child you birthed and raised was becoming a monster and it was totally and completely out of your control. She felt the eyes of the neighborhood on her as she walked Vinnie down the street. All of them gathered in a little circle on John and Jessica's yard, gossiping. She had only paid them a cursory glance. She'd heard the things said about her son, about her, about her family. She still had her pride. None of them were any better, but everyone always wants to point the finger, kick you when you're down.

Amber heard the dogs roaming the woods behind the house, barking and howling, chasing something. The other dogs in the neighborhood were now barking, the whole world a cacophony of mindless baying and ceaseless yapping.

Amber walked from the kitchen into the living room and surveyed the scene: Vinnie and Tommy on their phones, thumbs rolling over screens; Joe still in his jeans, his big goofy feet in white socks with colored tips that made him look like an oversized child. Somehow, the sight of his feet set up in the reclining chair disgusted her. It was almost too comfortable, too plain, too ordinary. It lacked future and, in that moment, she had a strange feeling of dread. This was her life now till her death. She was thirty-six years old and this was it, this was all it would be until the end, and it was so devastatingly disappointing. Self-help books talked of hopes and dreams and achieving goals. But she had ceased to dream a long time ago, her nights merely forgotten hours between days, and she didn't know what else to hope for because there seemed nothing left. She had done it, she supposed. She had achieved the American dream – a family, a house, two cars in the garage. They all looked so contented in that moment, but contentment was a form of spiritual death, an excuse to just give up. She tried to give up, she tried to be content, but there was an energy inside her; she wanted something she couldn't comprehend. She thought of the dogs running and baying at the edge of the trees. They sensed something they could not see and it drove them mad.

"To your rooms, boys," Amber said, but no one even looked up. It was as if they hadn't heard her at all. "Tommy, Vinnie, wrap it up and get ready for bed. Night is over." Thomas sighed, feigning the attitude of his big brother, which seemingly spread like a virus. Vinnie jerked his phone down and stood up suddenly. He wasn't speaking to her, angry she had forced him to rat out his friend. She heard a low mumble from his lips, something about 'bullshit'.

"What was that?"

He said nothing. His tall, lanky body seemed to take up so much room. He was taller than her now, big bones and dark eyes. He intimidated her at times, invaded her space, this stranger.

Joe watched Vinnie from the recliner. Joe was her last refuge when it came to their oldest son. Joe could sufficiently and physically scare him; she could not, and so the boy had no respect for her even though she had birthed him and fed him and raised him.

She watched him go with a fire in her eyes. She refused to let him know he intimidated her. She refused to be cowed by her own adolescent son. He slammed the door and she saw Joe wince and purse his lips.

"I'm gonna have some words with that kid," he said.

"Don't. Just let him settle down for a bit," she said. She just wanted peace and quiet for a moment. The dogs barked and howled; the news talk show host on the flat screen above the fireplace squinted and contorted his face with a look of bow-tied faux confusion to make the woman he interviewed look an absolute buffoon or possibly insane. Amber looked at the program for a moment; the face on the screen seemed so huge, devoid of blemish, his knowledge superior, as if he were a god that stood twelve feet tall. The colors were bright and vivid and schizophrenic, alarms sounded as another headline raced across the chyron; facts and figures scrolled down the side of the screen. There was cell phone footage of people fighting in the street.

She sat down on the couch and looked at her husband, but had nothing to say. In fact, she couldn't think of more than ten words they'd said to each other all day. After fourteen years of marriage, it seemed there was nothing left to say, nothing more to learn about each other. But that wasn't true. There were things she wanted to say, things about herself she wanted someone, anyone, to know, but the weight of those fourteen years kept her quiet. There would be no point in it, revelation changes nothing. A prisoner can find Jesus and tell the world of his new, born-again life, but it does not set him free, it does not ease the physical burden.

"The dogs are at it again," she said finally. "I'd say we should get them bark collars but I think they'd electrocute themselves to death."

"They'll settle down. Probably just smell a bear or something." Black bears were a constant problem in the neighborhood, tipping over trash cans, scattering garbage across lawns at night, occasionally trundling through someone's yard in the middle of the day as their children played outside. The bears were a bigger problem than the car break-ins. "It's good we have them to keep those bears away."

"Just wish they'd shut up for once," she said.

"Dogs bark, it's what they do."

"Can you call them back in? They never listen to me."

"That's because I'm the alpha to them," Joe said. "The big dog."

"I don't think I can even respond to that," she said.

He winked at her, went to the sliding glass door to the back porch, and started yelling, whistling, and now there was even more noise. She stared at the television screen. A commercial now, a drug to cure incontinence, the fate that awaits us all. The dogs came bounding into the living room and jumped up on the couch. She swatted them back down and brushed the dirt from their paws off the cushions.

"They were digging at something," Joe said. "Probably chasing a gopher or something."

"Get me a drink, Joe?"

That night, she made an effort. All the books and television talk shows said marriage takes work. She stared at herself in the full-length mirror of their bedroom. She wore a sexy little chemise she bought years ago and wore only once during a weekend getaway. She knew she looked quite good. After two pregnancies – the first of which derailed her quest for fame – she hadn't lost her figure. She was an objectively attractive woman, but when you grow so accustomed to seeing yourself it's difficult to fathom what others may see. The alcohol helped. It dulled her senses, gave her a certain hazy euphoria, helped her ignore the fact that when she watched Joe begin to strip his clothes off she wanted to turn away.

He left his socks on in bed, slowly grunted on top of her and came so quickly she wondered why she bothered. The dogs whined, scratching at the bedroom door, trying to get inside.

"Do you ever wonder if this is it?" she said to him. "If this is all there is?"

"What do you mean?"

"I mean, where do we go from here?"

Joe rolled over onto his back and stared at the ceiling a moment. "I don't know what more you could ask for," he said.

"Maybe that's the difference between you and me," she said.

"The boys will grow up and move out," he said. "We'll work and save our money. We'll be able to sell this place and move away and retire. Someplace that's always warm, maybe near a beach. You won't have to work at the Package Depot anymore, I'll have my pension. We'll have a good life, the kind of life you're supposed to have. There's nothing wrong with that, it's a good thing."

"It just seems like there should be something more," she said.

"There isn't anything more," he said.

"I'm not unhappy," she said.

"Could have fooled me," he said. There was an uncomfortable presence between them now. He was angry and hurt. She sensed it. Revelation changes nothing, perhaps it just makes things worse.

"It's nothing, really," she said to him. "Don't be upset. It was just a tough day."

"I work my ass off to give us this life," he said.

"We both do."

"And you don't appreciate it."

"I do," she said. "I'm sorry. It was just a thought. I just wanted to talk."

Joe rolled onto his side and was silent, breathing slowly and steadily, allowing himself to slip easily into sleep.

She was restless. She picked at her cuticles, bit a fingernail. The lights were out, and she stared at the bedroom ceiling fan that spread like flower petals.

Amber got out of the bed and opened the door. She pushed the dogs aside and blocked them from barging into the bedroom and walked to the kitchen to get a drink. She passed Vinnie's room and heard the distant sounds of something digital, saw a glow from beneath his door, but she couldn't be bothered to try. She was done for the day. His future would have to be his own and her feeling of responsibility for it was quickly fading. Her worry and concern and attempts at raising the quintessential good son who would grow to become a productive and successful member of society seemed like a long shot now for him; she rested her hopes on Tommy.

A couple more drinks and she could fall asleep. She took out a bottle of vodka from the freezer and poured two shots into a glass and choked it down like medicine. It made her feel hollow and slightly sick. She choked back so much. The house was dark but for the gray light that shone from the surveillance monitors and gave faint outline to the things, all the things, in her world.

She took another drink and tried not to vomit. It wasn't the vodka. It was something else. Her eyes were drawn to the monitor screens. There was something about seeing the world through an electronic medium that just made it different, more stimulating, like she was removed from it all and could watch from a distance.

But, for a moment, it appeared as if something was there. She looked closely at the backyard monitors and saw something indistinct, grainy and dark at the edge of the trees. It didn't move and she wouldn't have noticed it, but that she somehow felt it noticing her. It was not a man. It was not anything. It stood like a pillar of blankness, as if there were a malfunction in the lens of the camera, a hole where there should be image.

She turned and looked from the kitchen to the sliding glass doors and out into the yard. It was too dark to see. She looked back at the monitors and still there was the pillar of nothingness, seemingly closer now. She grew slightly afraid.

Glass in hand, she walked slowly through the living room. The faint blue and green glow of electronics cast a flat pallor over the walls and couches and family photographs. She stood at the sliding glass doors and stared out into the night. She couldn't see it, but it was there. She could feel it. Something that awaited her. Her hand reached for the outdoor light switch.

CHAPTER FIVE

He dreamed of a strange world, with smooth, concave streets like pipes cut lengthwise, and beneath the streetlights were piles of bulky white sacks that reached halfway up the light poles and everything was flat and two-dimensional like a painting he'd once seen of a diner in the night. The road led out into darkness, into infinity, and he was terrified; an unsettling anxiety crawled from his bowels and walked across his skin like a thousand insects exploring a corpse. There was a deep, dawning blood-red horizon just over the hills.

John woke on the couch at five in the morning and waited for a moment. He felt the fear of his dream inside him. It confused him. He thought of the white sacks beneath the flat, yellow streetlights. The world of his dream was insane and terrifying. He recollected the previous night as best he could. The house was so still and silent and, in that moment, it felt cheap and false. He was still dressed in jeans and a t-shirt, and he felt regret and shame and knew Jessica was angry with him, and he had broken yet another promise, and his week would be a long one of trying to make it up to her again. He just needed to spiral down into a hole at times. Some people would never understand. Work today. That would do him good. Sunlight broke over wet trees and he recalled the great fire yesterday, which seemed to have suddenly vanished from relevance and life returned to normal. He looked out the window to the backyard and patio-in-progress. He hadn't finished putting down the gravel. He would have to finish that tonight, he supposed, before it got too dark.

John found a Coke in the refrigerator and drank it down. He slipped on his boots and walked out to the mailbox for the newspaper. He wanted to see the article about the fire, to see if his name was in it, if the reporter had quoted him. It would be something to show the kids, to impress them that their father was in the news. Perhaps it would be a little something to gather the family around and diffuse Jessica and they could all have a moment of pride and smiling.

Jessica occasionally criticized his subscription to the newspaper. It was a needless expense, she said, and just made for more garbage to pile up. He never read the whole thing but there seemed a certain importance to it. He remembered his father, an old Vietnam War vet who finally had children late in life, sitting at the breakfast table, reading a newspaper in the early morning light before heading off to work at an insurance company. It seemed important to John, as if there were stability and certainty and wholesomeness in such things. It was a tradition that should not be lost. When Jessica complained, he always said it was the American thing to do. Part of the nuclear family tradition. "We need that more than anything these days," he said, because it seemed everywhere the world was falling apart.

It was already warm and humid. Work today would be a beast and he would return home soaked through with sweat, hidden by his reflective Public Works vest. The world was silent in the morning light. There were no cars, no wind, the air heavy and saturated with dew. He took the newspaper from the mailbox and flipped it open. Nothing on the front page, although he supposed that was to be expected. He finally found the article under the local news section titled, 'Abandoned house catches fire in Harington', and below it a picture of Elizabeth Tutt handing a water bottle to a volunteer firefighter, the smoldering house in the background. *How lovely for the Hillary wannabe,* he thought. He quickly scanned the article as he walked back into the house and sat down at the kitchen table, but his name was not there. There was only a quote from Elizabeth, something about cleaning up blight in neighborhoods, absentee landlords and whatever else might play for her city constituents, but nothing from the person who reported the fire and rushed to help, even if there was no help to give.

Police found remnants of fireworks in the grass near the house and believe that led to the fire. They are searching for a local youth who was reportedly near the scene.

He stared at the lines in disbelief for a moment. It was bullshit. The fire, he knew, started inside the house. He heard it burst through the side window, he saw the flames roar out and catch onto the roof. There was no way the fire was caused by fireworks. Besides, he'd been outside all that morning; there was no sound of fireworks, the little pops of cheap bottle rockets and Roman candles that could be bought at the local convenience store. Nothing like that. It was all bullshit, a flat-out lie, and the cute little reporter had just taken it at face value. He looked again through the article for his name or even a reference.

Neighbors reported the blaze Sunday afternoon and the house was fully engulfed by the time firefighters arrived on scene.

He tossed the paper aside and then retrieved it and looked at the reporter's name again. Anyone and everyone who was there knew that fireworks had nothing to do with it. There was no way, and the police were lying to protect that crazy little shit across the street. For what reason, he had no idea. Lucas had been a goddamned problem his whole life. Why not just find more reason to put him where he belonged? Young people were spoiled, coddled, and then when one of them acted like the degenerate he was, they made up mental health excuses to keep him from actually being punished. They just didn't want to deal with it. No wonder everything was going to shit.

John looked up and his son James stood in front of him, eyes half open, pajamas drooping from his shoulders. The boy said nothing to him and they stared at each other a moment. James walked stiff-legged like a newborn giraffe to John and crawled into his lap and John held him, feeling suddenly that there was nothing more important in the world than this boy. He thought that childhood must be terrifying, to have no control over what happens and even less understanding, that it must seem incomprehensible and chaotic. Perhaps it was why young children had nightmares. He tried to remember his own childhood, but there were only flashes of a dream remembered. It was as if it had never happened at all and, maybe, that is all the past was – a remembered dream, something that only exists in our minds. The past was gone, the future imagined; the only reality was the moment and even that was littered with fractures and falsities. He looked again at the newspaper.

James stretched on his lap and spoke in a half yawn. "Are you and Mommy getting a divorce?"

He looked down at James for a moment. He had asked it so casually. "Of course not, buddy," he said. "Why would you ask that?"

The boy said nothing, slid off John's lap and went to the couch. He found the remote and scrolled through kids' programs until he found one with sufficiently bright, amorphous colors and inhuman sounds. John let the boy's question go. He just needed to get out of the house for a while, to clear his head. He showered in the kids' bathroom to give Jessica her space. They just needed time; time and space and tranquility. That was what was needed, but life gave little of it.

He felt like a stranger in his own home, or perhaps a guest who'd overstayed his welcome. It seemed that the family consisted of Jessica, Caitlin and James and he was just some guy who hung around and occasionally did odd jobs, like the super of an apartment building. At times, it felt more primal; Jessica the female of the species, guarding her offspring from the male. He was sure he saw that in a documentary at some point, maybe something about lions, the male just being this big, dangerous problem – necessary for the continuation of life but, in general, just a pain in the ass who occasionally needed to be scared off by females. The male lion's sole job was protecting the pride. It gave the male lion purpose over and above mere sperm, John supposed. But there was little in their neighborhood, in this civilized world, that required John to protect his pride, his family. He was a source of income, to be sure, but Jessica earned more money than him. When they started out their life together, it was a matter of love. Now, it was a matter of value, and he feared his value was fading.

By eight in the morning he was sweating in the August heat. The sun beat down, the hot asphalt they poured radiated from the ground, and he was caught in the middle. Still, he felt at home here with his crew. He felt needed, even when they stood around doing nothing as the roller packed down the stone base. And when the job was done, he could say he did something useful, something that mattered; he fixed a road that needed repair, something no academic egg-head, buried in his journals and papers that would never see the light of day, could say.

He sweated out the poison. He forgot about home and concentrated on the job. When he thought about Jessica, he sparked up a conversation with Roy or Mike and they complained about everything under the sun. Complaint, the great communion of men. They complained and bitched and whined and pontificated on solutions; they developed their own answers that were probably wrong but no one really cared. He knew none of them would go home that night and try to solve any of these complaints. It was just a way to pass the time, a way to watch the molten asphalt congeal and cool – the passage of time. The asphalt, like the La Brea Tar Pits, sucked in time and held it for millions of years. They were all insignificant and he grew older by the second.

The burned-out house and newspaper article still bothered him, wriggled at the back of his brain, annoyed him with its implications. There was a threat. There was a lie. A lie printed publicly was also a threat, and it seemed there was a concerted effort to establish the lie – the police, the newspaper, the idiot politician down the street. It wasn't a matter of fireworks and wasn't a matter of blight; it was a matter of truth. Reality shouldn't be a dream of half-truths.

"It's fucking fake news," Roy said.

"Fake news," John said.

"It's all the media does. They just give you the line the government wants you to hear and then they repeat it a million times. You look at the news. Some senator ass-hat says something, gives it a nice turn of phrase, and not just one news story or talking head will repeat it, but they all will. A million times over. And soon you're repeating it, too, and then, just like that, it's the truth because no one bothers to question the narrative. They set the narrative and the media just gives them a loudspeaker. Fucking fake news, man."

"I don't know," John said.

"What's there not to know? You know what you saw, right? You know you saw the fire explode out of the house, right?"

"Yeah."

"So who you gonna believe? Some reporter and a shitty cop or your own eyes? They need to be called out on that shit."

"This fucking kid," John said. "I know this kid lit this fire. The whole street knows it and he knows it and that's why they can't find him anywhere."

"Little psychopath."

"He is a little psychopath. They got files on this kid two miles long and he's still running around out there and they want to tell me it's fireworks?"

"See, they didn't put you in the article because you were there. You saw the whole thing. They don't want people to know what you know, they only want people to know what the cops want them to know and they have Little Miss State Representative Pantsuit to make it official in the story. Nothing to see here, everyone go about your lives. They're not looking for that kid. They couldn't care less. Coulda burned down the whole damn neighborhood."

"So what do you do, then? Nothing *to* do, I suppose," John said.

"Don't sound like a fucking cow, man. You just gonna stay in your pen, occasionally moo for the people while they milk you for all you're worth?"

"Well, what the fuck do you do, Roy? Talk a big game."

"Hey, I do plenty. There's plenty of us that decided we ain't taking this shit anymore."

"But what do you do?"

"You'll see one day, my man. I'll let you know."

"Okay then," John said.

Roy was full of shit. He wasn't going to do anything. But his overall point was solid, made perfect sense. Sometimes it seemed nothing was real, and yet here they all were, stuck in it like some computer matrix, because deep down, everyone knows it's all a lie.

But it didn't have to be. Sometimes, you had to do just one decent thing, right one wrong, to start things in a better direction. The newspaper story was wrong, the reporter was wrong, the cops were wrong and they needed to be told about it. Everyone did. Because it was bullshit and it shouldn't be tolerated. Maybe he could do this one thing and make it right. He knew what he saw. He knew the truth and that mattered.

The rest of the guys loitered in the parking lot of the Public Works building near Roy's truck. They took out a cooler and opened some beers and called him over to join them. It was hot and bright and he wanted a beer more than anything in the world, but he waved them off. Jessica would surely be angry about yesterday. He was on restricted driving; he could only go to and from work during his set hours. If he was pulled over again with even a single drink in him it would all be over and his license would be gone for years.

John pulled his Ford truck from Route 4 into the dark, leafy cave of his neighborhood. There were three ways in and out; two from Route 4 and one that crossed the wetland swamp in the valley and ran up another hill to a nicer neighborhood with big houses where you could catch the road into the next town. Their little enclave was secluded, isolated. No one drove through. No one needed to.

He turned right onto Ridgewood and looked at the politician's house and felt the need to insult her. Such a glory-sucking bitch, a typical politician. Who were these people anyway? So eager to do or say anything to get into the limelight for even a brief moment. Who thought they could run the world. They thought they were better than everyone else.

He looked again at the Widner house as he passed. The far side of the garage was largely intact, the side nearest his neighbors nothing but black bones beneath a velvet-blue sky. He saw Vernon there in the soot and rubble, bent over, examining something on the ground. John stopped the truck and rolled down the window. Vernon looked up and saw him.

"What are you doing?" John called to him.

"Looking around."

"Find anything?"

Vernon walked through the long, unkempt grass and came to John's window. He was sweating.

"Did you see the newspaper article?" John said.

"The fire started from inside," Vernon said. "You can easily see where it spread."

"How can you see that?"

"You trace the line of the fire, how badly things are burned. I can't tell if there was an accelerant used, but it looks like it went up pretty quick."

"There was a lot of stuff stored in there, from what I heard," John said. "Could have been a lot of chemicals and shit to catch fire."

"I would need a gas spectrometer to know exactly," he said. Vern was a pretty smart guy, even if he didn't have a job and lived with his mother.

"They said it was fireworks," John said. "That Lucas was playing with fireworks in the long grass and the house caught fire from there. I didn't hear any goddamn fireworks that day, did you?"

"The grass isn't burned," Vernon said. He pointed to the burned-out wall of the house. "You see? No burned grass, no soot, nothing. These guys don't know what they're talking about."

"I'm gonna contact that reporter," John said. "She didn't even try to listen to what I said."

"They just don't care," Vernon said. "Someone burns down a house in our neighborhood and they say it was fireworks. It's not scientifically possible."

"She has to come out here and see this," John said.

"I can show her," Vernon said.

"I'll let you know," John said. Vernon backed away from the truck and John drove one house down to park in his driveway.

The sun was just beginning to dip and heat the back of the house. He almost dreaded coming home on days like this. He told Jessica he'd stop drinking but yesterday was just too much, too tempting to sit and commune with everyone. She had stayed away. She wasn't interested in socializing, a clear indication of her anger with him. She had spent the day filling in gravel for the back patio while he opened beers with the neighbors and, eventually, a bottle of whiskey had appeared and then it was dark and there was little to remember but his dreams.

Caitlin and James were on the couch, the mounted flat screen running through some crazed cartoon. They didn't look up as he walked into the room and didn't answer when he said, "Hey guys." They just stared and some part of him felt slightly sick.

"Where's Mom?" John said to them.

"Upstairs," Caitlin mumbled.

He dropped his keys on the dining room table and left his boots at the door. Their bedroom door was closed but he needed a shower and a change. He walked into their room but it felt like he was encroaching on someone else's property, as if he were a thief sneaking through the house.

He immediately regretted entering the room. There was a presence there. Jessica sat upright and cross-legged on the bed, laptop open in front of her, typing. Her dark outline stood out against the violet wall. Lone pictures in cheap black frames hung in suspended animation. The curtains rustled slightly, and she, in the middle, seemed to control it all like some small statue an ancient Amazon tribe would worship. The bed looked small with her in the center; it was a wonder he ever slept in it at all. It felt crowded. She looked up at him as if he were a stranger she'd just seen for the first time but whom she hated more than anything in this world – more than her father, who left her when she was a child, more than her bitch mother, who abused her, more than every disappointment that had piled up throughout her entire thirty-five years. All of it in that one look that filled the room.

John stood in the doorway and tried to speak but couldn't. The words wouldn't come and he was suddenly overwhelmed with fear.

"You're taking something from me," she said. Flat, monotone, emotionless. "You take and take and that's all you do."

He tried to say he was sorry but he couldn't. He stood there in stunned silence and stared at her, searching for the words, the meaning, of what he felt.

"You love only yourself," she said.

John backed out into the hallway and shut the door. He walked back downstairs and sat down at the computer desk with their old desktop. He needed to let this be for a while. He found the article about the house fire online. He found the name of the pretty reporter who got it all wrong, who had sold the world a false story, who had snubbed him in favor of some dumb politician. He found her email address and tried to write.

Tried to make it sound serious, official, critical and, most of all, worthy of respect.

Deep down, he knew he was smart, smarter than people gave him credit for, particularly when confronted with his size. But now, in this moment, he could only conjure one line of simmering rage that he ashamedly borrowed from Roy: *You lied. You're supposed to tell the truth and all you gave us was fake news, you little bitch.* He wasn't necessarily angry at her, but he had to make her wake up and understand, and sometimes the only way to get someone's attention is to yell fire in a crowded theater or call them a bitch.

Cartoon characters danced in the background. Multicolored lights played shadows across the walls, rearing up behind him like a kaleidoscopic fire. It all seemed so monstrous. For the first time in his life, he was afraid, but he couldn't say of what.

CHAPTER SIX

Amber was asleep on her feet behind the counter of Package Depot, where packages arrived and departed, and people asked complex questions about shipping and arrival dates, terrified that their precious package of cheap crap might not reach the middle of Bum-Fuck, Ohio, at the holy preordained time so they may gently touch, with their consumer love, their long-lost cousin who ached for human contact.

Her inner monologue these days was atrocious. She cursed like a sailor in her mind and wore a gentle, if shopworn, smile on her face. She was tired and the store was dead and that made her more tired and she wondered what the hell she was doing with her life. Maybe life was nothing but sitting in an empty store, getting older, watching packages, people, things come and go to destinations unknown. She was dour. She knew this and embraced it, because why not? Why succumb to all those advertisements, those flashy videos, those digital billboards that sold positive thinking? They were all selling you something and trying to make you happy for having bought into it.

She was tired. That was part of it. On nights they made love – or fucked or humped or lazily rubbed up against each other like two flabby sea mammals – the dogs were kept out of the bedroom. The first time they tried fucking when the dogs were puppies, the two of them just barked and watched with rapt attention until she couldn't stand it anymore and after that they were shut out on 'date nights'. At least there was one thing Joe loved more than the dogs, for a few minutes anyway. But on those nights the dogs stood at the door to the bedroom, frustrated, confused, scratching at the doorjamb, sniffing at the sliver of air beneath, whining that high-pitched, incessant noise. Joe had fallen into a beery sleep almost immediately afterward, passed out when she returned from gazing out into the line of trees where she felt something staring back at her, looking into her. She had wanted to tell him but he was gone, and now, in the daylight, in the flat, monotone nothingness of Package Depot, it seemed a stupid flight of fancy. Getting herself worked up over some imaginary fear meant bringing some kind of excitement to her life. It was that bad.

The dogs kept at it until two in the morning, when she finally gave up and let them inside. They crowded between her and Joe and she was pushed to the edge of the king mattress by some dumb animal who cared nothing for her inner life and was thus an integral part of the family.

So she was tired and cranky and filled with a soft hate for everything and everyone around her when she received an email announcement from the Parent Teacher Association: 'We have an exciting announcement! Tonight, at our planning meeting for the new school year, the executive committee will bestow a new Parent of the Year award for the person who has been diligent and faithful in working on the PTA all last year despite challenges both personal and professional. We look so forward to seeing who the first annual Parent of the Year will be!'

This was one of her extracurricular activities. She had felt partially summoned to join and did so more out of peer pressure and guilt than anything else. One has to be invested in their child's education. One has to be involved in making a difference. Plus, she thought that perhaps her presence on the association would confer some kind of extra leeway for her wayward eldest son and defer responsibility of his being a burgeoning fuckup through signaling she was an active, wholesome and involved parent. She had planned to skip tonight. She had never skipped before, but figured she could feign ignorance of the first meeting of the year. Now, with the email reminder combined with the thought of returning home at an hour when everyone would still be awake and requiring dinner, she rethought her plan.

She got out of work at five. The meeting started at seven. That gave her two hours to herself and a good excuse not to go home. Her gym bag was in the car. Maybe a light, quiet meal afterward.

The evening was warm and inviting in a way that made her feel like anything was possible and lifted her spirits. She locked up the store, nearly invisible in a strip mall, bordered by a dance studio for kids on one side and a home heating store and showroom on the other. One could drive right by and never see the place and that was fine with her. If you must be a ghost, better not to be bothered by the living.

She followed through on her plan and was proud of herself for that. She didn't return home and instead went to the gym just two miles down the road and again felt more lifted. The sweet, end-of-summer air, the feeling of being on her own, of having a few moments to move muscles, work up a sweat and feel like she was doing something exclusively for herself. She was in good shape for her age, but it wasn't about getting in shape, really, it was about time. And there was something about the wall of mirrors that lined the gym, where she could constantly sneak looks, observe herself, judge herself at all angles to affirm her existence as it appeared to others. *There I am: that's my ass, my hair, my face, my chest – this is how I look to people around me.* And, naturally, she watched others, watched how they contorted their bodies as they strove to be something different, to make themselves more appealing. It was a funny thing about gyms and exercise, it was all about sex but few wanted to admit it. From the tight or skimpy clothing to the machinations of the exercises themselves, there was always a lot of thrusting, contorting and sweating. All eyes were on the mirror like a form of masturbation.

How she would love to be alone with all these mirrors and truly examine every inch of herself from every angle. It would be better than a vibrator, she imagined.

Amber left the sheen of sweat on her skin and changed back into her normal clothes. She stopped at a cafe and had a salad and a glass of white wine because no one can actually attend a PTA meeting without some form of drug in their system. Joe texted, asking where she was, and she let the phone sit for a whole five minutes before finally succumbing to the electronic urge that had now embedded itself in the very DNA of humanity: *PTA meeting tonight. You're on your own for dinner.* That surely meant a pizza or two would be delivered to the house. She drank a second glass of wine and popped a breath mint before driving to the school.

Their school district was separate from the city schools, a top priority for all homeowners in Amber's little squelch of a neighborhood. They may have to vote with the city but at least they didn't have to send their kids to school there. Everyone knew the horror stories of city schools. No parent in their right mind would willingly send their child there if they had an alternative, what with all the fights and metal detectors and drugs and shitty teachers. And yet, here was her boy in their quiet, high-performing school system acting like a little sociopath, following in Lucas's footsteps – another product of the fine school system. She wondered if they had found that boy yet, pinned him down for questioning. Whenever she began to grow despondent about Vinnie and her role as a mother, she thought of Lucas and his parents. The boy was out of someone's nightmare. She empathized with them having to watch their son unravel in such awful ways and she feared it.

The high school was set atop a small hill with sports fields carved into the earth below. It was big, holding both middle and high school students for two towns. The football goalposts rose up lonely and pale over the neatly trimmed grass, the soccer goals wide enough to fit a truck through, and the track encircled it all, clean and symmetrical. A chain-link fence bordered the property and students put keg cups through the chain links to spell out 'Welcome Back Seniors!' How fitting, nice and lame, she thought. It wasn't like when she was a teenager. Everyone hated school back then. They sought rebellion. Such a display would never have been conceived of in the first place, and would have been immediately defaced or torn down if any class nerds had deigned to try. It was a different time, a time when teenagers, like her, didn't give a fuck. When she was their age, she was sneaking beers in the woods, dropping acid before school in the morning and giving hand jobs in the back of the bus. Maybe that didn't play out so well in the long run – Amber never even attempted college and would probably be stuck at Package Depot until the day she died – but there seemed a certain nobility in it: raging against society, even if you had to wipe the cum off your hand before checking into homeroom.

These days, it seemed high school students were so very…lame. All united in friendship and understanding and social activism and internet self-advertisement. They gloried in the unity of doing the right thing for society, advancing their future careers and their social worth and it all seemed so conformist and empty.

But then, Amber wanted the same for her sons. She wanted them socially engaged and kind and successful; she wanted them happy and compliant and soft to the touch. She wanted them to be part of this push for a better place, as much as somehow, for some reason, she hated the idea of it.

Maybe that was where the Lucases of the world sprang from. The last rebels bursting forth from the oppressive, pious normalcy like a fireball of Hell through the window of an empty house.

She felt old now. She sounded old. All she needed was a shotgun, rocking chair and a *Keep Off the Lawn* sign while she awaited death.

Death was Melanie Stillwell. Her dyed blonde hair cut razor sharp across her jawline, a bright white and completely manic smile on her face. Melanie Stillwell, who was so overwhelmingly happy to see the other parents that it just had be fake. The walking dead, the parenting dead, the involved-in-their-childrens'-lives dead, the PTA-member-of-the-year dead. And Amber wandered into the horde like the last survivor of a zombie apocalypse finally giving up and deciding it is better to join the masses than remain the last woman on Earth with a functioning brain. Amber wasn't entirely sure what excitement she sought, what her 'ideal life' would be if asked by a therapist, but she knew this was not it.

"Amber, it's so great to see you again!" Melanie's hands were like bony knives, as sharp as the rest of her. "How was your summer? We took the kids to Rome! Isn't that fantastic? It was such an educational experience for them. I think it's essential that children experience the larger world, don't you?"

"Oh, of course!" Amber said, fake smile and all. Amber had never been beyond the Eastern seaboard, let alone outside the country. The airfare alone for her family would be a month's pay. That's what you got when your neighborhood was lucky enough to share school district lines with the wealthier suburbs. Sure the schools were great, but you had to contend with an entire army of kids whose parents will buy them cars, have five bathrooms, designer clothes and take them on international vacations.

"We always talk about a European vacation someday," Amber said. "But our schedules! There's just so much to do." Thank God she stopped for a couple drinks. She moved quickly as possible past Melanie and found her seat in a conference room where the other thirty or so parents now sat, making small talk and shuffling their things.

There was all the usual shit. They had to take and approve minutes from each meeting. Roll calls, votes of yay or nay, subcommittees to subcommittees, who's going to chaperone the dances, who's going to organize the bake sales.

Is there anything more suicide-inducing than the idea of a bake sale? Crumbling brownie squares and rock-hard chocolate chip cookies on napkins to raise enough money to make cheap posters to advertise the Snowball Dance? Amber did not pose this question to the group.

And then on to the most bewildering aspect of the evening – the Parent of the Year award. Melanie Stillwell took to the podium as if she were about to announce the latest lotto winner, joy and pride trembling beneath her skin.

"So, the executive board decided this year we would begin a Parent of the Year award to show our thanks and gratitude for someone who has shown themselves to be, not only a great and involved mother or father, but a real and true asset to the PTA, a team player, and a trusted friend to all of us. It's not always easy making it to these meetings while trying to balance raising your children and work and home life, and the executive board wanted you all to know how much it means to us that you take the time and put in the effort, not just for your own children, but for all the kids and for this school. Since this is the inaugural award, we've based our decision on looking at who really stepped up last year, who faced hardship and difficulty but still found time to make PTA a priority."

Melanie brimmed with joy, her own joy at being able to bestow some kind of honor on another person.

"Amber? Won't you please stand up so we can thank you for all your hard work last year and present you with this small token of our appreciation?"

Amber's body reacted but not her mind. She stood, she smiled, she even spoke a few words about how honored she was to receive the first Parent of the Year award. Her fugue state still managed to go through the proper motions: show humility, say you don't deserve this, that we're all, each and every one of us, a true Parent of the Year, and that she looked forward to making this another great school year. Her performances on the high school cheerleading squad were less spectacular than this impromptu speech, which her brain had called forth from countless hours of watching television award shows. There was an easy formula, and she just spouted like an automaton, the walking, talking dead. If the dead could speak, it would probably be in the form of award acceptance.

And then, in her hand, was a gift basket wrapped with a bow: bottle of wine, crackers and cheese and chocolate and bath salts. "We hope that you might be able to use this as a little self-care for a night," Melanie said as Amber nodded her thanks and quickly, quietly sat down, waiting for the eyes of the room to leave her, once again, nameless, faceless.

Amber sat alone in her car beneath the high school parking lot lights and cried. She cried because of everything that was and everything that was not and everything that could have been. She cried because there was no way out, ever. She cried that Rome existed; she cried that her life was half over but the path already set, unfurling like a ball of yarn, the thread to lie limp and flat and unmoving till the end.

She drove back home. It was nearly nine o'clock and dark and she unwrapped the gift basket, thanked God it was a screw-top bottle of Pinot Grigio. She drank from the bottle, long gulping chugs like she was sixteen and drinking in the woods with her friends around a fire again, the darkness of the trees closing in around them, only firelight and laughter and a warm, beautiful, hazy togetherness keeping the dark at bay. She thought of this as she drove alone through those awful streets and took pull after pull from the bottle and secretly wished to veer off the road into a telephone pole because she knew no other way out and the only response must be severe and life altering.

The streetlights came and went. The darkness grew. The bottle half-gone, she went for more and still she couldn't stop crying. No bonfire now. No immortal teenage life. Only the end looming somewhere out there and the knowledge of a life wasted and gone. What is left when the ball of yarn is completely unfurled? Nothing but the empty space of unfulfilled possibility.

She could drive these streets with her eyes closed, let alone drunk, and for a moment she did. She shut her eyes and just let the car roll along and when she opened them again nothing had changed. She was in the same place, driving in the same direction, in her same neighborhood. Maybe in some alternate universe at that moment she crashed and died, but in this one she came back to the world the same way she had momentarily left it.

Ridgewood Drive was empty, its two lonely streetlights sitting sentry, as she turned onto it from Beechwood. She saw her house, dim light in the windows behind curtains, soft and lonely. *What are these strange constructions in which we confine ourselves*, she wondered. *They seem so small from the outside and yet inside they are whole worlds.* She finished the last of the bottle while sitting in the driveway and left the rest of the gift basket in the car, not wanting to explain it to Joe. She stepped out into the warm night air. It made her feel more drunk, and yet made the world feel eternal; this same warm darkness once surrounded the Earth at a time when humans were not even a forethought. She looked up and down the street. There was no one, nothing, just the empty silence of lonely houses and, trapped within them, lonely people all destined for the same place.

Out of the darkness there was fevered, loping movement and from the corner of her eye she caught the onslaught of something fast and intractable emerging from the trees. In her haze she was startled, scared, and then just annoyed. The dogs had come around the house. They ran close together as if conjoined twins, legs galloping over one another, heads at once lowered and then raised baying into the night. And then, in an instant, the beasts stopped and raised their heads, silently staring directly at her. She paid no attention and began to walk across the grass toward the front door and then stopped. The dogs were silently staring at her. Normally, they would run up and jump and wiggle and beg for attention, but now they were silent and staring, eyes full of light and she, in turn, stared back at them, confused.

The dogs separated from each other and slowly circled to each side of her. She heard a low growl. It sounded as if it came from the trees behind her. She turned to look but there was nothing there. She turned back again and the dogs now faced her, the hair on their backs raised stiff. She heard the deep, low growl again. The dogs stood still as statues, their heather-gray hides barely visible in the night, but their eyes shone, trained directly on her. Helmutt began to move sideways to her right, Otto to her left. They worked in unison, a well-oiled hunting machine. It was their nature, what they were meant to do. Amber turned and looked behind her again but there was still nothing there. The dogs were not looking behind her, they were looking directly at her. Their heads were low, their legs bent slightly.

She hesitated, confused and worried now. "Guys, it's me," she said, but it was as if she were a ghost trying to speak to the living; nothing but a slight breath. "Helmutt! Otto! Get going!" she said, now showing her anger. The growl deepened and intensified. Amber waited and then took a step back. The two dogs took one step forward. *These are not my dogs*, she thought. *These are something else.* The dogs took another step closer, one from her right, the other from her left. Amber felt behind her for the door handle to the minivan.

★ ★ ★

That night she lay in bed as far from her husband as possible without sleeping on the floor, the dogs sniffing and whining at the bedroom door, banished for insubordination. He tried to talk to her but she was silent.

"They would never hurt you," he said. "Dogs can sense things we can't. They can pick up on things we don't see or hear. They know things we don't. There was probably something in the woods that you couldn't see."

She said nothing back to him.

"Oh, you're giving me the silent treatment now. Isn't that productive?"

Her silence was something much more. Her silence was a levee. If she were to speak, all would be swept away in her rage. It came from deep within her and seemed to keep coming and building, and she could feel it, and she knew that if she spoke, she would not be able to hold back, that she would lay waste to everything, everyone in her life and would accomplish nothing. In the end, she would wake tomorrow to the same world in which she was trapped.

The dogs sniffed at the door. They would never be still, they would never be silent. So single-minded in their pursuit, their desire to unmake her and tear her piece from piece.

The threat came from the outside and from within. It was everywhere, all around her. It lurked in the past and the future, in the outside world and in the bedroom. Her life unfurling to that last bit of string and everyone, everything hastening her undoing.

"They love you," he said. "I love you," he said.

But there was nothing that truly loved her, because, in the end, they all wanted her dead.

CHAPTER SEVEN

Shondra Waite stood bold and beautiful against the deep sky. Her dark, perfect skin shone with a nearly metallic gleam in the sun. She was young – early thirties – a skintight black neoprene shirt hugged her body, her dashiki skirt hovered just above the grass outside the Amherst Museum of Modern Art, and her perfectly tied head wrap, flecked with orange, green, red and black, rested like a crown on her head. Elizabeth was both in awe and envious, still shaking from her morning of campaign door-knocking. Shondra had earned that envy; the daughter of a single mother raised in the slums of Bridgeport, she worked her way into the Yale School of Art in New Haven and her post-modern architectural sculptures that examined technology opposed to the natural world won her instant fame, rocketing her nearly overnight into the auction houses that every artist dreams of. Now she was here to deliver her newest creation, and Elizabeth Tutt had brought her here. It was meant to be a gift to the city, but Elizabeth couldn't help but feel that it was a gift to herself, a piece of her own legacy. She was now the giver of culture to the city.

Shondra wandered the property just outside the museum's entrance, instructing the curator and the builder how her Tree of Life display would encapsulate a small sapling on the museum green. "It is the Tree of Life," Shondra said, seemingly to no one and to everyone. "Surrounded by the imitation of life, a technological window through which we see a distorted version of the world that is unreal and yet appears real. It is a lie that represents nothing more than a death of the natural. Here, the tree is preserved, a reminder of our reality in the world of unreality.

"In the cultural traditions of Western Africa, the tree stands as a bridge between heaven and Earth, a maternal figure that provides food, comfort, protection. When a child is born, a tree is planted and it is meant to grow with the child, to produce good fruit to nourish the child as she grows into an adult. But here, it is surrounded by the falsity of our modern world. The sapling will stand in defiance, beset by these ghosts in the machine."

It was a beautiful, profound proclamation and Elizabeth's pride was tinged with envy because this creation would never be hers. She hadn't artistic skill in any amount.

Elizabeth was exhausted. The political forces that aligned against her were already in full swing. Before coming to the museum, she had spent the morning canvassing the neighborhoods of the city, the poor neighborhoods in particular, where she spoke of socioeconomic inequality, equal rights, and warned against the fallout of an austerity budget that would surely beset a state deep in debt that refused, year after year, to tax the rich. Her constituents should not bear the brunt of the oncoming fiscal disaster. She knew the buzzwords to perk their ears. She walked with Meghan through the neighborhoods of South End, the haunch of her dog leg district. She walked past the abandoned houses, single-story boxes that looked little more than cardboard, leftovers from the manufacturing days, dropped along faded streets years before she was even born. The overgrown yards scraped the legs of her pantsuit. Even the houses that weren't abandoned seemed forgotten, haunted little dollhouses. She kicked trash on sidewalks and streets out of her way: nip bottles, Styrofoam food containers with the rotting remnants of fast food, plastic bags like tumbleweeds, soda and beer cans not yet salvaged, forgotten grocery carts, the skeletal remains of mattresses and box springs resting against telephone poles covered with pictures of a missing nine-year-old girl. A hypodermic needle broke underfoot. She felt the heat and heard the dogs bark. She watched the young men and women eye her suspiciously and then ignore her, felt the rattle of screen doors so loose they nearly fell to the ground with each rap of her white knuckles.

These were her constituents, but they were not her people. And they let her know at every turn. It had been a difficult summer. There had been protests and marches, chants and occasional violence. They were worthy causes but, despite her support, they were not her causes and it created a rift she struggled to bridge. People were hurting and when they looked at her – a smart, navy blue pantsuit reminiscent of Hillary, carefully bobbed hair straight from Elizabeth Warren's congressional photo and face perfectly white and without blemish – they saw money and privilege and pandering, and perhaps they were right. The city was on edge.

An emaciated woman held a child in her arms, stared out from behind a screen door, nodding uh-huh until she gently, timidly, reached out and took Elizabeth's campaign flyer like an abused child. Elizabeth strained to see her behind the screen. There was a darkness in that house. Some great shadow that loomed behind the frail woman with the frightened eyes. It was as if she had stepped forward from it, for a single moment, and now receded back into shadow, only to disappear again. A man in a stained tank top, smelling of cigarettes and alcohol, talked for fifteen minutes about his constant rejections for social security disability. She stopped and talked to a group of men and women in lawn chairs between a community health center and a used furniture store. They were here every day, they told her, smoking cigarettes and watching the neighborhood. She didn't stop to talk to the young men with sagging pants and bandanas playing basketball with a rusted hoop. Fifty houses, Meghan had told her. We need to hit fifty houses, at least. Her feet were tired and sore. It was hot and the street rippled in the sun. Who else were they going to vote for? She pointed to Washington D.C.; she talked of police brutality; she talked of community services, youth programs; she said they had to get guns off the streets. Everyone agreed but come election day, would they be there? She didn't know.

One more house now. Maybe no one would be home and she could just leave the flyer in the mailbox. The dogs inside barked up a storm, causing her to step back. Every time a door opened she felt herself an intruder on something real and personal. One more house and then on to the museum to meet the great Shondra Waite. These were Shondra's people. She should be out here, not Elizabeth Tutt. But she was the only one running in the campaign who wouldn't try to gut everything that had been built so far. There was only one direction to move – forward. But forward to what? Where? It was like a great wheel that had begun to turn, she was only along for the ride.

The dogs in the house barked and finally a man, older and hard in a soiled tank top, answered the door. "Yeah, I remember you," he said, the screen door swaying before him. "I remember you. What have you done with your time?"

"Well, I—"

"Nothing. That's what you've done. Come down here talking we're gonna do this, we're gonna do that, and what happens? Nothing. Where you been up there? Lost?"

"No—"

"C'mon now. You see us? I don't think you see us. You see what you want to see but you ain't seeing us. We go out into the street. We march and hold signs and chant and shut down traffic and then you pop your head up and say it all over again — what're you going to do?"

"Well, as a representative I can be your voice—"

"My voice? My voice is out there! My voice is in the streets! My voice is all over this place. Look around South End. This is my voice here! Where are you? Where's your voice?"

"I will fight for you—"

"We fight for ourselves. We fight, we get beat up, dragged down the street and shot by your cops. But we keep fighting. What are you fighting?"

He wouldn't let her speak. She couldn't say what she had rehearsed. She couldn't say what she really felt, that she was alone and overwhelmed and as lost in this mess as everyone else, and there was nothing she could do. She couldn't admit that, so here she was deaf, dumb and mute because it was all too much to say.

"What are you afraid of?" he said. He stared at her, eyes wide, sclera like white saucers tinged with red filaments. He moved closer and closer, out of the door now, onto the front porch. The dogs behind him were barking with more intensity. She felt so small. "What are you afraid of? Think on that. What scares you here?"

"I...I don't know. Now, if you'd just let me—"

"I ain't stopping you from doing anything. You stopping me! You all stopping me! I'm bigger than you, I'm bigger than this whole world. You trying to stop me! You afraid of that, aren't you? Tell it like it is! Tell me now! Do I scare you, bitch?"

She turned and ran, nearly tripped over a crack in the concrete, bumped up against the chain-link gate, spilled out into the hot street.

"Keep running!" he screamed after her. "Run for president after this! Don't make no difference down here!" He laughed as she ran.

And now she watched Shondra Waite glide across the grass of the museum property. She heard the traffic in the background; she watched as Shondra directed the curators and builders. Shondra was a product of the system she fought for, an example of what could be. If only they could see it. They would see it. Shondra's work would be here for all to see, a testament to what could be done, if only....

"You're making a difference," Meghan said and Elizabeth trembled.

★   ★   ★

As Elizabeth drove back to Ridgewood Drive, as she left the haunch of her district and traveled to the last paw-like section of her quiet neighborhood that now seemed so small and isolated, she felt a great sense of relief. Politics was a stage and for the first time in her life she felt overwhelming stage fright. She needed to hide behind the curtain. She was no longer sure which part of her was real – the person or the performer, the great show or the inner workings, the spotlight or the darkness surrounding it. She turned onto her street and her heart sank. Nearly every yard bore a sign: 'Let's Kick Tutt!'

Then another sight caught her eye. Parked just two doors down from her was a police cruiser in the driveway of the Lovetts' house. She looked from the cruiser to the charred remains of the structure across the street and back again. Last she'd heard they still hadn't located the boy. He was still missing, hiding from the police and his family. They were probably beside themselves with grief and worry. Elizabeth was exhausted and feeling old, but she also felt a sense of ownership and responsibility in the matter.

These were also her constituents and her neighbors. She wondered how many from the neighborhood had offered this mother and father a smile or kind word. As ostracized as she was, she still caught bits of gossip: the boy was a bad seed, disturbed and dangerous, routinely followed by police and school officials, a budding nightmare. Naturally, the burden and guilt for such a child would fall on the parents. She had never seen them at the neighborhood block party. She had rarely seen them outside of the house. It was a small house, single story, probably two bedrooms on a little third of an acre with trees in the back and the window blinds constantly lowered. She thought about the timid, emaciated woman staring out at her through the screen door with the haunted look in her eyes and thought about this poor couple just two doors down. *These little haunted houses*, she thought.

She went inside and changed out of her pantsuit into jeans and a light blouse and rubbed the soreness from her feet. She ran a load of dishes, glanced out the window and saw the police cruiser had left. It was nearly evening on a Saturday and the neighborhood, the world, was dead still. Nothing moved, suspended for a moment of time in the last heat of a dying summer. She put on her tennis shoes and walked down the street. She struggled to remember their first names. She knew their names, but still, nothing came to mind. They were like ghosts among the living, their only proof of life a disturbed child who burst forth like a ball of fire.

There was a decorative lamppost in the yard. The hedges were trimmed and ran beneath the bedroom windows. She knocked on the door and readied herself, more nervous about this intrusion than she'd been during her morning door-knocking. A thin woman with curly black hair that dripped down over her shoulders answered the door. Her eyes were dead tired, her face a pale gray with lines etched into it by years of work and worry. She could see the boy – Lucas – had her looks: feminine, long face, ridged long nose. In him, however, it had appeared faintly beautiful.

"We haven't decided who we're voting for," she said, her voice tinged with embarrassment for Elizabeth.

"No. I'm not here about that," Elizabeth said and tried to laugh it off. "I…I just wanted to check on you and see how you were doing and see if there was anything I could do to help. I'm Elizabeth. I don't think we've ever really met."

The woman looked her up and down, sizing her up. An offer of help was rare enough to be suspicious. She pushed the screen door open and held out her brittle hand. "Tonya Lovett," she said. A man appeared behind her, thick salt-and-pepper hair swept over his forehead and big glasses. The man looked as if he had never left the seventies. "This is my husband, Frank," she said.

"I just wanted to see how you were holding up. If you've heard anything about your son?"

Frank stepped forward and seemed to overwhelm Tonya. He pushed the door open farther. "Why don't you come in?"

Everything in their house was covered in Christian paraphernalia. Everywhere Elizabeth looked there was a bone-thin figure hanging from a cross; an angelic, pale, bearded face surrounded by a corona of light; quoted scripture on soft-colored photographs of clouds, waterfalls, sandy beaches; Precious Moments figurines of fat little children bent over in constant prayer. The whole place left over from some bygone era. It was as if they were elderly grandparents already, begging entrance to heaven through symbolic gesture. The stale smell of used and moldy furniture accompanied the overwhelming sense of quiet loneliness.

Tonya sat cross-legged at the kitchen table with Elizabeth. She held a cup of coffee. There were no pictures of Lucas on the walls.

"The police haven't found him. Nobody has heard from him. We don't know where he is," Frank said, his voice bellowing but hardly sad, more like fed up. "I'm sure you saw the cop here a few minutes ago. Telling us the same stuff all over again." He seemed bored with it all now, impatient. "Hell if I know where the kid went."

Elizabeth heard his voice, but she kept her eyes squarely trained on Tonya. Tonya looked at her as if she were pleading.

"Lucas was born before Frank and I met," she said. "But Lucas doesn't know that."

"I understand," Elizabeth said. "I'm sure that would be difficult for a child to process."

"I didn't want him to know who his real father was."

"We don't need to talk about that," Frank said. "What's done is done."

"I'm not trying to intrude."

"His biological father—"

"Is a piece of shit," Frank said.

"—owns the house across the street," Tonya said. "The one Lucas set fire to."

Elizabeth looked at Tonya tenderly and touched her hand. Elizabeth had encountered this before when people would contact her office looking for help, an oversharing that was really more of an unburdening, the desire for someone else – anyone else – to know their plight, their story. It often came out as word vomit; in this case, overly personal story vomit. Rarely was it something Elizabeth could even hope to fix, but that wasn't the point; they just wanted to be heard, to be validated. It was uncomfortable, and usually Elizabeth feigned listening while making a steady and polite move toward the exit. But it was not possible here. Seated at a table, before two people she had approached out of kindness, she couldn't turn tail and run. She had to listen and, she could tell, Tonya was desperate.

"I grew up in this neighborhood," Tonya said. "This was my parents' house. I grew up right here. When I was twenty-four, my parents moved south but I had just started a good teaching job at the elementary school and I didn't want to leave and start over so I stayed. I was on my own for the first time. He had moved in across the street. Mostly kept to himself, but we would see each other every now and then. He was different."

"He was a drug addict," Frank said. "Plain and simple. He was crazy, too."

"He was always working on those cars of his outside," she said. "I hadn't dated much in my life. People make bad decisions, sometimes."

"He hurt you," Frank said.

"The way he talked," she said. "It was like a song that lulls you in. The way lyrics make sense with the music but if you just read them – really just read them – they don't? He was like that. I ended up with some problems. It was my first time really on my own. We partied a little too much maybe."

"You nearly died."

"Stop."

"It cost you your job for a while."

"I had to go to rehab, myself, for a while," she said. "He had a penchant for heroin, LSD. I just couldn't help myself. It felt so good. All of it. And then it just leaves you broken the rest of your life. I remember seeing the light at the end of the tunnel – the way you always hear about? I remember seeing that and then just feeling cold, shivering dark and cold. I woke up in a hospital alone."

"Since we're just leaving it all on the table here," Frank said.

"I was pregnant at the time."

"It doesn't matter now, that's all in the past."

"You don't have to tell me all this."

"Why shouldn't I tell you? I may never get another chance. I'm not ashamed. I'm just trying to understand it all."

"He took off the second he heard she was pregnant," Frank said. "Just left the house there to rot but has refused to sell it – and he's had offers. Ask any of the neighbors, they'll tell you."

"It's an odd place, that house. I wouldn't ever go back into it. There was always a sense when you were inside that something else was there. It felt heavy. It could seem so big inside but it's not."

Frank sighed. "We told Lucas to stay away from it, but you know how teenagers are."

"Of course."

"Lucas has issues," he said.

"Lucas's father had – shall we say – different beliefs. He experimented. We experimented. Altered perceptions, altered realities. He would talk about Helter Skelter, the coming race war. He covered the walls with symbols – things he said were older than the Bible, and crosses that didn't look anything like what you see in a church, swastikas. He said they were doorways, means to tap into the beyond, but we never went anywhere. We never left beyond our own heads, and it was terrifying."

"He was out of his mind," Frank said.

"I don't know why I kept going back," she said. "It just felt so rebellious at the time, so...unique. Maybe I just thought it didn't really mean anything. All those symbols, they work into your mind and change you. That's what people don't realize about symbols. They get inside your head, they alter you, even if you don't know what they mean."

"Everyone knows what a swastika means, Tonya," he said.

"And the eyes," Tonya said. "He painted eyes all over the walls of the house, kinda like the eye on a dollar bill? The all-seeing eye, he said. The Illuminati, the global conspiracy. He talked about a cabal that ran the world, that stole and sacrificed children and coded subliminal messages into television commercials. I could feel the walls looking at me, like they were alive. It was its own world, completely separate, but it felt like we were uncovering something secret, something real when everything else just seemed so fake. The world was operated by this mysterious force and we were the only ones who knew about it."

Tonya looked now at Elizabeth, as if she'd forgotten she was there. "You must think I'm awful," she said. "I swear I'm not like that. I would never be like that now."

In a way, Elizabeth did think she was awful, but she felt pity, too. The past was unforgiving. It was hard to look at this frail, haunted creature and condemn her for past sins, to strip her of forgiveness.

Elizabeth took Tonya's hand. "Not at all," she said. "I understand. You went down a dark path. We all make mistakes, but it doesn't mean you're a bad person."

"But how long do you have to pay for a mistake?" she said. "How long? A lifetime? Your son's lifetime? It will outlive me."

"Well, I'm sure with some help Lucas can turn things around. I'm sure they'll find him and then he can get the help he needs...."

Tonya gripped her hand tight now, a wild, intense look in her eye.

"I don't want them to find him," she practically growled. "I don't want him to come back here. They should take him away. You don't know what it's like to have your son – your child who you birthed and raised and fed and loved – become a complete and total *stranger*. He's different people one second to the next and never the same person twice. I'd have to yell at him, not because I was mad, but just so he could hear me. It was like he was that far away. Like you could see him but he was somewhere else entirely. You could yell as loud as you want, maybe he would hear the echo."

"Things have been difficult," Frank said and he gently put his hands on Tonya's shoulders and pulled her away from Elizabeth.

"He terrifies me," Tonya said. "He doesn't sleep, he walks around the house at night talking to himself. He's on the computer all day doing God knows what. We had to lock up all our medications because he kept stealing them and then when we tried to take his marijuana he threatened to kill us both in our sleep. He said he heard voices from that house. He said it was calling to him. And we couldn't stop him. He cut Frank with a kitchen knife. Show her, Frank. Show her the scar!"

She was becoming hysterical and Elizabeth felt herself slowly leaning back in her chair.

"Do you know what it's like to live with someone like that? Before he ran off, you know what he told us? That he was a god. A god. That is what he thinks. And what can a god do? Anything it wants. I've raised a monster that thinks he's a god."

"I'm sure he's not—"

"You don't know," she said. "You can't know. The doctors don't know, the teachers don't know. Nobody does. What am I supposed to do with someone like that? We're lucky he didn't burn this house down with us in it. When they find him, if they find him, I want him in a state facility because I can't do it anymore! He's killing me either way. He wants to send me down that tunnel again, just like his father."

"I'm so sorry," Elizabeth said.

"You said you wanted to help," Tonya said. "You're in the government. You want to help? You get him put away somewhere. That's what you can do."

Elizabeth looked at Frank and he shook his head.

"I understand," Elizabeth said.

"Do you know what it's like to live in fear?" Tonya said. She gripped Elizabeth's hand, bone on bone. "I hope you never do. It breaks you. It breaks your mind."

★   ★   ★

It was dark by the time Elizabeth left. Where had the time gone? It had seemed little more than minutes inside that pathetic, sad place. She stood at the end of their short driveway and looked down Ridgewood Drive to where the dim yellow streetlight hung over the intersection with Beechwood, and then she looked in the opposite direction toward her own home on the corner of Ridgewood and Leadmine where another dim streetlight cast a lonely glow onto the pavement and not much else. Then she stared straight ahead at the burned-out, abandoned Widner house, the place where Tonya had briefly, innocently trod down a dark path in her early adulthood, a place where she had become infatuated with a strange man, inebriated by drugs and impregnated with a son who had become a disturbed and possibly dangerous young man who felt that same house calling to him. Is it possible that Lucas found out? That he knew it was his father's house? Or was that just too easy? Too neat an answer? Life rarely had such neat and tidy answers.

Her mind was lost and exhausted, as if she had just summited a mountain peak and was now falling back down. The day itself seemed long and insane, a maelstrom that blew her about in the winds. Wasn't that one of Dante's levels of Hell? A constant windstorm where trapped souls reached for each other but could never touch, torn away by the gales. Lust: that was the one. Perhaps she was among the guilty.

There was the sound of a pop and sizzle. It startled her for a moment and she turned in time to see the streetlight over Ridgewood and Beechwood fade to a dull orange and then black, and the street became dark. There was no moon and no stars; there were no lights on in the houses, not even the one she had just left. It was odd. More than odd, it seemed uncanny. There was a certain wrongness to it all, as if something was just slightly off. She turned to walk home and another pop and sizzle left the only other streetlight, the one at her corner, dark and dead. She walked quickly now, the darkness falling over her shoulders.

Elizabeth shut the door to her house and locked it and turned on all her lights. She chastised herself for becoming an old, fearful woman subject to flights of fancy and paranoia. Was she afraid of the dark now, too? Was she pushing aside a lifetime of education in rational thought just because two light bulbs burst? This was stupid and illogical. This was not who she was. She was just exhausted, physically and emotionally. The stories over the course of the day, the highs and lows, had left her vulnerable and beaten up. She needed a stiff drink and noise and sleep. She needed to turn her mind off. An exhausted and hyper mind could be a dangerous thing.

She poured herself a scotch and turned on the television. No news, no documentaries, just something stupid to watch to shut off her brain. She had a secret, guilty love of reality television shows, something she would never admit in public. Her latest fixation was a show about couples paired together by a panel of experts who meet the day they are married and try to make a lasting marriage out of it. Clearly, this was nearly impossible and, if she wanted to intellectualize this petty little obsession of hers, she could argue it showed the futility of expertise when it came to issues of the human heart. But really, she just liked to watch and judge the participants, to criticize their motives, their decisions, their looks, and most of all, root for them all to fail.

The sound of the television crowded her house with the voices of others, crowded out of her mind the fears and trials of the day. The scotch settled her into a happy, hazy mist of reality twice-removed, and she sat curled on the couch in sweatpants and t-shirt, enjoying this moment of peace.

*   *   *

Ten-thirty at night, three knocks at her front door startled her, roused her out of a sleep-like trance of false reality feuds and flashing colors. The knocks came again, harder, more insistent, reverberating throughout her house, proclaiming itself real. Her senses were up now, heightened, nervous adrenaline pumping through her body because someone unannounced was demanding entry at night. There had been car break-ins in the neighborhood before, generally youth from the city looking for a joyride or something they could sell. The occasional burglary occurred, though far less often. But she was alone and it was night and someone was standing at her door knocking – harder now.

Elizabeth went to the living room window, touched the curtain aside a few inches so that she could see the front doorstep. There was no one there. She opened the curtain wider now to get a better look around, to see if she could see someone walking away, possibly in the yard, but she could see nothing; the street was too dark, the glare from the light inside her house made it impossible. She turned off the lights and returned to the window to look again. Still, there was no one there. She walked cautiously, tenderly to the door, turned the dead bolt, opened it a crack and peered outside. She could feel the night air on her face and knew it was real. She could hear the tree frogs chirping in the last night of summer. She opened the door wider and looked out into the darkness along both sides of the house to see if someone was lying in wait for her. No one, nothing, gone like the fleeting fear of a lonely woman.

She shut the door and locked it, but the fear had found a home inside her now. She was relieved no one was there but still scared that someone had intruded into her space for the purpose of frightening her. A prank perhaps, but an intrusion nonetheless and one that left her feeling vulnerable to the outside world – in a word, unsafe. This little neighborhood, this quiet enclave, was now falling apart, invaded by others.

She turned to walk away and then, quiet as a whisper, so light as to be chalked up to her imagination or a childhood memory, there were three more raps at the door.

CHAPTER EIGHT

Did he just see that? It was hard to say, so quick and momentary, the flash of a red vehicle parked in his driveway as John passed the turn for Ridgewood Drive and continued down Leadmine toward the small bridge over the wetlands. Why would a red car be parked in his driveway? He had just left an hour ago; left as his two children readied themselves for school; left as his wife stared into her computer and typed furiously, snapping quick orders at Caitlin and James, warning them of the impending bus; left as he glanced over his shoulder and she said, "Are you coming home tonight?" and he said, "Yeah." In that moment, he felt everything was wrong and over and done with, except for maybe one last moment, one last chance where he could save it, save it all, their lives, their marriage, their family, their whole world. Just one more split, one more crack in the foundation and it could all come crashing down.

"You're not sleeping," she had said to him.

"I'm sleeping down here," he said.

"No. You're down here but you're not sleeping. You're up all night on the computer. What are you doing?"

"Research."

"Research on what?"

"Nothing, don't worry about it."

"It was just some dumb kid playing with fireworks, John. No need to get obsessive about it."

He kept his head down. She was smart, sure. Smarter than him. She went to college and everything, but that didn't mean he couldn't know something she didn't, that he couldn't be aware of something she was blind to.

He had a tendency toward obsession, but thought it more of a strength than a weakness. Shortly after Caitlin was born he became obsessed with physics, trying to understand the mysteries of the universe, how it worked. Maybe seeing her born into the world started him down the path of trying to understand it all. After reading countless books, he thought he had mastered the language and theories well enough to try his own hand at submitting an article to academic journals. Sure, he couldn't do the math and had zero letters after his name, but he thought his philosophical and theoretical approach to bridging classical mechanics with quantum mechanics would be enough to pique the peer reviewers' interest. Besides, he told himself, Einstein was a nobody before he was Einstein. Every journal to which he submitted his paper about light speed invariance and electromagnetic symmetry dismissed it out of hand until he finally gave up and determined that the institution of science, itself, was so far up its own ass that it couldn't recognize when an amateur had beaten them at their own game. They suppressed him to keep order, to maintain the impenetrable wall between science and the rest of the world, just like the news media, which similarly suppressed the truth in order to maintain their own facade.

"It's more than that," he said. "It's bigger than that. It's important."

"It's not some big cover-up, John," she said and then she laughed.

John arrived at the Public Works Department only to be told he would be on his own for the day, to take the pickup and go fill potholes near Leadmine Bridge – complaints of cars bottoming out and whatnot – and so here he was, less than a mile from home with a lingering question in his mind. He couldn't bring himself to turn the truck around and go back to see if his eyes had deceived him. A red car in his driveway at nine in the morning and she fucking *laughed*.

The asphalt was old here, dull, faded gray. The road heaved and cracked. The harsh winters left chunks missing, torn out by snowplows, run over by three-ton vehicles till they were wide and empty and then the snow would melt and they filled with enough water to drown a cat and when they froze again the ice pushed and expanded and the holes grew larger still. There were holes everywhere. It was a particularly rough patch of roadway but one that cars flew down regardless, because drivers loved the descent from his neighborhood to the straightaway across the wetlands with its tiny bridge over a deep brook and then its ascent into the next hill, the nicer neighborhood with the big houses and two-acre yards. To the east and west stretched the swamp, filled with long, brittle reeds between the two hills. Here was a beaver dam; here was a heron; here was a place he would occasionally walk to with his children to look for trout hiding in the shade of the bridge midday. A breeze ran across it all, the reeds whispered and he was very alone.

He took the shovel from behind his seat.

It was hot enough to make him think summer would never end, and he could feel the heat from the asphalt in the truck bed radiating outward, pulsing against him. He'd be drenched with sweat in fifteen minutes, but it didn't matter. All he had to do was keep his head down and fill holes. All day long, fill holes. All he had to do was think through this thing and it would make sense. He could fill the holes. There was a red car parked in his driveway; the fire started inside the house; the police claimed it was an innocent mistake; the reporter wouldn't respond to his emails or take his calls; the reporter worked for a newspaper owned by a corporate conglomerate. Somehow it all pieced together to make sense. Somehow they all worked together to deny the truth: the fire started inside the house, intentionally set by a young psychopath, and the government didn't want to investigate, and the reporter just did what she was told by the corporate monster and so now reality was skewed, even for his own wife, who laughed – *laughed!* – at the truth. No one really knew but the four people there that day who saw the fire in the beginning, saw it rip through the windows and the roof. He had little use for the cops. Who was he going to talk to – Badgely? No. Badgely just thought he was an overgrown drunk. The cute little reporter – the little bitch. Aren't they supposed to seek out the truth? Aren't they supposed to be unbiased? He had tried calling her desk but it always went to voice mail. He had emailed her several times over the course of several nights, recounting his statement as the first eyewitness to the fire; sending her pictures he'd taken of the supposed 'fireworks' debris left in the grass near the abandoned house that clearly showed they'd been sitting outside in the sun for weeks, their cardboard skins faded and weathered. He'd sent her videos and articles showing how modern store-bought bottle rockets were incapable of lighting that kind of blaze; he'd sent her weather reports showing it had rained just two days prior to the incident and clearly the ground and grass would have been too wet to spontaneously combust; and, last but not least, explained to her how the house was set on a concrete foundation, even if there was a flame it could not have traveled under the frame of the house to catch fire inside and then spark off the fireball they'd seen, the product of gallons of combustible chemicals that had been sitting for over a decade in that long-forgotten place.

She never responded. Not even a courtesy reply. She was so young and beautiful with her bright, stupid future ahead of her in the bright, stupid media who told everyone what to do and what to think and how to think. She couldn't be bothered with him, probably too busy taking dick from some boyfriend who looked like Justin Bieber, a scrawny, prepubescent douchebag wearing Ray-Bans, and had his own YouTube channel. Probably couldn't change a tire if his life depended on it. John was thirty-eight years old. What was she? Twenty-two at best? And thinks she knows enough to tell the world what's going on.

And then there was Lucas. A sixteen-year-old drug-addled little terrorist. Naturally, there were no available records, but everyone knew. That kid was insane and dangerous and they just let him walk around free, excused by the same system that locked John up and took his driver's license because he'd had a couple drinks. Locked up someone who works every goddamned day and fills holes in the roads and pays taxes to the same government that lets this fucking kid get away with arson and God knows what else. By the time that kid was grown he'd be Son of Sam. Yet he was still out there, wandering around, probably in the neighborhood, hiding in the trees, watching them every night. Stalking the very woods that John looked at now. He'd come out of hiding at some point. He would strike again. It would get worse. They never stopped with just lighting fires or pulling the wings off flies. But everyone wanted to ignore the coming reality, more proof that the whole world was going to hell and everyone was dancing along with the music.

He moved the truck just over the bridge to the other side of the brook and began to fill the holes there. He took a contractually mandated fifteen-minute break. He opened the passenger-side door and sat looking out over the swamp. He took two nips of vodka and tossed the tiny, empty bottles into the brush. He heard the sound of an approaching car, coming from the direction of his neighborhood. The sound carried far and he saw a red car dip out from the trees, coming toward him now on the straightaway across the wetlands. It bounced over the small bridge and passed him in a flurry of sound and wind. He caught a glimpse of the driver, a man who looked soft and pale with glasses, who stared straight ahead, not even a glance at John.

He took the shovel back in his hand, a touch of haze in his vision now, the sun brighter, the asphalt blacker. The potholes wouldn't fill themselves.

$$\star \quad \star \quad \star$$

Where does the time go? Old men ask that question but few actually stop to think about it. You're born and grow and then you're an adult and you never really know how it happened, as if each day you wake to a new world, a new reality, and you are left with a dreamlike memory of other lives, but it isn't real anymore, just imagined. And when you look back on it, everything has changed, but you're still a kid – a child – now trapped in a man's body, with a job and a house and kids of your own. And you look around briefly and realize that everyone else is a child trapped in a body, that we have the same fights as we did in the schoolyard, the same fears as we did lying in bed at night in the dark, the same yearning for selfish pleasure at the expense of all. Time passes slowly and then instantly. He had blinked and it was quitting time. He had only fixed half the potholes. Lost in his own mind, the long, flat swamp stretched out beneath a lazy sky, the air buzzed with the sound of insects fucking; time had stood still and then made an imperceptible leap forward. Maybe it was physics.

There was a message from Jessica on his phone from two hours ago. He had missed it somehow. Perhaps he had been asleep. He wasn't sure how much he had been sleeping lately. She said he was up all night but it didn't seem that way to him. Perhaps he was up late, but not all night. Perhaps sleeping on the couch was not giving him rest; perhaps the booze kept him from truly sleeping at all. He had certainly woken up this morning, therefore he must have slept. But he did not remember waking just now. It was as if he had begun to fill the potholes and then was suddenly conscious again five hours later.

Can you pick Caitlin up from dance at 6 tonite?

He texted back: *Sorry, was on a job. I guess I can. I'm not supposed to drive tho, remember?*

It's on your way home from work. And not being allowed to drive somewhere has never stopped you before, which is how we got into this mess.

He couldn't really argue with that, so he just texted back *Okay* and she didn't respond.

There was still asphalt in the back of the truck and it had cooled and congealed into a single hardened mass. His boss would kill him. He looked at the time and tried to gauge how long it would take to return the truck and get to his daughter's dance class. There was a pickaxe behind the seat. He took it out, climbed into the pickup truck bed, raised it over his head and brought it down, splitting chunk after chunk until it was broken up enough to shovel out and bury in the brush like a body. He looked at the remaining potholes. It was fine. No one actually cared. He'd sneak back later and finish up. Cars passed by and bounced up the road toward Harmony Hill.

When he dropped off the truck at the Public Works Department, he made it quick and spoke to no one so that no one would ask where he'd been all day, part of the magic of unseen government work. With fifteen minutes before he had to pick up his daughter, he took his pickup and stopped at the liquor store. He bought a few more nips for the evening and then, with a second thought, went back inside and bought a ten-pack of them. It was just to keep himself numb and steady. It was to keep himself thinking clearly, calmly. The assault of his coming home, of facing the life he had blinked into, would not cut as deeply. He twisted the tiny caps and drank two more on his way to the dance studio.

He never liked this place. The studio had a waiting room where young girls waited for their next class clad in leotards and tights and all of them in middle school or high school with long hair and young skin and the look of everlasting hope on their faces. He felt so big and out of place. The folding chair felt like it would break under his weight, his work boots big and clunky compared to ballerina slippers and delicate bare feet. Mothers waited for daughters, building friendships and sharing mundane stories. No one talked to him and frankly he preferred it that way. He snuck a peek through the doorway to see his daughter. She stood, chunky with the remains of baby fat, awkward and soft, but yearning to be graceful and perfect: arms akimbo, the toe of her right foot extended forward, touching the polished dance floor, staring into the mirror image of herself. He wondered what she was thinking at that very moment. She was the eldest, the perfectionist, the type-A personality who wanted to do well in school, who spent her free time creating crafts, who wanted to please those in authority. Every minor victory she claimed she immediately brought to John and Jessica's attention, so that she could be told it was a job well done. Every opportunity that presented itself to her, she took, even if it meant long hours of dance after school, or little jobs performed for neighbors. She wanted everything and tried it all: she acted in plays, a ski club during the winter, art classes, swim teams and soccer. He watched her hop in place, exchange one toe touch for another. She was not perfect, but she was striving for it.

John put his head back against the wall. His eyes went to the people in the waiting room. Fat mothers tended to beautiful daughters. Part-time dance instructors, still in high school or community college, waited and stretched and bent their heads to their knees. Everywhere around him was young flesh covered in a thin layer of Lycra. A man's gaze in the presence of young women could cut through any facade of decency and he felt big, awkward and guilty just sitting there. You could bury it down, you could pretend you were above it, but it was always there, turning your eye toward that tight little ass or those budding breasts or those young, bright eyes not yet beaten down by life. He wondered about these girls – sixteen, seventeen, eighteen years old – walking back and forth in front of him. Did they know? Perhaps they were too young to realize yet, perhaps it was just dawning on them, raising their walls – both physical and emotional – that would exist for the rest of time, passed down through generations. Music played in the studio, as the dancers went through their routine. He caught the eye of a mother who glared at him, lines in her face, hate in her eyes. He felt like he was falling asleep again.

Then Caitlin was there, hugging him, a light sheen of sweat on her face that rubbed into his skin. He held her and felt like a part of decent society again; loving father, husband, provider. Her affection meant he was good. At only ten years old she was not yet of the age where she would be embarrassed to openly love her dad. "Just let me get my things," she said. There was the smell of sweat and perfume in the air.

He hid the ten-pack of nips beneath the seat of his truck before Caitlin got inside and she told him about her day at school and then about her dance routine, and she told him she was happy that he would come and watch her dance. He felt normal and grounded. Perhaps for the first time in a long time. He meant something to her. He was her father and she loved him unabashedly and unconditionally.

"I have to get Ms. Nancy's mail when we get home," she said.

It was one of the many little jobs that she found around the neighborhood. Every day she would bring Nancy – essentially house-ridden, with an oxygen tank connected by tubes and plungers into her nostrils – her mail. The frail old woman could barely make it to the mailbox, so she paid Caitlin five dollars per week to get her mail and bring it to her. Caitlin had been saving her money. She had more cash put away in her little plastic safe than John and Jessica had in their checking account. Their frequent fights and fears over paying the bills, the number of times they had to tell the kids they couldn't afford a special vacation or the latest toys, meant Caitlin had grown into a girl with a healthy fear of poverty and a singular desire to not only succeed in order to gain praise, but also succeed in order to have the money her parents never had.

That's good, he thought. *Don't end up like me.*

He pulled his pickup into the driveway and Caitlin ran up the street to Nancy's mailbox. He waited and watched her go, never letting go of that old fear of a car speeding down the street and knocking her dead. It was the basis for all parenthood: keep them alive long enough so they can keep themselves alive. It was something that welled from deep within, that the child must live, must carry on at all costs. He stood and waited at his truck as Caitlin retrieved the mail for a woman dying of emphysema. He glanced down the road to the house that Lucas had burned and across the street to the house of his parents. He wondered if they felt the same way. If they would stop at nothing to keep their son going. If they would, perhaps, hide him from the police. He wondered if he would protect his own children from the same fate, from falling into those dark, black holes, formed by cracks and upheavals, into which countless fell and were lost. In the haze of his mind he saw himself slipping, ever more quickly, over the edge. He drank another nip while he waited, checking to be sure Jessica wasn't looking out the window.

"Daddy? Ms. Nancy isn't answering the door." Caitlin was beside him once again. In her hand were a few pieces of junk mail, sheets of coupons printed on cheap paper, mailers for septic cleaning services, lawn care and *Vote for Elizabeth Tutt.*

"Maybe she's just taking a nap or in the bathroom," John said. "What do you do with the mail when she doesn't answer the door?"

"I leave it at the door."

"Well, why don't you do that?" he said.

"She didn't answer the door yesterday either," she said. "The mail from yesterday is still there."

John stood up straighter now and looked through the small line of trees that separated his property from Nancy's, her old single-floor ranch looking dusty and pale in the waning light. "All right," he said. "Let me go over with you."

He felt odd walking up to Nancy's house. He'd hardly spoken three words to the old woman, his wife having fielded her questions and requests for help when they arose. He opened the screen door and yesterday's mail flopped onto the front step, just as Caitlin said. He picked it up and glanced through it. More junk mail: predatory lenders and credit card companies, advertisements and requests for donations. There was a folded piece of computer paper inviting Nancy to attend the annual block party to be held at the intersection in front of her house a few weeks from now. She had occasionally wandered over in past years during the festivities, but she would only take a small amount of food on a plate, exchange a few words and then wander back to her house to sit in the window, eat and watch.

John knocked at the door and called her name and then listened. Caitlin watched him from behind. No sound came from inside the house.

"Did she say she was going anywhere?" he asked.

"No."

Nancy's old car sat in the driveway and he breathed a deep sigh. He knocked on the door, harder this time, called her name louder and still there was nothing. He tried the door handle but it was locked. John walked to the bay window where Nancy would sit to watch the block party, put his hands to the glass and tried to peer through a gap in the curtains. He could see the old furniture, the sparse room that looked not so much dirty as it did undisturbed. Dust had settled over everything. Near the entrance to the kitchen he saw a pair of legs and an oxygen tank lying on the floor.

"Sweetie, go tell Momma to call an ambulance, okay?" he said and she immediately welled up with tears and fright.

"Is Ms. Nancy okay?"

"I don't know, sweetie. I'm going to find out, but I need you to go tell Momma now, okay? I want you to go. Quickly now, okay?"

Caitlin turned and ran back toward their house. John girded himself, took a few steps back and then kicked the door through, his strength and weight breaking off pieces of molding and splintering wood.

★   ★   ★

Blue and red lights flashed over the trees in the dark. He paced with his hands on his hips, watched as paramedics loaded the stretcher into the ambulance. Old Oxygen-Tank Nancy covered in white cloth, looking like a sack of laundry. The neighbors gathered once again.

He'd found her sprawled on the kitchen floor, the tubing from the oxygen tank to her nostrils wrapped around her neck. She was stiff, immobile as a piece of wood. Jessica had come over after calling the police and pronounced her dead as a doornail. "She's been like this a while," Jessica said. "Maybe a day or so. I found a home-care patient like this one time."

"I remember," he said. "But look at the tube wrapped around her neck."

"She fell and it twisted," she said. "Not uncommon."

"Her eyes are open," John said.

It didn't seem right. Before they left Nancy's house to wait outside for the paramedics and police, he looked around. It was a sad place, the home of someone left alone by her children, grandchildren. A place that had been slowly rotting away; the old carpet worn through in places, the wallpaper peeling, dust clinging to cheap trinkets, porcelain figurines and fake flowers in vases. He looked for signs of something missing, signs of a break-in or theft, but he didn't know where to look or how. The only thing missing was a sign of life.

Her eyes stared out at the ruin of time.

Outside, he waited. He had told the trooper on duty that he saw Nancy on the floor and then kicked through the door in an effort to save her.

"Why did you kick down the door?" the trooper said. "You should have waited for us."

John looked at him with a screwed-up face. "The door was locked and she could have still been alive," he said.

"Did you try to get into the house through another entrance? The sliding glass door on the back porch maybe?"

"No."

"Did you leave the house through the sliding glass door?"

"No. Just out the front, the same way I went in."

The trooper closed his notebook and said, "Well, you didn't have to kick the door down, the back porch door was open," and then walked away from him. John went to his truck and snuck another nip. He stopped and talked to Mark from across the street. "That's too bad," Mark said. "She was a nice enough lady."

"She had her oxygen tubing wrapped around her neck," John said.

"That sounds disturbing. The cops investigating?"

"I told them, but I don't know. Lock your doors."

"I always do. Got a small arsenal in there, too. I pity the person that comes to this neighborhood looking for trouble."

"First the fire, and now this, and Lucas is still out there running around."

Mark looked at him oddly and then let it go. John walked back to the outskirts of the scene, stood near the state trooper's car, waiting for someone to ask him what happened. At the intersection with Beechwood he could see Joe and Amber Locke; Dale and Becky Atkins watched from their inter-neighborhood golf cart with Jim and Julie Katz, who lived directly across from Nancy. Vernon Trimble studied the scene carefully.

Elizabeth Tutt now stood beside him. He looked down at her and then sighed. Everything seemed to be coming in waves, jumping from one face to the next.

"What happened?" she said.

"I found Nancy dead on the floor," he said.

"That's so sad."

"It might be worse than sad."

"What do you mean?"

"Just lock your doors at night," he said.

She looked at him for a moment as if readying herself to say something. Instead, she put her head down and walked away, back toward her home. He watched her go, a small figure fading into the night, and was glad to be rid of her.

Then he saw her – Meredith Skye. She had come from the direction of Beechwood and was speaking with a state trooper, writing on her little notepad, looking over her trendy glasses with big doe eyes up at the officer, jotting down every word he said and taking it verbatim as she had with the house fire, believing it, believing all of it, reporting the official line, the official lie.

She stepped back slightly when he jogged toward her, calling her name.

"Mr. Ballard, I'm not interested in rehashing the fire—"

"You never even responded," he said.

"I'm sorry. It gets very busy sometimes and I can't respond to everything. And you emailed me…a lot. And, for the record, I don't lie and I'm not fake news. You really expect me to listen when you write those kinds of things to me?"

"Did you even read any of it?"

"Listen, Mr. Ballard, I understand how you feel, but my job is to report what the police and fire marshal find. It was a house fire. It happens."

"It didn't happen like that, though. And you know that. I was there."

"And here you are again."

"I found her," he said. "Did you know that? Did they tell you that? My daughter was bringing her the mail and she hadn't come to the door for two days. I kicked in the door because I saw her lying on the ground through the window. Did they tell you any of that?"

"The officer said they were alerted by neighbors…."

"Did they tell you she had a cord wrapped around her neck? Did they tell you they still haven't found the little psychopath that burned that house down that you don't care about? Did they tell you any of that? You just take their word for it. Do they tell you to do that? Is that what reporters do now, just as they're told? Take the company line and ignore the truth?"

"You seem to be present when a lot of this happens, Mr. Ballard. You're the common thread. If there's something suspicious going on, maybe the police should start with you."

"You're twisting it," he said. "You're twisting everything and you don't know what you're talking about."

"And you're going to tell me?"

The lights flashed red and blue strobes. It cast shadows in darkness, twisted features and glimmered in eyes like a carnival. His head swam in it all, each glimpse of thought a flash of light that disappeared just as quickly. He talked, more animated now. His head was hot and he felt a pressure, the veins pulsing. He told her the truth, but he had already forgotten it.

She seemed to grow smaller and smaller, shrinking before him. Her face became a mask of horror and disgust on the verge of tears and rage. She was receding into the dark, sinking to the bottom of a black lake. He reached out toward her and realized she had backed away from him.

"Where are you going?" he said.

"I have to go, Mr. Ballard," she said.

"I'm telling you what happened!"

"You're scaring me, Mr. Ballard," she called back.

"Scaring you? What about her?" he yelled, pointing to Nancy's house. "Her eyes were open, Meredith! Her eyes were open! Yours should be, too!"

CHAPTER NINE

"Do you know who died today, Mom?"

Vernon held a spoon of rice to her puckered, wrinkled mouth, but she still refused to eat, turning away like a child.

"You have to eat, Mom."

"Did I die?"

"No, Mom. You're right here with me. Nancy up the street died. Do you remember Nancy?"

"I am dead. I died. And you're here to torture me. That's all you've ever done is torture me. This is Hell. What did I do? I don't deserve this. You're awful to me."

"Just eat the food, Mom. Aren't you hungry?"

She opened her mouth slightly and he forced the spoonful of rice between her lips but she didn't seem to notice. She didn't chew. It just sat there as she stared past him, toward something that was inside her mind and yet somewhere out there.

"Nancy couldn't breathe," she said.

"Yes, Nancy who had the oxygen tank. Do you remember her?"

"I see her," his mother said. "She just stares at me."

"Yes, she used to look out the window a lot," he said.

Vernon had watched the scene that night, the neighborhood once again populated with police, fire trucks and an ambulance, except this time it was different. The fire had been during the day and this was at night and it seemed more ominous to him. No one died in the fire, but with Lucas still missing and now Nancy dead, it all seemed connected. He heard it said many times by forensic investigators that there are no coincidences in detective work. Vernon had seen John Ballard raging at the reporter, at the police. The reporter had walked quickly away from him, the police put out steadying hands to calm him. Vernon found Ballard and got the whole story: eyes open, oxygen tubing wrapped around her neck, no obvious sign of a break-in, the front door locked and the sliding glass door to the back porch unlocked. If she was killed, it meant the killer could have come in and left through the sliding glass doors. There could be fingerprints, but contrary to popular belief, fingerprints don't end up on everything you touch. Plus, she was incredibly old and in poor health. The obvious and simplest explanation was that she had simply fallen over and died. But, then again, there are no coincidences.

"You're dead," his mother said. "We're all dead, just like her."

"Stop saying those things, Mom. No one here is dead. We're eating. Dead people don't eat."

She allowed him to spoon another bit of rice into her mouth. He wondered how much longer she could hold out like this. The human body is remarkably resilient, continuing on at all costs. Addicts pump ungodly amounts of every drug they can into their body for decades and still live on; coma victims live for years in a state of unconsciousness. His mother's mind melted away and yet her body continued. It was as if the mind and body were separate and yet together. Wasn't that part of Rene Descartes' philosophy? He would have to consult his books.

Vernon didn't have the energy to bathe his mother that night. After much cajoling and arguing, he convinced her to finally eat those little bits of cheese and thus take her pills. She stared at him as if he were vile for making her eat when she didn't want to, shook her head as if he represented every regret in her life, and maybe he did. He was without brother or sister. He was the lone product of her marriage and her life as a mother and maybe that wasn't good enough for her. More and more, it wasn't good enough for him. He grew tired of feeling alone and poor and most of all without consequence. He thought of Nancy. If she was murdered, at least her death would mean something – it would be of consequence, a force acted upon her by another that would have far-reaching implications: investigation, capture, prosecution, prison sentence, media reports. It would require attention. Otherwise, it would just be another candle that simply extinguished, and there was little drama there. People need drama, he thought.

He tried to put his mother to bed, but she kept pushing him away. He felt frustrated and grew increasingly impatient and angry. A sense of loss seeped into him. There was nothing worse than feeling like a failure and he wanted badly to have some kind of influence, some kind of meaning. He finally gripped her by her frail shoulders and forced her down into the bed and he screamed in her face, with a rage he hardly knew he possessed, to stay the fuck in bed. Her eyes were wide, frightened, and she went stiff and lay perfectly supine in bed, staring at him. The sound of his voice was now gone and everything was once again silent. He felt bad, but his mind was in overdrive and he had to retreat to his room, to get away, to become lost in something else.

"I'm sorry, Mom," he said. "It's just you just have to do what I tell you and it's time for bed."

"I hate you," she said, simply and quietly.

He lay in bed with the lights off. Only the light from his television cast a pallor over the walls, his small couch, his computer desk and piles of clothes he'd yet to wash. The soothing voice that told of horrors flooded his space, his mind, on a continuous loop. A woman answers the door of her house to find a man asking to use the phone, he forces his way in and stabs her to death; a little girl goes missing from a small town in Wisconsin, only to be found weeks later washed ashore, her hands and feet bound, strangulation marks around her neck; a successful businessman in Nevada returns home to find his wife shot to death. It was all out there, the ever-lingering presence of danger, but so often the danger did not come from without but from within the home, the family, the neighborhood. The knife-wielding home invader lived just two houses down in a trailer park; the little girl was murdered by a pedophile uncle; the woman in Nevada was shot by her husband. There was little coincidence when it came to murder. In Nancy's case it could have been Lucas. It also could have been her own family members, seeking to cash in on her house. He didn't know which option it could be, if any. He needed more information and that wouldn't be forthcoming from the police.

He thought of John Ballard at the scene. He seemed unworldly, out of his mind, raging. He would talk to John tomorrow, get his take on the situation, find out what he knew when he was in a better state of mind. Briefly, he thought of his own state of mind, and he finally admitted to himself that he was lonely. There was no one else to share this life with him. Most days, the only person he spoke with was his mother. He left the house only for groceries and his walks around the block. Sometimes he would walk several times a day. But winter would arrive in a few months and his walks would grow less frequent in the cold.

He stood up from his bed, dressed and put on his shoes. He couldn't sleep. He opened his bedside table and took out his bowl, packed it with some pot, and then walked outside into the night. He sat on the concrete front porch and sparked his lighter, leaving him temporarily blind as he sucked in the smoke and felt his head inflate and grow warm. He stared at his long gravel driveway, which led to Beechwood, cast in a dull glow from the moon, and waited as his perceptions shifted, changed, eased into that elated sense of being. He looked at his yard and the small Hyundai parked outside the garage. He thought of others, their work-all-day, watch-TV-all-night lives, straining, striving. It was an endless cycle. Why bother? Maybe he had it right, after all. For as much as others may look down on him as a societal leech, he'd stepped out of the rat race and was still living the same quality of life as everyone else in the neighborhood. He was just doing it without all the soul-crushing work. He was living his own way.

But not really. He was living his mother's way. His life was dictated by her illness, her growing insanity, her persistence. He was caught in a different cycle. He was dangled by the strings of a mad puppeteer who screamed in the night and oscillated between forgetting him, ignoring him and hating him. He thought he could hear her wailing now, but it seemed far away. There was a rustle somewhere in the trees, but it was too dark to see anything. Something moved, skittered amongst the leaves under the cover of night. A small field mouse, a squirrel, a bird.

A large crack of a branch now, something bigger, heavier. Or was that only in his mind? Everything seemed so much louder when he was high. The small crunch of a squirrel across dead leaves might sound like a bear trundling through the woods. The screams of his mother in the night pierced like the cries of a banshee, her jabberings as she lay awake in bed talking to the moon had the same effect as if she were kneeling beside his bed whispering them in his ear. Perhaps she was. Perhaps there were movements about the house he was unaware of. He knew that she would get up and move about when he was asleep. Occasionally he would wake and find her standing over him in the dark, staring down with her pale withered face illuminated by nothing more than the glow of his digital bedside clock. In that way, she haunted him. He'd seen countless real-life tales of hauntings during one of his earlier digital television binges: homeowner awakens in the night to find a figure standing over his/her bed. Or, perhaps, an alien abduction story, her tiny stature and gray skin like that of the small, alien creatures with black oval eyes and small slits for nose and mouth. What did she want from him? It was impossible to know and she was more difficult to communicate with than ghosts or aliens.

He didn't want to go back into the house yet. He suspected that she would wake, and he couldn't be bothered with putting her back to bed so he stayed outside. Better to be with whatever walked in the woods than what he knew walked inside his childhood home.

He needed to walk the neighborhood and think on it. He took his pipe and small bag of pot and shoved them in his pants pocket. The streets were dark. The streetlamp that normally lit the corner of Beechwood and Ridgewood had, like Nancy, extinguished, leaving the neighborhood with only the dull glowing eyes of lit windows, most of which were dark at this hour anyway.

He walked down his long driveway, away from whatever sounds came from the woods, and turned onto the street. Around the corner he could hear Joe and Amber's dogs baying at the sky. Their hunting howls carried over the trees like those of their wolf ancestors. He could hear them running the property. They seemed agitated, vicious even, and he wondered what it must be like to face down a pair of animals bent on tearing you apart. Clearly it happens; people are mauled to death by a dog or a pack of dogs on a regular enough basis. The statistics were there: more likely to be killed by a dog than a shark, etcetera, but in his heightened state of consciousness he tried to imagine the perspective of the victim, just as he did when watching his forensic detective shows. What does one think and feel as it's actually happening? When do you realize that you're not going to get out of this alive? How strange it must seem to be torn apart by the family pet. The dogs bellowed again and he heard Joe's voice calling them back inside.

He saw Nancy's house, now completely dark and devoid of life, the lights and vehicles all gone, the family members – as rare a sight as they had been in the neighborhood – all retreated home for the night to resume mourning tomorrow. John Ballard had yelled that Nancy's eyes were open. He knew from his forensic studies that the eyes often remained open in death, but the state of her eyes could determine time of death, depending on how much the whites had dried out and the iris bled into the rest. But what was he really saying as he bellowed out that line? That her eyes had been open? Perhaps John realized for the first time what awaits us all. Perhaps it was John's eyes that had been opened. Vernon's eyes were open, he was sure of that. He knew that at any time he could be snuffed out. Maybe John – a nice guy, but maybe not so bright – had such a realization in that moment too; perhaps the image of dead Nancy, neck wrapped up in her oxygen tubing, eyes open but seeing nothing, had stirred such a realization in him as well.

Or perhaps his eyes were seeing something different. Perhaps John saw something more than just the common fate of humankind; maybe it was something more specific and frightening. After years of watching every true crime show he could find, Vernon realized one thing: everyone walked a tightrope. The real question was when you fall and how far. It seemed the neighborhood was falling. This safe little haven felt less safe in the last couple weeks. The fire was an intrusion of harsh reality, as was Nancy's death. The fact that Lucas – a mentally ill possible arsonist – was still at large and probably hiding in the neighborhood carried with it a heightened sense of danger.

Vernon stood outside John Ballard's house for a moment. A gauze curtain glowed yellow on the first floor of the two-story cape, the only light on in the house. He thought he could see the shadow of a figure moving about.

Vernon's mind was lost in the darkness, the possibilities, churning in the marijuana haze, connecting dots not connected before. He barely noticed the slow approach of a car. He began to walk again toward Leadmine until he was nearly across the street from the burned-out Widner house, when a tremendous light fell upon him and he was forced to squint and hold up his hands. The light blinded him and he saw swirls of color. The light blinked out and he was blind again, this time in darkness, but he could hear a voice, heavy and authoritative, telling him not to move.

"Hold it right there. Keep your hands where I can see them."

And he did. He kept his hands raised, trembling, like a weak and frightened common criminal.

Vernon's eyes adjusted to the darkness again and he could see a police cruiser in front of him. He could see the state trooper, one hand on his flashlight, the other on his gun, circling the front of the car toward him. He was confused and suddenly scared and his mind immediately went to the weed in his pocket. He could smell it himself; the cop would surely have a nose for it.

"What are you doing out here?" the officer said.

"Walking. I live here."

"Where do you live?"

"55 Beechwood. Just around the corner. I'm just out for a walk."

"Little late at night to be walking," he said. "What's your name?"

"Vernon Trimble."

"You have any I.D.?

"At home. I walk at night sometimes. Everyone knows me here."

"Been knocking on any doors tonight, Vernon?" The officer shone the light right in his eyes. "Or have you been walking around doing something else?"

"No, I haven't knocked on any doors," he said, becoming angry now at this ridiculous intrusion. "If I wanted to talk to someone, I could simply call them and go over to their house."

The cop kept the light blazing in Vernon's face.

"My mother has Alzheimer's," he said. "Sometimes the only time I can get a little peace and quiet is at night, so I go for a walk."

"Have you approached anyone's residence tonight?"

"What? No. I only left my house five minutes ago."

"Can anyone at your home confirm that?"

"Only my mother but I wouldn't use her as a witness," he said. "What's this all about?"

"We've had complaints about someone knocking on doors and running away," he said.

"First I've heard of it."

"Well, it appears whoever is doing it is targeting just one house. But she's called many times now and we're increasing patrols in the area."

"Who's it happening to?" Vernon asked, but before the officer could say that he was not at liberty to divulge that information, Vernon caught a glance over the officer's shoulder to see Elizabeth Tutt standing in her yard looking on at the scene of his possible arrest.

"Are you under the influence of anything tonight?"

"Am I under arrest?"

"Not yet."

"Not ever," Vernon said. "You've stopped and questioned me and have your answers and this is my neighborhood where I live. I'm free to walk about all I like at any time I like. I'm not twelve years old playing ding-dong-ditch."

"You seem a suspicious person," the officer said.

"As do you."

"You enjoying this little back and forth? Maybe I could take you down to the station and we could talk a little more?"

"In the words of Bartleby, I'd prefer not to."

"I went to college, too, smart guy. Just do me a favor while you're out traipsing around: if you see someone, something, let me know. I've got a frightened woman who's being constantly harassed by someone knocking at her door at all hours of the night."

"I understand, officer. I'm happy to help. This is a tight-knit neighborhood."

"Fair enough."

"Can I get your name so I know who to tell?"

"Trooper Brett Badgely."

"I remember you from the house fire the other day."

Badgely shone the flashlight in Vernon's face again and mumbled something about seeing him around. Badgely returned to his car and continued down the road, and Vernon was left again in the darkness between Lucas's house and the one he burned down. He looked down the street and saw Elizabeth turning slowly, holding herself, walking back toward her well-lit front porch.

"Wait!" Vernon called out, now feeling unafraid of human interaction, adrenaline pumping from his brush with the law and this new information. "Wait, Elizabeth!"

He was out of breath and breaking a sweat by the time he reached her yard. Her arms were crossed, not in the way that implied judgment but as if she were comforting herself. She wore a cloth robe and sneakers and, standing before her in the dark now, he saw that she was pretty but with a pained look in her eye, as if she longed for something she feared would hurt her. She watched him and they both stood in silence as he caught his breath.

"Is someone bothering you?" Vernon finally said.

"It seems to have become quite the pastime for someone," she said.

"How many times has it happened?"

"Every night for the past week. All hours of the night. It wakes me up and I look out the window and there's no one there. There's never anyone there. I don't even see anyone running off down the street."

Vernon looked back up Ridgewood Drive, silent and dark, and then to Leadmine Brook.

"What are you doing out so late?" she said.

"I like to go for walks sometimes at night. Think about stuff."

"I saw you here at the fire."

"Yes. My opinion is that it was intentionally set. I don't care what the police and fire marshal say. I did a little investigation of my own."

"I tend to agree with you," she said. "It makes me nervous. I don't want my house to be next."

They were quiet a moment. Vernon could offer her no reassurances. She was right to be cautious.

"Maybe there's something we can do," he said finally. "Maybe as a neighborhood we can figure something out. Somebody must have seen something. Somebody must know who's knocking on your door."

"They never ring the doorbell," she said. "I wonder why that is sometimes. I dread coming home at night because I don't want to hear the knocking again. To know that someone out there has targeted you, it's just...."

"Scary?"

"Personal," she said. "But maybe personal is scary." Then she waited a moment and put out her hand. "I'm Elizabeth. I don't think we've ever formally met."

"I'm Vernon. I live just around the corner with my mother. She's sick. Dementia. So I take care of her full time."

"You seem like a kind person, Vernon," she said. "Do you want to come in for a drink? Or coffee? Anything at all?"

★   ★   ★

Elizabeth's home made him feel like a child. It was neat, orderly, clean, expensive, everything that his home was not. It looked like the home of a successful adult, someone who was educated, mature and had actually made something of herself. There was a fragrance in the air. But, like a museum, it seemed too perfect, too neat and not actually lived in or able to be lived in. He didn't want to touch anything for fear that it could be some expensive bauble that had to be perfectly placed in its assigned spot.

"This must seem odd to you," she said from the kitchen. "To be in here at this time of night with someone you've never really met."

"We're neighbors," he said. "Can't be too odd."

She set down a drink in front of him. Scotch. He never drank much liquor, the sickening burn left him feeling nauseated, but he made an exception and decided he would force it down out of politeness.

"I don't know how neighborly we really are," she said. "I can't say I've felt too welcome here."

"They're just not used to strangers," he said.

"I've lived here two years. I'm hardly a stranger, am I?"

"Not a stranger in that way," he said. "But in another way."

"Well, from the look of the signs planted in every yard up and down the block, they all certainly seem to know my name. They all want to 'Kick Tutt', apparently."

"That's why you're a stranger," he said. "It's not about politics. It's about letting your guard down so they can know you."

"And why should I have to make the effort, Vernon?"

"Because you're the one complaining about it," he said.

She gave him a wry smile and took a long drink. "You're a quick-witted one, aren't you?"

Vernon looked to the front door.

"Do they ever come back? The same night, I mean?"

"No. It's only been once a night. Then I call the police and they send some cruiser over to not find anyone at all."

"The neighborhood block party is coming up," Vernon said. "You should come. It would help, I think. Come. Have a few drinks, talk to the others, let them get to know you."

"I'm a politician, Vernon. Going to gatherings of random constituents is usually a recipe for disaster unless it's all planned in advance."

"You underestimate yourself," he said. "And everyone here."

"I'll try to make it."

"I want you to be there."

"Why?"

"I have an idea," he said. "And I think you being there would help, given what's happening to you."

"And what's that?"

"We need to form a Neighborhood Watch," he said.

"These matters are best handled by the police, not a renegade band of bozos running around the neighborhood probably armed to the teeth. They'll probably shoot the first Black kid that wanders in from the city."

"You said yourself, the police never get here in time to stop whoever is harassing you. We could be here constantly. You see the Carters' house over there? Completely outfitted with security cameras. So is Joe and Amber Locke's house. That's how they figured out Lucas was at the abandoned house the day of the fire. We could probably figure out who's harassing you if we all just came together to work on it."

"I'll let the police know about the cameras," she said. "I'm sure the Carters would be willing to help."

"The cops already know. That trooper who just stopped me was one of the investigating officers the day of the fire. They know, they just don't care."

"I don't think that's true."

"They care once there's a big enough deal for them to care and right now, that isn't the case. But you don't want it to get to a point where they do have to care because that would mean something bad for you."

"We have institutions for a reason," she said.

"And yet they fail and fail again," he said.

"Well, I'm trying to fix that."

"You won't fix it before the next knock on your door," he said.

"What good would I do for your Neighborhood Watch, anyway?"

"It would show solidarity, participation...."

"You want my political position to give it the air of authority. I won't do it. The last thing I need is that big brute down the street beating a kid half to death because he knocked on my door a few times and then telling the world that it was my idea."

"John's not so bad. He's just under a lot of stress."

"Aren't we all?"

"You saw that Nancy died tonight, right?"

"Yes, I saw."

"Did you know that she had tubing wrapped around her neck?"

"No, I didn't stick around very long."

"It's true. John found her. His daughter would get Nancy's mail and he kicked in the door and found her dead, with her oxygen tubing wrapped around her throat."

"I'm sure the police will look into it."

"It's out there, Elizabeth. The world is a dangerous place. It has dangerous people. We have to come together as a community, as a neighborhood, and look out for each other," he said. "Right now, we're all just isolated, separate. But something is going on here. I sense it. There's been a change. It's like something has turned its eye on us and is paying attention, but not in a good way."

She tipped her head to the side and smiled at him again. "You're not helping me get to sleep, Vernon," she said. "Let's change the subject."

"It's one of the few subjects I know well," he said. "I've studied it for years."

"And what is your degree in?"

He let that question disappear, as if he hadn't heard it.

"When's the last time you smoked grass, Elizabeth?" he said.

"Probably since before they stopped calling it grass," she said. "You sound older than me sometimes."

Vernon took out his pipe and his bag of weed and put it on the kitchen table where they sat. "I need it to help me sleep. My mother moves around a lot at night, screams sometimes in her sleep. It will help, I promise."

"Fuck it," she said, laughing. "By next year we'll have probably legalized it anyway."

He smiled. "If you could do that, Elizabeth, you'd have my vote."

★　　★　　★

Vernon left Elizabeth's house and walked home in the early morning depths. All around him was perfect, still silence. Nothing moved or chirped or hopped through the underbrush. The house lights extinguished, the people in a state of near lifelessness, as if hibernating from the world. *Sleep is a strange thing*, he thought. *We blink out of existence for a time and then wake suddenly into a new day.* Sleep was a mystery of the mind, truly frightening when you thought about it. Each morning we wake to a world that is slightly different, yet familiar enough that we can continue on – each day a new moment, each night an imperceptible gap between those moments. Even during the day, there is the immeasurable time difference between when light strikes an object and when we see it and process it. It is not instantaneous. There is a gap and in that way we see only the past. We see the world as we expect it to be, but maybe not as it really is, because something has changed and maybe we don't realize or recognize it yet. If it were up to him, he thought, he'd never sleep. He would watch it all change and shift, subtle and slow, the way a god may watch the universe unfold with no concern for time. If he could stay awake long enough, he could see it happen.

He turned onto Beechwood toward his home, toward the place where his mother lingered between the worlds of past and present, reality and imagination, and he realized that he was not the only one awake, not the only one watching. He felt another presence, something just out of sight, lingering in the dark of the trees. He felt it keep pace with him. From the silence of the woods another twig snapped, another branch broke, another footfall echoed soft but heavy in the night. Vernon kept his head down. He felt fear, but refused to look up, refused to gaze upon it, if it could be seen at all.

Vernon quickened his pace. His mind reeled, lost in a haze of weed and a bit of alcohol. When he'd left Elizabeth she was fading quickly to sleep. It was an intimate moment, to be near a woman again as she readied herself for bed, and he felt an affection for her now and wondered at the future possibilities of such an encounter. She had spoken with him, paid attention to him, was interested in him and that tiny spark of connection between strangers had lifted him so much that he felt a moment of joy and even love.

But those feelings gave way to his absolute aloneness in this moment, his sudden sense of physical vulnerability in the dark. He stood at the edge of his driveway and looked up at the outline of his home, crumbling under the weight of years of neglect and disease and loss and idleness. Like standing water, it seemed suffused with insects and rot. He slowly walked the crumbling driveway, his feet twisting in the uneven holes pinched with rocks; the overgrown grass that wasn't even grass anymore but just weeds retaking what was theirs all along; the house like a bad memory, something that should be burned to the ground as well so that its memories could be extinguished, sent up in smoke.

And with that thought he looked to his right and there, in the trees, he saw a pale white face staring at him in the dark. His mother, clad in nothing, stood at the tree line, gaunt, dark eyes wild and possessed, her blue- and red-flecked varicose veins like roots planting themselves in the soil, spreading tentacles through the dirt, crawling through the neighborhood, enveloping his life. She stood silent and unmovable as a statue and, for a moment, Vernon felt terrified. She was so stark and out of place. She glowed ghastly. He was suddenly a young child confronted by a witch at the edge of a dark wood.

His own mother was now unrecognizable, her face a mask of insanity, her body desiccated and chilling – a mere vehicle for something else, something other. In that moment he wondered what it was that he cared for, that he fed and put to bed at night. It was not his mother. It was as if some parasite, some worm, had wriggled into her brain and possessed her body as it slowly ate away at her from the inside out.

A long, bony hand reached out toward Vernon and something darker reached out to him from the void behind her eyes. He could see her, ephemerally changing form. As old as death, it became something new.

"What are you doing out here, Mom?" He said it quietly, choked by fear.

"I was talking to the boy," she said. Her voice echoed from the bottom of a well. "We talked for a long, long time."

"What boy, Mom?"

He could see now, just over her shoulder, another pale white face looking out from the trees. Lucas seemed to float in the darkness, black hair dripping over his dark eyes, skin smooth with childlike youth.

Lucas smiled at Vernon from the trees, big and wide-eyed and crazed, and then seemed to fade away into the night.

CHAPTER TEN

"You got to be kidding me, Joe. This weekend?"

It was early morning. Amber was already dressed and ready to open the Package Depot. Vinnie had already run out the door, chasing down the school bus because he overslept. She readied sweet Tommy for the next school bus and brushed her fingers lightly over his soft cheeks. Nothing ever worked around here unless she made it work and, in being married to and attempting to raise men, she had come to find them borderline useless when it came to getting the trains to run on time. The morning had been a mess. She knew Vinnie had been up all night online, probably jerking off into a sock. Tommy had refused to eat breakfast, creating a long-lasting standoff between herself and the sweet, but often stubborn, boy.

But there was no excuse for her man-child husband.

"I told you about this months ago," he said. "You said it was fine at the time."

Unless this was all her fault. She reached back into her memory, searching for a snippet of conversation, trying to recall Joe saying he and Vinnie would take a long weekend trip to a hunting lodge in upstate New York with his buddies and their sons. "It will be good for Vinnie," Joe said. "It will give me some time with him, maybe help straighten him out a little bit."

"You guys don't hunt, you just sit up there and drink the whole weekend."

"We hunt, we fish," he said. "Remember all the venison I brought back last time?"

"You didn't even shoot that deer," she said. "It was someone else's."

"Still...."

"Are you taking the dogs?"

"No. There's no room and they're not ready for hunting yet."

"It's because you never trained them, Joe. All they do is run around the yard, frothing at the mouth for something to kill. You bought them and now they can't even do what you got them to do."

"They'll get trained...."

"They're three years old. They'll be dead before they learn to hunt."

That wasn't particularly true. The dogs hunted all the time. They brought mangled and macabre 'gifts' which they left on the back porch: squirrels, tiny moles dug up from the ground, even a full-size wild turkey one time. Amber would come to the sliding glass door and there they would be, wagging their tails, eager eyes, an expression on their faces that resembled a human grin. God knows what germs they brought from those animals into the house, where they licked everything and everyone.

"It's the neighborhood block party this weekend," Amber said, not that she particularly cared. And that was the funny thing: she didn't particularly care that Joe was leaving for the weekend. Frankly, it was a relief he was taking Vinnie with him. She just wanted to lash out for any reason she could find. And she knew it. She could feel it, this need in her gut to tear into him – for something, for nothing, for everything – and now she felt helpless to stop herself.

"C'mon, Amber. You're going to have a great time at the party. You always do. It will just be you and Tommy. You'll be able to relax. He'll play with the other kids, you can mingle. It will all be fine."

She did enjoy the block party. Every year she made a Mexican dip that was completely gone by the early evening. She scrapped any diet she was on for a single day and wolfed down hamburgers and hot dogs and one of the nineteen different desserts – homemade cookies, moon pies, cupcakes, death by chocolate – that lined the dessert table. The intersection was essentially shut down and blocked off but for some unsuspecting driver who took the wrong turn off Route 4, ended up in the infinite loop of their neighborhood and was quickly glowered out of existence by the irritated looks of fifty partygoers. The kids played, rode their bicycles together up and down the street and, when it became dark, played hide-and-seek or ghost in the graveyard while the adults drank and sat around a big bonfire in Jim and Julie's yard as music blared from speakers. Everyone brought beer and shots. People laughed and sang and joked and, late at night, Jim would round up whoever was left to hang out in his giant hot tub. Two years back, Amber had stayed late, allowing Joe to take the boys back home to bed. She'd been drunk and the idea of bonding with her neighbors and friends in a hot tub appealed to her. They all stripped down to their underwear and hopped in. The water was bright and warm and swirling with color. She had felt sexy and young again in that moment, noticing she was in far better shape than any of the other women, and the men shamelessly ogled her, and she didn't care. The hangover the next day was brutal.

But it was fun. It was the way things were supposed to be. During those annual parties, it felt like they had all escaped back in time, to a simpler era, to a time of community and togetherness, where right was right and wrong was wrong. A time when there was almost a childlike wonder to the world, and the country was truly, actually great. It was not a time she had lived through in reality, but rather one that she felt, like a lucid dream that stays so long it becomes enmeshed in memory.

And now, she remembered Joe had mentioned the weekend a couple months ago. "You couldn't have reminded me about this anytime during the last two months, Joe?"

"I'm sorry," he said.

"You fucking should be."

"What's wrong?"

"Nothing," she said. "I just...I don't know." She looked at him now and he seemed so pathetic. It was difficult to stay angry and she felt the tightening coil in her gut letting loose now, bringing her back from what amounted to an adult temper-tantrum.

"It'll be fine," she said. "Just me and Tommy." It would be bonding time for her and him, too. Vinnie was far too gone for her to hold and love on as she did when he was a child, but there was still time with Thomas and, as a mother, she felt that plucking at her heartstrings as well. For all that she desired and all that restrained her, she found comfort in the idea of peaceful, intimate moments with her youngest child, who she could still hold at night and feel a bond that was still pure.

"It's fine," she said. "Really. I'm sorry I freaked out. I just didn't remember." Joe hugged her and she let him.

"That was a terrible hug," he said.

"I'm not there yet," she said.

In the driveway, her maroon minivan sat warm in the morning sun, a million pebbles of shattered glass scattered on the asphalt and in the driver's seat. She stared at it for a moment, processing what had happened and then feeling defeated, frustrated and more furious. She looked inside the minivan, careful not to place her hands near the shards, and scanned for signs of theft. Loose change from the cupholder was gone, one of the boys' hats and Vinnie's gray hooded sweatshirt were gone. She called for Joe.

"Goddamn these fucking animals," he said and took out his phone to call the police. Amber called her manager and said she would be late.

*   *   *

It had happened to them before, but never had they gone so far as to smash the window. Now, as she waited for the troopers and Joe examined his high-tech security cameras, she walked out to the street in the bright morning sun and looked up and down the road. Cars were parked in driveways, but not a single one of them appeared touched. Nobody else was standing outside their car calculating the cost of replacing a window and wondering whether insurance would cover it; no one else was trying to figure out when and where they could get it fixed; no one else was standing among a million shards of auto glass.

She walked back inside and Joe stood at the security monitors rewinding through the night and then playing it back. "Police will be here shortly," he said. "I'll get it all cleaned out afterward and tape it up for you. I got a call in to an auto glass shop. I'll get it taken care of for you before I leave."

"Thank you," she said.

"But watch this. These little fuckers," he said.

On the screen was her minivan, colorless in the night vision, inert and heavy in the driveway like a beached whale in the ambient light of nearby porch lights. The digital video raced forward with nothing happening –

no car approaching in the darkness, no hooded figure jumping out and smashing the window with a hammer – and then, suddenly, the image jolts and spins and there's nothing to see but the underside of their roof.

"They turned the camera upside down," Joe said. "Pointed it up at the roof."

They waited outside for a few more minutes before the state trooper pulled onto the driveway and a short, wiry man stepped out and introduced himself as Trooper Kelly. He had his notepad out and was writing before they even explained to him about the video camera.

"Anything missing?"

"Probably about ten dollars' worth of loose change and some of my son's clothing," Amber said. "This has happened before."

They showed him the security camera footage and he watched intently and appeared to take it seriously. "Are there other cameras?"

"One out back," Joe said. "But there wasn't anything on it."

"Do you mind if I look around your property outside?" he said.

They watched as Trooper Kelly stared at the security camera, still pointed upward at the roof overhang, and then as he walked slowly along the side of the house. Their front porch was a concrete slab that ran the full length of the house, with outdoor wicker furniture where Amber sometimes sat in the evening warmth, enclosed by porch railing and bordered with evergreen shrubs. The trooper scanned the inches closest to the walls of their home until he reached the far end of the porch. He leaned over the railing and looked down into the mulch, and then turned back and looked at the camera again.

"Who do you know that would do this?" he said.

They looked at each other. "Uh….no one," Amber said. "I don't know anyone who would do this."

"It was someone who knew you," the trooper said. "They knew exactly where the camera was and exactly how to get onto your porch without being seen. There's a shoe print over there in the mulch, a scuff mark where they jumped over the railing here, and a small bit of mulch here where they walked along the side of the house.

"If it were the usual random break-ins they wouldn't have known about the camera and probably wouldn't have cared either. Plus, you're the only house in the area that was hit. Normally, I'd have five more calls in by now and I took a quick drive around before I stopped here. So, whoever did this knew about the camera and specifically targeted your house and your van. Now, think again, do you know anyone who would do this. Anyone younger perhaps? A friend of your kids, maybe?"

"Goddamnit," Joe said.

"There's been some issues in the neighborhood with Lucas Lovett," Amber said. "My oldest son is friends with him."

"Has your son been in touch with Lucas? We've been trying to locate him."

"Not trying very hard, it seems."

"Excuse me, sir," Trooper Kelly said, "but we have been trying to locate him. He's being treated as a runaway and we're concerned for his safety."

"*His* safety?" Joe said. "What about the rest of us?"

"I don't think Vinnie has heard from him," Amber said. "But we can ask."

"Let me know when you do," the trooper said. "In the meantime, I'll write this up and give you the paperwork if you want to put it through insurance."

Joe had already pulled the wet-vac out of the garage to suck up all the glass.

"We'll keep the dogs outside at night until it gets too cold," Joe said.

"What good would that do, Joe? The dogs love Lucas more than they love me."

The trooper said he would go down the street and speak with Lucas's parents.

Amber watched the officer drive the short distance down Ridgewood Drive and stop in front of the Lovetts' house.

"Those poor people," Amber said. "Can you imagine?" But the truth was, she could. She felt it in Vinnie. Maybe not as pronounced, maybe not as visible, but it was there. Everyone knew of Lucas's 'issues'. In a neighborhood filled with teachers who worked in the same school district their children attended, word traveled fast, spreading like wildfire from the teacher break room to the very street on which the boy lived. And, of course, Amber had known the boy for so long. He was in the same grade as Vinnie; they'd grown up together. He'd been in their home on countless occasions. She watched as he grew from a quiet, brooding young boy to a young man with a faraway look who always seemed distracted, as if he were listening to something no one else could hear, his mind working in ways that made no sense to anyone else. There were times when she would ask him something simple – how's school going this year? – and he would look at her as if she were speaking a different language, struggle to bring any words to his lips. Lucas looked frail at times, haunted at others, but now it seemed he'd turned a corner. Had changed so completely as to be a stranger to them, a criminal, a threat. Maybe the house burning had been an accident, but after listening to the trooper's thoughts on the smashing of her window, it was a logic too perfect to refute. The simplest answer is often the correct one.

"Yeah, well those poor people have got to get their kid under control," Joe said. "Everybody has had enough of his shit."

"It's not their fault."

"Like hell it isn't. Are they gonna pay for a new window?"

"Don't you dare ask them to," she said. Joe grumbled, half his body in the car, vacuuming up the pebbles of glass.

Amber walked back into the house with a suspicion and entered Vinnie's room. Like many modern parents, they sought to allow the teenage boy some privacy, to let him keep his room as he saw fit, provided he contributed to the household by meeting school expectations. Naturally, the school-expectations part of the deal didn't last – Vinnie was a straight C student – but the privacy part of the arrangement was just easier for everyone involved. No arguments over cleaning his room or making his bed, no constant monitoring of internet activities, which was frankly impossible anyway once he had a phone that could access anything a young man's mind might want and, frankly, she didn't want to know about it. But there was a feature on Vinnie's computer that could prove useful: text messages would appear and be recorded on the laptop, a feature she discovered when she confiscated Vinnie's cell phone last year and watched as he continued to text his friends, saying some of the most horrendous things about her, things that hurt and enraged and further ripped him from her embrace. If she were honest with herself, she had yet to forgive him for it.

Vinnie's room was a mess, the floor barely visible beneath a covering of clothes, dishes from late-night eating piled on his desk gathering fruit flies, soda cans on his nightstand, the remnants of things that he had loved as a child – books, model airplanes, Boy Scout projects – broken. His laptop was open on his desk. Vinnie would have preferred having a password lock on his computer, but part of the deal when they purchased the laptop was that Amber and Joe had the password, not him, and could lock him out of it at any time. They had yet to employ such drastic measures.

Amber found the messages application and clicked into it and there they were, texts between Vinnie and Lucas, going all the way back to the day of the fire. Vinnie had been in touch with him since the beginning.

8/24, 4:41 PM

Dude, police are looking for you. Where are you?

What do they want?

Did you set that house on fire?

I had to let it loose. It was trapped there and I set it free.

Set what free?

The past, the future, all of it, bro. It was all trapped in there and now it isn't. It is out there in the world.

My mom made me talk to the police. I didn't rat you out. Just said that we played with fireworks there sometimes.

You there, bro?

Lucas, you still there?

I didn't rat you out, I swear.

Where are you?

Everywhere, bro. I am everywhere.

8/27, 3:32 PM

Bro, the resource officer pulled me into his office today asking bout you. Where are you?

Don't matter.

Are you around? I need to get high.
I am high.
You got some weed?
Always.
Meet up?
The pond.
How much?
Idk…bring what you got.

8/27, 6:16 PM
That was fucked up, yo. I find you, you're dead.

8/27, 6:25 PM
I want my money back, bro. You gonna play me like that? I find you, I'm gonna beat your ass. Better not show your face around here again.

8/27, 10:52 PM
I'm watching you.
WTF does that mean? Best back off, bro.
I'm watching all of you. I am God.
Come off yourself bro.

9/1, 8:27 PM
Can you hear it? It's everywhere. I hear it all the time. The voice of the ghost.
You talking crazy.
It's angry. It's coming for you. It's coming for all of you.
I saw it. I saw the ghost. It spoke to me. You can never unhear it.
Stay the fuck away from me, yo.
See you soon.
Fuck you, bitch.

9/6, 11:16 PM – Just last night.
I need food.
Too bad.

You gonna let me starve?

Maybe use the money you stole from me bitch.

I'm cold yo.

Don't care. Hope the police bust yo ass.

Do you hear the house calling?

Shut up. Stop texting me bro. Sick of your shit.

Do you hear it?

Do you hear it?

Do you hear it?

★   ★   ★

That night was bad. Joe was enraged. Vinnie fought back. None of it went well. Amber took little Tommy into her bedroom and cuddled with him in bed with the television turned loud to drown out the sound of their voices, but it was impossible to keep Tommy from hearing it. Then there was the sound of breaking glass, and Amber wondered how it had all come to this. She left Tommy in her bed and found Vinnie sitting on the floor, knees up, holding his face in his hands with Joe, breathing hard, standing over him. A glass vase was broken on the floor, shards like knives scattered over the hardwood. Outside, the dogs bayed at a black sky. Vinnie's cell phone was on the floor, broken, stomped into oblivion by Joe's work boot. Vinnie was crying. Joe, red in the face, stood with his fists clenched. "Let's see you go to the police this time, you little sonofabitch," Joe said. "You gonna tell them about your drug-dealing friend? You gonna tell them you've been hiding this kid all along? What are you gonna tell them now?"

Vinnie began to stand up and Joe lurched forward, growling, "Stay down!" and the boy slid back down to the floor. Amber could see now there was a bruise on his jaw and she wondered if they had finally become that kind of family, the kind where physical violence was just a natural part of it, something passed down from generation to generation. She could see their family tree becoming engulfed in a swamp of low expectations, disappointment and resentment.

"From now on, I'm on you like white on rice," Joe said. "You're not going anywhere, doing anything, speaking a fucking word without my allowing it."

Vinnie sat on the floor, back against the wall, holding his face, eyes glassy and far away, too far away to ever be reached again.

"Next thing we're doing is getting you out of this school and into some boarding school somewhere."

"Joe, that's ridiculous...."

"We're not raising some degenerate criminal," he said. "And yet here we are. With a degenerate criminal. Living with us. Not much longer, boy, I can tell you that."

"I'm almost sixteen. You can't make me do anything." Vinnie's voice was childlike now, quivering, rasping between breaths.

Joe loomed over him, bigger, bulkier, decades of anger built up to assert its dominance. "Like hell I can't. You're about to learn the hard way."

"That's enough," Amber said. "Go outside and cool off, Joe."

Joe seemed to waver for a moment, her voice bringing him back. He pointed his finger down at Vinnie. "This is all going to come to a head soon enough," he said. "You and me, boy. We're gonna be having a long, long talk this weekend and by the end, you'll be straightened out or I'm gonna leave you up there in those woods. See how you like it then."

Joe walked out the door, but not before grabbing a bottle of Jack Daniels. She knew this routine. He would sit on the porch, cool off and get drunk, and she would have to go out and make sure that he could safely come back inside without hurting anyone or breaking anything else. But that was fine for now. She would let him be. She looked down at Vinnie, who still held his face in his hands so that he couldn't see the world around him.

Amber pulled a chair close to the boy and sat down in it.

"What happened to you, Vin?" she said. She couldn't help her motherly instinct. She couldn't help the way she felt on seeing him broken, hurt and crying. She couldn't help but empathize suddenly with his being lost in youth.

"I'm not even friends with him anymore," he said.

"Yeah, I caught that part in your text messages."

"I'm sorry."

"I'm sorry too, honey. But the problem is, I don't know that you're actually sorry. I wonder what it is that you actually feel."

She put her hand out and laid it gently on his shoulder and he shook silently.

"I don't know, Mom," he said. "I don't think I feel anything."

"That worries me, Vinnie. I love you, but that worries me a lot."

"I know," he said. "Mom? You don't think I'm like him, do you? That I'm crazy like him?"

"No, honey, I don't. Lucas needs help and that's why they need to find him. He's sick, but it's not contagious."

Vinnie looked up at her. "Are you sure?"

She ran her hand over his curly hair and stared down at this big, gawky, lost stranger in her home. It was a moment of vulnerability, when she still saw a child in his face, a scared, confused child that desperately needed his mother's comfort and yet she found that comfort hard to give. She looked at the shattered vase on the floor. It had been her mother's, passed down from generation to generation. She thought of little Thomas in the other room, watching cartoons at full volume. She thought of her husband on the front porch, quelling his anger with whiskey. She thought of her desires that would remain fantasy and her fears that had become reality and it gave her a sick, nauseous feeling in her stomach. How could she tell him that things would get better when everything she felt cried out that life was nothing more than a downhill slide?

"Yes, hon. I'm sure. We just gotta get you straightened out. We have to get all of us straightened out," she said. "It will all be okay. I promise."

It was just a lie we tell others.

CHAPTER ELEVEN

The dream came back, night after night. When he slept he lived it all over again, but with small changes, additions that pointed him in new directions. When he was awake, it lingered in the back of his mind like a warning. It was that same, lonely streetlamp in the night, the pile of white bags like discarded laundry rising at its base, slightly yellowed in the electric light. And all around it, the sky held a foreboding redness. It was desolate and lonely and the more he saw it the more terrifying it was. He felt himself moving closer to it, pulled by a morbid tide. He saw a landscape in the background, the silhouette of the Widner house. He knew what was in the bags but still had to see. That lone light in the darkness held so much at bay. He wondered whether he was the light or the darkness or the burned-out house.

John woke on the couch again. James slept beside him, wrapped in John's big arms, calm and angelic in his sleep. Pure innocence that would never be known again. Every day was another strike against it, every moment another step into the darkness – or was it another step closer to the light? He couldn't tell. He felt the boy's small body beside his own, as if the boy were part of him. It was the closest he'd felt to anyone, anything, in years and he placed his big hand on the boy's head and felt the life pulsing through him for a brief and fleeting moment.

John was tired. He hadn't slept in his own bed in weeks. Jessica now ruling the castle from above, swaddled in the bed he bought when she was pregnant and her back hurt from their old mattress. He had stopped asking to join her. She had frozen him out, and he was alone. There had been a time when she was his best friend and lover, when they seemed to move and think as one, but now she was gone far away. The only tether that remained was their children. He felt a dizzying anxiety pulse through his body at the thought of another day, of continuing this sad dance waiting for the music to stop. It was all a waiting game at this point and he was tired of waiting. It was as if all he had done in his life was wait until he was told to move. He did not act; he was acted upon. He waited to be told what job to do next; he waited to be told what was needed to keep the house, the family, running; he waited for a paycheck and he waited for the paycheck to be taken away to pay the bills. It all left him in a state of suspended animation. He was aimless. He waited aimlessly for his wife and family to come to him and tell him that they loved him, that they needed him, that he wasn't just some big dumb anchor holding them all down. He waited, but they never came.

He waited to be acknowledged. He tried to make himself known to them, tried to assert his existence, but was routinely ignored, looked through, or met with a shrug. Like some lame poltergeist whose only power was to occasionally move some small trinket. He kissed the boy's head and wondered if James would even realize if John left and never returned home. He could disappear and everyone would just keep on with their lives, no longer wondering why that trinket had stopped moving on its own.

John wasn't sure how late he'd been up last night and his head felt like he'd been hit by a truck. On the coffee table beside his couch and makeshift bed his laptop was open, and a pint of vodka sat empty on the floor. His email box was open with seventeen new messages, all from Meredith Skye: *Please stop emailing me, Mr. Ballard, or I will be forced to go to the police with a complaint.*

He didn't remember emailing her and searched through the messages he'd sent, feeling suddenly embarrassed and ashamed. His web browser was opened to numerous articles on arson, breaking and entering, the flammable components of store-bought fireworks and bottle rockets, the basics of investigatory journalism, instances among the elderly when they had been scared to death by an intruder. He had sent them to Meredith, along with long messages – complete with misspellings that, in his waking sobriety, made him look and feel all the more stupid – outlining what he knew had happened to the abandoned house, what he knew had happened to Nancy, and what he knew would happen in the future.

Our neighborhood is being terrorizzed and you won't even pint the obvious truth so you can protect you little liberal world-view where psychos are jest 'misunderstood.' That its the rest of us who need to be better. Fuck that. My famibly and my kids are here and I won't let nothing happen to them. Hell keep doing this. All you care about are the scumbags living in the ghetto, so you can get more of the money I work for and give it people who dont worked in a decade because there too lazy. I know who owns your newspaper. I know who they vote for. I know you can't be objuctive because youre whole corporat media empire is pointed in one direction and that is to ignore US! Well you won't be able to ignore me! You think your scared? The TRUTH doesnt care about your feelings!

Despite the spelling errors and the thought of having a police complaint filed against him, he was somewhat proud of that last little line, although he was unsure if he had thought it up himself or picked it up from somewhere. All subsequent emails he'd sent to Meredith had been returned as 'blocked'.

John was still in the clothes he'd worn yesterday and they smelled like wet dirt and rotting leaves. He left his young boy sleeping on the couch and took the empty pint bottle outside and threw it in the recycling bin, pushing it down deep so Jessica wouldn't wave it around in front of his face when she found it in order to shame him. Was he ashamed? Yes. But she didn't understand. He needed that release. He needed that slow, settling cloud over his mind. He felt so scattered all the time, like he was trying to keep up with ten thousand things at once, all of them flying through his consciousness, and all he desired was relief. She wouldn't understand, she never tried to understand, and all she wanted to do was ignore him, just like Meredith.

The morning air was heavy and wet with an autumn chill. The sky was overcast with rippling clouds that stretched for eternity. John walked to the top of his driveway to get a look at the ruins of the Widner house; a few load-bearing walls remained, the brick edifice of the front of the house was scorched and brittle but still stood nonetheless; blackened beams and two-by-fours pointed in the air like spikes. The image haunted him. Sometimes he wondered why. It was just a stupid abandoned house that everyone wished had been either sold or burned down a long time ago. But it was also a lingering violence, an intrusion, that had beset them. To hear the old timers talk, it had always been the product of a sick mind, and now it had been burned down by a sick mind, one let loose upon the world. He glanced across the street to the Lovetts' house, wondering if they were even trying to find Lucas, and he saw something bright and shiny and new: a For Sale sign was planted in their small lawn.

Now they're trying to run from it, he thought. *They're dumping their sweet little psycho and getting the hell out of Dodge.*

John stared again at the remnants of the house, walked down the street and stepped onto the overgrown lawn, the weeds and tall grass pulling at his boots. He crossed the border onto the burnt-black wood and ash, stood between the lingering beams and the blackened brick. Everything had been reformed, melted, molded and turned to soot, stub and cinder to be blown about the world. Matter is never destroyed, only reformed. He remembered that from school and it always stuck with him. It seemed mystical and made him think about death. How one could go from a living, breathing, thinking person to nothing more than deteriorating flesh and bone in just an instant, with the simple stop of a heart. What makes the heart stop? The answers seemed simple – blood clot, age, loss of blood – but in another sense, it wasn't so simple. Where does the animating force go? Looking at the ash and cinders of the house, John thought it was no wonder all those preachers talked about a soul. He stood among the ruins and thought about how when you change the form of something, the essence of it is gone. What's worse is you can't bring it back.

Life is change, he was told at an AA meeting Jessica forced him to attend. If life was change, then the essence of everything and everyone is constantly shifting, changing, dying over and over again, never to be the same. He thought about Jessica. He thought about their relationship, what was left of their marriage. Had that much changed? Where had the essence gone? He looked around the mess of ash and burnt wood. *Things can be maintained*, he thought. *Things can be rebuilt.* He refused to accept the terms of this shitty deal. No. The terms of this deal could be met with willpower, force, pushed back and made to wait for another day, forced to wait for someone else who would bend to its will. But it would not be him.

He gave one last look around the place that rose like a mountain in his dream. He looked at the For Sale sign on the Lovetts' lawn, and beneath the vapid gray clouds of a crushing sky, he walked back home.

★   ★   ★

John took off his boots and walked upstairs to his bedroom. He didn't knock but just opened the door. Jessica had stashed herself away up here for a long time but it was still his room, too. It was still his house and he planned to hang on to all of it.

She seemed startled when he walked in and began to remove his clothes in the walk-in closet.

"What are you doing?"

"I'm taking a shower," he said. "I called out of work today."

"Are you sick?"

"No."

"Then why did you call out?"

"Just because. I have the time, I'm going to use it. I need a day."

"You're not using the kids' shower," she said.

"No, I'm not. I'm using our shower. Because it's our shower. I've had enough of this. Tonight I'll sleep in our bed, too. It's time this little game ended, Jessica."

"It's not a game," she said.

He walked out of the closet, still in his jeans but without a shirt, his broad chest exposed to her. "So what is it you want then?"

"I think it's time we talked about separating," she said. "I can't live like this."

"Live like what? I'm the one sleeping on the couch every night."

"If you want the bed, then I'll sleep on the couch. But I'm done with this. I can't handle it anymore. I never know what you're going to be like. I never know if you're going to be drunk or sober, angry or kind. I can't depend on you. The kids can't depend on you."

"Look around you, Jessica," he said. "Our kids, this house, this entire life? I helped build this and now you say you can't depend on me? Who do you think keeps this place going? Who pays the bills here? You just want to throw it all away?"

"I'm not throwing away anything. I'm saving myself."

"From what?"

"From you."

He looked down and nodded. "From me," he said. "Like I'm some curse put on you. I still love you, Jessica. Maybe I haven't always done the right thing but I still love you. And you loved me. But now you need to save yourself from me?"

"You're not right anymore, John. You're up all night on the computer, drinking constantly, you don't know where you are or what you're doing half the time. Do you even remember past eight o'clock last night?"

John said nothing but just waited with his head down, listening, wondering if his kids were awake, wondering if they were listening to her attempts at unraveling and reforming the world. Her attempt to burn it all down and make something new out of the ash.

"You know what happened when I picked Caitlin up from dance class the other night? I was brought into the office and Melanie sat me down and – very cautiously and politely, I might add – asked that you not pick Caitlin up from dance anymore or, at the very least, wait outside in the car."

"What? Why?"

"There were complaints by the other mothers, John. They said you were leering at the girls, the fucking teenage girls, John! And mumbling to yourself, saying dirty things to yourself! Sitting there staring at children, sweating and mumbling to yourself. It made them so uncomfortable they threatened to pull their daughters from the program if you were allowed to return. Do you know how embarrassing that was for me? I mean, what is wrong with you? Staring at teenagers, saying those kinds of things? Is our own daughter even safe with you?"

"You shut the fuck up, right now." He walked toward her, big chest straining. The very thought that she would threaten to take his daughter away from him inspired a murderous rage. "I would never hurt our daughter in any possible way. And I have no idea what those bitches are talking about. I didn't say a word to anyone when I picked Cait up the other night. I just sat there, waited and left. I'm not staring at any girls! This is bullshit. They just hate men and I was the only one there for them to point to. They'll find any excuse to label some guy a child molester or rapist or whatever. And they'll do it over nothing. Nothing! I'm not staring at any underage girls, for Christ's sake. You and all of them have lost your damn minds."

"You don't see yourself, John," she said. "You think the world is the way you see it, but it's not. It's not. And you aren't the man you think you are. I've been with you for sixteen years now and I've watched you, I've watched this whole time, and maybe I should have said something sooner but I can't wait any longer. You don't see how you are to other people. You're stuck in your own head and you're ruining what's left of your mind, John. And I'm not going to sit here and watch it, and I'm not going to let my children watch it either."

"You're the one who's lost it, Jessica," he said. "You're all wrapped up in this holier-than-thou bullshit and you're willing to break up our family just to prove it. You're going to believe a bunch of gossipy bitches over your own husband? What the hell is wrong with you? And, you know what? Maybe I wouldn't have to drink if my wife – my best friend and partner – were not freezing me out, leaving me completely alone night after night. You know who else is on the computer all night? Take a look in the mirror, Jessica. How are all your little Facebook friends, anyway?"

"I need someone to talk to…."

"And so do I! It was supposed to be you. You've dropped the ball as much as me."

"But the ball has dropped, John. And I don't want to pick it back up again. I'm not going to spend any more of my time trying to rebuild something that just won't work."

"You go ahead and give up," he said. "I'm not. You'll see. I have enough love for both of us. I can get us through this."

"You don't love me, John. You just think you do. You don't love all this, you love the *idea* of all this," she said. "And as long as you have that idea in your head, you'll never see the reality of it for me and for the kids. You'll never understand it."

"Yeah, so I'm the dumb one who can't see reality," John said. "Who's too stupid and drunk to understand anything. Of course. My thoughts and feelings aren't worth shit. Gotcha."

"I'm just saying—"

"You've said enough," he said. "You've ignored me long enough. Frankly, everyone has ignored me long enough and I'm done with it. You want to see a new me? You want to see someone change? You just watch."

"I don't have the energy."

"I'm going to do something great one day. You'll see. Something that matters."

"I don't need you to do something great...."

"No. You just want to run away. That's fine. But I'm not going anywhere and neither are my kids. You'll have to figure that out on your own."

With that, John walked into the bathroom, shut the door and turned on the shower. He stared at himself in the mirror for a moment and tried to stop crying but he couldn't. He covered his mouth, but his body shook and trembled and heaved.

He could hear her just outside the door.

★   ★   ★

John stayed in the shower a long time, letting the hot water run rivulets through the grime on his skin. For a while he sat on the floor of the shower and shook and cried. He couldn't remember the last time he cried and he wasn't sure why he did so now. Jessica's words, her threat to leave, undoubtedly hurt him but it seemed like so much more than that. It wasn't just heartbreak or fear – it was disappointment. Not at her nor at anyone else, but at himself, and it seemed infinitely worse. His entire life history seemed a maelstrom of forces he could not control, as if everything had been preordained from the moment of his birth. He had simply gone with it, become a cog in the machine, moved about by outside forces, powerless to stop it. No one grows up wanting to work for a municipal Public Works Department, but you need money so you get a job and then that's your job experience so that's the job you're stuck with, and then after so many years you've got a house, a mortgage, a family and debt, and by the time you realize half your life is gone and you wish something was different, it's too late to reverse course. Better to continue on at the same place and do the same job to continue the same life because now you had dependents, now you had to provide, and you're too old to learn anything new, too busy and broke to go back to college, too boring to find new friends and you're totally and completely stuck. So, now you might as well have a couple drinks to ease the thoughts, to put them to bed, but those thoughts are with you all the time and just one drink won't do and now your wife hates you, says she doesn't know you, and now you're facing divorce and are going to be pushed by another force – insurmountable legal forces – into an even greater trap of exile, child support, loneliness and irrelevance.

It was a prison of his own making, he supposed, but he marveled at how he made it. Like it was instinctual; the way a rat automatically knows how to build a nest, John had the instinct for trapping himself in a downward spiral.

He toweled off, let the steam clear his senses. He brushed his teeth and shaved, and by the end felt new and refreshed and clean. He dressed, and by the time Caitlin and James were ready for the school bus he looked like a dad in a television commercial – the highest aspiration a father can achieve: clean cut, good looking and smiling, content with his life, whose children and wife adored him, whose job valued him; a man who had reached the pinnacle of the American Dream. All those commercials just doomed everyone else to feeling like a failure, but today he looked the part and he walked his daughter and son to the bus stop and waited with them, hugged them before they boarded, an ideal, picturesque moment, something he hoped they would remember for the rest of their lives.

He walked back to the house as Jessica was leaving for work in her nursing scrubs. He always found her sexy in them, despite the fact that she treated him like an unwanted guest.

"What are you going to do today?" she said.

"I don't know," he said. "Think. Try to straighten some stuff out. Get my head right."

"I meant what I said."

"So did I," he said. "You'll see. Everything will be okay."

"You keep telling yourself that but you keep doing the same thing over and over."

"You need to know that none of those things said about me are true. I would never—"

"Normally, I would believe you, John. But I don't know you anymore." She waited a moment and then said, "I'm going to take some time for myself tonight. Go out for a little while on my own after I get home from work. Think things through."

"Fine," he said.

John stayed away from his computer. He stayed away from the articles and websites that had captured his mind as of late. By all accounts and as far as he could tell, the world was ending over and over again, every day. It bred a luscious fear in him. It drove him to stop it some way, somehow. It drove him to prepare for it. He had to get his head right so he could be the hero his family needed. But it also drove him to darker places, and right now he needed clarity. He needed to be a part of life rather than death. He needed to come to grips with who and what he was. Maybe he didn't matter in the grand scheme of things but maybe there was freedom in that as well.

In the afternoon John made his way downstairs to the basement. He felt a longing to look back on his history and he found his old high school yearbooks from junior and senior year, photo albums from his childhood with his mother and father, and he sat on the cool basement floor and flipped through them, marveling at and mourning his youth, when the world seemed so open and full of possibility. His father had been a quiet man, but there was an anger beneath his rough, tanned skin. His father sold insurance for most of his life. John's mother ran a small bakery that had set up shop in a strip mall. Times were always tight and that gave him a sense of normalcy. It was not just he who had difficulty supporting a family and paying the bills; it was the birthright of the entire goddamned country – to struggle and strive and ultimately be left with little. Contentment had to be reached in other ways. His parents seemed content, as far as he could tell. They never seemed to strive for more than what they had, yet he had this bug in the back of his brain that kept gnawing at him, something that told him he wanted to be remembered for something other than just getting by, remembered by more than just his children and a handful of old friends he never heard from anymore. The photo album from his childhood and high school years captured so much that memory could not hold. All-American varsity football linebacker; varsity jackets, big, young muscles and a youthful face with a cut jawline. His high school football team had won state championships his senior year. His picture in the newspapers, which actually meant something then. He went to college and played for a division three school, but in the end he couldn't keep up with the studies. He dropped classes, faded out of the dorms and found himself back at home with Mom and Dad. His father got him a job at a construction company and he dug ditches like a madman in the heat, hauled lumber or roof shingles, used every ounce of his muscle every day and made good money for it. He wondered why he'd tried college in the first place. All those suckers were still in school and he was making fifty grand per year.

Then there were pictures of Jessica. She was a waitress at the local Chili's, a couple years younger than him and paying her way through nursing school. He and some of the boys from the construction site would go in after work on Fridays for some tall beers and she was there, cute and tender and unassuming. But she was tough. Wouldn't give him the time of day at first, but he kept trying until she agreed to one night out with him. It was summer and he took her to a local music and food truck festival with no-name bands from around the state and trucks lined up serving fried food and together they walked and talked and laughed. He was a gentleman. He made her laugh. He showed her that he was big but gentle and caring. That night she told him that, more than anything, she wanted a life without regret, one that she made for herself on her terms. "I promise, I won't get in the way," he told her. A year later, she had graduated nursing school and they were married.

A year and a half after that, his parents died in a car accident when a big-rig jackknifed on the highway and then he was completely on his own, alone but for her.

They used his inheritance and his parents' insurance money to travel: Mexico, France and a long trip to Australia, and when she became pregnant with Caitlin, they used the rest for a down payment on the house in which he now sat on the cold cement basement floor contemplating his history. He took the town job because of the benefits. Pay was pretty good, too, and with overtime he thought they could do pretty well.

All that time, however, he kept expecting something to happen. Something big. He kept expecting that he would somehow become more than what he was. He expected it, but it never came, and now that he thought of it, he'd never really done anything to facilitate a great change. He just got so caught up in the moments, the inevitable rolling wheel of life that pushed forward no matter what: marriage, death, birth, job, house, bills. It came at him every day and days rolled into months, into years, wrapped up in those moments where he felt he was making great strides forward, reaching the commercial dad level of the American Dream.

And then it all stopped. He wasn't sure how or when, but he suddenly found himself in his early thirties with nowhere left to go and nothing left to do. He had the wife, the kids, the car, the job and the house, and now he was just supposed to exist like that until he retired and died. He grew fat around his formerly youthful muscles, had trouble getting it up for Jessica in bed; Friday nights drinking with the guys became weekend drinking with the guys, which then became weeks of drinking by himself. The inheritance money was gone and bills piled up and somehow there was always less and less, sucked down an eternal black hole, and he needed to drink just to escape the monotony.

His father once told him, "Life is hard, son," which seemed odd to him at the time because his parents' life hadn't seemed extraordinarily difficult. As a family they hadn't faced some of the more difficult life challenges others had – there hadn't been any serious illness or untimely loss of loved ones; his father hadn't been laid off and crushed by an uncaring economy. It seemed an odd thing to say and, as a young man, he was unsure what exactly was so hard.

But he'd come to a new understanding at this stage in his life: what made life hard was not the momentary difficulties one faced, but the long, unending days and years and decades when nothing much happened, when it was just the day-in, day-out monotony of life that wore you down like fine-grained sandpaper until you realized you weren't actually going anywhere but were just stuck like a jackknifed truck on an interstate highway and that could be deadly.

He stared at an old photo, him in his football-hero gear standing beside his parents, and felt a dim nausea in his stomach.

He heard a knock at the door upstairs and quickly shut the photo album and dropped it back in the plastic box. He lumbered up the stairs, turned the corner and could see part of a state police uniform through the window beside the front door.

Trooper Badgely was standing on his front porch when John opened the door.

"Good afternoon, John," Badgely said. "I was wondering if I could have a word with you."

This prick, talking to me like he's my boss or my father, John thought. "What's the problem?" John said. He didn't move from the doorway, although he felt like kicking Badgely right in the chest and launching him off the front porch.

"Well, it involves your contact with Meredith Skye, the reporter," he said. "Our understanding is that these emails you've been sending are threatening in nature."

"Bullshit, I haven't threatened her."

"I said threatening in nature. Not that you had made a threat. If you had made a threat, I'd be here arresting you."

"So why are you here then?"

"To ask you to cool down, stop contacting her, or else this might get escalated into something more difficult."

"Well, now, that sounds like a threat, Officer Badgely."

"I'm just asking you, man to man, to lay off of her," Badgely said.

John looked at him a moment, turned his head slightly sideways. "Is this official state police business or are you just happening by for a personal visit? You ask me, this sounds more personal."

"Nothing personal, Mr. Ballard. Just trying to keep things civil. I know your concerns about what's happened in the neighborhood lately, but let's just try to keep our heads about us, okay?"

"It's a free country. She's a public figure and I have freedom of speech," John said. "Simple as that. And if you guys did your job instead of just covering everything up maybe there wouldn't be an issue in the first place."

"We're not covering anything up, Mr. Ballard, I can assure you. But if you continue down this path, there might be more trouble for you in the future and I'm sure you don't want that."

John stepped from his doorway onto the front porch, close to Badgely, towering over him. John couldn't help himself. This was his house, his neighborhood. He wouldn't be threatened by some hack cop on his own property.

John stood toe-to-toe with the officer and looked down at him, a rage building in him that was both new and somehow familiar – the rage of a cornered animal.

"I'm sure you wouldn't want that either, officer," he said. "Now get the fuck off my property."

Badgely smiled and John could tell, deep down, he wanted this fight.

"Fine, Mr. Ballard. But just know, this is your last warning."

★   ★   ★

For the first time in more than a decade, John put on some shorts and a t-shirt and ran. It wasn't just a jog, it was a *run*, his feet pounding the pavement, his lungs straining, his body shaking, sweat pouring down his face and back. He ran like he was being chased; down Ridgewood, past the Widner house and the For Sale sign on the Lovetts' lawn; down Leadmine Brook and across the small bridge that traversed the wetlands where he'd left potholes to be filled for another day; a burning and long incline up the next ridge and a right onto Harmony Hill, where all the big houses of the successful people lay back from the road with football fields for yards. He ran to push back at it all. He ran because there would be a time when he would need all his strength and all his endurance and all his will. The headlines flashed in his mind, the news stories documenting the collapse weighed on his shoulders. It was all going to shit: his life, his marriage, the neighborhood, the town, the city, the country, the world. It was all a giant abandoned house set fire by a wave of insanity and lies. None of it made sense. All the sins of the world, the disappointment of his wife, the bleak future for his children rested on his shoulders and he needed to be ready to carry the weight, to fight back. The alcohol from last night evaporated through his pores as he pushed himself, running harder and faster down that street, a man trying to break some kind of record.

But as he ran, as sweat soaked through his shirt and his muscles burned, he saw something. He had seen it before a million times, driven past it at forty miles per hour, never paid it a single thought until now. Harmony Hill, with all its McMansions and in-ground pools and leafy overhangs, had its own spot of blight, just like Ridgewood Drive. Set far back from the road, shaded by an old and dying oak tree, stood another abandoned house. It had been there as long as John could remember; a saltbox-style house covered with brown shakes, dotted with windows of paper-thin glass, pieces of siding falling off, cobwebs visible in the windows, roof partially covered in moss. It was like seeing something again for the first time and John's all-out run slowed to a clopping jog and then a walk until he stood in front of the old, wooden house, staring at it.

The house reminded him of a trip he had taken with Jessica and the kids to Salem, Massachusetts. During the tour they saw the famous witch-house, the only house left from the days of the witch trials, and home to one of the judges who put those women and men to torture and death.

The abandoned house on Harmony Hill didn't have the peaked gables and severe angles of the witch-house, but rather it was the way the house was built, the color, the wood siding, the glass – it seemed a relic left from a time when men and women feared witches and devils that lurked in the forests of the night; when they told stories of dark rites involving children sacrificed beneath full moons and claimed visions of demons in human form riding broomsticks, casting curses. It was from a time when all the world was darkness. He imagined how easy it would be to believe in witches and demons back then, to be afraid constantly, to fear a force you could not see or understand because everything was shrouded in dark and cold and brute survival. *Maybe their fear was justified*, he thought. *We look back on them with derision and sneer or laugh today, but for them it was real and, in a way, true. We think we're better than that now, but we're not.*

John looked up and down the silent, leafy street and saw no one else. No cars passed, no people walked in and out of their giant, vinyl-sided houses. The sun was bright but there was no life to be seen or heard anywhere. He stepped off the street and onto the property, overgrown and choked with weeds the same as the Widner house. Frankly, he was amazed that such well-to-do neighbors had allowed its continued existence in their midst. John walked to the front of the house, cupped his hands and peered in through the windows but he couldn't make out much in the light – floorboards, dust and walls mostly – but it looked as if there was something there, signs of life that had passed through. He circled to the back, walking along the side of the house, noting its wood rot, how it shifted off its stone foundation. In the back he found taller weeds, brimming and buzzing with insects. The back door was locked but one of the windows was broken, a panel punched out and John tenderly tested the window. It slid up with a wooden creak and he could smell the air from inside – mold and dust and something else he couldn't pinpoint. There was no way he could get his big body through the window frame but he was able to reach through to the back door handle and unlock it.

John walked inside cautiously. He was trespassing on something but he wasn't sure what. It was a quiet little thrill, a rebellious transgression.

Inside, there were many rooms and thresholds and doorways. The old place seemed larger inside than out but was bare and lifeless. He came to a narrow staircase leading to the second floor and stared up into its darkness. He walked the stairs slowly, testing each step to be sure his weight wouldn't send him plummeting to his death, but they held sturdy and strong.

And there, in one of the rooms that looked out over the rest of the neighborhood through a window, was where he found it – an old mattress, clothes that would only fit a thin teenager piled in a corner, empty food containers and garbage. But it was the walls that truly frightened him; covered in blood-red markings, symbols, crazed writings like demonic graffiti. Some of the symbols he recognized – swastikas, pentagrams, an anarchist symbol he'd seen spray-painted on the side of riot-ruined buildings on the news.

And then there were the eyes. Seemingly hundreds of eyes painted in the same red color lining the walls. Some with giant Xs through them, others smeared with blood-red handprints, some contained within triangles like the all-seeing eye on a dollar bill. Hundreds of them, round or oval, in varying degrees of detail; some were passive and soft looking, others appeared like the eyes of a raging coke fiend – desperate, intense, murderous.

Scrawled in massive letters above it all:

I AM GOD.

I SEE ALL.

I AM EVERYWHERE.

John moved a pile of clothes with his foot and bugs scattered. He turned, taking in the whole place, feeling dizzy now, the exertion of his run catching up to him, his heart pounding for an entirely different reason, adrenaline pumping.

He wasn't scared of Lucas. Frankly, John could pick him up and snap him in two with his bare hands. But he was scared of what Lucas was; he'd already set fire to one house and John was convinced that he'd somehow been involved with Nancy's death. There was no telling what the kid might do next or who he might do it to. John thought about his children, so vulnerable and trusting. Caitlin and James may have been taught not to talk to strangers but they wouldn't think twice about engaging with a teenager they recognized from the neighborhood.

He thought for a moment about going to the police, but then he thought of Badgely and his veiled threats, the newspaper reporter and her snotty emails and eye-rolling dismissals. To them he was some big, paranoid drunk, but now he had Lucas. Now he could show them he'd been right all along. Now he could grab the kid by the back of his neck and drag him right down to the police station himself. He could end this haunting of Ridgewood Drive.

"I got you, motherfucker," he said.

John ran hard and fast again, back the way he'd come, plunging down from Harmony Hill, crossing the wetlands and back into his neighborhood. By the time he turned the corner and ran past the politician's house, he had a plan. He'd keep this to himself, he'd stalk the stalker and he'd bring Lucas to justice himself. Then everyone could breathe a sigh of relief, the specter hanging over all their heads would be gone. He'd be a hero.

He saw a red car slowly rolling past his house and had a momentary flash of recognition. He could see Jessica's car in the driveway beside his truck. He watched the red car turn right down Beechwood and disappear. Jessica was just getting out of her car, still in her nursing scrubs, reaching back in to take out her backpack. She saw him covered in sweat, a rejuvenated look in his eye, and watched him as he slowed his jog and walked up their driveway.

"Oh my," she said. "Is something chasing you?"

"I'm not running from anything." He stared at her hard, a hint of malice and knowing in his voice. "I'm running toward something."

CHAPTER TWELVE

It was Friday and Elizabeth was finally seeing the fruits of her labor to bring something of cultural significance to this broken and beaten-down city. Although the official grand opening of the Tree of Life exhibit at the Amherst Museum was still a week away, she and her small group of loyal compatriots, along with the museum curator and the docents, were getting a first look at Shondra Waite's newest work. Set on the grassy lawn of the Amherst's grounds, it looked from the outside like a small house, a boxy, single-story ranch without windows, almost like the ramshackle, cardboard-like low-income homes she had visited during her door-knocking campaign through the South End.

Elizabeth was eager for the grand opening, eager to give the speech that had been wording and rewording itself in her head for a month now; she thought of the newspaper headlines, the social media campaigns she could build around this; she thought of the quotes she could give reporters and her name appearing in high-end art reviews, caressing the eyes of high-dollar donors who frequent the arts and are therefore, almost inevitably, in her political camp. The election was just two months away. Andrew Whitcomb could stick as many 'Let's Kick Tutt' signs in the shitty yards of her dying, backwater Republican hold-out neighborhood as he wanted, he wouldn't be able to compete with this. And besides, she was already polling at fifty-five percent and trending upward. She comforted herself with that thought and tried to fight down the lingering fear of being voted out, quite literally losing a popularity contest. Her academic mind rationalized that popularity contests were inherently stupid, but this was for a greater cause. Few things in academia were more important than politics and politics has real-world effects. At its purest, politics was the enactment of a philosophy, rational thought made real. At its worst it was akin to running for prom queen, and while she had never in her life thought of running for prom queen, the idea of losing an election stirred an adolescent fear in her that her brilliant mind couldn't tamp down or rationalize: the fear of rejection. It was confirmation that most people in a given area didn't like you and that could be a hard thing to live with, especially when you were approaching sixty, living alone among hostiles, being harassed on almost a nightly basis, and your prospects were fading with each passing year.

When she really thought about it, she wasn't sure she wanted to be alone the rest of her life. Living alone was certainly easy in some respects: never having to feel the presence of another, never having to make the extra effort to mouth meaningless words like, 'I'm making coffee, would you like some?' or 'What do you want to watch tonight?' Living with someone was like boats moored at the same dock and feeling small, silent waves rocking your hull constantly. Frankly, living with someone – and, more so, marriage – was work.

But then, during some of those nights and, particularly, long and dull weekends, when there was no campaigning or work to be done, when she tried to lose herself in a book or keep abreast of the latest news or academic journals, she felt the desire, the downright need, for another. Her mind flashed forward into the not-so-distant future; images of herself old, alone, lonely and fading into the dustbin of history with absolutely no one giving a fuck. Even that Nancy woman who just died up the street, under circumstances Elizabeth's paranoid and reactionary neighbors saw as suspicious, had a family. She had died alone – as does everyone – but there had been people who cared for her, she had that backbone of family. Elizabeth didn't have that. No grown children to check in on her, no siblings, her parents long dead and her husband gone into the ether of ended relationships. If she kept moving in this same direction, she would spend the end of her days in a nursing home with the word 'Shady' in its name and some underpaid, undereducated staffer dropping a plate of shitty food on her tray three times a day and maybe wheeling her outside for a look at a couple scrawny trees and a pond covered with algae. Or maybe she would end up like Nancy, trapped in her house as her body broke down and she struggled for air. Those thoughts made her wish for someone else in her life, to wish for that false security that came from marriage. There was something comforting in 'till death do us part'.

Maybe she just needed a boyfriend. Or a girlfriend. Frankly, at this point she would be happy with either. Though at this age, having a 'boyfriend' or a 'girlfriend' sounded ridiculous, like trying to play high school all over again. She changed the term in her mind to 'partner'. She needed a life partner. That was a good way to think of it.

For now, she comforted herself with the fact that she would be remembered for this, for bringing Shondra Waite – an artist who could inspire an oppressed minority group with their strong cultural and artistic movements – to a city and a people who needed inspiration. She was doing that, and it would be part of her legacy.

Elizabeth waited with Meghan and Elliot Perkins, the museum's curator, just outside the front entrance to the museum. Perkins was exactly what you'd expect from a curator – dressed in finely tailored clothes, everything about his thin, distinguished frame arranged perfectly, the white hair ringed around his shiny bald head cut perfectly and beautifully, circular glasses to offset his long oval face. He was severely mannered, calm and tempered, probably hiding his latent obsessive-compulsive disorder just below the surface, showing itself only when some tourist wandered too close to the Caravaggio. Shondra Waite stood just outside the exhibit, which, from the outside, was looking more and more like a rectangular black wooden box, and Elizabeth's academic mind was ticking away at the possibility that it was engineered to look somewhat like a coffin. *Sure, that must mean something.* Then again, perhaps the great trick of modern art was that it actually meant nothing but everyone thought it meant something.

Shondra spoke one last time to the crew tasked with helping assemble her masterpiece and then she walked toward Elizabeth and the small group of attendees slated to get the first look before opening day. Once again, she seemed to float toward them. She seemed so powerful and yet her voice was so quiet and calm and serene, as if she were from another dimension entirely, unaffected by the trials of this world. She was at peace and that was the strangest thing of all.

"It's almost ready. They're just running the computer program now that will feed into the Tree of Life," Shondra said. "I hope, when you enter, you will see and feel the juxtaposition of the electronic world and the real world, of the world of lies and of truth, of hate and peace. I hope that you will understand through this work that what is precious in this world is not what we see on these ubiquitous screens that now fill our lives, but rather in the simple physical reality of our world. The Tree of Life is something that stretches back to the earliest civilizations. It is something that should give us hope and caution. We are sacrificing our world for the sake of technology. But we do so at the risk of our sanity."

Elizabeth, feeling slightly overwhelmed with glee, began to clap but she was the only one. Her staffers looked at her and then began a half-hearted clap as well that went on long and uncomfortably until a few others politely joined. One would have thought some mid-tier golfer had just sunk a putt and Elizabeth was briefly angered by their lack of enthusiasm. So be it, the grand opening would be much better. Shondra smiled politely at them all and then led them to the entrance.

"Inside is like a maze, a small, dark labyrinth in which you are assaulted with images, words, news media and sound from the internet. You walk through confused, your senses of sight and sound overwhelmed by something wholly unnatural, meant only to stimulate, titillate and envelop you in fear, anxiety, and insecurity," Shondra said as she led them to the dark entrance. "But as you search and make your way through, you will reach the center, the Tree of Life, where you find the sunlight, the sapling that is the basis for all life and its symbolic nature that reaches back to our very beginnings as a species. In this you will see both the illusion and the reality of our current world."

Shondra looked to one of the assemblymen and he nodded. She stepped aside and motioned for them to enter. Elizabeth, more excited now, pushed to the front of the small group so that she could be the first inside the work of art she had midwifed into existence. Shondra watched as she walked into the dark entrance of what could have been a cheap house or, perhaps, an oversized coffin.

Despite it being light outside, the inside was dark and there was a brief tunnel through which she felt herself enter a new realm. And then came the digital assault of faces, words, images, scrolling through the internet like a social media shopping list: plates of food at fine restaurants; kittens crawling from a cardboard box and padding around on unsure paws; a woman, all legs and ass and perfect, beautiful breasts, being fucked from behind by a monstrous man; night-vision images of tanks firing shells that blew holes in a concrete tower somewhere in Palestine; protesters fighting in the street just before a car plows into the crowd; memes of Kermit the Frog spewing racist epithets; pictures of people holding funny and poignant signs written on cardboard; tear gas flying from grenade launchers just outside the White House; headlines from news stories that sounded more like middle school taunts – 'Watch as Sen. Tully Owns the Libs over Gun Control', 'Fact Check: Pants on Fire for President's claim about Founding Fathers'; some poor girl having a cock rammed into her throat caused Elizabeth to turn away for a moment and marvel at her newfound prudishness; advertisements for Viagra, Percocet, Prozac, Oxycodone and Humira; YouTube videos of young men playing video games or kicking each other in the crotch; a rendering of Jesus with one hand over the United States and the other hand clutching a handgun; memes of politicians and movie stars coupled with fake quotes; football players kneeling during the anthem as American flags swayed in the background and the audience hurled curses; opinion pieces from the *New York Times*, the *Washington Post* and *The Atlantic*; another video of street protesters colliding, threatening with guns; and images of happy, wholesome families posing at picnics and outdoor barbecues in nice leafy suburbs.

Elizabeth stumbled through the makeshift maze, the images and sounds assaulting her from every direction. She felt lost, dizzy with the unending spectacle of it. She could barely find her feet to move forward, the darkness of the cave-like interior illuminated only with digital media and, in that moment, she felt a great and urgent despair, the kind of despair that causes one to mourn their youth and contemplate whether suicide might, after all, be the most rational response to life. And then, as Elizabeth turned a darkened corner, feeling the brief presence of

Meghan and the curator behind her, she found the sapling tree bathed in sunlight. It grew straight and pure and real. Elizabeth's trip through the display felt like an eternity compared to this one moment of peace and beauty. She stood there, the small tree rising up out of the grassy earth, and as the rest of the small group gathered round, she breathed a quick sigh of relief and stared into the sky dotted with white clouds against the deep autumn blue, and knew that she had helped usher in a true work of art, something that spoke to the world. The sunlight reached down and touched her skin and she knew she was the sapling, reaching upward, not yet grown but growing, and in desperate need of nourishment from the natural world. It was simplicity and beauty. In a word, it was revelation.

Elizabeth listened to the murmurs of those around her and stood in awe of this tiny piece of life, standing in contrast to the darkness she'd just left. She saw the patch of sky and marveled at how tiny our window on the world could be, depressed at the fact that interconnecting the entire world was akin to interconnecting the basest of human nature.

Elliot Perkins stood beside her and motioned toward another darkened entrance on the other side of the sapling's little enclave. "We have to go through and out to the other side," he said.

"Is the rest of it like what we just walked through?" Elizabeth said.

"I believe so," he said.

She found herself wanting, more than anything, to just stay where she was, to not enter that dark place again. Perhaps that was the point.

★　　★　　★

At her home that night she thought of the sapling. Elizabeth decided to spend some time outside that evening. She walked the block in the warm evening air. She watched the trees move and sway with the breeze. She touched the branches and let her hand run along tall stalks of grass between houses and listened to the quiet that pervaded this little neighborhood. She began to understand her need for it at times, why she longed to come back to this little backwater when, rightfully, she believed she despised it.

There was some sense of calm security here that she'd never found in city life, with all the concrete and cars and constant sirens.

But, as night fell and she secured herself behind a dead-bolted door, poured herself a scotch and turned on the television for one of her guilty, non-academic pleasures, a pervading sense of insecurity fell over her. It had been a few days since there'd been a knock at her door, and she hoped her tormentor had finally become bored with her and moved on. But the anticipation – the fear – of hearing it once again still lingered. She had stood before the sapling that day and felt a childlike wonder at the world, and now she felt a childlike fear of the dark. The knocks, the intrusion, came only in the dark.

It had been three days, and she wondered if that was a long enough trend to establish the mysterious door-knocker had gone for good. The feeling of physical security was something she'd taken for granted until the door-knocking started. Somehow, making her way through the ghastly images in the Tree of Life display made her feel even less secure. *No wonder gun sales are through the roof,* she thought. She hadn't even glanced at her social media page since leaving the exhibit. She felt it almost necessary to abstain out of reverence, recognizing that it wasn't just the world that was the problem, but herself as well. Maybe that was the point, that we were all doing it to ourselves, driving ourselves insane.

She thought about that funny little man, Vernon Trimble from around the block, and his Neighborhood Watch idea. What would the harm really be? Was it so bad for neighbors to look out for each other? Particularly as she'd become the target of harassment by God-knows-who? Maybe the perpetrator could be caught with just a little coordination between the neighbors. Maybe, if she was lucky, it would be a targeted harassment campaign by her rival or someone who worked for him. Hell, even if it was just someone sympathetic to his views, she could spin it into an election-winning issue. *Look at what the other side is doing – harassment and intimidation – that's all they stand for.* She felt herself backsliding from enlightenment into the muck and mire of gamesmanship and politics and all the things Shondra Waite's work sought to purge. *Maybe we could never be more than playground children with toys,* she thought, and then turned on a new episode of a show that placed one naked man and one naked woman in a jungle for three weeks to see if they could survive. A brief reminder that for all the beauty of that little sapling, nature, more often than not, wants you dead.

And, as quietly and naturally as a secret lover returns, what Elizabeth knew would happen once again, happened. There was a knock at her door. She instantly seized up and felt a profound sense of disappointment and fear that this would never, ever end. In a moment of scotch-fueled anger, she decided she'd had enough. There were always several rounds of knocking and she wanted to catch him this time mid-knock, before he'd had a chance to scurry off into the night. She was done caring for her personal safety. This person was a coward and a bully and should be confronted. It was probably some dumb high school kid who would cease this stupidity once confronted by an adult. She was done calling the police, waiting for them to arrive and find nothing. This time, she slipped quickly and silently off the couch, stayed out of sight and then, a knot curled in her stomach, waited at the door for the next sound of knuckles on wood. She readied one hand on the dead bolt, the other on the doorknob.

Like the sudden tug of a fish on a fishing line, the knock came – the first of three, as was custom – and Elizabeth twisted the dead bolt, turned the handle and swung the door open as the second rap landed on the heavy door.

There was no face beneath the gray, hooded sweatshirt, only blackness. The figure, druid-like, stood over her, cast in the yellow glow of her porch light, and it did not move, did not speak, but she could feel its hate-filled stare reaching out from the black hole of its head. She screamed briefly, and cupped her hand to her mouth as she stumbled backward, tripped and fell against the wall and onto the floor. She kept her hand over her mouth, trying not to hyperventilate, and stared up at it, into it, the tall thing in a gray hoodie with a black oval where there should be a face. The dark buzzed electric, crackling like radio static. She saw filthy hands reaching for the screen door, covered with black and red. She pulled her hand from her mouth and screamed again.

★   ★   ★

Once again, the quiet solitude of Ridgewood Drive lit up with blue and red police lights, except this time they flashed across the front of Elizabeth's house. She stood in her doorway and saw down the street where neighbors stood at the edge of their yards looking at the scene she created.

"So he never actually came into the house?" the officer said to her.

"No. I kicked the door shut before he could come any farther."

"How do you know it was a he?"

"Just the height and the clothes, I guess," she said.

"Could you tell what race he was? Black, white, Hispanic?"

"It was hard to tell. His hands, they seemed caked in dirt and... something red."

"Like blood?"

"I don't know."

"Did he say anything?"

She thought of that black oval of nothingness, the static buzz that seemed to emanate from it like a swarm of bees. "Nothing."

"And no face that you could make out?"

"Like I said, it was so dark I couldn't see his face." Elizabeth knew it sounded crazy to say that he had no face, that it was akin to the Grim Reaper in an Old Navy hoodie.

"Even with this porch light on?" the officer said.

"I couldn't see him beneath the hoodie," she said. "This has been going on for weeks. I call you guys and it keeps happening. This is the first time anyone has been there when I opened the door."

"We have patrol cars searching the area right now, Representative Tutt. Rest assured, we'll find him."

But she wasn't sure there was anyone to find. How do you find a person with no face? Is it even a person?

"Do you know anyone who could be targeting you? Anyone who has threatened you in the past, sent nasty emails or letters?"

"I get nasty emails and letters all the time," she said. "Usually to my government address."

"Any that stand out? Multiple emails from the same person, perhaps?"

"I'll put you in touch with my campaign manager," Elizabeth said. "She keeps much better track of that stuff than I do."

The officer was taking notes while standing with her on the front porch. "We're gonna see if we can get a fingerprint off the screen door handle," the officer said. "If he touched it, there's a chance he left something behind. Attempting to enter the house marks an elevation in seriousness, so we want to be cautious."

"Yes, great," she said, but her mind was elsewhere. She couldn't stop picturing the figure standing over her, couldn't stop looking into the black mirror of what should have been a face.

"Our technician here will take a look at your door," the officer said. "I'm going to speak with some of your neighbors and see if they saw anything. Don't worry, we're not leaving and you can go back inside and try to calm down. Everything will be fine."

The officer walked away, notepad in hand, and was replaced by a rather geeky-looking younger man with a kit who asked her to clear the area so he could do his work. She walked back inside. She'd turned on all the lights. She sat on the couch, called Meghan and explained the situation, asking her to find any and all threatening emails she'd received in the last few months. Meghan said she'd grab her laptop and be at Elizabeth's house in no time.

"That's not necessary," Elizabeth said.

"Yes, it is," Meghan said. "You shouldn't be alone tonight. Listen, you could even come stay with me for a while. Till this all blows over and they either catch him or he gives up."

"No," she said. "I'm not running from anyone or anything. I'll stay right here, thank you." And then she hung up the phone. Fear and anger; they drove people to do dumb, irrational things, herself included.

She had just hung up the phone when the interviewing officer asked her to come outside. Her head swam from the lights and fear and the lingering thought that she might have easily been killed by this intruder.

The fingerprint technician had left, saying he was unable to find anything on the rickety metal door handle, and Elizabeth walked outside where she was met by several state troopers.

"We picked up someone matching the description you gave just a couple streets away," the trooper said. "We'd like you to take a look and tell us whether or not this is the person you saw on your front porch."

"I didn't see his face," she said.

"I know you didn't, but maybe just take a look and see if this person matches what you did see, the clothing, height, stuff like that," he said.

"But I don't want him to.... What if he comes back?" she said.

"You let us worry about that," he said. "If you think this is the guy, you won't have to worry about him coming back anytime soon. We'll make sure of that. What we're going to do is put you in one of our patrol cars and drive you past the suspect. You'll be able to see him but he won't be able to see you. How does that sound?"

She wanted this to end, she wanted it to be over, but now the prospect of identifying someone, of giving a firm yes or no answer, made her nervous. She couldn't be sure. It was impossible. Guilt was supposed to be without a shadow of a doubt, but a shadow was all she had seen.

"Okay," she said.

Elizabeth sat in the back of the patrol car, the seats deep and heavy. Just sitting in the car felt like being imprisoned. The officer pulled out of her driveway, drove down Ridgewood and took a right onto Beechwood, going the full length of the road before turning right again onto Woodland, headed toward Route 4. Up ahead, she could see the lights of another patrol car and several figures standing in the street.

"We found a couple kids from Waterbury in the area," the officer said. "They say they're selling raffle tickets for their high school football team, but we've heard that line before. Generally, they're just casing the neighborhood, seeing what house might have the most stuff in it they'd want to steal. Then they come back when no one's home, break in and make off with whatever they want."

"Then why would they keep coming back?" she said. "Why would they keep knocking and running away?"

"Who knows?" he said. "We're not dealing with the brightest bulbs in the pack. Now, I'm going to pull up and talk briefly with one of my guys here and give you a good chance to look these two clowns over. Just stay quiet and seated back there, and when we're done you tell me if you think one of them is the guy you saw on your porch or not."

The officer pulled up to the scene and rolled down his passenger-side window. As his fellow trooper leaned inside the car to talk, the other trooper paraded the two young men near the cruiser. Elizabeth could see them now; both Black, probably in their late teens based on the information the officer gave her, but they looked even older. They were both big boys, tall and strong, stony looks on their faces that gave away nothing, their arms behind their backs in handcuffs. She could see one of them had on a gray hoodie. She stared at him, trying to piece it together from her recollection. The figure she had seen: gray hoodie, nothing but dark where his face should have been. It could have been a trick of the light, the angle of her porch light combined with his dark skin that made the figure seem faceless. He fit what she could remember, the very little she had actually seen. But one little detail bothered her: the gray hooded sweatshirt he wore had a Nike logo on the front. She didn't remember a logo, certainly not one so recognizable. But she had been terrified, in fear for her life. And she hadn't seen anyone with him, although it was possible his friend had been waiting in the street.

The officer said a few more words to his subordinate and then glanced at Elizabeth in the rearview mirror before rolling up his window.

"What do you think, Ms. Tutt? Is it possible the person you saw on your front porch is that boy right there in the gray hoodie?"

"It's possible," she said.

"That's good enough for us," he said, pulling the cruiser away and turning back toward her house. "We got priors on one of them for shoplifting and possession of marijuana. Plus, they don't have a good excuse for what they're doing way out here at this time of night. You know all the car break-ins we've had over the years. These kids come out to where they think cars will be unlocked late at night and start rifling through them, stealing what they can."

"I'm well aware," she said, now exhausted with it all and feeling a deep, heavy weight in her stomach. "I'm not sure if I want to press charges."

"You don't have to. Frankly, even if it was that particular individual, he didn't actually do anything we could charge him with. But we're going to take them both in for questioning in connection with some vehicle break-ins. We'll check out their story, see if it adds up. That will at least keep them out of this area for a good long while and you won't have to worry about them anymore."

The pit in her stomach, the feeling that she had just made an irreparable mistake, grew deeper and heavier, dark as the hooded figure she'd seen on her doorstep.

"Don't you worry, Ms. Tutt. We know how to handle these kinds of guys," the officer said.

"I'm just not sure," she said. "I'm never sure...about anything."

"That's life, Ms. Tutt. You go on the best information you have and let God sort it out."

CHAPTER THIRTEEN

It was the day of the annual neighborhood block party and by ten a.m. tents were erected and long plastic tables with folding metal legs set beneath them. Anthony from next door used his ATV to haul a trailer full of plastic folding chairs from his house to the party site that spanned the three-way intersection of Ridgewood and Beechwood, overlooked by now-dead Oxygen-Tank Nancy's house, currently sporting the second For Sale sign in the neighborhood as her children attempted to sell off the property for a nice little windfall.

John watched Anthony drive past with the chairs in tow from the living room window. He strained to see around the patch of trees at the edge of the yard to get a glimpse of the tents and tables.

"You should go out and see if they need a hand," Jessica said to him.

He wondered if the Lovetts would bother showing their faces. He hoped they wouldn't. He didn't want to see them looking all nervous and hollowed out among the people their errant boy was terrorizing. He didn't want to see them before he returned to the house on Harmony Hill to snatch Lucas up, choke a confession out of him and then drag him to the police station.

"I'll get around to it," John said, but it was his day off and he didn't feel like working for free. Besides, most of the work was already done. The neighborhood elders having planned and now executing said block party, he'd go up there and stand around so it would appear as though he'd contributed something. There were already some big plastic coolers sitting on the grass filled with cold beer. There was the sound of barking dogs.

Caitlin was on the couch, her head buried in her phone, ears covered with headphones. James played a video game. Jessica worked

on some kind of nacho cheese dip recipe – one of many that would
be at the party.

"Yeah, fine," he said.

★   ★   ★

Joe couldn't take the dogs. The very fucking dogs he said were good for
hunting, for tracking animals to their deathbeds or whatever it was that
hunting dogs did. He had to leave the two biggest pains in her ass here
while he took the third biggest pain in the ass to a hunting cabin for a long
weekend of father/son bonding, the last-ditch, pointless effort to make
sure Vinnie didn't turn out like Lucas, or perhaps worse.

Amber was unsure why her mood was so dour. She'd locked the dogs
out of the room last night so she could actually have the bed to herself and
after about two hours of scratching, sniffing and whining they had finally
slept somewhere else and, judging by the nest of dog hair magnetized
to the cushions, it looked like they'd taken the couch as their bed. She
was done caring. For the first time in a long time she felt somewhat free,
a weekend off from work, the burden of her husband and eldest son
rendered merely a shadow from far away, and a day ahead that promised
to be full of food, sunshine and drink; it was like a mini-vacation. She
had her sweet Thomas, who was a breeze to care for. He'd run about the
neighborhood with the other kids, eat too many cookies or cupcakes, and
sack out early as she got drunk around the traditional bonfire at Jim and
Kristen's fire pit.

Thomas was eating pancakes she made with pre-mix. She could
already see the Atkinses rolling up and down the road in their decorated
golf cart, Dale with his fake leg propped on the dash at an angle, a beer in
his hand, an open bottle of cheap white wine in the cupholder as Becky
held a plastic cup.

Yes, despite everything, it would be a good day.

The dogs were going nuts with all the activity, running, baying.
They were abysmally stupid creatures – all they could do was see and
react. They could never stop for a moment and realize that all this energy

expenditure was ridiculous, that these people didn't warrant barking, while simultaneously letting some psycho neighbor kid bust out the window of her van or, worse, corner her from getting into the house in that weird and unsettling little incident.

She wondered if the dogs realized she hated them. Animals have those kinds of senses, people say, but right now, as the two idiots ran up and down the invisible-fenced length of their yard howling and yapping, such otherworldly senses seemed far outside the realm of their capabilities. People probably claimed dogs had all these superhuman powers to convince themselves the unnecessary addition of an animal into their presence carried some kind of value.

The party officially started at noon. Enough time for her to ready her nacho dip.

She leaned down and kissed the top of Thomas's head, pressing her lips to his thick brown, bowl-cut hair.

"It's gonna be a fun day," she told him. "You have to wear your helmet when you're riding your bike, though, okay?"

"Okay," he said and went back to his pancakes.

★   ★   ★

Vernon dressed his mother as he remembered her from a picture he was unsure actually existed. In his mind, he remembered seeing her in this yellow, white and maroon striped jumper, sleeveless but with a collar, something he remembered her wearing when she was younger, her skin smooth, glistening in the heat of a summer day at the beach, big sunglasses like insect eyes covering her face, a breeze about to blow the floppy hat from her head. He couldn't remember the context of this image. He couldn't remember where it was taken, or if he'd even been born yet. Perhaps the image in his mind was a picture he'd seen of her from her youth, or perhaps an advertisement for women's beachwear he'd seen in an old copy of the *Saturday Evening Post* onto which he'd supplanted his mother's face. He was unsure of it all but the jumper itself, which had hung in her closet for as long as he could remember.

Maybe we all have a form of Alzheimer's, he thought. *Maybe we shouldn't fear forgetting the past because so much of it is a figment of our imagination anyway.* One thing he'd noticed about his mother in the grip of brain degeneration was that everything was seen as new and startling and therefore without the lies and presumptions brought about by memory.

She was without context. And now, it would seem, he was without context as well.

"Oh my, won't I look nice," his mother said. "Is this outfit new?"

"Yeah, Mom, it's new. You'll look great."

He helped her slide her arm through the shoulder strap. The skin of her arm was so soft it felt like it would fall away from the bone at any moment.

"Are we going to the beach? I remember we would go to the beach at Rockwell Park and Harry and I would lie out in the sun or swim. But the water was cold, so I would just get cooled off and go lie in the sun and watch Harry swim. He'd go so deep and I'd get so nervous for him way out there."

"No, Mom. We're going to visit with the neighbors. It's the block party, remember? We can go see the Atkinses? You like them."

"A party?"

"Yeah, Mom. A party. Lots of food and people to talk to."

"Oh! I should get ready."

"That's what we're doing right now, Mom."

"Will that boy be there?"

Vernon thought of the night he found his mother naked, standing near the tree line, talking to Lucas. Who knows what he said or even did to her that night. He should have called the police but he was high and slightly drunk and, most of all, startled and scared.

"You remember that, but you can't remember my name half the time?" he said to her.

"Oh, stop that, Vernon. You care about too many small things."

Today he was going to make his pitch to the others about starting a Neighborhood Watch. He'd mapped out his strategy perfectly; he'd pepper the conversation with hints and innuendos – the 'did you hear?'

and the 'it just keeps getting worse' – that would get the dire nature of their recent crime wave into the general atmosphere. Then, later at night when everyone had plenty to drink, he'd approach a select few with the idea and they could team up to present it around the bonfire. He thought of that night with Elizabeth Tutt. The police had been at her house again last night, although he didn't know why.

He hoped she would be at the party today. He hoped to talk with her again. He enjoyed how their conversation that night seemed to roll so smoothly, as if they were somehow old friends. The way they tried to one-up each other on the logic of argument, the way they each seemed to see through the other and be, for once, truthful.

He hoped that maybe she'd come around to seeing the logic of his argument.

"We should bring my nacho dip," Vernon's mother said. "Everyone always loved my nacho dip."

*   *   *

Elizabeth firmly committed herself to attending the block party, not out of actual desire but as a responsibility toward building community at home and a disciplinary exercise in trying to find common ground with others. But now she agonized over what to bring to this suburban backwater potluck. The pressure of deciding on an appropriate dish had rendered her paralyzed; she couldn't think, she couldn't act, she could only spiral in mental circles over the implications of potential food selections. She wanted to be accepted into this group of people who, based on the campaign signs dotting their street, would reject her without a proper culinary offering.

The flyer said there would be hotdogs and hamburgers. She thought about bringing some vegetarian hot dogs and burgers and then decided that would probably further alienate herself from the group. You have to meet people where they are, after all. She pondered different forms of casseroles listed online but they were thick and heavy, more suited for a midwestern winter than a New England summer. She considered various nacho dips but worried about cultural appropriation. She could fit in according to her values, she decided, and reached into her memory, asking what her mother would have done, but this didn't look like a group of people who would welcome caviar and smoked salmon dishes.

She was tired. She'd barely slept since the intruder at her door last night. She'd racked her brain repeatedly, the image of those Black boys in handcuffs haunting her conscience. She decided that she'd sneak away and call the trooper barracks at some point to find out what happened. She didn't want two more kids in jail because of her. She second-guessed her reaction to the figure at the door. She had been terrified, but she could have just said, "Hello." Perhaps it was as innocent as selling raffle tickets.

But then there was that feeling, that sense of evil, when she stared at the figure in her doorway, the figure whose face was hidden in darkness; there was the constant intrusion of the knocks at her door over the past weeks, the feeling that someone was out to get her, and they had finally made their presence known.

Perhaps it was those boys the police questioned, but it seemed counterintuitive for potential burglars to harass the occupants of a house they wanted to rob, potentially drawing police attention. It really wouldn't make much sense.

Then she thought about Lucas Lovett. He'd already been involved in a fire and, from what Vernon had told her that one interesting yet awkward night, the neighbors were all suspicious about the death of the old woman – Oxygen-Tank Nancy. She wondered if they had a nickname for her too and then thought it better if she avoided the subject with herself.

If she had to be completely honest, she was scared; scared of whoever was harassing her; scared of involving herself with the police now that they'd taken in those boys for questioning; strangely scared of the recent spate of incidents around the neighborhood, even though she had lived in a city with far more crime most of her adult life; and scared of facing all her neighbors as a public and political figure.

But, most of all, she was scared of being alone when it came right down to it. Especially right now when she felt so vulnerable. Now that she'd had at least one – possibly two, if you count the Lovetts – positive interactions with people in the neighborhood, it was finally time for a real block party debut.

She hoped Vernon would be there to talk to, so the others could see that she was accepted by at least one person.

She decided on a bruschetta with goat cheese – refreshing, delicious and perfectly vegetarian without being obvious.

★   ★   ★

There was the constant sound of Big Wheels rolling down the street. Children – at least a dozen – riding bikes, scooters and plastic whirligigs racing down Ridgewood from the intersection with Beechwood. Bright orange traffic cones warned foreign cars of people in the street, an ATV parked on the grass, the For Sale sign of Nancy's home glinted in the sun, tents rippled in the breeze. A classic rock station played Jethro Tull. The sound of bottle openers and aluminum can tabs cracking open, the drabble of polite conversation filled the air like spawning locust. *Grab a paper plate, grab a beer, find an empty chair and have a seat, my friend, let's talk weather and sports; let's talk about the real estate market. What do you think Nancy's home will go for? What about the Lovetts'? They're pulling up anchor and heading out. They find their kid and taking him with? Nah, they ain't found him yet, probably off in the city somewhere; say, grab me another beer. Let's talk beer brands. What's with all this alcoholic seltzer shit? Would have gotten you kicked out of any decent bar back in my day. If you're gonna drink seltzer throw some vodka or whiskey in it. What a day, man, the kids love this shit, hand me another, we got some conversation to tend to here. You think they'll show? Who? The Lovetts? Nah. I don't think so. Last I heard they're already gone. Out looking for that psycho kid, I hope. Cops ain't done shit except show up and write reports. That's all they're good for. There are enough guns on this block to take care of anything, who needs 'em, anyway?*

The first beer went down like nails – leftover effects of a hard night of passing out on the couch again. That was a mistake; he couldn't fall back into that trap. He'd gone running and it felt great and he'd managed to find the hideout of the very sought-after Lucas Lovett. In no time,

John would haul the kid in and put an end to all the problems and be the neighborhood hero. He watched his daughter load up a paper plate with brownies and cookies and thought twice about telling her to ease off. It was the end of summer and it was a party, after all. He watched James racing up and down the street on his scooter. He watched Jessica, clad in white jean shorts that showed off her lovely legs, talk with one of the women whose name he couldn't recall and he suddenly realized what a pretty woman he'd married and noticed that she had not once spoken to him since she arrived, not even glanced in his general direction.

He squinted in the sun and looked at the rest of the partygoers. Dale and Becky held court near their golf cart; Jim and Kristen sat by their sides, Jim already with a glazed look in his eye, his big body sweating beneath the Hawaiian shirt; Anthony and Rachel moved around, chatting up the crowd; the young hippie guy from down the street who installed solar panels and his wife with all the tattoos and long, jet-black hair. Now here came Amber and her youngest, riding his bike. Amber carried a tray and wore shorts and a little tank top. He'd never really looked at her before and now that he noticed, she was quite pretty, with a nice figure. She clearly kept in shape, although he had no idea what she was doing with her husband. She looked like the type of woman who needed a good toss in bed from a stranger every now and then. She caught his eye, winked and smiled, and he smiled back. Vernon directed his feeble mother to a table, sat her down before a plate of food, put a plastic fork in her hand so she could eat and he could mingle on his own. She just sat like a deer in headlights. She looked like death warmed over and he wondered how much longer Vern could keep up the charade. The would-be Hillary was walking toward the party, tray in hand, gracing everyone with her presence, hanging with the common folk, he supposed. This should be interesting. She looked awkward trying to smile and talk as Dale and Jim showed her where to put her contribution of food. She tried to act like this wasn't her first rodeo, but it so obviously was. Christ, now Jessica was talking to her. *Who needs this? Hey, pass me that bottle, a quick shot, hair of the dog and whatnot. Try not to get sloppy. Try to hold sway. Try to be the man you're supposed to be.*

The sound of Big Wheels rolling down the street, plastic on pavement, children screaming into the sky.

* * *

Freedom and a beautiful day; outside with barely a care in the world, food and drink catered by people to whom you owed nothing. Amber marveled at the sensation. How long had it been since she'd been free of Joe and Vinnie? Sure, there were the couple hours a day when she was alone, but when was the last time Joe had been literally hundreds of miles away and she was left with only Thomas in the house? She couldn't recall, but the feeling was practically orgasmic. It was Saturday, it was beautiful, and she had nothing to care about.

She'd locked the damn dogs in the laundry room.

With this feeling of freedom, she'd taken a look in the mirror, run her hand over the contours of her butt and then threw on some tight shorts and a cute tank top and walked to the block party, giving John Ballard – handsome, if anything, because of the sheer look of raw strength on him – a little wink when she noticed him noticing her. It was nice to be noticed once in a while for something other than being mom, wife, expendable employee at The Package Depot. She dropped the nacho dip on the table and didn't even remove the tin foil. She grabbed a spiked seltzer drink from the cooler, pounded the first one, took a second and laughed, flipping her hair over her shoulder. John Ballard noticed her again. She saw Thomas on his bike, riding with the others. With forty or so adults around, it meant she could shirk some of her motherly duties for a while. Someone would feel compelled to clean up the messes or shout 'car!' when a vehicle slowly rolled up the street so the little ones could move onto the grass; someone would feel compelled to do it, but it wouldn't be her.

She heard the name Lucas pop up in conversation and she immediately left the area. Any mention of Lucas would automatically, in the minds of her neighbors, implicate Vinnie as well, and thus the anchor of her eldest son's continual fuckups was dropped to keep dragging down her good time.

She grabbed another spiked seltzer to go and found more convivial, conversational pastures.

★   ★   ★

Vernon appreciated the free food. He'd brought some store-bought cupcakes in a plastic tray, left them at the end of the table and loaded his plate with everything hearty. Today, he and his mother would eat for free rather than draining down her social security payment to survive on pasta and cereal. He made his mother a plate, trying to get as much protein as he could for her, and plopped her down in a chair with a good view of the neighborhood children, which should keep her as fascinated as the squirrels in the backyard.

Vernon was on a mission. It would take some careful tweaking, gathering the right people and the right voices, but he had his targets: John Ballard, for one. He was fiery and forceful enough to push the issue through. Then there was Joe Locke, but he wasn't here, although his wife Amber was laughing, dancing to 'Sweet Home Alabama' and holding a drink in her hand. Naturally, he would have to appeal to Dale and Jim, just because they were retired, home most of the time and, as the village elders, literally knew everyone on the block. Their voices would count for more than anyone else's, except, perhaps, Elizabeth Tutt, if she'd come around to the idea. She wasn't wrong when she accused him of wanting her support to give the watch an air of officialdom. She may not be loved because of her politics, but she still carried the heft of being a legislator and having serious connections.

He was shocked when he saw Elizabeth shaking hands with Dale and Becky, Jim and Kristen as she set down a plate of what appeared to be a fancy Italian appetizer. She shook hands as though she were on the campaign trail, and maybe she was. A campaign to be accepted by her neighbors, he supposed. He was flattered she'd taken his advice and come to the party.

He gave a glance to his mother to be sure she hadn't wandered off. She sat alone at the table, plastic fork in hand, staring silently at Nancy's old house across the street. Her eyes were empty, her plate was full and her face pulled into a countenance that can only be described as full of rage and offense.

Vernon quietly snuck behind Jim's house and smoked a quick bowl, letting the high spread over his mind like water, making the food taste that much better, making the drink so much more vital. He found Elizabeth's tray and ate from it. He found Elizabeth and she said, "There's my old friend," and he took her to meet his mother.

"I've reconsidered your proposition," she told him.

It was all coming together.

★ ★ ★

Poor Vernon's mother was a sad sight and, deep down, Elizabeth feared a fate worse than hers: no son to care for her when she couldn't think or remember anything. Sure, she might have a nice little life right now, but none of that lasts forever.

"He was wearing a hoodie, I couldn't see his face," she told him. "It was all I could do to kick the door closed. It was so terrifying. I didn't expect anyone to be there and I could tell – I could just tell – that he was there to hurt me. I don't know why."

Vernon had pulled her away from the group for a private conversation in whispered tones. "We have to be careful this doesn't get out of hand. I don't know who it was."

"*I* know."

"How?"

"I've seen him. Lucas. He was at my house, in the woods. He'd lured my mother out and she was just standing in the dark near the trees. I thought she was talking to herself but then he just appeared out of the darkness."

"Oh my God…those boys the police picked up…."

"That's not all. Amber had her car broken into that night. They seem to think it was Lucas as well. He stole her son's hoodie from the minivan."

"I think we need to go to the police with this information."

"The police already know. What we need is to come together, form the Neighborhood Watch, like I said. I just don't want anyone to get hurt. Well, I don't want you to get hurt. This is escalating. This is only the beginning."

She was lulled by the happy atmosphere, the music, the food, the sunlight, the children laughing and playing. Everyone getting along – community – something strived for by today's youth. *Maybe they just need to get off their computers and actually have a neighborhood block party with some old fogies like this*, she thought. Sure, the conversation turned to politics, probably in more hushed tones because of her presence, but it was fine. She didn't care today. She didn't want to care today. Some days all that needs to be left behind in order to build relationships.

She could tell the Atkinses and Katzes were celebrities, two couples older than she, heavy with partying over the years, they remained a good time, which is all they really wanted from life. Later in the afternoon, Dale's big voice boomed out over the tents, saying he had an announcement: both the Atkinses and the Katzes were putting their houses on the market and moving. Maine, they said, to a collective groan of disappointment followed by congratulations all around. Dale said the torch of the block party would be carried on by someone else. Everyone nominated the Carters. There were hugs and drinks and toasts and everyone took the news with a bit of humor. Elizabeth had been to Maine before: pretty much just like this state but drunker with uglier people and a beach. She figured they'd do just fine there. They seemed like lovely people.

Someone shoved a cocktail into her hand and she took a drink and she felt light for a moment. People ate the bruschetta and she was pleased. She saw Vernon engaged in hushed conversation with the big oaf from down the street. The beer bottle looked tiny in his massive hand.

★   ★   ★

John felt he was lost. Lost in what, he did not know and that made it worse. He couldn't take it all in and then rest easy and relax with his people because, deep down, he knew they weren't his people. He had no people. He was alone even amongst this throng of neighbors. Everything moved in a blur. He'd had too much to drink maybe, but that wasn't quite it. He saw his daughter with her pale skin that reddened so easily in the sun playing babysitter to the younger kids as the air darkened and grew heavy with dusk. She was so damn good, it sometimes baffled his mind. She possessed those wonderful character traits of responsibility, kindness and a desire to help. She wanted to be good. In that he recognized himself: he, too, wanted to be good, but it seemed there was always something in the way, a perpetual guilt that just never left its suffocating perch. Any goodness he could ever hope for rested in his daughter, that maybe people would see her as she grew into a teenager, a young woman, and then a mature adult and see just a brief glimpse of a light buried deep within his own heart.

His head twitched this way and that, looking for James, but he knew to look in the direction of noise, the sound of children at play. He saw his youngest in the street, riding his scooter as he had been for hours now, racing the other boys. He was always in the mix, always had to be around others, always making his presence known. When he was only two years old, he and Jessica had nicknamed James 'Jimmy the Bull', not for the mobster but for the fact that he was bullheaded, quick tempered, prone to breaking things and built solid and heavy. John saw much of himself in the boy and that worried him. There were so many pitfalls for a boy guided by intense emotion and a competitive nature. In thinking these things about himself and his child, John wondered if, in his growing age, he was finally shedding some of that innate toxicity that plagued his nature. Jessica would look at him now and give a resounding 'No', but John felt that he was growing, changing, becoming someone more educated and thoughtful, reflective, even. Maybe it was just the setting, the warm waning sun and the deepening sky that fueled these thoughts. He looked for Jessica and she was nowhere to be seen: these appendages of his life – his wife, his children – were separate from him, out there in the world, unconnected and untethered, and that made him feel worse, his shoulders sagging, his head drooping...where was he going?

★   ★   ★

Night. The sound of kids playing hide-and-seek. The bonfire threw its light in the darkness, shadows moved, playing in the trees. John found himself sitting beside Amber Locke, her glistening legs crossed, a drink in her hand, eyes staring into him in a moment he quickly recognized as intimate. He was speaking but what was he saying? It all came in waves of recognition, as if waking from a dream.

"Sometimes I'm just scared," he said.

"Of what?"

"I don't even know. But it will be night and everyone is asleep and I'm alone and I just feel this fear, like everything is wrong."

"Everything?"

"All of this. The whole thing. It's terrifying. We live only for seconds at a time. Do you realize that? The past is an illusion, a memory stored in our brain. It's gone, it doesn't exist. The future is our imagination. So there's only right here, right now, and it feels so goddamn disconnected. If I'm alone at that moment and that moment is all that exists then I'm lonely forever, if you think about it. It's bigger than past and future combined because it's literally everything, right then. My wife, my kids, the rest of the world might as well not even exist and you realize that maybe this is all some kind of experiment, some kind of test. It's not real."

"I don't know how my life got here," she said to him, leaning closer now. "I'm surrounded by this life that I somehow made, and I can't figure out how I did it, or why I did it, and what it's supposed to be. I don't even know if I did the right thing. I did what everybody said I should do and now here I am, but I don't know if I actually did it or not. Maybe we're all just puppets on strings."

"I think about death. It's so strange. One second you're here and the next you're gone. And I don't care what all the preachers say, they don't know. It could just be lights out, like turning the switch off. Do you realize how impossible that seems? I can't even get my head around it."

"There's so much I don't understand and I don't know. Do you realize that almost everything we think about the world, we have not experienced?" she said. "It all comes to us from these images, words, written on something so thin we can't even see it. It's not even on paper, it's these little markings on a screen, ones and zeros put together and presented to us in bright, flashy colors. It's insane, when you think about it. That we've come to live this way. It makes no sense. And how can we truly believe it when we can't see it for ourselves? It's like we're communicating with ghosts. Every time we turn on the computer it's a goddamn seance. The world isn't real anymore, it's all manufactured, packaged, presented to us and we're supposed to just go right along with it."

"I tried to tell them the truth. I keep trying. The truth is that we're under siege and we don't even realize it. It's still all being stripped away, little by little."

"I try to turn it off," she said. "I don't know how my boys are supposed to grow up in this world. I don't know how they're supposed to survive it."

"Things are happening. Things we don't know and can't see. And then, sometimes, it just reaches down and touches you."

He stared into her eyes, aflame with the light of the fire, wet with drink and deep beyond words. She stared back at him, beautiful, tragic and daunting. He reached out and touched her bare leg to know she was real and she let him and, for a moment, he felt a connection, a tether in the night, and she leaned over and whispered in his ear.

"Have you ever seen a red car at your house?"

"I couldn't tell if I was imagining it," he said.

She stood up from her chair and said, "I'm going to find Thomas and tell him it's time for him to go home. Save my seat." Then she was gone and John stared into the fire and watched it burn.

★　　★　　★

The time was right for Vernon's announcement. The core of the neighborhood, about twenty or so people, all gathered around the bonfire. The kids still played in the night but their ranks diminished. Amber took her seat next to John. They both looked as if they were on another planet, staring through each other or into the fire that burned so large now. John sat back in his chair and, in the night, looked like the stone carving of a god or king set upon his throne.

Hours ago, Vernon had finally, delicately, removed his mother from the party as he felt she had started to disturb others with her ramblings, her constant questioning of everyday things and asking people repeatedly who they were and where she was. She had talked of squirrels and 'the boy in the trees' and those around her had grown disturbed and dispersed, leaving her alone at the table and perhaps a little depressed. So he'd taken her home and set her up in her bed with some old movies to keep her company. Perhaps now they better understood his plight.

"You ever think about getting her into a home?" Dale said to him. "It just seems rough to care for her like you do."

"The second I put her in a home they start drawing down on her funds and then, eventually, our house," Vernon said. "You know what the price of those places is?"

"I'm just saying, she might get to be too much for you," Dale said. "You're young, you need to live your life, too."

The fact that the Atkinses and the Katzes were moving was a bit of a setback to his plan, as they generally directed the loose social governance of the neighborhood, but he'd never really had them in mind for leading the watch, anyway. That responsibility he planned to bestow on John. Vernon would act as the organizer, the brains behind the operation. He hoped John wasn't too drunk to participate in the conversation. There was a sadness in his eyes that worried Vernon.

Music played in the background and the circle around the bonfire engaged in their own conversations. Vernon asked Jim Katz if he could turn down the music for a moment to make his own announcement and Jim quietly got up, walked to the sound system and lowered the volume. Few seemed to notice.

Vernon stood outside the circle and yelled out, "Can I have everyone's attention please? Can I have your attention?"

He waited as the talking died down and everyone turned to look at him, their eyes shining in the night.

* * *

As Elizabeth left the party, she felt some disturbing misgivings.

Despite the campaign signs posted in nearly everyone's yard, she felt a sense of acceptance when Vernon brought her into the fold of her neighbors. That much she appreciated. His announcement about the Neighborhood Watch went off well. The others had eagerly encouraged him. Vernon took the lead of setting up a private social media page, identifying the houses who had outdoor security cameras and facilitating a shared text group to monitor all the goings-on in the tiny little hamlet. He ominously recounted that someone had been stalking in the woods around his house; Amber told of how her minivan had been broken into; and Elizabeth, in giving her endorsement, told the group about the weeks of terror she had endured with the constant knocking at her door, culminating with the police taking two boys in for questioning.

But she held her tongue as the conversation then turned toward guns and the thinly veiled racism in their talk about 'thugs' from the city constantly breaking into their cars. She felt she had betrayed herself in the name of fear and the desire to be liked and now there was a sick feeling in her stomach.

Vernon nominated John to be the head of the group and everyone agreed. John had stood up and said he was 'honored', and that together they wouldn't let this place go to hell the way the rest of the country was – another thinly veiled attack on her worldview.

"We'll catch whoever is terrorizing this neighborhood," John said. "Because the police sure as shit ain't doing it and we have children to protect. First there was the fire and now all this? It doesn't take a genius to figure out what's going on and I think we can get this matter settled pretty quick." John was drunk but he had a knowing look in his eye that concerned her.

"Let's just try our best to keep it peaceful and safe," was her addition to the conversation.

"Just think of what could have happened to you," Vernon said. "It would have only taken seconds. You saved your own life."

Elizabeth was unsure on that count.

The party was now firmly behind her. She could hear their voices fade away as she passed John's house and then the Carters' and Lovetts' and the burned-out husk of the old abandoned house. It was dark. The town had yet to restore the streetlights and she could see her house, the lone porch light shining in the night.

She heard something, a stifled voice, a rustling in the long grass and overblown shrubs bordering the Widner house. She stopped for a moment, startled and, she had to admit, scared. She looked but could see nothing. It was too dark. But still, she felt there was someone there, moving about the ruins. She looked back at the block party and wondered if she should go retrieve the newly minted Neighborhood Watch to investigate, or perhaps, escort her home, considering all that she'd been through.

But no, that was just being paranoid and illogical. There were neighborhood kids everywhere, still out roaming and playing in the night. If anyone was there, that was the simplest and most likely answer.

She heard what sounded like a stifled laugh from the depths of the ruins and then, farther up the street behind her, the bellowing laughs of the partygoers beside the fire.

★   ★   ★

When Vernon arrived back home his mother was in a panic, wandering through the house as if blind, arms outstretched, wiry hair standing on end. In her panic, she knocked over vases and brushed framed photos from the walls and the glass shattered and she stepped on the glass with her bare feet and bled throughout the house so that it resembled a murder scene from one of his true crime shows. He could hear her screaming about 'the boy' as he walked from the road up the driveway, and he began a shuffling run to the front door only to find the stairway red with smeared blood and footprints and the house ransacked. He called his mother's name and ran up the stairs to find her virtually spinning about the living room, the image of an insane, swirling witch.

Vernon bear-hugged his mother and picked her off the floor to protect her bloody feet. She suddenly went silent and limp and then he could barely hold her deadweight. He rushed her to the bathroom, his high and slight inebriation worn down to just a nub of time delay. He sat her on the toilet and propped her feet on the edge of the bathtub.

He breathed heavy now, sweating from the exertion. "Mom," he said, "what the hell are you doing?"

"It's the boy," she said. "The boy is talking to me."

He searched the cabinets for something to disinfect her wounds. He wrapped her feet in layers of gauze and knew that he would have to take her to the hospital for stitches.

CHAPTER FOURTEEN

Amber woke with the obligatory hangover and the sound of whimpering dogs at her bedroom door wanting to go outside or be fed or just reclaim what they considered their bed. She already knew she would have a mess of shit and dog piss to clean up in the laundry room and that dragged down her elation at having had a night almost entirely to herself full of laughter and even a little sexual intrigue; she recalled her bare leg resting against John Ballard's as the two of them shared a moment of intimate conversation. Poor guy, she thought. She tried to give him enough of a hint, but the big, beefy lug either couldn't see it or was actively blocking the possibility from his mind. Either way, she felt she connected with him on a deeper level through the power of drink and that always meant a good and fun night. The hint of something sexual blossoming from the dried gardens of parentage still carried with it the aroma of youth. She felt new and invigorated.

Eight in the morning still counted as sleeping in, and she listened momentarily for the sound of Thomas watching television in the living room, but all she could hear were the whimpering dogs, their levels rising to a point that forced her to get out of bed and grumble beneath her waxing euphoria. The boy had played all day and night. She hadn't sent him home till nearly ten-thirty, well past his normal bedtime. He was likely exhausted.

The dogs jumped at her when she opened the door, swirled between her legs, nearly knocking her down as she tried to get to the front door and let them out. They slid like snakes through the doorway and bayed at the rolling, overcast sky. She let the door swing shut with its own weight and shuffled to the laundry room to assess the damage. A couple piles of shit, but not as bad as she expected. She ran the coffee maker and stared for a moment at the dishes in the sink, remnants of her work in preparing the nacho dip. She tried to remember getting home last night but came up short. There had been multiple bottles passed around the bonfire, everyone partaking of a sip, sharing each others' saliva in a communal toast to the newly founded Neighborhood Watch while they drunkenly discussed the details and waxed poetic about the fate of the nation.

The last she remembered was laughing and nearly tipping over in a camping chair as John Ballard, shirtless, stood over the fire like King-Fucking-Kong.

With her memory of coming home drawing a total blank there was a brief moment of panic, a niggling sensation and realization that she had not actually checked in on Thomas to make sure he was safe in bed. Coffee cup in hand, she quickly walked to his room, assuring herself that he was fine, there was nothing to really worry about; nothing could have happened to him when the streets were crowded with the people she knew and trusted, a growing guilt in her stomach that she had, for a few moments at least, neglected her duties as a mother in favor of partying like a teenager.

She opened his bedroom door but Thomas was not in bed. She called for him, questioningly at first, only loud enough for him to hear if he was in the room. Then she walked, more quickly, to the living room, calling his name, louder and louder, wondering if there was some way on God's green Earth that she had somehow gone about these first five minutes of the morning without noticing him in the living room, but he was not there. She went to Vinnie's room, her own bedroom to see if he had crawled into bed with her and was wrapped in the sheets and blankets; she checked the basement, garage, backyard, the laundry room and his room again, opening the closet doors, screaming his name now, over and over until it lost all meaning. Thomas was not the name of a boy now, it was a cry of fear and longing.

Then she was standing in the driveway, in nothing but a t-shirt and some tattered boxer shorts she'd stolen from Joe, and unable to speak or think past the tightening anxiety in her chest. Up and down the street, she saw nothing, no sign of life, everyone still in their beds. There were so many children last night, he must have gone home with one of them, an impromptu sleepover without telling Mom – or maybe he did and she couldn't remember. She took out her cell phone and started calling every number of every neighbor with a child, all the kids that Thomas had played with in the past or was playing with last night.

"Is Thomas with you? Is he at your house?" Her fevered panic carried through the phone with a trembling, shaking voice, to which the other end of the line – whomever it was – would answer: "What? No. I haven't seen him. What do you mean you can't find him?" and she would hang up and dial the next number.

She could imagine their conversations now; the mother turning to her husband and saying, "Amber says that little Thomas isn't home. She was asking if he was here," and the husband commenting on her state of mind last night, saying that everything is probably fine before rolling over to sleep off his obligatory hangover, as well. And then the mother would go to her children's rooms to check, to be sure that Thomas wasn't there, because they weren't sure themselves. They would find their children sleeping or watching television or playing their video games or surfing online and they would know that everything on their end of the street was okay, they were safe, but there still wriggled in the back of their mind something horrid. Slowly, front doors began opening, mothers and fathers began glancing out, looking up and down the street, seeing only Amber standing in her driveway, frantically making a phone call to 911 that she so badly didn't want to make. Was it really an emergency? Was he really missing? *He's not here, so where is he? This is what the police are for. Am I a bad mother? What will people think? He can't be gone. Where would he go? Who would take him?*

"This is 911, what is your emergency?"

She ran back inside when a sudden realization flashed. She plowed into the living room to the computer and quickly pulled up the security camera software. A two-way screen pulled into focus showing the front driveway and backyard. She rewound the footage through hours, back to the time she sent Thomas home, when she was too preoccupied to walk him there and tuck him in the way she should have. She slowed and stopped as she herself approached the door, stumbling up the slate-stone walkway and letting herself inside, the image of herself weighing like a ton of bricks; she saw people pass in front of the house at one a.m., neighbors returning home from the party. She scrolled back further; she saw older kids on bikes, more partygoers passing by, the occasional car. She scrolled to roughly ten-thirty and then stopped completely. A feeling of overwhelming dread fell over her.

A figure in a gray hooded sweatshirt appeared out of the darkness, and through the grainy black-and-white of the night vision, stood at the edge of her lawn and stared directly into the camera. There was no face, just blackness beneath the hood, but she knew who it was. She could tell by the way he stood, his gait, his dirty clothes; she could tell it was the gray hooded sweatshirt that had been stolen from her minivan last week. She couldn't see his face but she knew it was Lucas. She stared at the screen, the fear growing inside her like an overwhelming sound of buzzing flies, and he stared back at her, through the electronic screen, through time itself. It was as if he knew she would watch; it was as if he were sending her a message.

And then she was out the door again and running. She could hear sirens in the air, police cruisers coming closer, tracing their way through the neighborhood's outer layers. But all she could hear was herself screaming Thomas's name; all she could feel was the inexorable pull, like gravity, toward the Widner house, where Lucas would perch on the roof like a demented gargoyle.

Doors opened as she passed, awakened to her screams, so human, vibrant and tortured. Screams no one in the neighborhood had ever heard before. She could see the remnants now, approaching fast, her bare feet cut and bleeding from the asphalt. She could see the overgrown grass and scorched brick of the garage; she could see the slight rise of the blackened foundation; she could see the heaps of ash and burnt wood; she could see something pale white and bright red lying in the soot.

CHAPTER FIFTEEN

He woke to the sound of screaming. It was enough to instantly pull him out of sleep and send him leaping to the living room window in two steps to catch a glimpse of Amber running down the street in boxers and a tank top as she screamed for her child.

John was out the front door, not even putting on his shoes, just pounding across his front yard and onto the road in his socks, trailing behind her, last night's feeling of intimacy and connection frothing up from a deep well, as she ran for the burned-out house that haunted his dreams.

And then, when he saw it, he could never unsee it.

That poor boy – merely seven years old – stripped to his underwear, his core turned inside out, bright red and deep brown and everything held within splayed to the world. John's mind was overcome; it seemed to retreat so that only his body moved.

Amber was on her knees in the soot. She tried to scream over and over but nothing came from her mouth but a wheeze. John grabbed her in a bear hug from behind and pulled her away from her boy and she lashed out suddenly, elbows to his face, heels to his shins, but they glanced off him like raindrops. He turned her away from Thomas and at that moment she found her voice again and the pain in her scream was nearly enough to cripple him. He felt her weight and she seemed impossibly heavy, as if suddenly turned to stone.

Then, as if out of nowhere, gentle, tender hands seemed to lift Amber from him, carry her into the air like an angel bathed in morning light and then those warm and tender bodies surrounded her, holding her as she gnawed into their shoulders and trembled. John saw them now: Rachel and Kristin and Maryanne and Mark. He looked around and saw others streaming toward the scene, the people of the new Neighborhood Watch come to rescue one of their own. The sirens were close now and John knew he must look once more on the dead boy before he too would be dragged away.

Thomas lay on his back in the ash heap, the invisible parts of him spilled into the light of day, the glint of a big kitchen knife smeared with red just a few feet away. There was a circle traced in the ash around Thomas, partially trampled now by their feet, and the boy seemed to lie at the intersection of some design that seemed at once familiar and entirely foreign.

He couldn't stomach the sight any longer and turned away, pushing the visual memory down.

John walked from the body and stood beside the coterie of people consoling Amber as she trembled on her knees beneath their hands like a worshipper at the altar, baptized in the Spirit. John reached down and laid his hand upon her shoulder and, as if sensing his intimate, heavy touch, she whipped her head around and glared into his eyes and growled, "I know who did this."

He said nothing back, but he felt a rage grow like fire, burning bright and blinding heat. The police were here now, everything was done.

Yet there was one last thing.

★   ★   ★

John walked quickly back to his house, avoiding the police, letting them sort out the whos and whats of the matter because they didn't matter, none of those useless sacks *mattered*. Jessica stood in the yard, arms crossed, a worried look on her face. She asked what happened and John merely mumbled, "Thomas is dead," and she gasped and put her hand to her mouth and began to rush toward the rest of the neighbors as John rushed away from them.

The police would canvass the neighborhood soon, knock on every door, interview every household, everyone who was at the block party. They would be looking to talk with him and he had to move quickly and without their notice. In the partially finished basement, behind a cheap sheetrock wall and even cheaper door, was his old fishing gear from when he attempted to replace drinking with fly fishing but just ended up fly fishing while drunk until he eventually gave up on trying to tie knots with invisible fishing line while ten beers deep. But he had gone through the motions: purchased all the equipment, even took a class at a local fish and game shop where a guide took him to a heavily trafficked river and pointed out exactly where to catch river trout and helped him clear tangles from his guide lines. There, in the corner, was a musty pair of waders that hitched up over his shoulders and kept him clear of ice-cold river water up to his stomach. He put them on, a little tight now with ten years of extra bulk, and then left out the basement door in the back and walked into the woods toward the swamp that divided their neighborhood from Harmony Hill and the old witch-house. He knew Lucas was there. There was no justice for this. What he had just seen was too much, an unimaginable image, so real he could still smell it. This was bigger than the police, who would merely slap handcuffs on him; this was bigger than the so-called 'Justice system' that would probably declare the boy sick and send him to a home. This was what haunted his dreams, this was the threat that needed to be eliminated. He practically ran through the dense underbrush until he came to the edge of the swamp and his wader boots sunk into the black mud.

He stared out across the wetlands. He knew it wasn't deep. He'd spent enough time repairing asphalt on the tiny bridge crossing the muck to know he could walk through it. He had to do it in secret, he couldn't capture the attention of the detectives who were now descending on the neighborhood. This had to be silent and secret.

The water and mud closed in around his legs. His foot sunk into the swamp and the swamp, in turn, latched onto his leg and tried to stop him, to hold him back from what he must do. But he was big and strong and he ripped his leg up out of the mud and moved forward, step by step, through the water. The other side was a mere one hundred yards away but every step was like moving through cement; it clung to him, choked him with its smell, tried to trip him with scattered logs and branches on the bottom, sucked him into its depths only to have him tear away from it and move forward. He powered through the swamp. He powered through everything. Nothing would stop him, not even himself. He was the president of the Neighborhood Watch, he was a father and husband, and this breach could not be allowed to stand. He was out of his body, watching it unfold like a movie over which he had no control. He was out of his mind. Today it was Amber's son split and splayed over the ashes; tomorrow it could be his own. It was only a matter of time unless someone did something.

Anyone who saw him wading through that place would think they were seeing some kind of Northeastern Sasquatch; a lumbering man-like creature rocking its big body and long arms through the morass, the water at its waist, a furrowed, primitive forehead pointed downward as it pushed on and emerged dripping and caked with black mud on the other side. The water sloughed off from him as he broke through the saplings and ferns until he was on dry ground. He dropped the waders and left them in a pile and then continued through the woods until he saw the sprawling, manicured backyards of Harmony Hill. He cut over to the road, not wanting to be noticed by paranoid rich people who might alert police that some neanderthal was trucking through their lawn.

He found the street. Just a few steps further now....

★　　★　　★

Lucas slept on an old mattress in the abandoned house, its walls covered in red symbols and all-seeing eyes he'd painted that looked strikingly like the one traced around the body of Thomas Locke. John stood over him as he slept and stared down at the boy with his effeminate face, watching him for a time, trying to talk himself out of what he knew he must do. Indeed, when the boy woke it would be to a nightmare, to the grim fact of his own dying. John had no weapons, no guns or knives, just his bare hands and that was good enough. John waited for a moment, felt the sun warming the inside of the room through the single window, taking mental notes of the eyes scrawled on the walls, the garbage littering the floor, the rumpled clothes the boy wore and the faint dark hairs that traced his upper lip and chin. This was an act of mercy, if nothing else.

John looked for a moment out the window and onto the street, quiet and flooding with Sunday morning church light and then there was a sharp pain, a pressure in his thick calf causing him to stumble slightly, and a fire that reached up through his nervous system. John looked down and saw the handle of a pocket knife jutting from his calf and the wide brown eyes of Lucas staring up at him.

John's leg buckled for a moment. He found himself unable to look away from the sheer oddity that was a knife sticking out from his leg. The pain dulled somewhat in those brief seconds and it appeared more of a curio one would find at a flea market than something attached to him. Then both he and Lucas stared at each other – Lucas looking like a child who'd just been caught in a lie, staring up at his father about to punish him.

So, John punished him. Lucas tried to move from the mattress; John clenched his big hand into a fist and smashed it down into Lucas's face, surprisingly soft and delicate. The boy's head snapped back down toward the floor, a look of confusion at first as his nose and mouth were suddenly burst open. John's fist was nearly the size of the boy's face, and he felt nothing from the impact, like striking Lucas with a rock. John hit him again, this time square across the eyes, and the boy's head twisted. He scrambled and panicked and then John's big body was on top of him, straddling him, and John wrapped his hands around Lucas's throat and began to squeeze. Decades of wielding shovels full of asphalt and gripping jackhammers made his grip a pneumatic vise and John squeezed so hard that his thumbs grazed the vertebrae in the boy's neck.

Lucas's big brown eyes popped outward, fixated on John, watching him as he continued to squeeze and hold. The boy's body shook but couldn't move under John's weight. John stared into the boy's eyes, brought his own head nearer still, until they were mere centimeters apart, till he could see a redness budding in the white sclera. Lucas was going to die now, and John felt it surge through him. He tightened his grip again, the boy's throat folded in on itself. Not a breath nor a word passed between them but something else did. John felt it. He felt something flow into him the moment the boy stopped struggling. It was like watching a ticking clock come to a halt; the inner gears ceased to function and time disappeared.

John felt a pit in his stomach and then an overwhelming panic. Like a suicidal jumper realizing halfway through his fall that he wanted to live, it was too late. John released his grip and whispered, "Oh my God," to himself as he stared down at Lucas, a kid he'd watched grow up over the years into the monster he'd become – a monster, yes, but still a human being. John tried to wake him, as if Lucas were stuck in a deep sleep.

John lay there with the dead boy for a moment and all around them were eyes watching. John stared at Lucas's face, waiting. His big eyes bulged like inflated balloons.

★   ★   ★

John left his waders to sink in the swamp and limped through the cut of forest back to his home. He walked through the basement door and could hear Jessica scurrying about upstairs. He could hear his daughter and son watching television. He wondered what she had told them when they asked about all the sirens and police cars and the god-awful screaming. He wondered what she had told them when they asked where their father was; he wondered what she had told the police.

He shut the basement door and he heard Jessica now come to the stairs. "John! John! Is that you?"

"Yeah, it's me."

She came down the stairs and peeked around the corner to see him standing in the basement, exhausted and crying.

"Where were you? The police are asking to talk to you. I didn't know where you were."

"I just needed some time," he said.

She softened a moment. "Are you okay?"

"I can't get it out of my head," he said.

She approached him gently, mother-like and wrapped her arms around him. "I know," she said. "I can't stop thinking about it either."

John kept thinking of those bulging eyes staring upward, open and lifeless.

"It's all I see," he said.

He felt her grip tighten around his chest.

"You're bleeding!" she said and he looked down to a small pool of blood that had gathered at his right heel, dripping out from his pant leg.

"It's nothing," he said.

CHAPTER SIXTEEN

What must it feel like to be stabbed?

It pained Vernon to think of little Tommy Locke's final moments, of the innocent boy's bewilderment and surprise and confusion. Rarely does someone die instantaneously of a knife wound. There is time to think and contemplate, to feel the life slowly fading and feel the other metal stabs into your body. Do you feel them? Or are you numb with shock and disappointment?

Vernon, secluded in his dark basement room, sleeping off the night, hadn't heard Amber's screams as she'd run down Ridgewood Drive. A fire, a runaway teenager, a death, a car break-in and the constant harassment of an elected official, it all came quickly and quietly and was far more excitement and foreboding than he'd ever experienced before. He hadn't stirred till he heard the sirens, which overwhelmed the air, and then the Neighborhood Watch group text began exploding with "Oh my God," and "How could this happen?" and "This has to be stopped," and "I don't even know what to say." Vernon threw on some clothes quickly and did his best to half-jog to the corner and see all the police cars and ambulance at the scene. Jim and Kristin stood in their front yard, the tables, tents and coolers left out from the night before wet with dew, and they shook their heads, stifled tears, and told him of little Tommy Locke. Vernon tried to catch sight of Amber somewhere in the flashing mess of it. "They've taken her to the hospital," Jim said. "It was too much. I can't imagine." Already, uniformed police were working their way up and down the neighborhood, knocking on doors, asking questions.

Vernon rushed back to his home to tend to his mother and her feet, still bandaged in gauze. She was up and trying to get out of bed. Putting her feet on the floor caused her pain and stranded her on the bed, calling for help from her room. Vernon picked her up and brought her to the bathroom and waited outside the door.

"We have to take you to the hospital for your feet, Mom," Vernon told her through the door. "You might need stitches, or a wheelchair, or I don't know...."

"I won't let them take me!" she screamed.

"They're not going to take you anywhere, Mom. I just need them to check the cuts on your feet."

He knew it would be a struggle to get her into the car.

"I don't need them! I don't need those doctors!"

"Someone got hurt last night," Vernon said, more to himself than to her. "A little boy was murdered last night, Mom. Just down the street. Can you imagine that? Do you understand that?"

"Who killed the boy?" she said, suddenly sounding lucid.

"I think I know," Vernon said. He felt like he wanted to do something, to be in the mix somehow, but, at the same time, felt completely and utterly useless. He realized with a sudden, gripping vigor just how fantastical his television-fueled dreams of crime solving and detecting truly were. He was a nobody. He was less than a nobody. When push came to shove and an innocent life was now gone, it was the professionals who would take the case, had all the information and the facts that they would never, in a million years, share with some jobless, pudgy thirty-something burnout living in his mother's basement. For all his self-supposed crime-solving instinct, the officers would have heard a thousand times that they should be looking for Lucas from every other neighbor on the street before they got to him – and he was confident they would get to him. Contrary to what he tried to demonstrate to his friends and neighbors, he had no real insight, no knowledge outside the superficial; he had nothing real to offer the world now that it was faced with true, real-life tragedy.

He thought of Amber; he thought of her husband, Joe, and her eldest son, Vinnie. He thought of what they must be going through right now. For all his ability to picture what it must feel like to be killed, he had far greater difficulty understanding such a loss. Perhaps it was because he had no family, no children the world could take that would leave him devastated. He had only his life and his bodily autonomy encased by skin; the only tragedy he could picture for himself was having that skin pierced by the blade of reality.

He thought of his mother's feet, of the blood on the floor and on his clothes as he tried to bandage her up last night. It wouldn't be a good look if the police came searching; any bloody clothing, despite the truth of where it came from, would make him suspect until otherwise cleared. He had to take her to the hospital for multiple reasons and he knew that when he got there they would eye him suspiciously, wonder if he were taking proper care of her. Maybe they, too, would investigate who Vernon Trimble really was, what he was capable of. Perhaps, such an investigation was warranted.

★   ★   ★

Elizabeth couldn't imagine that such a horrid thing had taken place within sight of her home. Most of all, she couldn't imagine that she had likely been a small witness to it all. But that was undeniably true. She told the police everything she'd heard and seen when she was walking home from the block party last night. As far as she could gather, the time of her passing by the Widner house coincided with when they thought Thomas Locke was killed. Elizabeth didn't have much to tell; she'd heard whispers; she'd figured it was the neighborhood kids playing in the dark as they had been all afternoon and evening; she paid it no mind and continued on her way home. She heard no screams, nothing out of the ordinary besides the sound of what she thought were kids snickering and sneaking about. It was dark, the streetlights were still burned out and so she saw nothing. That was all the help she could offer. She ducked back into her house the second detectives left and kept a vigilant watch out the window. There were detectives at the Lovetts' house. They'd been there for some time now. If Elizabeth was ever the outcast in this neighborhood, the suspicion surrounding the Lovetts' only son had banished the couple to a realm of otherness so extreme that Elizabeth was widely accepted by the group as a whole. The neighborhood had a common enemy, and it wasn't the woman featured on the campaign lawn signs.

She watched as police escorted the Lovetts into a patrol car. She could briefly see the look on Tonya's face. There was so much pain in the world that, even in a position of mild influence, it made her feel useless – mere window dressing for a society that wanted to claim some semblance of order and virtue as it slowly imploded all around them, unimpeded by moral stances or carefully worded press statements.

Her phone buzzed with text messages from the new Neighborhood Watch. Everyone cursing, crying, pontificating, calling for arms and an official request that anyone with video surveillance turn their data over to the police immediately.

Then came the inevitable text message from Meredith Skye asking her for comment about the awful murder that took place a stone's throw from her house. Elizabeth thought for a moment: Who was she to say anything at all? What even was there to say? Her words would merely cheapen the tragedy. The publication would relegate a true, heartbreaking loss to the superficial and trite pages of some dying newspaper and website. Her campaign manager, Meghan, texted her now. Lots of 'OMGs' and exclamation points and then a brief reminder about the museum opening of Shondra Waite's Tree of Life exhibit.

Reporter is asking for comment about the murder. I don't even know if I want to. I don't know what to say, Elizabeth texted.

Tell them it is a heartbreaking tragedy and that no child or family should ever suffer this kind of loss. Tell them it merely highlights your push for more youth services, mental health counseling and rehabilitation that your opponent has vowed to undercut.

I don't know....

Every crisis is an opportunity. Everything we're saying is true. Add that you hope the perpetrator is caught and faces justice. Add that you are making a donation to a youth crime prevention nonprofit in the name of the murdered boy. Depending on what the outcome of the investigation is, we could probably push legislation called 'Tommy's Law', or something of that nature.

Am I selling my soul, Meghan?

You're exposing your soul. You're fighting for positive change. Don't get down, get mad and get ready to fight. Toughen up, buttercup!

Elizabeth dropped her phone onto her table and looked out again at the scene. The police were spread out across the neighborhood; she could catch glimpses of their uniforms in the woods behind the burned-out house. Dogs on long leashes arrived in specially marked cars and were now pulling and tugging and barking into the trees, noses to the ground.

It's only a matter of time before we're all caught, she thought. *In some way, we're all implicated, we're all guilty.* You could only stay ahead of it for so long before it caught up with you and made you pay. Everybody paid, one way or the other. Justice was not only meted out through courts.

She wasn't exactly sure of the sins she'd committed, but she knew they were there, she felt them in her soul, if she indeed still had one.

The police dogs barked and pulled at their tethers. She texted Meredith Skye.

★   ★   ★

John changed his pants and socks, dumped them in the washing machine and ran it for a quick cycle to get rid of the blood. He was sure he needed stitches. The knife had pierced deep into his calf, nearly striking the bone, and at every step it ached and burned so much he winced. He heard the dogs outside, roaming through his backyard and into the woods where he'd just walked. They were tracking a scent, but he had no idea whose scent.

There were heavy knocks at the front door. He heard Jessica answer and say, "Yes, he's upstairs. Let me just get him," and now John steeled himself for questions, tried to be sure that nothing in his face gave him away. He squashed any guilt, knowing that this was justified vengeance, necessary for the preservation of life, liberty and the pursuit of happiness here on Ridgewood Drive, but knowing that others wouldn't understand. His mind still reeled from it. It had happened so fast and so easily. It was as if he'd suddenly altered the position of the universe. This single, violent, immutable action had let him slip from one reality to another in a matter of seconds and now he had to face the world a brain-fogged, limping murderer, tasked with keeping a massive secret.

John was sweating. He splashed some cold water on his face, dried off and then walked down the stairs, each step nearly causing his knee to buckle from the pain but he didn't let it show. Naturally, it was Officer Badgely at the door, who was apparently his new handler.

"Hi, John. Was hoping to have a word with you." Badgely seemed so much bigger all of a sudden, his hat and mirrored sunglasses crowding the entrance to his home.

John just sighed, said nothing and walked outside. The air was electric with movement, as if an unfelt wind swirled across the world. Even when he couldn't directly see the crime scene, he felt it. A small army of police lay just out of sight, working, trying to find Lucas, and eventually they would come after him as well. It was only a matter of time.

"John, you know I have to ask you these questions, right?"

"Sure."

"I was here earlier. You weren't. Where were you?"

"I had to get out, clear my head," John said. "I've never seen anything like that before."

Badgely seemed sympathetic for a moment. "Me neither," he said and looked down at the ground. "You okay, though, John? You seem a little tense."

"I just saw the body of a boy all cut up and gutted. I just held his mother when she found it. No, I'm not okay. No one should be okay."

"Where were you last night around eleven p.m., John?"

John pointed up to the intersection with Beechwood where the tents and coolers and foldout chairs still stood from the night before. "I was at the block party."

"Who were you with?"

"Mostly everybody. We were all sitting around the bonfire at that point. But I wasn't keeping close track of time." John shifted his weight and pain ripped up his leg. He stumbled a moment and tried to play it off. Badgely eyed him.

"Did you see Thomas Locke last night?"

"Uh, I'm sure I saw him here and there. The kids were all running up and down the street with their bikes and toys."

"Were they running or riding up and down the street?"

"Both, I guess. You know what I mean."

"Did you see anything or anyone that stood out to you? Do you remember anything out of the ordinary?"

"Not at all. It was all so perfectly ordinary. It was all so normal."

"Were you drinking last night?"

"Yes, everyone was."

"Did you see Thomas Locke leave to go home?"

"No, but I was sitting next to Amber at the bonfire and she said she was going to tell Tommy it was time to go home and go to bed and she walked away for a while to talk to him."

"About what time was that?"

"I think it was around eleven or so. Hard to tell."

"And did Amber come back to the bonfire?"

"Yes."

"Did she seem different to you at that point?"

"No. She seemed…happy. We were all having a good time."

"Did you leave the group at any time?"

"No."

"Not even to use the bathroom?"

"There was a porta-john right there," John said, pointing up the street to where the port-a-potty still stood, all hot piss and plastic baking in the morning sun.

"What did you two talk about?"

"What?"

"You said you were sitting next to her. Did you have a conversation with her?"

"Yes." The pain kept coming. He tried to keep his weight off his right leg but the dull throb grew now to a thunder.

"So what did you talk about?"

John thought for a moment. He remembered the feeling of intimacy, of truly connecting with someone for the first time in a long time, and now he felt that budding closeness ripped away in the aftermath.

"We were just talking about life, I guess. We talked about all sorts of stuff. We had all just decided to start a Neighborhood Watch group because of everything that's been happening around here."

"A Neighborhood Watch, huh?"

"Yeah," John said, growing a bit bolder, feeling a sense of righteous anger well up from inside him. "Being that we've had a fire, car break-ins, harassment and now two deaths and the police have done jack-shit about it, we figured we better get organized and start handling this ourselves."

"Handle it how?"

"Any way we need to," John growled, staring Badgely directly in the eye.

"Do you have any idea who might have done this to Thomas Locke?"

John looked down the street to the Lovetts' house. It was surrounded in shadow, quiet and still as a grave, the For Sale sign the only splash of color that somehow made it seem even more lost. Police dogs barked somewhere in the woods; it echoed throughout the valley.

"No. No idea."

Badgely shut his notebook, sighed and looked around. "I'm sorry this happened, John. It shouldn't have. And I'm sorry you had to see that. It wasn't easy for me either."

"Are we done?"

"We'll be in touch if we have any more questions."

John turned to walk back into the house and gingerly took the step onto his front porch when he heard Badgely's voice again.

"John, you're bleeding."

"What?"

"The back of your leg. It's bleeding."

John looked down and saw that blood had soaked through the bottom of his pant leg.

"What happened? How did you get hurt?"

His mind was suddenly blank and he fumbled for words. "Just a cut," he said.

"Looks pretty bad," Badgely said. He opened his notebook again.

"Not that bad. Just a little trouble getting home last night. Came in through the garage and it was dark. Got a lot of tools, lawnmower and stuff in there."

Badgely stared at him and John could see his reflection in Badgely's sunglasses.

"Best get that checked out. Wouldn't want it to get infected."

"I'll be fine," John said and moved to shut the door.

"One last question!" Badgely called out and John stopped in the doorway. "Did you see a weapon of any sort around where you found Thomas?"

John thought for a moment and he remembered the gleaming blade of a kitchen knife in the black ash just a few feet from the boy's insides.

"Yeah. I saw a knife there. Looked like a kitchen knife. From one of those block sets you get."

"Did it look familiar to you at all?"

"I don't know. They all kinda look the same."

"Do you have a set of kitchen knives like that?"

"Who doesn't?"

Badgely shut his notepad again.

John looked at him from the doorway with a deep-set rage in his eyes. "Am I a suspect, Badgely?"

"Take a look around, John. At this point, the whole neighborhood is a suspect."

John shut the door and left Badgely on the front porch. Jessica stared at him. Caitlin and James were asking what happened and watching the police and ambulance and fire engines out the window. The police dogs emerged from the trees, barking at his house, pulling at their tethers, showing their teeth.

★   ★   ★

Vernon sat in the emergency room of St. Mary's Hospital downtown waiting for the doctor to finish stitching and bandaging his mother's feet.

It was midday and there were only a few people, but they all wore the same expression on their face of bored restlessness, waiting for answers that would seemingly never come. He, for one, relished these moments when someone else was responsible for his mother, when he turned her over to professionals and was able to let go of her for a few moments.

In a strange way, he felt he was betraying Amber by even leaving the house. Such a tragedy warranted a somber showing of respect and grief by isolating oneself in mourning, as if the whole neighborhood should cease living for a single day because Amber's life was forever changed and little Tommy would never see another day. But his mother's diseased mind did not know rest, could not recall grief and empathy when appropriate, and would not allow her to stay put in bed with her feet up to let them heal. The cuts were significant and the doctor said they would need to sedate her in order to stitch up her feet. It also meant Vernon would probably have to carry her around the house more. He figured at this point he should be in better shape just from physically lifting her so often, but he remained portly and tubby and soft. He would have time in the future, he figured, to get in shape and live his life. He just had to hold out a little longer.

Of course, when he first brought his mother into the emergency room there were questions and suspicions of whether he was really caring for her or actually abusing her. He told the nurses and the doctor the same story repeatedly: she had knocked over a vase in the middle of the night and proceeded to walk across the shards. He didn't mention the fact that he wasn't in the house, but had left her alone while he got high, drank with friends and organized the launch of the Neighborhood Watch. He left that part out of the story, but figured he was entitled to it; he was a human being, and he deserved the chance to relax and socialize like anyone else. He deserved a life, too. He told the doctor he was asleep in his room when it happened.

He was fairly accustomed to trips to the emergency room at this point. He knew it would be hours here. It was already hour three. On the flat-screen television hovering in the corner of the ER he could see television news footage of his neighborhood; a dogged-looking female reporter holding a microphone and speaking into the camera, a solemn look of concern on her face, as if she were about to cry but holding back in order to deliver the salacious news everyone in the world required. In the background of the shot, he could see police tape cordoning off most of Ridgewood. The camera cut to filler footage of other streets in the neighborhood. He saw his own street for a moment combined with flashes of small houses, all in an editorial effort to show how this small, quiet community had been rocked by a gruesome child murder. A true crime show playing out in his backyard. Cut to interviews with neighbors: he saw Mark and Maryanne on screen, a microphone pointed in their direction, their mouths moved and flapped but there was no sound, just their heads shaking, the look of complete helplessness in their eyes, and, for a moment, he wondered if this is how we truly experience the world. Images spun through the air, brought to a form of half-life on the screen, and without it, we would know hardly anything beyond the four walls of our solitary lives. In a way, the screen seemed more real; the colors brighter, the people and their lives bigger, the incidents more important. It was as if everything you saw on screen was right next door, encroaching on you, even if it was a million miles away. Except, this time, it truly was right next door, and watching his neighbors on television, he felt sympathy even though, as one of them, he should have felt that anyway. On screen they suddenly seemed so much more important, so much more *human*, and Vernon wondered if there was something inherently wrong and terrifying in that fact. Was anything real if it wasn't acknowledged on the screen? Or did everything become fictionalized?

Amber had run down the street screaming that morning; she had found and cradled the bloody body of her dead boy. The police and neighbors were on television. It was both truth and fiction now and he could no longer tell the difference.

Vernon's mother appeared out of the hospital doors in a wheelchair, pushed along by a large male nurse with a doctor in tow. He could see his mother was sedated, her head lolling on thin shoulders, her feet thickly bandaged, the nubs of her toes peeking out.

"We cleaned out the wounds to prevent infection," the doctor told him. "She needed nineteen stitches total. Some of the cuts were pretty deep."

"I just didn't think I could get her to the hospital at that time of night," Vernon said.

"The timing isn't an issue," the doctor said. "I'm a little more concerned about your ability to continue caring for her, though, Mr. Trimble."

"I told you, I was asleep. She gets up sometimes in the middle of the night."

"I completely understand. I'm not blaming you for anything, Mr. Trimble. Caring for patients with Alzheimer's and dementia can be very difficult and it just gets more difficult as the disease progresses. It's not your fault, but at some point I believe she may require more care and help than you can actually give. One person can't do it alone, especially when we get into later stages."

"I understand that, but—"

"Mr. Vernon, it's my recommendation that you get your mother into an assisted living facility with a team of people better able to manage her condition."

Vernon stopped and thought for a moment. He'd already had these discussions in the past; he'd already listened to the lessons and lectures.

"There are several programs and facilities—"

"I know," Vernon said, rather abruptly. "It's just…they're not cheap and we don't have much other than our home."

"I understand, Mr. Trimble. But the cost of caring for her in your own home – the financial and, frankly, the personal cost to you – will exceed what you can afford to give. Now, with her unable to use her feet for a while, it's going to be extremely difficult for you."

"I know."

"As it stands now, I'm assigning a visiting nurse to come by the house once a day to check on her feet, change the bandages and to assess her overall condition. She was fairly combative when we tried to administer the anesthetic and seems to have a delusion about a boy she keeps screaming about."

"Yes...."

"If I were you, Mr. Trimble, I would get your finances in order, check out programs available through the state and Medicare and see about getting her in a home as soon as possible. Because it won't be tenable for you much longer and, frankly, we may have to intervene for her own good."

Vernon looked down and pursed his lips. He felt a weight on his shoulders. He was being pushed toward making an actual decision on his own, one with actual consequences.

"I understand, doctor," was all he could say.

"If you pull your car around, we'll assist you in getting her seated," the doctor said and walked away. The nurse waited with his mother, who sat in the wheelchair silent, head lolling about shoulder to shoulder. Vernon walked alone outside and into the parking lot.

CHAPTER SEVENTEEN

I told you so I told you so I told you so I told you so I told you so I told you so I told you so I told you so I told you so....

You didn't want to listen. You didn't care. You just wrote what the government told you to write and now look at you. Another fake news hack 'journalist' for another fake news hack newspaper.

You've gotten everything wrong that you've written about in this neighborhood. I TOLD you that fire started inside the house. I TOLD you we all knew who did it. I TOLD you that Nancy didn't just die of heart failure. And now a little boy is dead and that's on YOU as much as anybody else. Because you didn't care enough to write the TRUTH! You just want to hide the truth from everyone so they don't ask questions. So they BEHAVE! So we don't believe our own EYES! I'm on to you now. You should tell the TRUTH of what happened. You peddled a lie and now a boy is DEAD!

John's emails to Meredith Skye no longer bounced back. They went through. She saw them now, she was listening, and he emailed her once a day, sometimes twice. Late at night, in a haze of whiskey, a new angle would occur to him, a new point to be made, a new rock to pile on her body, and he'd fire off another email. Now she would realize the truth of what he'd said all along and in that sense he felt triumphant.

But he was also scared, terrified. After an extensive search throughout the woods surrounding their neighborhood, the police came up with the all-too-obvious idea of searching all abandoned and blighted properties within a one-mile radius and quickly happened upon Lucas's hideout on Harmony Hill. But they had not found Lucas. They found the etchings, the eyes that he had drawn on the walls, but they had not found him. John remembered the feeling of Lucas's body going limp; he remembered the light fading from his bulging, reddened eyes; he remembered the kicking feet and flailing arms that suddenly ceased as the boy slipped into a deep sleep; he remembered slowly loosening his heavy grip around that thin, pale throat.

He left Lucas there, dead on a mattress, but his body was gone. Was it another lie? Was this the BIG LIE the police would peddle next?

He wondered if the blood from his calf had puddled on the floor beside Lucas's bed. His leg ached, the muscles cut through. He walked with a limp when no one was looking. His calf was red and swollen, his skin trying to close over the oozing cut. If they found his blood there, they would have his DNA. The dogs could have followed his trail from the house to the swamp. They could have found his old waders left in the water. They could follow the trail right to his backyard and then detectives would be back with questions he couldn't answer.

It also meant that Lucas was still out there. That he would want revenge on the man who tried to kill him. That he could take that revenge by killing Caitlin or James the way he'd done to little Tommy Locke. John and Jessica had already talked to Caitlin and James about running away if they ever saw Lucas and telling an adult immediately; they'd already answered their questions, trying to tenderly skirt around the horrific image of the boy cut open and splayed on the ash heap of the old abandoned house. They'd set rules about coming directly home after getting off the bus and either Jessica or John was always watching them outside.

John had barely slept for three days since the murder. He would close his eyes and that haunting dream would return, but so much clearer now. It wasn't a dream, it was a premonition: the blood-red haze in the sky above the Widner house, the single pale streetlight with bodies in white sacks piled beneath it. How many bodies were in his dream? How many bodies would be counted by the time this was all over? He had never seen a murdered human body – much less a child's. Movies didn't do justice to the raw reality of it. It had a dizzying effect that left him sick, and he would wake in the middle of the night in a sweat. In the darkness, he reached out for Jessica but she was not there. He was on the couch again, alone. And then he would reach for another drink to black out his mind, stuff down the images so he couldn't think of them, and then realize that he was silently crying.

The fear was too much. Lucas had killed that boy and John had killed Lucas. But now Lucas was still alive and there was no way John could protect his family twenty-four hours a day. There was no way to know how Lucas might return, what he might do, what weapon he would bring to the fight. Nowhere was safe, nothing was certain, all was in flux.

John called an emergency meeting of the Neighborhood Watch. Mark from across the street said he'd host the meeting and the rest of the group started responding, saying they would be there, saying it was time to take back control, to watch out for each other, to protect children and families by any means necessary.

That evening, at dusk, John crossed the street from his house to Mark and Maryanne's. He hid his limp, stuffed the pain down, but it was hard. He looked up the street to the Lovetts' house, now abandoned. He'd seen them packing their things the day before and now it sat dark and silent. He looked up the opposite direction of Ridgewood and saw the For Sale sign in front of Nancy's house and, more recently now, in front of the Katzes' home. Despite this little gathering, the whole neighborhood looked silent and empty. It was as if everyone were hunkering down, putting plywood over their windows in anticipation of a coming storm.

Inside Mark and Maryanne's small house he could feel the tension. They all wanted to do something, but there was nothing they could do but remain vigilant. John had done something, and, in the end, it turned out to be futile. Maybe all their efforts were futile. Maybe nothing done by good people actually worked in this world anymore. He couldn't even kill a boy half his size. Like so many other things in his life, he felt the failure of impotence, powerlessness.

In total, there were eight people in the living room, sipping beers and talking quietly. Mark and Maryanne were there; Vernon, looking anxious and distracted; Elizabeth Tutt sat in the corner, prim and proper, tucked into herself like a wallflower at a party; Becky and Dale were seated on the couch; Anthony Carter from next door talked quietly with Mark; and Jim Katz attempted to maneuver his bulk around the coffee table toward a snack tray Maryanne had laid out. They all waited for him to get started. He took a seat in the center of the living room couch.

"This will decimate our property values, for sure," Jim said. "Just as we need to sell."

"It'll take years to recover from this," someone chimed in.

"We don't have years to sell our house. We already put a down payment on the one in Maine."

John wasn't sure what to say at first, but he decided to just be as simple as possible.

"We all know why we're here. And I think we all know what's going on," he said finally. "What happened this weekend can never happen again. There's no one to protect us but ourselves. The cops just come clean up the mess afterward, and they're not even doing a good job of that. We all know who did this, we all know what he looks like and we all know that he's still out there. He never left the neighborhood. He's been hiding amongst us somehow. Vernon, you saw him."

"I did. A couple weeks ago. I wasn't sure at first, but now I am. He'd lured my mother out of the house in the middle of the night. I found her at the edge of the woods talking to him."

"And you didn't tell anyone?" Maryanne said.

"There was nothing to tell at the time," Vernon said.

"And from what we heard from Amber, it was Lucas who broke into her van and stole some things from it." He then looked at Elizabeth. "And we know that you've been harassed for several weeks now, someone knocking on your door in the middle of the night?"

"Yes," she said. "Although the police think they arrested the right people. A couple kids from the city…."

"I wouldn't trust anything they say for a second," John said. He paused for a minute and breathed deep. "I can't unsee what I saw the other day. I can't get it out of my head." His calf burned and throbbed and he tried to exhale the pain. "We're dealing with a murderer and that means we have to be on guard, we have to be ready to use lethal force to catch this kid."

"Wait a minute…" Elizabeth started.

"Wait for what, exactly?" John said. "Another dead kid?"

"The first response should be to call the police," she said.

"By the time they get here you'll already be dead and he'll be gone. That's how it works. If this kid is going to be stopped, he'll be stopped by us."

"They don't know for sure that it was Lucas," Elizabeth said.

"I gave the police my security footage," Anthony said. "I saw it. One tall kid in a hoodie walking with Tommy past our house that night. I saw it, it was Lucas, all right. They know it."

She looked at the floor, growing more uncomfortable.

"What we need is an immediate alert system," Vernon said. "One text to the group and everyone comes running to that location. We can get there quicker. It wouldn't be the first time citizens captured a wanted criminal. Did anyone see the Night Stalker documentary?"

"You get the alert on your phone and you come running…preferably armed," Mark said. "He's already used a knife. Who knows what's next."

"Keep your phones charged and on you and make sure you can hear the alerts. You see someone walking past your house, you let us know. You see someone on your security cameras, you let us know. You see something, say something. That's what the government wants for terrorists, well that's what we're going to do to protect our lives and this place," John said. "And keep your kids in sight when they're outside. Don't let them out at night. Keep 'em close to you until we get this all worked out."

"I think everyone should post updates to the Facebook page, too," Vernon said. "Every day, check your security footage and let us know, even if there was nothing."

"Agreed," John said. "I'm looking into getting some security cameras for my house. Elizabeth, I would recommend you do the same, especially that he seems to be targeting you."

"I can't say for certain—"

"It would still be best. For you and for everybody else," John said. He thought for a moment of Lucas's hideout, the room covered in graffiti in the shape of eyes. "I want eyes on this neighborhood twenty-four seven. We're the Neighborhood Watch, right? So let's watch. Let's watch for him. Let's watch for strangers, anyone out of the ordinary. Most of all, let's watch out for each other and our kids. That's the most important thing."

Afterward, John watched as Vernon escorted Elizabeth home, walking silently and quickly past the crime scene and the now-abandoned Lovett house. John waited in the growing dark at the edge of his yard as Vernon plodded back toward his house on Beechwood.

"I have a quick question for you, since you seem to know so much about police work and forensics and all that," John said.

"Sure," Vernon said, suddenly seeming more confident.

"It's a weird question, but, can someone survive being strangled?"

"Oh sure," Vernon said. "It actually takes a lot to strangle someone to death, it takes a long time. The person passes out first from lack of blood to the brain. They might even stop breathing temporarily and appear dead, so the killer releases his grip. But the body can automatically jump start the breathing process again. There's a final spasm of the body to breathe and it can suck air back into your lungs. It all depends, but it's not an automatic death sentence. Why?"

John looked down the street. It was the same view he held in his dream. "Just thinking if I ever get ahold of that kid," he said.

"Yeah," Vernon said. He looked at the ground and appeared to shuffle his feet. "I feel so guilty, John. I feel like if I'd said something when I saw him that night, maybe the police would have found him before all this."

"It's not your fault, Vern," John said, putting his big hand on Vernon's shoulder. "Next time, though, call me and I'll come get him. We'll all come get him."

"I will," Vernon said.

"We can't do this without you," John said. "This was your idea. You're as much of a leader here as any of us."

"Thanks," Vernon said and then continued on down the street. John watched him as he went and turned the corner toward his home.

John went inside and called Roy from work.

"You see the newspaper?" John asked him.

"Yeah, I saw it," Roy said. "Should I believe any of it?"

"I was there, Roy. I saw the kid all cut up. I held his mother while she screamed."

Roy was quiet for a moment.

"I need something from you, Roy," John said.

"Yeah, I can do that."

CHAPTER EIGHTEEN

They spent the day filling potholes. Dozens of them, as if a pride of meerkats had taken up residence beneath the old asphalt and burrowed their way to the top. The heat from the asphalt in the back of the truck warmed John to a sweat and the fall air, ripe with the smell of leaves turning and burning wood, rolled across the sweat on his forehead and gave him a chill. John's leg seemed to hurt more now than when he was first stabbed, the area around it a deep red. He did his best to work through the pain, hid the wince in his face when he put too much weight on his right calf. No one noticed; they were all wincing from various pains built up over a lifetime of outdoor physical labor. Together, Roy, Michael and John rolled all over town like vagabonds; they found a pothole, turned the yellow lights on atop the truck, threw a couple orange cones onto the street, grabbed a shovel, and filled another hole. There were holes everywhere. The system is breaking down, Roy said.

Afterward, John hopped into Roy's Ford truck, leaving his own at headquarters, and together they drove out of town, farther away from the city, into the surrounding hills where the suburbs gave way to long stretches of trees, old farms and fields that produced nothing but long grass and locusts. Part of the scam, Roy said.

John was quiet and Roy asked him if there was something on his mind, but he just said no and they kept on driving.

"It's a hell of a thing you had to see," Roy said to him. "I guess I'd be rather quiet, too. Gotta be concerned for your own, right?"

"Yeah," John said.

There were so many turns in and out of wooded, empty roads, bypassing small houses on lots of land, ducking into hills and shadows. John couldn't get back here if he had to. "You drive all this way to work every day?"

"I like my privacy," Roy said. "The fewer people, the fewer problems, I've found. Simple as that. I don't need neighbors in my business."

Roy's house was small, set back from a road barely wide enough for two cars to pass. His driveway was long, nothing but dirt and gravel, but there were several other trucks parked in front of the house when they arrived.

"I think you'll enjoy this," he said.

John could hear the sound of music playing and Roy led him around the house to the back. The yard was a long, low upward slope toward a thick congregation of trees. There were fake animals made of wood and Styrofoam and hay, set at varying distances, and wooden stands with paper bullseye targets set in them. On the back porch four other men lingered, talking in low, monosyllabic words, smoking cigarettes and sipping Budweiser, faces dark from outdoor work and beards of varying length. One wore a camouflage t-shirt, another a red hat. Classic rock streamed from a radio turned loud. Roy handed John a beer, grabbed his own and introduced John to the others. He couldn't remember all their names and didn't try.

Guns were lined up, leaned against the porch railing. Shotguns, hunting rifles and the infamous black 'assault rifle' he'd seen in countless news stories, magazine covers and videos of American troops streamed from wars in deserts. Handguns were on the table: revolvers, semi-automatics. John held the basic, requisite knowledge of firearms that came with having grown up a boy and become a man. There were things one needed to know as a man and could be gleaned from the cover of any gun magazine in any magazine rack in any grocery store in the country: Dirty Harry carried a .44 Magnum; an automatic and a semi-automatic were not the same thing; the U.S. military never should have switched from .45s to 9 millimeter handguns; guns don't kill people, people kill people and, if it were up to the Democrats, only criminals would have guns.

They stood on the porch and talked about the weather and lower back pain and supervisors who ride a desk all day. They were all workers, thick calloused hands, skin tan from the sun, bellies that spurt out over jeans and hid a tremendous amount of aging muscle. Their t-shirts were stained with sweat and dirt. These were his people and with the music and drinks it felt like an initiation ritual into some kind of club.

"Jesus, Roy, you said he was big, but it'd take a tank to put this guy down," the one in the red hat said. The others laughed and John felt self-conscious for a moment. "We could use a guy like you. Make people think twice before trying to breach our lines."

"Breach your lines?" John asked.

"You know, all those clowns holding their protests and rallies, tearing down statues and burning down their own cities and shit? We go there, we form a line and we push back. The government sure as shit ain't gonna do it, and the cops aren't doing shit, so someone has to push back on these commie fucks."

"You shoulda been there when they tried to tear down a statue of Columbus," the other one said. "Roy here knocked this Antifa motherfucker clean out, took his sign. Haha. He's got it hanging on the wall in his house."

The others all smiled. John could see a certain satisfaction in blasting one of those whiny, good-for-nothing dipshits in the face. He wanted them to feel his power.

"Well, John here is in the market for home protection," Roy said. "He's got some maniac running around his neighborhood killing children and since the cops won't do anything about it, John here has set up a righteous Neighborhood Watch and needs a little extra firepower."

"That's how it goes," the one in the hat said. "You organize at home. You build up, you arm up, you protect your own and then you protect our freedoms."

"What you need is a shotgun," Roy said. He picked up a pump-action twelve-gauge that leaned against the porch rail and handed it to John. John had never really fired a gun. When he was a boy, an uncle let him shoot a little .22 rifle at a fish-and-game club's outdoor shooting range. He had worn bulky plastic earmuffs and plastic glasses that were too big for his head. The pop when he pulled the trigger brought a smile to his young face like setting off a firecracker. Still, John held the shotgun in his hands and looked it over as if he were judging its quality. Really, he had no idea.

"Twelve-gauge, pump action," Roy said. "Full of double-aught buckshot and it's perfect for home defense. You won't miss and whatever you're shooting at will be dead, no questions asked."

The man in the camouflage shirt walked ahead of them into the yard, steadied himself, took a handgun from his waistband and fired one shot after another at the paper targets twenty yards away. John felt each pop of gunfire reverberate through his jawbone, down his gut and tingle the tip of his cock. The man fired until the magazine was empty and then turned around and lit a cigarette. Then the man in the red cap took a few steps forward and fired some rounds from his own gun. The radio played in the background. It seemed on endless repeat, an eighties synthesizer beat strung together over and over, a saccharine female voice strained to rebellion.

"No ear protection?" John asked.

"Would you have ear protection in a gunfight?" Roy said. "Best get used to the sound, be able to function with your ears ringing and, believe me, when you fire this baby, your ears will ring."

Roy took the shotgun from John's hands and opened a box of big, plastic shells. He showed John how to load the shells into the magazine, showed him the safety button – 'red means dead' – how to chamber a round by pumping the forearm like he'd seen in countless movies. "It's simple, cheap and effective," Roy said. "Everybody should have one."

Roy handed the shotgun to John and motioned for him to walk into the yard and give it a try. "You'll never feel the same way again after firing this puppy off," he said.

John tenderly walked down the porch steps, protecting his bad leg, and stood in the center of the backyard. Roy stood behind him. John pumped the shotgun and racked a shell into the chamber. Roy whispered something he couldn't quite hear or understand. It was like he was praying to himself in tongues. John was nervous, heart racing. He held the gun, leveling it down range toward a Styrofoam cutout of a pig. The music made him want to dance with it, fire away on endless repeat.

The blast rang his ears, jolted his shoulder, sent a shockwave of power and electricity through his bones. The pig stood idle, nothing moved, nothing exploded. It was like a dream where nothing you do actually matters. He pumped and fired again, pumped and fired again, and still the pig stood, absorbing the pellets, blue smoke drifting into the sky.

The sound was so much louder, stronger, than the handguns the men had fired earlier. Roy clapped him on the shoulder, the sound of his laughter barely audible beneath the ringing in his ears that reminded him of his childhood, when the television would suddenly cut off and a long, high tone would play, commies launching nukes from ten thousand miles away.

This is a test of the emergency broadcast system....

John pumped another round into the chamber and fired.

He felt Roy's presence behind him, the muted laughter of the other men.

The broadcasters of your area in voluntary cooperation with the Federal, State and local authorities have developed this system to keep you informed in the event of an emergency....

He thought of Jessica, of sleeping on the couch, of Meredith Skye. He thought of Amber and of little Tommy dead and gutted. He thought of a red car parked in his driveway, of the red haze in his dream, of the red cap worn by the man standing beside him.

If this had been an actual emergency....

He fired again and the Styrofoam pig wobbled, a piece of white flesh dropped off. Another pothole to be filled in an endless sea of potholes. He thought of that strange fear in the middle of the night that he could not define but somehow left holes in him, pieces of himself exposed to the world, chunks falling off bit by bit.

The attention signal you just heard would have been followed by official instructions....

He thought of Caitlin and James, a close-up of their faces, like a photographer capturing the essence of childhood in their eyes. He fired again. The ringing never stopped, the emergency broadcast was forever, you dance to the music all your life until you die.

Once again, this is only a test....

John pulled the trigger again and this time there was nothing but a hollow click. Empty. He held the shotgun pointing down range and looked over his shoulder at Roy.

"Can I try the other one?" he whispered, and motioned toward the black rifle leaning against the porch.

Roy clapped him on the back. "You got it, brother."

⋆   ⋆   ⋆

Roy drove John back to headquarters, where he'd left his truck. It was dark, and Roy pulled into the parking lot and turned the truck off and they sat together quietly, awkward for a moment as if it were the end of a first date in high school. Roy turned toward him, pulled his leg up slightly so that his knee rested on the bench seat between them and his elbow on the headrest.

"I'm glad you're coming around," Roy said in a solemn, fatherly voice. He was older than John by a whole three years and yet somehow John felt like a child in his presence, as if there was something Roy knew – that maybe a huge swath of men out there knew – that he didn't. "What you're experiencing is just the tip of the iceberg of what's happening all over this country. It's good you're taking the initiative, taking control of the situation, organizing your people, making sure you're ready to defend your family. Because they're trying to eliminate men like us, little by little."

"Who are they?" John said.

"Who do you think, John?" Roy said. "Look around. Look at your own situation. The government runs our schools, tells our kids what to think. The government runs the media and tells us what to think. When we catch them in a lie, they say we're the ones who are crazy. They're trying to eliminate the family. They're trying to change this country. They push the gay agenda, the communist agenda, the Black agenda. They're forcing this down our throats every day and then they want to come take away our only means of defending ourselves. But now you have to protect your family from a monster they created. That kid should've been locked up years ago but they keep coddling and now look. Your own government just allowed a little boy to be murdered because they were so busy trying to crack down on people like me – law-abiding people – that they ignored the real problem."

John sat there quietly, awkwardly, and nodded. He felt something encroach on him but he wasn't sure if it was the government or the intense intimacy with which Roy evangelized.

"Family," Roy said. "It's all about family." He paused for a moment. "You remember when my wife left me, right?"

"I remember you talking about it," John said.

"Shit. She took my kids, too. Now I only see them twice a month because some judge thought they'd be better off with her. Why is that? Why would they be better off with her? Why not me? What's so wrong with me?"

"I don't know. I'm sorry."

Roy looked at him. There were tears in his eyes. "You have to hold on to what is yours," he said. "You have to hold on to what you love and never let them go. You have to protect them. Sometimes you have to protect them from the big government agenda, sometimes from the thugs and crazies they let run in the streets, and sometimes from those closest to them. I didn't hold tight enough, John, and I lost everything."

"C'mon, Roy. Things aren't so bad. You got a good place, you got friends...."

"Those guys saved me," he said. "They pulled me back up, they gave me purpose. What do we do all day? We drive around filling potholes, fixing roads that just break up next winter anyway. You have to have a purpose, John, you have to have a line to stand on and, most of all, you have to be willing to fight for it. This country is falling apart. And it's just going to get worse."

Roy reached over and hugged John and held him tight for a moment. "We all need to stick together," he said, breathing into John's neck.

They quickly and quietly transferred the shotgun and a box of shells into John's truck where he laid it down behind the driver's seat of the front cab. John paid cash – four hundred – and then Roy drove away and

John was alone with songs and emergency broadcasts and schizophrenic images of collapse and death pulsing through his brain. He stopped at the liquor store around the corner from his neighborhood and bought a twelve-pack for the evening. He drove through the dark streets and turned onto Ridgewood. He scanned the trees, the sides of the road, looking for anyone, anything that could be Lucas. He eyed the politician's house, then the Lovetts' house, then he stopped his truck and stared for a long time at the burned-out frame where they'd found Tommy.

His street was empty. The houses empty. The children were gone from this place as night darkened the little neighborhood that used to belong to them and now belonged to something else, taken over by this deep, fearful emptiness. The trees bent under its weight, the yellow police tape, fallen into the long grass, seemed to move and twist and wrap itself around the whole world.

CHAPTER NINETEEN

Sometimes Elizabeth feared her own sense of intellectual detachment. Here she was, standing in a somber black dress beneath a melancholy, overcast sky as the body of a young boy killed in a horrific manner was laid to rest and, rather than truly feeling anything, her mind was lost in trying to piece together a moral puzzle in which none of the pieces actually fit.

It was midday and she stood among literally hundreds of people who had gathered for the funeral of Thomas Locke, who'd likely been butchered by her next-door neighbor. The extended family of Amber and Joseph Locke had rallied across the country to show up for this funeral in a show of strength and solidarity. Neighbors attended, school teachers, administrators, the first selectman and fellow students; there were arts and crafts murals at every school in the small town, although, she noted, there were no murals for little Tommy Locke at the city schools where losing a kid or two each year to murder was just a part of life; a mural for Tommy would have just been one more mural piled atop too many.

But here, in these little, isolated and homogenous societies, there was an orchestrated display of grief, an outpouring of support and constant, breathless news coverage. The town rallied when one of its own was taken in such a manner. It was a rare event for them and in that rarity was power and in that power was corruption. It was a kind of moral corruption, the desire to be part of something horrific. People who'd never known or seen Tommy Locke or his family rallied around the dead little boy, attended the funeral, made gushing statements online, helped organize the murals and a candlelight vigil where a hundred or so town residents released little Chinese lanterns into the night sky.

It was like when someone mentions a movie star and another says, "Oh, I met him!" to make their own life more interesting, gleaning some of that fame for themselves. She'd done it, too. Having met and been photographed with the Rev. Al Sharpton during a visit he made to the governor, Elizabeth had used the photo for social media and campaign mailers, sending it to all her constituents so she could claim the mantle of racial justice activism by proxy, even though there was no way the reverend would ever recall her face or name. She'd been in a long line of people wishing to be photographed beside him. It was valor by association.

The same went for acts of horror, she supposed, except when it came to horrors it seemed the lure was all the more powerful because it played on tragedy, sympathy and a dark fascination with the macabre. It was horror by proxy, victimization by association, tragedy as social commodity. But none of them were Amber Locke. None of them could possibly understand or know what she'd been through finding her son like that, the gut-wrenching guilt she must feel, the absolute and total devastation.

Elizabeth's election opponent, Andrew Whitcomb, had already seized on the tragedy. There were new lawn signs popping up: 'Protect Your Kids! Kick Tutt!'

Whitcomb wasn't here, though, *she* was. But even now she questioned her motives.

All eyes were on Amber during the funeral. Elizabeth could feel it. She could hear the occasional whispers. Everyone watching, waiting for the moment when Amber would let loose a torrent of grief, perform a primal scream, exorcising the pain, but it never came. Amber stood stiff, stolid, and unemotional as a statue. She didn't cry, she didn't speak. When her husband went to wrap his arm around her, she quietly, almost imperceptibly moved away.

Elizabeth had attended as a show of solidarity for the Locke family and out of a sense of obligation, having been a partial witness. She felt she owed it to somebody to be in attendance even if it created a scheduling nightmare for her. Today was the opening of the Tree of Life and Elizabeth was to give a short statement praising Shondra Waite and her new piece for reporters and art connoisseurs alike. The opening was at two p.m. and already she was cutting it close. This was the lynchpin of her campaign, bringing a great, new Black artist to the museum to inspire the young inner-city kids to new heights and possibilities – all after attending the funeral of a butchered white kid from a forgotten neighborhood just outside city limits.

Just a couple days ago, news broke that a Black teenager from the city, Antwone Diller, had died in state police custody in what the police spokesman said was a rare and adverse reaction to tasing the boy as he resisted being put in the barracks' holding cell. Antwone was asthmatic and the product of childhood abuse by foster parents, which included being locked in a closet at a young age, giving him a severe case of claustrophobia, according to the activists quoted in the papers. When they tried to force him into the cell he had an outburst and was tased, triggering an asthma attack, sending his heart into strange fluctuations and eventually stopping altogether. He was fifteen. His life had been short and brutal. Marches, protests and vigils were being scheduled. Tommy's funeral would be just one Elizabeth would be attending. Another tragedy coinciding with the opening of Shondra Waite's exhibit.

Her mind churned through all of this; less so, her heart. And that made her wonder at her own motivations. What was she doing here? What was she doing later at the museum? What on Earth was anyone doing anywhere? It all seemed stupid and ridiculous in this moment. Even the act of coming together for this funeral seemed an arbitrary and pointless endeavor: it would change nothing, it would not bring Tommy back, and humanity would just go on as it always had – there would be killing and death, rich and poor, smart and stupid; there would be tragedy and inspiration, success and failure and, in the end, none of it would truly matter.

The preacher raised his hands toward the sky in prayer and hundreds bowed their heads.

And so we appeal to the unseen, the unknown, the arbitrary and imaginary, because what else can you possibly appeal to?

Naturally, in the middle of the prayer and the absolute silence of the mourners, Elizabeth's phone began to ring. She'd forgotten to turn it to silent. Heads tilted, eyes slit, people stepped slightly away from her so others would know it wasn't their phone ringing. It rang three times before she could get her hand to her pocket and turn it off. She recognized the number as Meredith Skye – again – and wondered what could possibly be so important that Meredith would be calling her on a Saturday morning when she knew damn well that Elizabeth would be at the exhibit later. She threw the phone back in her purse and lowered her head. Her phone buzzed again. This time it was Meghan. Meredith must have called the campaign headquarters.

The prayer ended and the small casket was lowered into the ground and a line began to form to drop flowers into the grave. Elizabeth glanced at her watch, gauged the length of the line, the distance to her car and traffic implications. She held in her hand a small note she'd written to Tommy, telling him how sorry she was, how much guilt she felt at having been present in the darkness as he was taken from this world. The note had come to her in the night when she was slightly drunk and feeling deeply, reflecting on that moment, trying to reconcile what she knew in her mind with what she knew in her heart: she had borne witness, however minor and incidental, to his death and was also, therefore, guilty. Elizabeth wasn't religious but the note was a private confession to herself and to Tommy that she wanted to deliver to the heavens.

She glanced down at her watch. There were three speakers for the opening and she was the last before the exhibit was opened to the public. Then she, Shondra and the museum curator would be the first to walk through those panels flashing media toward the Tree of Life at the center.

Elizabeth clutched the note in her hand. The line moved forward slowly. She could be a little late. It was the least she could do.

★   ★   ★

Elizabeth drove at breakneck speed down the highway, cutting through traffic. She took the exit toward the museum, a blind turn into an intersection that had claimed countless traffic accident deaths over the years and was the subject of numerous city-planning meetings which she had never attended. It was on her list of things to do, but things move slowly when it comes to infrastructure. The blind curve gave way and she had to stop short before plowing into a car stopped at the intersection. She drummed her hands on the steering wheel, anxious to move. Her phone dinged with text messages. She glanced briefly while trying to avoid a car accident and becoming one of those statistics about driving and texting. Elizabeth's short speech was in a folder on the passenger seat and slid to the floor, scattering the sheets as she came to a final stoplight. She could see the front of the museum. There was a throng of people and seemingly even more reporters and news cameras, which she found odd. She knew there would be media coverage but this looked like the president was in town. She could see the curator giving his speech. He was supposed to be the second speaker and she didn't think she was running that far behind. Elizabeth parked in the employee lot, gathered her speech from the floor of her Volvo, and rushed around the side of the building to take her place standing beside Shondra.

The curator spoke of the importance of the Tree of Life, his words blowing past Elizabeth like a breeze as she gazed out over the small crowd and smiled, trying not to show that she was breathing heavily and nearly sweating from the brief run to the podium. She looked for familiar faces, she looked for Meghan, but she was nowhere to be seen. Meghan should have been here, but then, maybe that was the reason for her call earlier. She couldn't check her phone during another serious public gathering, and so she smiled at the crowd and whispered a quick greeting in Shondra's ear, to which the artist said nothing, merely leaning down to hear her words and standing back up straight and tall.

A hand touched Elizabeth's shoulder and she turned to see the events coordinator, a fussy, uptight, small woman who constantly wore flowing dresses and scarves. She leaned in to Elizabeth's ear. "We're going to move right into the initial walk-through," she said. "Given the circumstances, we thought it best if we limited remarks."

Elizabeth stared at her for a moment and the small woman appeared to have a fearful, guilty look in her eye. "What circumstances?" Elizabeth whispered.

The events planner seemed to stare at her in disbelief.

"I have my speech right here. It won't take long. I was told I'd have an opportunity to speak. I put a lot of work into this!"

Still, the woman just stared at her. On stage, the curator announced the exhibit was now open to the public. He handed Shondra a pair of giant scissors to cut the blue ribbon at the entrance to the exhibit.

"You can still be one of the first walk-throughs," the events planner said and then quickly walked away before Elizabeth could register her anger. Instead, she turned back toward the crowd, flashed a false, beaming smile and clapped vigorously, laughing slightly as if the events planner had told her a joke. The ribbon fell to the ground. The reporters in the crowd erupted and Elizabeth heard her name called over and over again, but the curator boomed into the microphone that they would be taking questions after the walk-through.

Now she was furious, being herded along with the others on stage toward the entrance to the Tree of Life. She was pushed to the back of the line. She tried to call out to the curator but she could only see the back of his bald head. She called his name, but he didn't turn around. Nobody turned around. No one acknowledged she was speaking to them, or to anyone at all, as their small, exclusive little group shuffled like schoolchildren into the house built of black screens now dazzling with digital flashes. She looked for Meghan again. She felt herself on the verge of crying, not out of sadness but out of frustration and anger. She held it back with a smile and small waves to the crowd, some of whom were yelling her name. As she was hustled into the Tree of Life, she heard only disambiguated voices.

The group moved ahead of Elizabeth quickly, disappearing around a corner into the maze-like infinity of the structure flashing constantly with digital memes, videos, headlines, articles, do-it-yourself instructional videos, pornography, racism, politics, images of anger, revolt, protest. She felt lost in it again, but the transcendent awe that she'd first felt was gone; now a sense of foreboding and fear began to overtake her. She was out of the loop for some reason. Something was wrong, she could feel it. It seemed to emanate inside the walls of the Tree of Life, like the echo of a small voice in a cave.

And in that cave she heard her name spoken. It was a woman's voice, curt and official, a news broadcast somewhere. She turned to find the source but it was gone, now replaced on the screen with an image of two men in an embrace. She heard her name again from another part of the cave and spun around again only to see a video of a teenage girl attempting to dance but falling on her head. It was as if she were haunted by the voice of a dead news anchor. She kept walking through the maze, toward the Tree of Life, alone now. The rest of her elite group was gone. The images, the sounds, came at a frenetic pace, the constant flashing lights and words boring into her brain. Her anxiety increased. She felt lost, started worrying that maybe it was all too much and she was headed toward some kind of light-induced seizure. Around the next corner she could see a hint of true sunlight, the breath of fresh air, the anchor to the real world.

She walked quickly toward the corner and then stopped short. Her face was on the screen before her. It was an image she recognized, an unflattering photo of her in mid-sentence, face and lips and eyes screwed up as the camera caught her in the midst of delivering a passionate, angered argument, the nature of which she could not recall. But there was her strange, screwed-up face on the screen before her.

The headline: "State Rep. Elizabeth Tutt called police on a Black boy selling fundraiser tickets. Now he is dead."

She turned the corner. The Tree of Life glowed stoic, perfect in the sunlight.

★   ★   ★

Her voice was gone. She tried to speak, but all she could muster was nonsense, stuttering half-words. The throngs of reporters were on her as soon as she exited the Tree of Life and all she could say was, "I don't know," and "That's not what happened," and "I've been at a funeral all day, I'll have to get back to you." Phones and cameras were held in the air, snapping pictures of her, recording her as she tried to get through the crowd, get to her car and get away. She didn't know what was happening.

Antwone Diller – was that the name of the boy arrested the night she called the police? She'd never asked, only happy that maybe the late-night harassment would cease. She didn't know what any of them were talking about. She didn't know what had happened. "No comment," she said. "I'll be releasing a statement later," she said. The museum curator was gone. Shondra Waite was nowhere to be seen. People standing in line outside the exhibit glared at her. There were protesters in front of the museum now chanting her name.

She was overwhelmed and terrified and now she was breaking down. Elizabeth pulled away from the reporters and ran to her car, cameras recording the awkward flight of a woman running away in high heels.

★　★　★

It was nearly dark before she could bring herself to actually read the online news reports. Meghan, ever the political animal who prided herself on winning, was gone. Resigned as campaign manager the instant the first reporter called and, just like that, every ally she'd ever had wasn't answering her phone calls or texts. None of the staffers to her small campaign – mostly college kids – answered the phone. Even if they had, what could they tell her? They did phone banking and sent mailers for minimum wage. Meredith Skye wasn't picking up. She called the state Democratic Party chair, got nothing but his voicemail and two hours later he still hadn't returned her call. She called again, this time screaming into his voicemail that he was about to lose a House seat. Politics was traitorous. Everyone ran for cover to protect their own asses. She wasn't important enough to mount a defense this late in the game, particularly against this kind of bombshell, but still, they had abandoned her. This wasn't her fault, she'd done nothing wrong.

Video of her running from the Tree of Life exhibit was broadcast across social media, the local news stations and now the national news programs. It looked awful. *She* looked awful. All afternoon there had been a television news crew outside her house, finally packing up and leaving when it grew too dark.

The story: after Antwone Diller died, Meredith Skye and her back-stabbing cronies filed a Freedom of Information request for all 911 calls from the area, found her call reporting someone harassing her, a threatening figure in her doorway wearing a gray hoodie. They tracked her call to the arrest of Diller and his friend, guilty of nothing but being Black and going door-to-door selling fundraiser tickets for their football team in a white community. It was another case of scared white woman syndrome, another suburbanite terrified at the prospect of a Black youth in her neighborhood, another example of a liberal hypocrisy. She was skewered across every form of media available in a matter of hours, if not minutes.

"Calls to Rep. Tutt were not answered and Tutt's campaign manager, Meghan Brooke, indicated that she has resigned from her position and could not offer comment."

"Officials from the Amherst Museum of Art said they hoped the importance and artistry of Shondra Waite's new Tree of Life exhibit – which was championed by Rep. Tutt – would not be dampened by this tragedy. 'In light of this confluence of unfortunate and reprehensible events, we feel that Shondra's work is more important than ever for the city as it mourns the loss of a fine young man with so much potential,' museum curator Elliot Perkins said.

"Tutt's Republican opponent in the upcoming election, Andrew Whitcomb, called for Tutt's immediate resignation. 'This is just another example of Rep. Tutt using the communities she claims to champion for political gain, meanwhile undercutting them as she always has,' Whitcomb said in a statement."

Elizabeth was drunk. A glass of scotch in her hand, she slammed her laptop closed and, for a moment, sobbed pointlessly and quietly to herself while sitting on the couch. She didn't know what to do. She didn't know what to say or who to talk to and, even if she did, they likely wouldn't take her call. For the first time in a long time she felt utterly and completely helpless, trapped, and beaten for good. In the course of one morning, her entire political career, the culmination of her life's work to this point, had been ripped out from beneath her. She knew how this worked. She knew there was no coming back from this within two months. Her biggest voting bloc would either stay home on election day or cast their vote for her opponent and her name would forever be associated with the death of a child – two children, she supposed, as she had given comments to the media regarding Tommy's death.

In her spiraling, she thought of Amber Locke and the funeral, which now seemed far in the past. Yes, her professional life was now stripped away, but Elizabeth tried to put it in context. She thought of Amber and Tommy. She tried not to think of Antwone. She rose, half-heartedly, off the couch, glass in hand, and walked outside. The cool night air perked her up, sobered her up for a moment. She walked into the middle of Ridgewood Drive and stood still, looking at the burned-out ruins where Tommy was found dead and then across the street to the Lovetts' house. She stared down the street, which seemed to reach endlessly into the dark beyond, the houses merely blocks placed side by side by some unwell child, the pavement disappearing over the bend, the haunting hills suffocating the life from this place. It was, if anything, a quiet place to settle down and watch yourself die.

She stood for a long time there, watching night settle over the neighborhood, watching it turn from a quiet little haven into an isolated and frightening wilderness. And when the light was gone from both the sky and her eyes, she walked back inside and locked the door and poured another drink.

Late that night there were three heavy knocks at her door. She stumbled to her feet from the couch, drunk and wavering, and looked through the blinds of her window. There was no one there, just the lonely glow of her porch light. She fell back to the couch and sobbed once more to herself. The knocks came again, louder, more insistent this time.

She couldn't possibly call the police now. She thought of texting the Neighborhood Watch and thought again. That was all she would need; a small army of idiots descending on her house in the middle of the night and probably shooting someone. Then another death would be on her shoulders. *How many deaths do we contribute to?* she wondered. There'd been enough for now and, in her moment of weakness, she wished for her own.

CHAPTER TWENTY

Amber hadn't spoken in over a week. Not a word since that morning, that god-awful day when she found the last good, innocent thing in her life butchered. She had screamed that morning, but it wasn't her voice. It was a sound that had emanated from within, from deeper than her lungs or her stomach; it was a scream from another world because that is what she saw: something from another world. This couldn't be her world. This couldn't be her life. That couldn't be her boy cut open in the dirt and soot and dust, eyes gone misty with pale blue, mouth hung open, a rictus of perpetual surprise. No. That was something otherworldly, and in the face of it, there was nothing she could say, nothing at all.

So, she had been carried. Carried at first by the people around her, carried again by the paramedics and the police, carried again by stretcher to the hospital, carried again to a psychiatric ward for evaluation and care. They kept urging her to talk, urging her to say something, but there would never again be anything to say other than that scream. Eventually, they stopped trying. Joe and Vinnie tried to get her to speak and every time they tried, she hated them for it. Joe, forever trying to put his arms around her, talking to her – *C'mon, honey, I'm here, just tell me what happened, it's okay, I'm here, I'm so sorry, I can't believe we lost our boy, just talk to me, please, we need you* – and then he would sob and she would stay silent and not look at him, not look at anything, because all she could see, all she would ever see, was her boy cut open staring into the sky. Vinnie kept saying, "Mom? Mom, please talk to me," but she couldn't talk to him. She couldn't abide this stranger, this thing she'd created that had brought such pain into her life. He stared at her with those big, brown eyes and curly hair and all she could see was the face of Lucas Lovett, and she hated him for it.

They needed her, they said, but she didn't need them. She needed nothing. She wanted nothing. She just wanted it to all disappear. They came to her with funeral arrangements, she didn't care and she didn't speak. The police came to her with questions, but it didn't matter, they could find out on their own. None of it would bring him back. None of it would erase that image from her mind. She was no longer Amber Locke. Sometimes, she couldn't remember her name.

She spent three nights in the hospital before Joe and Vinnie brought her home. She walked inside, looked around, went to the bedroom, shut the door and left them standing in the living room wondering what to do. *Let them wonder. Let Joe sleep on the couch. Let Vinnie stare blankly into the screen of his computer. Let the dogs bark and scratch and whine.* Her husband and eldest son had left her alone and weren't there when it happened – *let them wonder.* If they hadn't left, things would have been different. Life balances upon fractions of a moment, coincidences, decisions that seem meaningless and then, in hindsight, are a direct, unflinching road to that one big moment that changes everything.

The cloudy, flaccid eyes of her youngest son looked into her soul and then took it. She was a ghost now and ghosts cannot speak, they exist only as an afterthought, a living memory prone to poltergeist rage.

So she floated along, cowed by prescription antipsychotics and a perpetual fever dream where everything appeared close up, huge and balloon-like, and people asked her inane riddles like, "How are you?" and "Are you doing okay?" and she could only stare at them like a doll made of flesh. The dogs barked at her as if she were a stranger. The noise was far away but still close. Their howls trembled the air. She felt the vibrations. She floated along, carried by Joe and Vinnie; carried by the mortician and the funeral home; carried by waves of people extolling their grief as if they knew such grief. It didn't matter.

The day of the funeral, she stood among a crowd of strangers, people she'd never met or seen before, children from little Tommy's school and their parents, adults from town trying to share in her grief as if it were something they, too, desired. She stood on the grass in the cemetery, with its rows of gray headstones, and marveled at the strangeness of it. It seemed such an odd place to lay her child, in the ground among the thousands of anonymous dead. She heard the words of the pastor of a church she never attended. She didn't thank God for the life of her boy, instead she hated God for putting her boy in the ground.

I am God.

That is what Lucas had texted her oldest son. I am God. And perhaps he was. He had taken life like God. Why ascribe such power to anyone or anything else? All these killers, little gods in the making, taking life where they see fit for reasons known only to them. The casket was lowered into the ground, the crowds dressed in black came and stared at her, quietly asking themselves why she didn't cry, what had broken inside her; quietly thanking the little god for not choosing their own son or daughter.

All your little children will have their time, too. All roads lead to that same place.

The house was covered in flowers, the smell of Eden, and they too would wilt and die. The flowers mixed with the smell of food and blood – mounds of meat in tinfoil pans and plastic-wrapped plates. People crowded into her home, milled about, spoke in soft tones, and stifled the occasional smile or laugh because they couldn't help themselves. She recognized them all. Friends, family, neighbors; her Aunt Eliza sat beside her on the couch holding her hand as if she were a dementia patient waiting out her last days in a convalescent home. Amber just stared out the sliding glass doors, across their small, grassy lawn and into the dark copse of trees. She remembered the night she stared out those windows and saw something out there, a meaningless black hole on their security monitors. She remembered the image of Lucas, clad in her son's hoodie, standing at the edge of their driveway the night he killed Thomas, just staring into the camera, his face in shadow, his lithe body grainy with night vision.

Something was coming for them all. It took many forms but she could see it now.

She watched Joe, standing in the kitchen, so far away he might as well be on another planet. A small cadre of black-clad mourners surrounded him. He wiped a tear from his eye and nodded, looking down at the floor as someone put a hand on his shoulder and whispered in his ear. She watched Vinnie, surrounded by his friends from school, sitting on the back porch on lawn chairs, laughing – laughing! – as they talked. She heard the dogs locked in the laundry room scratching at the door, whining, pleading to be released. All of it seemed so small and yet so huge. *Look at them*, she thought. *They keep moving on like little robots, fleshy machines that for some reason or another keep going until they finally wind down – or are put down. We're all winding down, one second at a time.* Looking around the room, she felt surrounded by the lifeless; nothing but walking, talking automatons, grateful their gears had not come to a stop or been splayed out all over the front yard. Their mouths flapped open and closed; their eyes sparkled and hid secrets; their arms and legs moved in a mockery of life. Each would approach her; each would try to talk to her with their flapping mouths and tongues. The words were worthless, stupid, inconsequential. They insisted she join them, they insisted she talk, but all she really wanted – from the second she found her baby in the ruins of that Hell-house – was to be alone and in silence, and when she wasn't allowed to be alone or silent, they locked her up in a hospital and fed her medication that made the world go blurry. They gathered round her like a church congregation bent on saving her soul through a laying of hands. All they wanted was for her to talk, to sing, to join the chorus in mourning. She would not join them, because they just wanted to move on with their lives and what she needed was an entire lifetime of silence and solitude.

They would never give it to her. Not these strangers in her home, not her husband nor her eldest son. Instead, they talked and laughed, ate and drank, and tried to forget. She needed escape. When she looked back on her life, she wondered what it was all for; what the sacrifices and hardships and the giving away of herself was truly for. If her child could be killed in such a manner by a boy who'd been in her house countless times, if she was forced to look upon it, to hold his hollowed-out body, then there was no meaning to life.

She looked at Joe, who had abandoned her that weekend, gone fat and boring and useless with age. She cooked him dinner every night, fed his stupid dogs, listened to his constant talking, his reconciling of their shabby little life, and then, at night, let him strip down and hump her like a mutt. She looked at Vinnie, whose lifelong friend had brought this terror to her home, who had actively hidden and communicated with Lucas when everyone was trying to find him. Had he told someone, anyone, things might have turned out differently. Instead, she would be expected to continue cleaning up after him, cooking his meals and pretending not to hear him jerking off in front of his computer when she passed his bedroom door at night. They wanted her – all of her. She was trapped in their desires, their needs, their world. She was done with this life, the life she hadn't chosen but rather succumbed to.

And they kept trying to break her.

The eyes of the room were on her. She could feel it. She radiated anger and resentment like a dying star collapsing into a black hole. They looked at her, terrified that they too would be sucked into this dark place where the rules of the world are bent and strange; where time ceases to be linear and right and wrong become one and the same.

Amber stood from the couch where she'd sat silent the whole afternoon, and everyone stared at her, unsure of what she would do next, waiting with anticipation to see her grief, but she would not give it to them. Instead, she walked slowly, stoically through the now silent and waiting crowd to the front door and then outside. From the front porch she stared into the street, to the place where Lucas had stood that night, a druid figure that disappeared into the night for a child sacrifice. The sky had grown overcast, the low, gray cloud cover rolling out for miles. It was cold, the leaves turned over in a wind, their soft white underbellies exposed. She looked up and down the street for a moment. Just past the corner of Ridgewood and Beechwood she could see John Ballard stuffing a black bag in the trash bin outside his house.

She walked down her short driveway and then past the line of cars parked along the side of the road. She walked slowly at first and then faster as she watched John stand for a moment outside staring into the woods behind his home, still dressed in black slacks and a white shirt from the funeral. He looked up and saw her and stood transfixed, like seeing someone again for the first time after decades of absence. He walked up his driveway and stood in the road and waited as she came to him.

Then she was there with him in the middle of the street. He towered over her. She looked up at him and he back down to her and a wind swept down the street.

Then she grabbed on to him and hugged him and she felt his arms engulf her.

"There's something I have to tell you," he said.

★ ★ ★

That night she could not sleep. In the darkness, she saw Lucas Lovett. She saw him watching her and she felt exposed, naked and vulnerable. She felt the house crawl with his presence. Maybe it was Lucas; maybe it was Vinnie or Joe. Maybe there wasn't a difference. Maybe they were all one and the same. Everyone was asleep. Joe had drunk too much and was snoring on the couch; Vinnie was in his room, asleep with the television on.

The dogs were outside, left there so that they would stop trying to scratch their way into her bedroom, into her bed, and now they were out in the darkness running, barking, howling the words of John Ballard.

"I knew where he was. I knew and I didn't say anything. I don't even know what to say, Amber. I'm sorry. I never thought...."

"You never thought...."

Amber got out of bed and went to the kitchen where she could see the video monitors. In the grainy night vision she could see the dogs charging into the trees, disappearing, and reemerging with something in their mouths, dropping it outside the sliding glass door before issuing a lonely howl and charging back into the woods for more.

She walked past Joe snoring on the couch, oblivious to the sounds that kept her from sleep, that kept her from peace. She stood at the sliding glass door and looked out into the night. Her hand moved to the back porch light switch.

The porch lit up fake and pale in the night, suddenly obscuring her view of the trees. The dogs began to yip and bark with more fervor.

Amber slid the door open and stepped outside. The cold autumn air ran up her nightgown, touching her naked body, her bare feet cold on the pavestones, pinched by tiny pebbles trying to gouge through her calloused heels. The dogs circled in the distance, and one of them hefted something into its mouth and trotted toward her.

She couldn't make out what it was at first. A thick stick, perhaps, some rotting wood, black with age. But as the dog came into the light she could see it was pale and fleshy and soft. She saw the unmistakable divide and curl of human fingers, twisted and stiff in death. She saw where the forearm had been chewed through, separated at the elbow, the bright white bone peeking out like moonlight.

"But I found him. I found him that morning and I wrapped my hands around his throat and I squeezed till he didn't move anymore. It was the easiest thing I've ever done. I don't know why it was so easy but it was."

"Maybe that's just who we are now."

The dog dropped the arm at her feet and ran back into the darkness. She stared at it for a moment. The arm was thin, longer than a child's but not large enough for a man, smooth and hairless, the fingernails held flecks of paint.

The second dog dropped a hand before her, light and delicate and frozen in a grip. One by one, they brought her these offerings and laid them at her feet, wagging their tails, howling in the night: an upper arm and shoulder, a piece of spine, a jawbone with teeth and a chin, a chunk of hip, a thick thigh that looked too large and heavy for the dog to carry, but he dragged it to her anyway.

The pieces began to pile before her in the yard, more and more of them. Some just chunks of flesh, others with bone. It was amazing how a person could be reduced to something so small, a pile of parts. Amber felt she must be dreaming, but she could feel the cold air, she could feel the wet grass, she could hear the panting breath of the dogs and the soul-stirring sound of their howls. She could smell death – it permeated the night – and she remembered the abandoned house and that morning.

"I don't know how he survived. I just don't know. I knew he was gone. I felt it."

One of the dogs emerged out of the darkness and dropped a foot before her and then, staring up at her as if waiting her approval, backed up and sat at the edge of the light. The second dog dropped the other foot before her and he, too, sat back on his haunches and waited.

Amber stared down at the feet and noticed something small and familiar on the ankle of the right foot. It was a small tattoo of a blue butterfly. She looked down at her own right ankle and saw it there, faded with age, a remnant of her youth. The dogs brought her the pieces of her own broken life. Limbs and chunks torn from her over the years. Her body nothing but an inanimate pile of parts.

The dogs sat at the edge of the light, their eyes glowed, staring at her. She heard a low growl somewhere in the darkness. A cold wind moved through the trees. She turned in horror and stared at her house where Joe and Vinnie slept, the place that had been her final undoing.

"Maybe he was right all along. Maybe he is God, risen from the dead. But my boy is buried and gone and he's not coming back. None of us are."

CHAPTER TWENTY-ONE

When Amber had grabbed on to him, John had never felt a force so powerful in his life. It wasn't in the grip of her arms that couldn't even reach around his midsection, it was something else. She hadn't hugged him so much as seized him, and in it was desperation so severe that he felt something change inside himself. He realized now, more than ever, the tenuous grip he held on his life. That it was slipping from him and he was powerless to stop it. The world was unraveling, like a reel of film spinning toward its end. His life nothing but a series of still photographs raced through at breakneck speed and he, the main character, suddenly left to wonder how he got from one place to another all the while seemingly standing still. His life was not his own. He was being acted upon by outside forces. They all were. There were machinations behind the scenes. He felt it in those moments of fear in the dead of night. His existence, his physical strength, was not able to change it, to avert the next great seismic shift. He was too weak. Something loomed in the red sky of his dreams. His calf burned and itched and spread fever up through his head.

And yet Lucas had somehow forced the world to change, to bend to his will. He had forever changed Amber's life; he had forever changed John's life; he had changed the entire world for their little enclave. There was power in insanity; there was power in the fanatical willingness to kill. Lucas was doing it, he was bending the world, changing the film in profound ways.

He had felt it for so long, but now, for the first time, he truly realized what it was he feared: his own powerlessness.

For all his size and strength, he hadn't even been able to kill a boy half his size. He hadn't been able to keep his wife happy and, no matter what he tried to tell himself, he couldn't keep his children safe. There was always something out there, always a threat. It could be Lucas; it could be a car crash, cancer, drowning, dog attacks, kidnapping, child molesters, choking, heroin, suicide, fire, a school shooter. It could be any of those things and he could not stop them all. He could not save them from life. The people who deigned to run the world couldn't save them either. Instead, they just twisted reality, told them that girls were boys and boys were girls and everyone is gay and if you're white you're privileged and racist and if you're poor and Black you're a hero and if you're a killer and a criminal it's not your fault and if you don't go to college you're an uneducated idiot and if you wanted to raise your children traditionally that you were somehow unworthy, that you needed to be overruled by the elite know-it-alls in government – the same know-it-alls who let Lucas run around on his killing spree because they chose to ignore John's warnings, decided his opinion wasn't worth shit, chose to keep their eyes closed. He knew this. He saw it everywhere now. It was real. Sooner or later, everyone is offered up as a sacrifice.

"I saw you outside with her," Jessica said. "Anything I should know?"

John sat on the far end of the couch, away from her. The television was muted for a moment, a talking head on cable news. John could see fear in the broadcaster's eyes. He rubbed an ice-cold beer bottle over his forehead to cool the burning sensation.

"I was there when she found him. I guess that means something," he said.

"You're not telling me something," she said.

"What is it you want to know?"

"The truth, John."

He looked at her for a moment. "Yeah, the truth would be nice, wouldn't it?"

She looked away from him and back at the flapping head on television.

"You want to know the truth, Jessica? The truth is that I'm sick of sleeping on the couch. The truth is that I'm sick of wandering around this place at night, wondering why my wife won't let me into our bed."

"You know the answer to that."

"I don't think I really do," he said.

"It's the drinking, John…."

"No. That's what you keep saying, but that's not really it."

"You tell me, then, John. You tell me why you're a stranger in this house."

He couldn't look at her right then. He had to look away. He had to lose himself for a moment in everything that he felt, that he knew.

"I'm so fucking alone," he said.

"I'm sorry you feel that way," she said.

"You're doing it again," he said. "You're treating me like a goddamn psych patient at the hospital."

"I don't know how else I'm supposed to treat you at this point."

"How about treating me like you actually love me? How about treating me like we've been together for sixteen years and we've made this home, this family and this life? How about treating me like I'm not unforgivable? That I'm not completely lost, because, to be honest, I'm feeling pretty fucking lost at the moment. I don't even know what to do to bring you back to me. I don't even know where to start because I can't figure out how I got here in the first place. And it scares me, Jessica. It scares me so bad, and I'm the only one who seems to want to do anything about it."

She just stared at him, cold and unmoving. He felt his words choking him but he couldn't stop now.

"Is this what it's supposed to be?" he said. "Is this how it was supposed to turn out? I look at myself and I don't know what happened. I'm nearly forty, Jessica. I have a go-nowhere, do-nothing job. My friends, I don't even think I really have any anymore. They're all gone. Remember the good times we all used to have together? Where are they? They're all off with their tiny little families and their tiny little lives and we're all separate and alone and no one seems to notice or care but the whole time our lives are slipping away. We get older and fatter and balder and poorer and we just shrug our shoulders and say, 'Oh well, there's nothing I can do,' and that's just fucking awful, Jessica. Everything just goes along until you suddenly realize that you haven't felt happy, or even content, in fucking decades and we're all supposed to be okay with that? It's like your whole life, you have this vision of the future, this future where things are, for once, okay and going well, and it just never fucking happens and all the while you get weaker and sadder and more desperate."

"You keep saying 'we' and 'us' but you're not talking about me. Those aren't my thoughts or feelings," she said.

"You're not listening to what I'm saying," he said.

"I'm hearing you. I'm just saying that what you're describing is how you see your life, not how life actually is."

She was doing it again. Speaking to him in that calm, therapeutic manner taught to her in some nursing class seminar about conflict resolution for mental health patients. He hated it. There was no emotion to it, no true feeling. She couldn't even pretend they'd once been in love, that she once cared about him. She refused to even remember a time in their lives when she would have held him close, let him quietly, sadly sob on her shoulder, cupping her hand to the back of his head, letting him feel protected and safe, like a child running into the arms of his mother.

"Your life here is so much better than mine?"

"My life is going just fine," she said.

"Because you can't be bothered with me anymore."

"It's not all about you, but you always think it is."

"How else am I supposed to look at things? We're all trapped inside our minds. We can only think about things through our own lives, Jessica. You're as self-centered as I am but you just don't want to admit it."

"That's enough," she said, and began to gather her laptop and stand up from the couch.

"What are you doing on that thing all night anyway?" he said. "Who are you talking to? It's like I sit here next to you but might as well be completely alone because you're on that goddamned thing all night talking to God-knows-who."

"You want to talk about feeling alone?" she said. "Try living with a drunk. Try talking to someone who's slurring their words and not making any sense. Try spending the evening with someone who passes out sitting upright on the couch when you're trying to enjoy a night together. Try not knowing if I'm going to have to pick you up from jail again when you don't come home right after work. Try knowing that the money I earn is going to pay thousands of dollars for a lawyer instead of the things we need around here. Try keeping the kids upstairs and telling them Daddy's not feeling well because he's downstairs on the couch drunk out of his mind and I don't want them to see you that way. You made your choice, I'm just trying to deal with the fallout, and you want to put this on me? Fuck you, John. You don't even try, you never have."

"I'm just...." He couldn't quite find the words he meant to say. "I can't change the past, Jessica, and I'm sorry about that. But I think I can change the future. I want us to be good again. I want us to be okay and I'm scared. I'm just so scared and most of the time, I don't even know what I'm scared of."

"There is no future here, John. Maybe that's why you're scared," she said. "But I can tell you one thing: I want you out of the house. You want to crash and burn? That's on you. I won't have you dragging me and the kids down with you."

"I'm coming to you," he said, "asking for help and you just want to put me out? That's it? You're just done and giving up?"

"Why not? You gave up a long time ago."

"I never gave up on our family."

"You gave up on yourself."

Jessica turned to leave. To walk up the stairs and spend the rest of the night huddled in her bedroom with the door shut to him.

"I'm going to be somebody," he said. "I'm going to make a difference. You'll see. And you're not taking anything away from me. Not this house and not my kids."

CHAPTER TWENTY-TWO

His mother screamed in the dark about the boy all night and kept getting up from her bed and walking on her bandaged feet till they bled. Vernon kept having to return her to bed and feed her pills stuffed in pieces of cheese, wondering why she wouldn't sleep, until he finally succumbed at three in the morning to tying her down spread-eagle with his father's old neckties in what looked like a scene from an incestuous S&M porn flick. The pills didn't touch her and he could barely keep his eyes open and only the marijuana prevented him from losing his temper. But he could feel it welling up inside him. She kept screaming about the boy and he asked her which boy but she would just scream at him, telling him to stop hurting her, to get out of her house, whoever he was, until Vernon just decided to let her scream, went to his basement room and tried to drown out her voice with the deep, melodic narration of *Forensic Files.*

He didn't remember when her screaming stopped. He didn't remember drifting to sleep, but he woke to the sound of the doorbell ringing at eleven in the morning and the sudden rush of panic as he realized the visiting nurse was here for her scheduled assessment and his mother was still tied down.

The doorbell rang again. Vernon scrambled out of bed and looked through the blinds of the small basement window and saw a young, pretty, dark-haired woman dressed in plain clothes with an identification badge hung around her neck and a laptop in her arms.

He was a wreck: still in an undershirt and boxer shorts, what little hair he had left was matted from his pillow. He smelled, and he had his mother tied up in her bedroom. It wasn't his best look.

The doorbell rang a third time.

"Just a minute!" Vernon called. He struggled quickly into his jeans, grabbed a button-down shirt from his closet and made sure to shut the door to his room. He ran up the stairs to his mother's bedroom and undid the knots as quickly as possible. She was asleep and he threw the ties into the closet, shut the door and covered his mother so she looked like a comfortably sleeping, ancient angel.

He answered the door breathless and was stunned by her eyes. For a moment, they were both silent, staring at each other. Vernon felt a sudden, disorienting dizziness in seeing her. He was overwhelmed.

"Mr. Trimble?" she said.

"Yes. Uh. Vernon, actually. Sorry, it was a long night and I overslept."

"My name is Jillian and I'm here for your mother's assessment. Is everything okay?"

Vernon caught himself for a moment. "Yes! Uh, I mean, yes. Everything is fine. My mother is sleeping."

"Well, I still have to come in to see her."

"Of course," he said and stepped aside so that she could enter the house, which, he now realized, smelled of age, rotted carpeting and microwavable food.

"Can you take me to see her? I'm afraid I'm going to have to wake her up," Jillian said.

"Normally we're up long before now."

"You said it was a long night. Did something happen?"

"No, nothing happened, it was just…she wouldn't go to sleep, she kept trying to get up and walk around on her bandaged feet and the medication didn't do anything."

"And how did you resolve the issue?"

He felt like he was being interrogated. She spoke with such bureaucratic precision; her calm, non-confrontational tone somehow made it seem so much more ominous, as if she were part of a machine, rather than this beautiful living person standing in his living room, and that made him feel sad and alone, a strange outsider to be graded on his performance today.

"Well, she eventually fell asleep. Like I said, it was a late night."

"I'd like to check the bandaging on her feet," Jillian said.

"Right this way."

Jillian sat down at the edge of his mother's bed and gently shook her awake, saying, "Mrs. Trimble? Mrs. Trimble? It's time to get up, sweetie," and his mother's eyes fluttered open, pale and still panicked, searching the room for the voice and landing finally on Jillian and then over to Vernon.

"You!" his mother screamed again, raising a bony arm and pointing directly at him. "You hurt me! You tied me up. Help me! Help me, someone!"

Jillian turned to look at him. Of course she remembered this, right here, right now, of all times and places.

Vernon trembled for a moment, stuttered. "I…uh…that's not really…."

Jillian turned back to Vernon's mother and said, "Are you feeling okay today, Mrs. Trimble?"

"The boy," his mother said. "They have to find the boy."

"Which boy?"

"The beautiful boy from the trees. He's everywhere, don't you feel him? He comes to my house, he comes to talk to me."

Jillian looked at Vernon again and he just shrugged and said, "I don't know." It was too much to explain.

"Let me take a look at those feet of yours." She began to tenderly unwrap the gauze dressing. Vernon watched her do this in such a loving and caring way that he suddenly felt like the worst human on Earth. How was it that the more familiar a person becomes the less we care? The less patience we have? Of course, Jillian would only be here for an hour and then head back to her presumably perfect and happy life, while Vernon would be here twenty-four hours a day, seven days a week for the foreseeable future. *Compassion and love are not infinite*, he thought, *no matter what the storybooks and romantic comedies tell you*, but as he watched Jillian checking the stitches, cleaning them, rewrapping his mother's feet, he felt a deep sense of dread and anxiety. No matter which path of decisions he traced out in his mind, it all came back to the same place.

He wondered about Jillian's life, right then. He imagined her – a beautiful, gleaming beacon of what life was meant to be – returning to her own home, perhaps to a boyfriend (there was no ring on her finger), heading out for drinks at night with close, meaningful friends who she'd known since college and all the while financially secure, saving money every month, saving for retirement, building a life in the future with children where they would all grow up happy and secure, not rich, of course, but doing well enough to take vacations and buy new clothes every school year. He saw Jillian in his mind as she would be in twenty years, still beautiful, probably in a new position at her job, content, living life in the perfectly prescribed way for success.

She was everything that Vernon was not and that made him yearn for her in a way far more powerful than sexual attraction. He wanted her life and, as modest and normal as her life probably was, it seemed far out of reach. He couldn't even imagine where to start. He thought of all the people out there, the people he would see online or on television, making something of themselves, being celebrated, admired, loved. Every one of them an act that he could not follow. He had nothing to offer the world.

His life, like his mother's mind, was one of decline and decay. Her consciousness had birthed him into a world of her own making and as the pieces of her world fell apart, so too did the pieces of his. The world he knew was a product of her – this woman who no longer recognized him, and, when they finally took her away, his world would go with her and he would be left with nothing, destitute, and robbed of past and future.

"Can I talk to you a moment outside, Mr. Trimble?" Jillian said.

Vernon said nothing, but walked quietly, head down, with her to the door and together they stepped into the light and then stood face to face in an almost intimate moment. Although she said nothing at first, he felt he wanted to stand closer to her, to breathe in more of her, to maybe take her hand in his and walk down the street beneath a canopy of leaves.

"Mr. Trimble, I have to say I'm a bit concerned," she said, her voice so clinical.

"It was just a bad night, they happen sometimes," he said. "I would never do anything to hurt her."

"I'm not suggesting that you are trying to hurt her – can I call you Vernon?"

"Please." He said it almost too joyously.

"Okay, Vernon. My concern is that you're fighting a losing battle here. You're delaying the inevitable and, frankly, I don't think it's good for either of you."

"I didn't tie her down," he said.

"That's beside the point," she said. "Your mother needs round-the-clock care and help. It's only going to get worse as time goes on. It's not healthy for either of you. Her feet are in rough shape, to be clear, but she's also showing signs of malnutrition and some skin rashes from lying in one position too long."

"It's very hard to get her to eat sometimes," he said, "and then other times she won't move and I don't want to force her. She'll just lie there staring at the ceiling forever. Won't even get up to use the bathroom."

"I know, Vernon," she said, and placed a comforting hand on his arm. "This is how it goes. Trust me, I saw it with my own grandfather, and I've seen it a hundred times at my job. It's inevitable but there are ways we can make this much easier for her – and for you."

"I know what you're going to say…."

"I'm recommending that your mother be placed in a specialized facility."

Vernon shook his head. "There's no way we can afford it."

"The state offers programs and the facilities offer payment plans…."

"I'd have to sell the house," he said.

"Do you own this house?"

"No. She does."

"So, oftentimes, her assets will be retained by the facility to cover the cost of her care. When she passes away, if there is any money left over, it will be returned to you…."

"That's not the point!" Vernon almost yelled and Jillian winced in surprise. He looked at her for a moment and felt embarrassed. "I'm sorry," he said. "I didn't mean to yell, but it's just that this is all I have. I don't know what I'd do."

"What you'd do is live your life, Vernon," she said. "This is her life, not yours. And I know you love her and you've done a great job taking care of her, but it's time to let go and let some professionals take care of her."

"This is all I've done for five years...."

"I know," Jillian said. "And now it's time to start living your life, too."

He stared into her eyes, bright and shining in the sunlight and felt the world collapsing around him. She gave a sympathetic smile.

"Sometimes it takes doing something very hard in order to turn your life around," she said. "Either way, I'll be making my recommendation to the doctor, who will then be in touch with you and possibly with a judge to issue the order if he sees fit."

She turned and walked back to her car, a baby-blue hatchback shining in the driveway, just the kind of car she would drive, he thought.

★   ★   ★

Vernon moved his mother to the kitchen and fed her scrambled eggs. He took her to the bathroom, wiped her down with a washcloth and changed her diaper. She yelled and criticized and occasionally swatted at him, but he ignored it. His head felt heavy and while he knew there were a million thoughts churning in his mind, he couldn't focus on a single one; they just came in flashes of mental conversation and images, like he was a wallflower at his own cocktail party, catching snippets amid endless chattering and the clink of fork tines on china.

He had to get right. He had to get free and clear so he could think, but his mother kept trying to stand up and then losing her balance because of the bandaging on her feet, so he finally put her back into bed and tied her to the posts again. He knew they did the same thing in hospital wards, so what was the difference? He left room so she could bend her arms and legs and, as she was lying on the bed spread-eagle, he could see her stomach cave downward and her ribcage shoot toward the sky. She was like the living dead, a reanimated skeleton that just kept moving and making sounds. Looking at her for a moment, he felt the fear, confusion and revulsion he imagined characters felt in zombie films. He put the television on to keep her occupied and she seemed to calm down a bit. She watched in wonder and amazement as infomercial hosts sold their wares like televangelists.

Vernon walked outside and smoked a bowl, taking a long drag and letting the elation set in before he began his walk around the block that, just an hour ago, he pictured taking hand-in-hand with Jillian. He stood on the street a moment and then made his way toward the intersection, which brought him out from the tree canopy and let him stand in the full warm light of autumn. He looked up and down the street, trying to see it for what it really was. To his left, Jim and Kristen's house with a For Sale sign; directly before him, Nancy's old house, now empty, with another For Sale sign at the edge of the street; two doors up was Amber's house, silent and sullen with the death of their youngest son and, across from them, Dale and Becky's house with another Realtor sign in the yard. In the opposite direction, he saw the Lovetts' house, now empty with a For Sale sign as they fled the scene of their son's crime in the ashes of the abandoned Widner house, and for a moment time seemed to stand still; the trees stopped swaying, the birds went silent, the clouds sat motionless as a Kodak picture.

We're all dying here, he thought.

It had become a neighborhood of ghosts, each of them with one foot in reality and one foot somewhere else, just waiting for the final moment when they would eventually move beyond this lonely, forgotten place.

Vernon's phone chimed with a text message: *Strange car and van outside Elizabeth's house on Ridgewood, been there for a while.*

Vernon glanced down the road. He could see Elizabeth's house on the corner with Leadmine and parked at the edge of her yard a white van and a small hybrid hatchback.

Going there now, Vernon texted back.

Vernon walked toward Elizabeth's house. He tried not to look at the crime scene. For as much time as he spent watching and thinking about murder and death at night, he didn't want to think about this one. The police tape danced in his peripheral vision.

As he approached, he could see it was not just any van. On its side was a Channel 8 News logo and there were two men and a woman standing beside the van talking. He recognized the woman as he got closer: Meredith Skye. She waved to him, but he didn't wave back. She walked toward him, anyway.

"You're Vernon, right?" she said, smiling. "I remember you. Do you remember me?"

"I thought you worked for the newspaper," he said.

"I have an assignment with News 8, now," she said. "Covering the story about Representative Tutt. You're aware of what's going on, right?"

"Not really," he said. "We had a child get murdered right over there, everyone has been pretty concerned with that."

"Well, another child was possibly murdered," she said. "A teenage boy died in police custody after Rep. Tutt called the police on him. She said someone was knocking on her door and harassing her. Would you be willing to talk to us for a bit and give us your take?"

"I'm going to go check on Elizabeth," he said and walked past Meredith, onto the grass of Elizabeth's yard, and then knocked on her door. The television crew was immediately up and pointing the camera directly at him.

He heard Elizabeth's voice through the door. "Go around back," she said, and her voice sounded strange.

At the back of the house, Elizabeth quickly opened the sliding glass door and waved him in saying, "Hurry, hurry, so they don't come around!" She pulled him by the arm into her home, shut the door, locked it and lowered the blinds.

Inside was dark and the air was stale. There were delivery food containers and pizza boxes mixed with half-empty liquor bottles and clothes hung over chairs. Everything seemed displaced. It was a far cry from the perfectly neat and assembled home he'd visited previously. Elizabeth's hair was disheveled and she wore a robe over a t-shirt and pajama pants. She smelled faintly of alcohol, her eyes wide and frantic.

"Did you talk to them? Tell me you didn't talk to them!"

"I only said I was coming to see you."

"Okay." She breathed a sigh of relief. "That's okay. They can't do anything with that."

"Are you okay?"

Elizabeth's head snapped up, looking at him, and then she inhaled deeply to collect her thoughts. "They've all left me! They've all abandoned me! Can you believe it? My campaign manager, my caucus members, the state party, the fucking media!" she screamed, pointing a finger outside. "They've all turned against me! Why? I didn't do anything wrong! You know! You know what was happening to me!"

"I know," he said.

"The knocking. It kept happening and there was no one there and it just kept happening and it would get louder and louder and I thought someone was trying to break in and then one night there's just this person, this thing, standing there and I couldn't see his face but I know he meant to hurt me, I could feel it, and so I call the cops and they arrest this kid and now he's dead, but I don't know. How was I supposed to know? I didn't kill anybody, I did what anyone else would do, right?"

"Absolutely," Vernon said. He was becoming nervous. Elizabeth's erratic hand gestures, her frenzied words, the intensity in her eyes reached into him. In his marijuana haze he had trouble keeping up.

"I don't know what's going on," Vernon said.

Elizabeth clutched him by both shoulders and stared into his eyes and Vernon was scared and lost in them. "You have to go out there and tell them I didn't do anything wrong," she said. "Someone has to stick up for me!"

"But I thought you didn't want me to talk to them...."

"I'm going to lose my seat! They're slandering me, Vernon! You should see the Facebook posts! Twitter! Instagram! You should see the comments! They hate me! After all I've done, everything I tried to do, they all hate me! And that little bitch out there! I always helped her, I always made time for her, and now she stabs me in the back! She's literally standing across the street from a murder scene and she's hounding me over something I didn't do! Someone has to stick up for me! Someone from this neighborhood who knows what's going on and that's you, Vernon! You know everything that's going on. You could tell them!"

Suddenly Vernon pictured himself in front of the cameras delivering facts, information, about a series of crimes in his neighborhood, directing the reporters to the truth, just like when detectives gave press conferences to warn the public about a killer on the loose. Words began to flow into his mind, the thought of giving a great speech, something that would rouse the world to their plight. The reporters were getting it all wrong. They needed to be set straight and the grandiose words flowed through him, he could feel them.

"Yes," he said. "I can do that."

Elizabeth clutched him around the neck and started crying. "No one has helped me. They all left me and there's no one left but you. No one in this neighborhood will stick up for me but you."

Vernon nodded vigorously. He wasn't exactly dressed for television cameras and the words that had just been flowing through his mind suddenly seemed to dissipate and he couldn't remember them. But he felt, for a moment, strong, like he could actually help someone.

He girded himself, puffed out his flat chest beneath his undershirt, opened the front door to the light of day and walked out to Meredith Skye, looking at her as she held a microphone in her hand. She knew he was coming to speak to her and snapped the camera crew to the ready.

"My name is Vernon Trimble," he said. "I began the Neighborhood Watch here partly in response to what was happening to Elizabeth Tutt on a nightly basis, and I'm here to set the record straight."

He'd never felt more alive.

CHAPTER TWENTY-THREE

Elizabeth finally felt she had a hold of this thing, this amorphous, nebulous thing that had run rampant in the news and burned like a forest fire on social media and sparked protests on the city green. In just a few short days she had begun to right her own ship. She'd sent out her own press releases with a full explanation of the events leading up to that night; she'd offered condolences for the family of the boy who died in police custody, proffered her own innocence in the matter, pointing to the police report that noted she had never seen the face of the figure standing in her doorway, leveled the blame directly on the arresting officers and, finally, state Democratic leadership had reached out with offers to help. Promises of a new team, an influx of campaign funding, a last-minute pushback on the narrative. Who were the real perpetrators here, anyway? If someone calls the police because they are being harassed, should they expect to be tied to the death of a juvenile? This was a wake-up call for reform. A rallying cry. There were still two months before the election. They couldn't afford to lose this seat.

It had all begun when Vernon walked out of her house and straight up to that snake Meredith Skye and told the true story of what happened. Elizabeth was forever grateful to Vernon for it. His delivery wasn't perfect, but it got people talking. Not always the right people, but people nonetheless, and that afforded her a chance to mount a defense.

She had texted him afterward: *You're my personal hero. Thank you.*

Now she welcomed the news crews, put her face on television and in the newspaper, set aside her self-doubt, fear and second-guessing and replaced it with righteous anger. She pointed to the events taking place in her neighborhood, she pointed to the failure of the police; she took the bull and bullshit by the horns and decided to come out swinging.

A 911 call should never be a death sentence, she told them all. Children of all colors from all places should be safe. This was failure on a monumental and deadly level. The cops had shirked their responsibility to find the true perpetrator of these crimes and harassment and instead found some random inner-city football players to arrest and one of them died. She reached out to arrange a meeting with the family of Antwone Diller; she pushed an online fundraiser to support the family. She told the world that this story would not be swept under the rug for cheap political points. She had to rally her base, who had been shaken in their support.

"My opponent has made crime the central issue of his campaign," she said. "But what he really wants is oppression without consequence, not justice. We demand justice."

Now she was scheduled for a full interview with the state CBS affiliate in three days to clear the record. No more of this social media, newspaper bullshit. She was going to tell the whole story, the full story, and lay blame precisely where it should be.

She was prepped and ready. Since Vernon had made his statement to the news, she'd sobered up, cleaned up and felt reinvigorated, ready to take on the world, the police, her opponent, even these goddamned village idiots surrounding her with their 'Let's Kick Tutt' lawn signs.

Meghan had always insisted on door-knocking, and as angry as Elizabeth was over Meghan throwing her to the wolves with zero notice, she understood the utility of her advice. Elizabeth decided she would start right here at home, right in this neighborhood, which was so clearly in Whitcomb's camp. She gathered up her campaign flyers and set out to walk the neighborhood, knock on doors and let these people tell her face-to-face why they wouldn't vote for her, their own neighbor, a member of the Neighborhood Watch, a victim of whatever was going on in this formerly quiet little place.

She started at the house just across the street from her, home of an elderly couple so old that they appeared to be the walking dead, or, in the husband's case, the wheelchair dead. Seniors vote, so she spoke with them, smiled, laughed, listened to their concerns. Oddly, they seemed far more concerned about what was happening in cities like Chicago and New York than they were about what was happening in the city right next to them, let alone in their own neighborhood. They talked about riots and protests and the breakdown in the rule of law. In the background the television was turned to cable news, bright lights, flashing colors, security camera footage of a smash-and-grab robbery on the West Coast, a makeup-caked blonde intermittently beaming a pageant smile coupled with a look of horror and fear.

"Well, as I'm sure you know, I'm part of the Neighborhood Watch here, and so I'm deeply dedicated to safety for everyone," she told the elderly pair.

"But you're a Democrat," the old man said. His skin was practically see-through. So thin he looked starved beside his plump wife, who demurely abstained from offering an opinion on anything other than: "They're killing babies before they're born."

"I am," Elizabeth told him, and then she smiled. "But I'm your kind of Democrat. I want to preserve social security and Medicare and ensure safety. We can do it all, we don't have to pick and choose."

"They're burning down the cities and nobody is doing nothing about it. The government is giving the goddamned country away," he said. "A bunch of socialists."

She left them with her campaign literature and moved on. Some were unreachable, but she needed this, like a boxer training for a fight. She needed to get into the ring with these people, sharpen her skills.

She moved down Ridgewood.

She stopped at the Carters' house, a lovely family, as far as she could tell. Even had rooftop solar, courtesy of a bill Elizabeth had co-sponsored in her first year as a state representative. Anthony let her inside, warm smile, calm demeanor, soothing voice.

"I'm sorry for what happened to you," he said to her. "That wasn't fair or right."

"Thank you," she said. "But my real concern is for the family of the boy who died when he was arrested."

"What's being done about it?"

"It's under investigation, obviously, but I want to ensure something like that never happens again," she said.

Anthony sat for a moment and stared out the bay window to the street. "I agree, what happened to that kid was awful and shouldn't have happened. But I have to be honest, what terrified me more is what happened right next door to my house," he said. "That could have been one of my kids that night. Frankly, I think if the police had taken the fire seriously from the beginning, actually tried to find Lucas instead of saying it was just kids playing with fireworks and a runaway teenager, maybe this wouldn't have happened. That kid should have been in an institution or something with his history, but we just don't do it anymore. I see it at the hospital all the time. Kids come in for mental health problems, but we have no room, we have no treatment. The beds are full, and even if they do get treatment for a week or whatever, they're turned loose again, go off their medication and we're right back where we started. I don't know. You can't fix people, I guess."

"Maybe not, but you can fix systems," she said. "And the mental health system, the police system, even the education system are broken in ways that are causing harm, real harm, for people like you. I get that. But I also understand they can be fixed."

Anthony kept staring out the window. "I hope you're right," he said.

She skipped the Ballards' house. John intimidated her with his size and the wild look in his eyes. He seemed unbalanced, manic. Besides, it looked like no one was home, anyway. She stopped at Mark and Maryanne's house across the street where they'd held their Neighborhood Watch meeting. Maryanne answered the door, let her in and gave her coffee. Then, instead of talking politics, they just talked for a half hour. Maryanne, with a leftover southern accent, told Elizabeth how nervous she was these days, how scared she was that everything was falling apart, that the neighborhood was emptying, that a child had been murdered, that every other week it seemed there were police here investigating something.

"I'm worried when I come home and Mark isn't here," she said. "We've had car break-ins in the past, but now it's different."

"How is it different?"

"I'm not sure," she said. "But when it keeps happening over and over again, you get the feeling you're on your own. No one is coming to save you, so you just have to look out for yourself. It's like we've been forgotten."

Elizabeth reached out and took Maryanne's hand. "I'm here," she said. "I haven't forgotten you. I live here, too."

Maryanne started crying.

"What's wrong?" Elizabeth said.

"Did you ever think it would be this way? That it would come to this?" she said. "We always think of the future as this bright, gleaming hope, and then when it comes it just gets worse and worse. People get worse and worse. You can't even feel safe. Mark is already talking about moving. Getting out of here. That poor boy, that poor family."

"This is a difficult time," Elizabeth said. "For everyone, everywhere, and I understand. I feel it, too. But we have to get through this together, with compassion and understanding. We can make changes, but we have to set ourselves on the right path."

"It's just a matter of time before they come for all of us," Maryanne said.

"Who do you mean by 'they', Maryanne?"

"I don't even know," she said. "I just feel them out there. I feel it and I know they're coming."

And that was it, she thought. That was the true problem: 'THEY'. She could talk about systems constantly, she could talk about government programs, she could talk about policy changes, she could talk about safety and reform, but none of it would matter if THEY were out there. And most people had no idea who THEY were, so it was easy to substitute in your preferred boogeyman: the government, Democrats, Republicans, communists, Blacks, immigrants, gun-nuts, white nationalists, Islamic terrorists, all the way down to the local zoning board. It wasn't fear outright – like the fear felt when you're alone in the night and someone is knocking on your door – but more like a sense of unease left dormant for too long, the feeling that something that was once right is no longer right. That disquiet settled into the soul and had a voracious appetite, consuming every bit of information, channeling it through the psyche, amplifying their belief. Things that had once been familiar had been rendered unfamiliar.

And yet, the crimes in their neighborhood had all come from within, from something else left long dormant, ignored for too long.

We are all strangers now, she thought. *We're all 'THEM'. We're all the enemy.*

"What causes you to feel uneasy at night?" she asked Maryanne, doing her best to play the role of therapist politician.

"I guess that I just don't know what's going on anymore," she said. "I have two grandchildren, did you know that? When I see them they spend most of their time staring into their phones or their tablets. They talk about things I don't understand and it all changes so quickly. I can't keep up, and I don't think they can either, really. They might as well be speaking a foreign language. They show me things, videos, video games, all nonsense as far as I can tell. But, it's more than that. It used to be that what was right was right and what was wrong was wrong, and it was like we could all agree on that. But now no one agrees what's right and wrong anymore and so you're left on your own to figure it out and I don't want to be alone in that. Because maybe someone out there thinks you're wrong and they might be coming after you next."

"I can't imagine you being in the wrong about what's right and wrong, Maryanne," Elizabeth said, smiling.

"Maybe, maybe not," she said. "But still, I feel alone. Even here. Even with my husband. I can't tell if the world has gone crazy or if it's just me who's crazy. It's hard on the soul."

"You know, I once had a professor who said the reason so many people are obsessed with sports is because in sports everyone knows what the rules are," Elizabeth said. "A luxury and an escape in this day and age, I suppose."

"I don't care for watching sports much," Maryanne said.

Elizabeth thought for a moment. "Me neither. Maryanne, would you come with somewhere? I have something I want to show you."

★   ★   ★

Elizabeth and Maryanne stood at the entrance to the Tree of Life exhibit, its dark mouth occasionally showing breaths of light from the interior walls of internet-streaming glass.

"I brought this work here for several reasons," Elizabeth said, "and I think it may speak to you. I've found it to be very moving."

Elizabeth motioned for Maryanne to go first, hoping to watch her reaction, hoping to see a moment of recognition, an epiphany that can only be brought out by a work of art. Maryanne shyly walked inside and the walls began to play their light show in its dizzying display. Elizabeth felt an unsettling fear that she would once again see herself displayed in these images, in these headlines, but this time she avoided the spotlight. Instead, she followed Maryanne through the maze, watching her tentatively and slowly find her way.

"It's all so unreal," Maryanne said.

"It is and it isn't," Elizabeth said. "It's real, but it's a new kind of reality."

"That's the scary part," Maryanne said. She continued to walk, continued to turn the corners, greeted each time by new flashes, new videos, the war-comedy of crime and yearning and jealousy and hate and love and heroism and cowardice and politics and sports and international relations.

Until she turned the final corner and came to the Tree of Life, light from above shining down like the hand of God and all the walls quiet and bare and silent. Maryanne stood there for a moment staring at the little tree as it stood alone and at peace in the center of it all.

Elizabeth stood behind Maryanne, watching her take it in, hoping beyond hope that she felt something real, saw the truth of the display.

"I never went to college," Maryanne said. "I don't have the degrees that you do. I don't know anything about art. It always seemed too... academic, I guess? I grew up in Georgia, got out of high school, married Mark, got a job and had babies and...I don't know. It just kinda went from there. Suddenly you're sixty years old and everything is different and you look back and wonder where it's all gone."

"It doesn't have to be academic," Elizabeth said. "It can be something you feel, something that strikes you."

"I see that now," she said.

"The real question is how do we keep that beauty in ourselves, when we feel like there is chaos all around us," Elizabeth said.

Maryanne stared up at the sapling and, for a moment, a breeze over the top of the display caught the uppermost reach of the little tree and it bent slightly toward Maryanne as if urging her to an embrace.

"I don't think I've ever talked about this with anyone before," Maryanne said.

For the first time in a long time, Elizabeth felt she had actually reached someone, not on a political level, but on a personal one.

"Just think of this when you feel overwhelmed," Elizabeth said. "Remember that there is refuge in beauty, in real things, in life. You're not lost, you're not alone and you're not crazy. You're just looking in the wrong direction. This is the Tree of Life."

Maryanne looked at her a moment, curiously.

"This ain't the Tree of Life," Maryanne said. "This is the eye of the storm."

"I'm sorry, what?" Elizabeth said, suddenly stunned.

Maryanne kept staring up at the tree. "When I was growing up we'd get the occasional hurricane. It would come through, destroy everything. We'd have to hunker down, board up the windows, save food and water. The first blow would hit hard and then came the eye of the storm. You could literally see blue sky in the middle of it. It was eerie, a moment when everything seemed at peace but it wasn't. You could feel it. Even the air itself was charged with this violent energy, just waiting for another turn. We knew that was the most dangerous place to be because you think it's over, but it's not. It's really just beginning all over again."

"It's supposed to be a place of peace," Elizabeth said.

"Only if you're blind to what's coming next," Maryanne said.

CHAPTER TWENTY-FOUR

The house was empty and silent and Amber was alone but for the dogs. Joe said he needed to lose himself in work; Vinnie wanted to be with his friends at school and soak up the sympathy and newfound fame. So she was alone for the first time in what felt like years, walking the house, invisible to all but the dogs. Amber looked around her home. It was a mess; dishes piled in the sink, clothes piled in the laundry to be washed, half-empty glasses formed rings on wooden tables and dust coated the windows, framed pictures and television screens; debris, dirt and pebbles visible on the carpeting. The air still smelled of others, of otherness, and she was dumbfounded as to what to do. She saw no way to clean it up. She saw no reason. She saw no justification for having to do it. Why should she? Her arms wouldn't move, her legs wouldn't carry her to the tasks at hand and she simply wandered throughout and looked at these things piled up, more remnants of her life, cheap and easily broken.

She sat in Tommy's room. The bed was still made from the morning of the block party. There was the usual scattering of toys and clothes; a small television on a dresser where Tommy would watch his streaming cartoons and YouTube videos of other kids playing Nerf gun wars or Minecraft video games; Lego creations he'd done himself; toy excavators, trucks, cars and castles, the remnants of an imagination never fully brought into the reality of life before he was plunged into horror.

Her phone rang with calls, dinged with messages, alerted with outpourings of hope and offers of care on social media, but she didn't look or listen and eventually turned her phone off so she could be with the silence.

The dogs were barking now.

Amber left Tommy's room and shut the door behind her. She opened the laundry room door and the dogs barreled out, nearly knocking her over as they charged to the sliding glass door. Inside, the floor was littered with shit and piss, wet and soiled newspaper. The smell hit her and suddenly she could barely contain her rage.

She opened the doors to the backyard and the dogs bounded out into the cool wet of a rainy day and she shut the doors and locked them. Amber walked back to the laundry room and looked at the mess. She wanted it gone, she wanted all of it gone, to be rid of its burden, so that she could sit and commune with the dead.

She put on some rubber dishwashing gloves and picked up the crumpled newspaper from the tile floor. Headlines about politics and crime coupled with advertisements for food and cleaning supplies, bleach and glass cleaner and scrubbing bubbles. She put the newspaper into a trash bag and then into the garbage outside. She looked in the cabinet beneath the sink and saw that it was practically bare. It felt like a decade since she'd been to the store, another lifetime in which she did housewife things, but she needed to cleanse the laundry room of the smell. She was barely dressed, but it didn't matter. She took her keys and pocketbook, went to the van and drove through the neighborhood, careful to avoid the burned-out house and the Lovetts'. She couldn't bring herself to pass by that place anymore and, when she thought of it, she couldn't stand to be in the same neighborhood or even the same state.

She turned onto Route 4 and crossed the town line into the outskirts of the city to the nearby grocery store and walked inside through the rain. There were very few people, the aisles bare as if a holiday had come and gone and, in the pale light of the supermarket, she stood in the cleaning supplies aisle and stared at the colors of bottled soaps and chemicals: the blues, greens and oranges, the fast-acting, quick-scrubbing, lemon-scented and lavender-tinged tides of all that was meant to clean and wash away the plaque of life. She stared at the bottles with their child-safe caps and held them in her hands and read the chemical ingredients on the back and put them back on the shelf. Someone asked if she needed help finding anything but she said nothing and continued walking down the aisle, staring at the colors, the packaging, the big, bold letters that promised cleansing. There were so many, it was almost overwhelming. There were too many selections for disinfecting one's life; pick your poison in the color best suited to your personality.

Purple would do.

She turned down the aisle reserved for dog food, cat food, chew toys, rat poison and bug spray. She left an hour later with three full bags. The plastic handles bit into the flesh of her hand. She loaded them into the minivan and drove home.

The dogs came bounding around the corner of the house as she pulled into the driveway and pushed the remote garage door opener. They stopped and lowered their heads and watched her from a distance. She got out, opened the sliding van door and took out the bags. The dogs waited at the edge of the house, staring at her as she hefted the bags from the car. She heard their low growls as she walked toward the garage. She saw from the corner of her eye the blue-gray hair on their backs stand up. She watched as they bared their teeth at her. She walked through the garage, more of a massive storage closet than a domicile for their cars, and noted all the things in this space: approximately four bicycles of varying quality and rust, plastic bins filled with winter clothing and boots, scooters, plastic toys that Tommy loved and would never again use, rakes, snow shovels, extension cords, a bucket of road salt, two old car batteries, a hydraulic car jack, two gallons of antifreeze, a case of car oil, Joe's work bench and tool cabinet with a mounted vise, a storage rack with spare food, two massive fifty-pound bags of dog food.

It was noon. Vinnie would be back from school by three and Joe, who set off early that morning, would probably be back not long after that. She set to work immediately, starting in the laundry room, scrubbing and cleaning and disinfecting until the whole room smelled of chemical cleaners and fake flowers. She moved on to the kitchen. She washed all the dishes and put them away. She washed the countertops, polished the dining room table, picked up all the glasses and bottles and discarded napkins left out by her husband and teenage son as they awaited her return to normalcy. She swept, vacuumed, ran two loads of laundry and washed

the windows. She turned her attention to her bedroom. She brushed aside
the curtains, letting the light stream in to illuminate the swirling dust in
the air and set everything perfectly right – the decorative pillows in their
proper place, facing the proper direction, clothes removed from the lone
decorative chair in the corner, folded neatly and placed into drawers.

Finally, she took a long, hot shower. She scrubbed her body, washed
her hair, tried to melt off the past. She wanted to look proper. She did her
makeup, styled her hair and then selected a sundress out of her closet, a
pair of matching heels and a pearl necklace from her small and largely fake
selection of jewelry.

She stared in the mirror and looked like an image from an old copy
of *Redbook*, a memory of a time she had never lived but still, somehow,
knew was expected of her. She looked the picture-perfect mother
and housewife. She glided through her immaculate house on heels, a
beaming smile on her face, dancing slightly to a song in her head, as
she prepared a meal for her family. Tonight, she would spoil them with
riches, with perfection. She would transform her small world into what
it was meant to be, what they all longed for but could never quite
put their finger on. She had figured it out and she embraced it. She
was the loving trophy wife, the former beauty queen, the PTA mom,
the Maybelline Girl turned Maybelline Woman, the ever-sacrificing
caregiver who spent her days cleaning and keeping herself fit and perfect
so when her men came home, they came home to a perfect house, a
perfect wife, a perfect mother. Everything would be perfect from now
on, everything would be the way it used to be in those memories she
did not have. She would sacrifice every ounce of her being to ensure
her boys were well taken care of, transfer all of herself into them. She
had already sacrificed her youthful dreams of stardom and riches for this
little life of mild discontent punctuated by the horrific murder of the
one person on Earth who seemed to truly love her. But part of sacrifice
was not holding back, giving it all. So she would sacrifice again and give
to them all that was inside her, all the thoughts and dreams and feelings
that she had. Now was the time to move forward into a new day. She
would feed them from her body and soul, just as she had fed Joe's need

for a perfect little working family; just as she had fed Vinnie and Thomas from her breast.

She fed the dogs. She loaded their bowls with dog food, giving them extra treats mixed in, and they loved her for it and gobbled up the food in the shade of the garage, lapping heavily from their water bowls. She watched them as they ate and they watched her, gracious and wiggling in their excitement to take from her. She smiled at the beauty of it.

By the time Vinnie came home, she had soft music playing in the living room and the air smelled of warm food cooking in the oven. Dessert was prepared, and she had lemonade in a pitcher with ice to be served at dinner.

He looked at her and said, "Mom, what's going on?"

And she said, "It's okay, sweetie. Everything is okay. I'm going to take care of you now."

He began to cry and hugged her.

She stroked his mop of curly dark hair and said, "It will all be okay now. I'm here."

She held him, but she felt nothing at all because there was nothing but emptiness inside her.

★   ★   ★

How happy they were to see her like this.

Joe returned from work, tired and hungry and still sad, and then marveled as he saw her, hugged her tight as she finally spoke to him, telling him that she was fine now, that they would soon be very happy, and he said how amazing and perfect she looked. He had tears in his eyes.

"I thought we lost you," he said.

"No," she said. "I had just lost myself. I'm fixing that now."

"It's so good to have you back," he said.

"I'm not back," she said. "I've changed. We all have."

Amber instructed Vinnie to go to his room and do his homework while she finished preparing dinner. She ignored the strange, sarcastic, almost hate-filled look he gave her and she ignored the obvious sounds of video games and YouTube videos that emanated through the closed door to his room. It was fine. She handed Joe a lemonade spiked with vodka and he drank it down quickly, commenting on how sweet it was, and then she told him to relax and change out of his clothes while she set the table. He smiled and reached under her dress, squeezed her ass as she coyly slapped his hand away and gave him a wink. He changed out of his work clothes and sat in the recliner, put his feet up and enjoyed the Tom Collins. He watched the news while she worked in the kitchen.

Their neighbor from down the street was on television.

"I don't like her politics," Joe said. "But what they're doing to her is no good. They don't understand what's going on around here. Those boys shouldn't have been here at that time of night, anyway. What else was someone supposed to think?"

Then Joe sat silent for a moment and took another drink. "I miss him so bad," he said.

"I know, honey," Amber said. "I miss him, too. But we'll see him again someday."

"God, I hope you're right."

"I know I am." She smiled and gently placed her hand on his cheek. He grasped it and stifled a sob.

"I'm sorry I wasn't here," he said to her. "I shouldn't have gone."

"You men needed your time away," she said with a smile.

"I don't know what to do about Vinnie," he said. "I can't seem to get through to him. I don't know what he's thinking or how he's taking all this."

"Vinnie will be fine," she said.

"All I know is that we need you," he said, looking her in the eye now, a sense of pleading in his own. "We need you more than ever."

"You have me," she said. "You have all of me. Everything I am."

He gripped her hand and said, "Thank God."

She called them to dinner at a neatly set table. A roast, sweet potatoes, green bean casserole, lemonade and an apple pie she baked in the oven.

"We should say a prayer before dinner," she said. Meals had always been a voracious and hectic time in the past, never commencing with prayer but rather with interrupted arguments, phone texts and time crunches between work and school. Vinnie rolled his eyes and Joe stared at her a moment before finally saying, "Yes, of course. You're right."

Joe lowered his head and reached out and they all held hands and recited the Lord's Prayer.

Give us this day, our daily bread, and forgive us our trespasses as we forgive those who trespass against us. And lead us not into temptation but deliver us from evil....

They gorged themselves on the meat and potatoes, the pie and lemonade. Joe looked at Amber and said, "Aren't you having any?"

"None for me," she said and smiled demurely. "I'm watching my figure."

CHAPTER TWENTY-FIVE

Vernon lay awake in the darkness, the sound on his television turned low as one episode of *Cold Case Files* concluded and another began. He watched and listened and smoked a bowl. It occurred to him that in all his research he had reached a basic conclusion: murder is human. It was not done by monsters, it was done by men and women who, apart from this indiscretion (or sometimes multiple indiscretions) lived like everyone else. They were fathers and mothers, brothers and sisters, sons and daughters, employees and managers, rich and poor, old and young. It made no difference. From all outward appearances they could be a perfectly fine, ordinary person, and then, one day, the world is shocked by their brutality, their cunning, their rage. But the world shouldn't be shocked. It was, in fact, completely ordinary. It is only treated as extraordinary in a society that willfully prefers to look away, prefers to ignore that they are no different from those whom they condemn to prison for the all-too-normal act of murder.

The funny thing about murder, he thought, *is that it always happens to someone else*. Because, if it happened to you, you weren't around to notice.

Sometimes, when he was completely detached, when he was high, seeing things from outside his own body, he wondered what the crime of it truly was. Everyone dies. Why should a person dying – even if by the hand of another – be a crime? That person was going to die anyway. It could be of old age a hundred years from now or it could be a car accident tomorrow. We try to place limits and rules on death. It's as useless as trying to control the weather.

And so, too, would his mother die. As would he. The only difference being that if everything progressed without interruption, she would die before him. That wasn't a guarantee, of course, just the likeliest of outcomes and one worth betting on. Though, depending on how the next few years turned out, Vernon may not have the money to place such a bet. It was not about when death comes or the manner in which it comes, because it comes at all times, in all ways, but it's about how we live until that point – or better yet, if we truly live at all.

Lying in his bed that night, feeling his room close in and then expand like a lung, feeling the sensation of blood coursing through his limbs, Vernon realized he had not lived at all. His mother had lived. She had grown up, worked, married and raised a family. She had lived the normal and expected life. Now she was old. Her death would be normal and expected. His death, on the other hand, if it were to come tomorrow, would be utterly devoid of meaning, because there was no loss. He could get hit by a bus tomorrow and people would shrug and move on with their day. Were he murdered, would anyone even try to find the killer? Or would they be forced to confront the truth that death only matters when it happens to someone with value? It's not that they are particularly concerned about the loss of that person, but for the harm that it inflicts on themselves. They only care because they, the living, are somehow inconvenienced. The dead are dead, no matter the circumstances.

In a way, he envied little Tommy Locke. His death was mourned by the entire state. Sure, he was young and conceivably had many years ahead of him, but then, he could have just as easily been run down by a car the next day. As we age, death loses meaning.

All this came to him in a flash. Like when you see yourself in the mirror and, for a moment, your brain forgets to filter the image through your preconceived lens. In that moment, you see yourself the way the rest of the world sees you every day. The lines in your face are deeper, skin more muddled, hair thinner, fat hanging from your bones. You think, "God, is that me?" and you realize it's the truest version of yourself and it's more pathetic than the fantasy in your mind.

So now, sleepless in the dead of night, Vernon was left with a decision. His mother had lived a long life and her mind was gone but her body, somehow, kept running. She was like a car on the highway whose driver had died at the wheel. The outcome is already set and the journey from now till the end will just create more loss. In a way, she was already dead.

And he was waiting to live. To live the way he should have been living this entire time. He too, would ultimately die, but he was still conscious and on the road, two hands on the wheel, his mind able to navigate the lanes. Why should he wait for his mother's car to crash into his? He could steer himself into a better lane. Her driver's license had already been revoked by the state six years ago.

That night she had gone to bed willingly, without the fight that accompanied so many of their nights together, and in that time he felt a certain sentimentality toward her. His memories of childhood came back to him like pictures from a photo album, but, just like those pictures, the memories were divorced from the present. They were snapshots of another time when there was much more road ahead.

The time was now. There was no other way to come out of this with what he deserved – namely, a life and a way forward. It was a sad truth, but one that must be accepted as entirely human. The pretty nurse would be back in a couple days with the paperwork and then the process would begin for putting his mother in a home. It wasn't right that the past should take so much from the future.

Vernon pushed back the covers on his bed and sat up. On the television, pictures of bodies and crime scenes and men in suits being interviewed in front of a green screen. He took his bowl from the nightstand beside his bed, pushed more flower into it, took his lighter and inhaled deeply, holding his breath until he coughed out a cloud of blue smoke. He stood up and accidentally kicked over some empty soda cans beside his bed. He pushed some old clothes on the floor out of the way with his foot and walked to his bedroom door.

The stairwell leading to the front door and then up to the living room was dark. It was nearly two in the morning and it all seemed so far away. A long, endless climb of stairs from bottom to top. He took them slowly, quietly, sneaking in his own house. Was it the darkness that caused his need for silence, or was it that he didn't want to look her in the eye one last time? He had given her extra pills this night in the hopes she would remain in a deep sleep and not wander the house on her bandaged feet, crying out in the night.

Just the thought of waking again to her insane screams was enough to cause him to shudder, to fear her. She had gone from nurturer to threat and he couldn't bear the thought of it any longer. At this point, doing anything else was cruel. There would be no questions asked because her death would cause no one else any pain or discomfort; because it would be expected, it would be natural and normal and fit neatly in the box of expectations.

Vernon walked quietly up the stairs, but for the creak on the fourth step from the top. He made no sound as he walked the worn carpet of the hallway past the bathroom and the two bedrooms on the top floor opposite his mother's. He pushed the door open and saw her sleeping face-up in the pale moonlight emanating from the window where she watched the squirrels and marveled at their existence. She looked dead already; withered face, mouth hung open, breathing so quietly it was as if she were not breathing at all.

He didn't want to make it hard on her. He just wanted her to slip out of this world while she slept in the easiest possible way. No violence, no blood, no bruises. This wasn't out of anger; it was out of compassion and desperation and the desire to live the life she would have wanted for him. She slept soundly in the bed she had shared with his father, the bed she slept in for more than thirty years in the house they purchased and where they raised their little family. Isn't that what everyone wanted? To die in their sleep in their home, rather than strapped to some hospital gurney surrounded by strangers in surgical masks? She lay peacefully, for the first time in a long time, beneath the sheets and comforter. There was no more fitting place. We should all be so lucky.

He quietly walked to his mother and sat down beside her on the bed. He thought for a moment about the past few years with her, caring for her; the sleepless nights, the humiliation, having to wash her naked body and clean her after using the toilet. He thought of all the times he was forced to tell a woman he was chatting with on a dating app that he lived with his mother only to never hear from her again. He thought of the cute and vibrant nurse who would be returning to his home in the next couple days with paperwork to be signed.

He loved his mother. He'd spent years of his life – what should have been great years of his life – caring for her, demonstrating his love. But now it was time to move on and, were she still capable of thinking, he was sure she would agree.

Vernon leaned down and kissed his mother's cheek, soft and delicate, and then slid a pillow out from the sheets beside her and placed it over her face and pressed the palm of his hand firmly down over it until he could feel her nose and mouth through the down. He waited a few moments, felt her body surge upward, felt her arms reach up. He moved his body over hers to keep her from fighting. Her arms pinned down by his knees, her frail and weakened legs trapped in the bed linens as they tried to kick and shake, her desiccated chest heaved, and then, after a few moments, she went still and silent. He held the pillow there a little longer and waited until the whole Earth felt still.

Vernon wiped some tears from his eyes and tried to tamp down the sick feeling in his stomach. There was no going back now. He could only move forward. He took the pillow away and placed it back under the sheets. Her eyes were open and pale, staring at the ceiling, and he closed them with his thumb and forefinger.

He walked out of her room and shut the door. He walked back downstairs to his basement and lay in his bed. In the morning he would call the ambulance and tell them his mother had passed away in her sleep.

★   ★   ★

It started with the dogs in the middle of the night. Amber hadn't slept. She had waited. She made Joe keep them in the laundry room that night and then let him writhe on top of her in a sad, sullen lust and pass out asleep. She lay in the dark, waiting, listening. First came the whines and whimpers and then the ghastly howls, like something from another world. Then the hacking sound of the dogs vomiting, forcing everything up. Joe woke up and then Vinnie and they went to the laundry room and then called for her. "We have to call the vet as soon as we can in the morning," he said. "They're really sick."

"Are they going to be okay?" Vinnie said.

"I'm sure they'll be fine, honey," Amber said.

The dogs lay on the ground, frothing at the mouth, vomiting, howling, seizing. They snapped at Joe's hand when he touched their stomachs, like wild animals caught in a hunter's trap.

"Is there a twenty-four-hour animal clinic somewhere? An emergency room for vets?"

"I don't know," she said.

"Well, go find one!" he shouted, and she left and walked into the living room and sat on the couch for a moment. Otto suddenly seized and jumped to all fours and bolted from the laundry room. He ran past her through the living room and smashed his head into the glass of the porch door. The dog stumbled, shook, retched with another ghastly sound and then collapsed on the floor. She watched it breathe quickly, in and out, ribcage rising and falling, until it finally stopped and the dog lay still. Foam ran from its mouth onto the carpet. There was blood and shit all through the house.

Helmutt was still crying in the other room and Joe was yelling something to Vinnie and Vinnie said he didn't feel well. "I think I'm going to be sick," he said.

"I need help!" Joe screamed. Amber stood up and went to the kitchen to make some coffee. The second dog was still in the laundry room spinning in circles, chasing its tail, whining and howling and retching blood on the floor.

She would clean it up in the morning.

★   ★   ★

Vernon woke in the night. It was not a sound or a touch that woke him, but rather a presence. He opened his eyes and there hovered over him a figure that glowed pale in the darkness and he was immediately afraid, needles running from his chest through his stomach and into his limbs, but he found he could not move. As his eyes adjusted, he could see that it was the ghost of his mother standing over him, clear and real, and he could see her pale eyes were wide and her mouth was open and he heard her voice – *murderer!* – and he realized she was alive. She held something that glinted metallic in the light from his muted television and then, suddenly, there was something in his stomach, something hard and sharp and foreign. He wondered for a moment what it could be. It felt so strange, so big and different and then, just as quickly and easily it was gone, and he remembered what he had told John that day on the street: it's actually fairly difficult to choke someone to death, murder isn't easy.

He felt something smooth and sharp again. This time in his side as he rolled over to stand up. It felt like a dream, and he didn't understand what was happening. His mother was screaming at him to get out, to get out of her house, but he was confused. He stood up and stumbled away from her. His legs weren't working right. He was having trouble keeping his balance and he was wet. Everything was wet but he wasn't sure with what or why.

The television screen flashed bright and in the digital light he could see her more clearly now in her nightgown, face gaunt, eyes wild, thin hair splayed in all directions and in her hand a knife from the kitchen. Vernon's hands kept rubbing at his belly, wiping at his shirt, and they were wet, and he looked at them. They were black. His mother was near him and screaming for him to get out and he felt a pain in his ribs causing him to keel over slightly to one side. He felt it inside him. He felt it moving around, moving things he'd never felt move before, and then it was gone again, and his hands were gripping part of his side, trying to feel what happened, to keep his insides from spilling out.

He tried to raise his hands as she came near him again, but they wouldn't move from his stomach. She moved slowly toward him and, for a moment, he thought she was going to embrace him, hold him. He felt her closeness, familiar and loving, and he said, "Mom," and leaned in as if to put his head on her shoulder and then there was the knife in his stomach again, this time just below his sternum and he felt the air going out of him.

He tried to scream, tried to ward her off now, but he couldn't find his breath. He wrapped both arms around his midsection, turned away from her and started to walk toward the door. His legs weren't working right. Nothing did, like his body was separated in pieces and the parts were not working together. He fell against the doorjamb and made his way to the stairs. He felt something slide into his right buttock and his right leg stopped working.

"Mom, stop," he said. He turned to look and she was right behind him holding the knife. He recognized it from the butcher's block in the kitchen. Her eyes were wide, alive with childlike wonder. She poked at him and he felt the tip of the knife hit his hip bone and it hurt badly. Suddenly his legs moved again and he climbed the stairs to the landing. He turned the corner and pulled himself up the second set of stairs to the living room. She followed behind him the whole time, poking at him like a child poking a dead animal with a stick, prodding with the knife. He tried to swat at her with his hands but every attempt was short and quick, his arms returning again to his stomach. He slipped on the last step and fell onto the living room floor. Vernon didn't know where he was going exactly, he was just trying to get away. He felt another deep run through his side, just above his hip and he felt his insides move about. It was like having the hand of a puppeteer inside him, causing him to move in ways he did not understand.

Then the metal shaft was gone and his mother was gone and he did not know where she went. He felt very tired and he couldn't tell whether his eyes were closing or if it was just the darkness of the house at night.

He saw the light from the kitchen and the old house phone sitting on an end table in the living room. He pulled himself up and tried to walk toward it. Only his left leg would work now and he was breathing so quickly, and he couldn't catch his breath and everything was slippery and black and only now did it occur to him that it could be the end, that this might be the culmination of his entire life, and it seemed so strange, so foreign, that it should end like this and yet, somehow, it did not cause him fear. It was only a fleeting thought, one moment there and the next far away.

Vernon stood upright for a second and girded himself. He limped slowly toward the phone. The house seemed to stretch, the distance growing with each step. He saw his mother again. She stood before him and jabbed him twice in the stomach. He placed a hand on her shoulder and pushed her aside. There was another pinching jab into his back, but he kept looking at the phone. He didn't know where his cell phone was. Downstairs on the floor near his bed perhaps.

Then the phone was sideways. Or rather he was. And he realized he was on the floor. Everything was turned the wrong way. He could see it sitting there a long way off but he could not move. Nothing worked right. It was all collapsing and he still couldn't figure it out. He had spent countless hours watching these scenes played out, wondering what it must be like, picturing the moment one realizes it is all over, and still it seemed so incomprehensible.

He saw his mother's feet now and the hem of her nightdress stained red, hanging over him, and his mind flashed to memories of his childhood, of being a young boy, looking up at his mother and father with a sense of bewilderment and awe.

He heard her voice in a moment of clarity. "Vernon? What happened to you?"

He didn't know. He couldn't look back on it all and tell where it had gone wrong. How do you account for an entire lifetime? It was all before him but too big to see. Maybe he just hadn't tried hard enough. Maybe he had taken it for granted and wasted his time. Maybe he was just cut into pieces since the very beginning.

"I don't know, Mom," he whispered. "I don't know what happened."

CHAPTER TWENTY-SIX

John didn't sleep. He didn't even sit. He drank. He limped around the living room in the night, swaying slightly. The wound on his leg was oozing bright red. He poured vodka on it and it practically sizzled. He didn't know where to go or what to do and most of all he couldn't think. The whole world felt strange and even though he was inside his own home, it didn't feel right. He felt like he was outside in the dark, homeless, left to wander. It all felt wrong. At one point he wandered upstairs and opened the door to the bedroom and he heard her voice, "Please leave and shut the door," and he did leave and shut the door.

He was guided by outside forces.

He looked into his daughter's room and saw her sleeping in bed and he went to his son's room and watched him for a moment in the sliver of light from the hallway. Their chests moved up and down beneath the sheets, barely noticeable.

John stood before the computer screen and let its blue light wash over him. He typed. He raged. He emailed and it was all for nothing. The floor creaked beneath his feet.

He went into the basement and stood there for a time. It was cold concrete surrounded by earth. He stared through the basement door window into the darkness behind their house, into the trees and the wetlands beyond. He thought of his march through the swamp that day. He thought of his hands clasped around Lucas's neck, the look in his eyes, the feeling when his body let go. And yet he had failed. The police would figure it out. They already had their eye on him. They would put it all together. It was just a matter of time. All of it was a matter of time. Everything winding down on some unseen clock.

This is what he'd become: the thing hidden in the basement.

He stood there in the darkest part of the house until the world outside began to turn a faint shade of gray and then slowly come into focus. He wasn't tired anymore. He was awake. Everything swam in his vision.

John waited and then pulled his body upstairs and stared at the clock. Six in the morning. He didn't change clothes. He just put on his boots and a hat and walked out into the pale, chilly morning, started his truck and drove to work, passing the For Sale signs that littered the neighborhood, the campaign posters stuck into the ground, the police tape lying limp on the grass. The world moved around him, but it did not matter. There was only one world, his world. His was the only mind that could contemplate it. *Everybody thinks different things,* he thought. *But we're trapped in our consciousness. The only world that exists is the one in our mind, fed by eyes, ears, mouth, skin. It is up to me to shape the world.*

He parked his truck at the Public Works station and walked inside, dragging his right leg behind him, sweating in the cold. He poured a coffee and a shot of vodka from a pint bottle in his jacket. He sat in the break room and waited for the others. Something was happening. He could feel it in his bones. He needed to not think. He needed to work. He needed to fill holes with black tar asphalt.

When the others filed in to get their assignments, he said nothing. Roy eyed him from across the room. His supervisor, Mitch, asked to see him in his office and John rose and followed him down the hall. John slumped into the chair beside Mitch's desk to ease the weight off his leg and Mitch shut the door and stared at him.

"I'm going to need you to take a breathalyzer test," Mitch said. "You reek. If you like, we can call the union rep, but I'm not letting you out there until I know you're okay to go."

John stared at him. "I'm fine."

"You can't even hear yourself," Mitch said. "You don't even sound right. When did you stop drinking last night?"

"Last night?"

"For fuck's sake, John."

"For fuck's sake, John," he repeated.

"I'm calling the state trooper and having them come down here to check you out."

"Why?"

"Are you not following this? Are you on something? Is this some kind of medical emergency?"

"Medical emergency?"

Mitch stared at him a moment. "Look, John, just go home. I can't have you here like this. We'll call it a sick day or something, but get your shit together."

"I can work," he said.

"No. You can't. Did you sleep at all?"

"I don't know."

"I'll have one of the guys drive you back."

"No. Just let me stay here."

"I can't have that. I can't have you sleeping off a bender here. This is a fucking workplace."

John stood up, towering over Mitch. "Fine, I'll leave."

"Be here tomorrow with your shit together. This happens again and I'm moving for suspension and treatment and all that shit, do you understand?"

John said nothing and walked out the door and outside to his truck. He stared at the steering wheel and dashboard for a while. Everything seemed in the wrong place. His arms and hands felt awkward trying to grip the steering wheel and shift gears. He drove down the middle of the access road. Jessica was off work today and he couldn't go back home. Not yet. He didn't want to face her like this. He needed peace for a moment. He turned into a secluded town park. It was up a small, steep hill that ended in a parking lot with a field and light breaking through trees and a small, rusting playground. This early in the morning, the lot was empty. He parked his truck and laid his seat back and shut his eyes.

★   ★   ★

John woke to the sound of a car door slamming shut. He didn't know where he was at first. There was a car parked in the lot and a woman was getting out, dressed in hiking gear. John watched and she walked out into the field, down a slope and disappeared into the trees. He looked at the time; almost eleven in the morning. He remembered the talk with Mitch, and a deep shame overtook him. His stomach suddenly twisted with the fear that he could lose his job over this. *You have to get your shit together,* he thought. He didn't know how that was possible.

He needed to be home. He needed to sleep in a bed. It had been so long. He didn't care if Jessica was there. He would tell her they were overstaffed that day and he was cut. He would tell her he wasn't feeling well and had to sleep. All he wanted right now was to sleep long and deep and then, when he woke, he would be clear, he would be able to think, to see. Everything was a haze and he felt crowded, hot and close as if he were being pushed along by a thronging mob of people.

He started the truck. The radio came on. The talk show host screamed through the airwaves. He left the town park and took Route 4 toward Leadmine and turned right. He felt an anxiety in his stomach the closer he came to Ridgewood Drive. He kept checking the clock, as if it might suddenly jump ahead six hours.

There was a red car in the driveway, gleaming in the sun. He stared at it for a moment from the road and then looked up at the windows of his house. John parked his truck right behind the red car and got out. He limped to the front door and turned the knob. It was unlocked, open to the world. He walked inside and stopped and listened. He could hear her upstairs. He could hear her moaning, her voice jumping in ecstatic bursts. He could hear the sound of weight being thrust on the bed. The whole house was alive with it, a life he hadn't felt in years. John looked up the staircase toward their master bedroom. The door was closed. He thought about their wedding day, all the hope and expectation. He thought about the way she looked when he was on top of her, the way her eyes closed and her neck arched back. He thought about Caitlin and James.

John walked back out to his truck. He didn't feel the pain in his leg anymore. He didn't feel anything. He sat in the front seat behind the steering wheel and waited. He was so tired. He waited and he thought without thinking. His mind could not land on any single idea; it all just swirled like a hurricane and built up and then left him with nothing more than a whimper of a phrase, a feeling of deep, wretched darkness. He heard a song playing somewhere in his mind. He saw Lucas's eyes, bulging, staring into his own as his pale face turned red and then purple. He saw the body of a young boy, hollowed out, lying flat on the ash heap of another life. He saw his children crying for him, wondering where he'd gone and why he'd left them. He saw a sad, lonely life, living out of a room somewhere no bigger than a walk-in closet. It was all being taken from him piece by piece, bit by bit, until it was all gone. There was no future for him anymore.

Now there was an invader in his bed, the bed he hadn't slept in for months and couldn't sleep in now even though he was tired. She had been setting him up. She had been planning and plotting and fucking her way into a new life without him. No wonder she didn't care when he told her of his fears; no wonder her cold, clinical demeanor, her unwillingness to offer kindness in his most desperate moments. She was already gone with this man and now that man was here to take her and his children away, to kidnap them. His children, his home, his wife; this life was all he had and it was all being stolen right out from under him. He had prepared for so many threats, spent so much time focused on Lucas, that he didn't see the real threat right under his nose. They were conspiring to kill him, to leave him with nothing, this whole time.

He thought of Roy that night when they sat in the truck together. The way his eyes looked when Roy stared at him and told him to hold tight to his family, so full of desperation and loneliness and hurt; the way Roy sounded when he said he couldn't see his kids because the government made him stay away. *They're trying to eliminate men like us. What's so wrong with me?*

He remembered sitting beside Amber at the block party: *Do you ever see a red car at your house?*

He knew no one considered him a particularly smart man, but he always believed he was actually smarter than them all. Now, he felt so stunningly stupid. The whole neighborhood had been watching. If Amber knew, then Mark and Maryanne knew; the Carters knew; Dale and Becky and Jim and Julie and probably even the Lovetts. They all knew and yet they said nothing. They simply watched as his life was slowly, methodically torn apart. They patted him on the shoulder, made him head of the Neighborhood Watch, and hoped he would continue to ignore the knife placed deeply in his back, bleeding him dry.

Now a stranger was here to steal his wife, his children, his home and his dignity. It wasn't Lucas or the government or the media or the managers at his job. Instead it was his own wife and neighbors. They were humiliating him. They had been humiliating him since day one. Laughing at him, ignoring him, letting him swirl in the depths of sadness and depression and impotence while engineering the whole thing. They thought they could get away with it because they thought he was a stupid drunk, the ultimate sucker. She would divorce him, take the children, kick him out of his own house, force him to live in some shabby apartment somewhere alone eating out of cans, keep him working in the hot and cold, breaking his back to pay child support and alimony for the next decade.

In the end, he would be left with nothing. Everything he worked for meant nothing; those mornings when he woke early, stressed with how to cover the bills that month, meant nothing. All the good times – which she had since forgotten, but he clung to for survival – meant nothing. It would all be stripped down and sold for parts to pay lawyer fees.

And the betrayal. The way she looked at him that night and asked if there was something going on between him and Amber. She couldn't recognize the goodness in him, the fact that he could be caring and compassionate and a source of strength for another person. She had rejected all that he was, they all had. The entire world had written him off. Just another big, dumb man in a hard hat and neon-colored vest filling the potholes so your car won't bottom out. His leg ached more than ever now, and his head was so hot, like he was burning alive.

But they underestimated his strength. They didn't think what would happen if he decided to rise up. They didn't realize he could take a battle-axe to whole world and make them all pay. He could do that. He was stronger than they knew.

John got out of the truck, reached into the back of the cab and took out the shotgun. He chambered a shell and walked back inside. It was quiet now. The moaning was gone but the house still felt electric with it. He walked slowly, quietly up the stairs. He opened the door to his room. A man stood there in slacks and no shirt. John didn't recognize him. He was pale and lithe, with a full head of dark, shaggy hair and brown eyes. The door to the bathroom was open and the shower was running. He appeared educated, effeminate even. He looked at John for a moment directly in the eyes and stood dead still, shirt in hand, surprise and nervous guilt in his eyes, and then he saw the gun and, in that instant, he knew.

The man opened his mouth to speak and John shot him in the face and there was a crack of sound and a pale red mist and the man's face was gone and he was on the floor and his body shook in spasms. John's ears rang, that old warning system, and his eyes watered with smoke and the song kept playing in his head.

This is a test of the emergency broadcast system....

Jessica appeared in the doorway of the bathroom, water dripping down her naked body, tense with fear and shock like an animal poised to run. Looking on her in that moment, he noted how sexless she appeared, nothing more than awkward moving body parts devoid of any interest to him, no different than if a naked man stood there, a child or even an animal. She opened her mouth to scream but nothing came out. Or maybe she did scream, he couldn't tell. Her mouth was open and her eyes wide and her hands near her face and John was saying something to her, although he didn't remember what, but she wouldn't look at him, she wouldn't listen. She moved toward the faceless body on the ground, and John shot her through the stomach and her small body folded, skin pulling apart like putty, and she dropped to the ground as if pulled by an anchor.

John walked around the body on the floor. His boots forced blood up from the carpeting. He picked Jessica up and laid her on the bed. Her mouth opening and closing, gasping like a fish out of water, blue eyes wide open staring into God-knows-what. He stood over her a moment, watching, and then crawled into bed beside her and shut his eyes. He just needed time with his wife. The kids would be home soon. He had till then, at least.

His phone buzzed, text messages from the Neighborhood Watch: *Did anyone hear that?*

★   ★   ★

Joe and Vinnie both stayed home from work and school because they weren't feeling well. Amber called the school and Joe's job and told them both that the boys were ill and, knowing the terrible tragedy that had just befallen the family, each administrative assistant listened intently and with compassion. Amber figured it would be a busy day ahead, trying to keep the house clean and tend to their needs, but she put on a fine sundress and apron and did her makeup so she could properly fulfill her duties as wife and mother. She began by ensuring they were well rested, cutting the wifi from the house and removing their cell phones so they wouldn't be distracted.

Joe tried to stand from the bed and walk to the bathroom but he just stumbled and fell like he'd had too much to drink and then vomited on the floor and kept shaking as if he were cold. His teeth chattered so loud she could hear them and he lay in a fetal position saying, "I think I have to go to the hospital," and she said that was ridiculous, it was just a stomach bug and he should toughen up a little.

"It's this twenty-four-hour thing that's been going around," she said. "The women in the PTA have been talking about it for a month."

That was the beauty of institutions like the PTA: there was always talk of some illness 'going around', no matter what time of year, and it was always the perfect excuse for getting out of anything, particularly PTA meetings.

She tried to help Joe back into bed, but he was practically stiff on the floor, shaking and trembling and sweating, arms wrapped around his midsection.

"I don't know what's happening to me," he said.

"You'll be fine, dear, just get some rest. I'll bring you some medicine to help calm your stomach."

On her way to the kitchen, she stopped and mopped up vomit in the hallway where Vinnie hadn't made it to the bathroom in time. The whole house smelled of vomit, but it didn't affect her. Fifteen years of motherhood had immunized her to such stomach-churning smells and sights. She should have purchased more paper towel rolls and might have to make a quick trip.

She opened the door to Vinnie's room and sat beside him on his bed. He was trembling and shaking and said, "Mom? What's happening to me?" His voice was slurred and slow like he'd raided the liquor cabinet again.

And she said, "Nothing out of the ordinary. It's just a stomach bug, sweetie." He cried out in pain and she said, "Shhhh…it will all be okay," and placed her hand on his head to check for fever. "Hmmm…. You don't feel like you're hot. You're not faking to get out of a test, are you?"

She smiled and he glared up at her, terrified.

"Don't worry, I'll bring you some medicine to help calm your stomach."

"The wifi's not working," he said. He could barely get the words out, garbled and disjointed, beneath a wheeze in his chest. "Where's my phone?" His eyes were rolling back slightly. "I need to call for help," he slurred.

"Well, the last time you called for help, you told the police I had stolen your phone and we ended up with an embarrassing visit. Wouldn't want that happening again, would we? And then, of course, you probably got your brother killed. So maybe the phone isn't really what you need at the moment."

"I think I'm dying," he said.

"Nonsense," she said. "Just a touch of the flu. It's going around, you know."

She bent and picked up the small bucket of vomit beside Vinnie's bed, took it to the bathroom and flushed it. She went to the kitchen, reached into a cabinet and took down a measuring cup from a bright pink bottle of Pepto-Bismol, and then reached into the cabinet beneath the sink and took out a bottle of antifreeze, pushing aside the rat poison, and poured it into the measuring cup until it was full. It looked like bright green oil and she took it to her husband. He had crawled to the master bathroom and now lay there on the floor still trembling like a child. She reached down and put the cup to his lips and told him to drink it down. He didn't even open his eyes to see. They trusted in her and she would take care of them because that was her only purpose, to care for them, to be sure they met their full potential, no matter what. Nothing else mattered. Not the pieces of her life and dignity left in their wake, not the loss of the one true innocent in all of this; not her personal needs and desires. She was a good wife who put it all aside for them.

She went back to the kitchen, refilled the measuring cup and brought it to Vinnie, who said, "What is this?" and she said, "They make such pretty colors and flavors these days," and he drank it down and sipped a glass of water and fell back onto his bed and clutched his stomach. She walked out and shut the door behind her so she wouldn't have to hear the retching.

The boys had taken ill pretty soon after the dogs had died and there was much to do. She kicked off her heels and put on her gym sneakers. Helmutt's body was still in the laundry room – which was going to require an entirely new deep cleaning – and Otto's body was beside the sliding glass door where he had smacked his head and then panted his last breaths. The stains in the carpet around his body were deep and dark and she was in serious doubt as to whether the carpet could be saved, which would be tragic as it was a fine Berber they had installed just three years ago.

Amber slid the door open, took Otto by the front paws and began to pull. He was already stiff and they were big dogs, probably eighty pounds, and she had to put her legs and back into it. She thought of the gym and all the work she put in to stay shapely and how useful her strength training turned out to be.

She dragged him in starts and stops across the backyard and into the trees where the dogs liked to disappear at night and then return with pieces of her body in their jaws. She returned to the house and then took Helmutt by the paws and dragged him from the laundry room, down the step into the living room and then onto the carpet, and out into the trees.

The neighborhood was quiet this morning and there was no one around; everyone had either abandoned ship or were hunkered down after the death of her boy.

Amber spent some time on her hands and knees scrubbing at the stains in the carpet. She moved on to the laundry room with a mop and ample disinfectant. Chores kept the house nice and tidy and kept her active. She made herself a pot of coffee and added a touch of Amaretto, just to take the edge off. She deserved it. It was a hard day, but she kept her cheer. She made herself a sandwich and ate while sitting at the kitchen island. Joe appeared in the hallway, falling, stumbling against the walls, trying to make his way toward her. He was saying something about the hospital again, as far as she could tell, but his speech was so slurred it was hard to make out.

He took another step toward her and then fell onto the tile of the kitchen floor, curled in pain, crying out and sweating. He was breathing so fast, it was as if he'd just run a sprint and she thought that maybe if he had just stayed in better shape like she had he might be doing better. He had something in his hand and she realized it was a handgun, the one from the small pistol safe he kept in the bedroom. He was grumbling and growling and trying to straighten his neck out to look at her, trying to raise his hand.

"Oh my," she said. She walked over to him and took the gun away, and he was staring at her, eyes bulging and filled with rage and he was gurgling "bitch" over and over at her.

"Honey, you're out of your mind. Don't take this out on me, we've all been through enough already."

He rolled onto his back trying to catch his breath, chest rising and falling with increasing rapidity, hands useless at his sides.

Amber heard two sounds like fireworks from somewhere down the road and her phone started buzzing again with Neighborhood Watch updates. It was Maryanne, such a Nervous Nelly. She said she heard screams, that she was calling the police. Amber went to the front door and looked down the street. She saw John's truck in the driveway parked behind the red car she'd seen there so often when John was at work.

Amber looked at the messages but wrote back nothing. She saw no sign of activity, she heard no screams, nothing out of the ordinary. She had seen the driver of the red car only once as he had walked quickly to the front door and been greeted by Jessica Ballard. He was a tall, handsome, well-off-looking man. Of course, there was little doubt amongst herself or any of the neighbors what was going on, but she had always felt bad for John. She had hinted it to him, but he wasn't adept at putting puzzle pieces together. Truthfully, she thought he was too lost in his own head to actually see the truth before him; he fought to maintain a facade that he himself was actively tearing down.

John was a man at war with himself, she had finally decided, and in that way he felt like a kindred spirit. But she knew it could never be maintained for long. Seeing his truck parked behind the red car at his home meant that perhaps the real war was about to begin. Truthfully, she reveled in it and hoped that John would finally be satisfied, would get his due from the world. What he had done after Tommy had been found made him a hero to her, even if Lucas was somehow still alive.

The poor man, what a terrible way to find out. But really, it wasn't her place to say anything. Families have to work these things out on their own.

She heard a noise from down the hall and saw Vinnie crawling out from his dark room, pulling himself along the hallway floor, trying to reach his father and calling her name. She watched as he struggled to pull himself along, messy, curly hair that she used to love when he was a child flopping wet with sweat into his eyes. He made this god-awful sound over and over again that wore on her nerves.

He stopped when he reached his father and laid an arm over his chest, his head on Joe's shoulder. It was nice, she thought, to see them like that, to see them getting along, that a son would reach for his father in his last moments.

Joe was silent now, face up on the floor, breathing slower and slower, his eyes open, staring into the ceiling plaster. She wondered what he was seeing right then. She wondered if his life reeled through his mind. Or maybe he was seeing God the way Tommy had seen the God who gutted him, or perhaps a swirling mass of colors like grocery store shelves. She had no idea, really. Everyone ultimately dies alone. It's a personal thing. But still, it was nice that they had reached each other. Family is all you have.

"Help. Mom," Vinnie said.

She leaned down and brushed the hair from his face and looked into his bloodshot eyes and said, "Honey, I've been helping this whole time. You just didn't realize it."

★　　★　　★

John stared into Jessica's pale eyes and she stared back into his. Her hand reached up to gently hold his face. She whispered that she loved him, needed him. Her eyes were open. They watched him. He touched her face and it was cold and stiff. The bed was wet and stained and there was a smell of meat and rotting earth.

There was knocking at the door, loud, insistent, heavy-handed. John, startled, looked out the window beside their bed and saw a state police cruiser parked on the road. He just wanted to be alone with his wife. There was no future. He knew where this would lead. He knew there was no way out. They were here for the taking. To take his children, to take his home, to take his freedom. As if they hadn't taken enough from him already. He just wanted time.

White sacks piled beneath a streetlight. The abandoned house in silhouette beneath a pale, blood-red sky.

He would do one great thing. He would save his family, his home and his pride. He would be remembered as a man who stood up, who put his stake in the ground and said this is mine and you can't take it from me. They all had it coming, anyway.

He got out of bed and took the shotgun with him. He walked down the stairs in his boots and leaned the shotgun against the wall behind the door. He peered out the side window and then opened the door.

Officer Badgely stood, hand on his hip near his gun, turned slightly to the side, as if ready to cut and run or draw and shoot.

"What is it now?" John said.

"We got a call of a possible disturbance coming from this house," Badgely said.

John made a show of looking around. "Nah. Nothing going on here."

"Did you hear anything out of the ordinary?"

"No. Who called?"

"Just concerned neighbors. Thought they heard a gunshot and screaming."

"We hear gunshots around here all the time. People hunt just up on that ridge and it echoes."

"This must have been a little out of the ordinary then," Badgely said.

"I don't recall hearing any screams."

"Whose car is this in the driveway?"

"Not really sure. Why?"

"There's a car in your driveway and you don't know who it belongs to?"

"I think a friend of my wife's," John said. "Why?"

"No reason, really. Is your wife home, Mr. Ballard? We received reports of a woman screaming."

John stared at him a moment. "Yeah, she's upstairs in the shower."

"Is she okay?"

"As far as I know."

"Did you two have a fight this morning?"

"Not that I can recall."

"I'd like to have a word with Jessica, if I could," Badgely said.

John shrugged, stepped aside and held the door open. "Come on in if you like. She'll be down in a minute."

Badgely looked at him a moment and then seemed to relax. They had enough history together that, despite being at odds, there was a certain friendliness about it. Badgely saw him as a big, dumb lug, not a threat. He said, "Yeah, okay," and walked past John into the house. Badgely took a few steps past the staircase leading to the bedrooms and in toward the dining room table when he suddenly stopped and looked the place up and down.

"I don't hear any water running," he said.

"She must be finishing up."

John waited until Badgely turned to face him and then shot him in the chest. A window shattered behind him from the scatter shot and Badgely fell onto his back. John watched him on the ground for a moment. Badgely had worn a vest. He was still alive, but he was bleeding from the neck, grabbing his throat, trying to grab his gun and kicking his legs. His eyes were wide but it was no use. His boots slipped on blood and his hands couldn't grasp anything but the hole in his neck.

John stood over him and fired another shot into his face and then he was dead. His eyes were still open but they weren't in the right places anymore.

The kids would be home any minute.

It wouldn't be long now.

CHAPTER TWENTY-SEVEN

John wrapped his wife in a white bedsheet stained red and placed her on the floor. He took another sheet and wrapped the faceless man and left them lying together in the bedroom. He packed some of his clothes from the closet into a bag, left the room and locked it behind him. He took another sheet from his daughter's room and wrapped Badgely, dragged him to the basement door and rolled him down the stairs into the dark. A wind flowed through the broken window where the shotgun pellet had gone through Badgely's neck and then through the glass. He checked the time. The kids would be off the bus any moment and he needed to meet them at the stop so they wouldn't walk inside. He took some luggage to their rooms and emptied their drawers of clothes and took the bags downstairs and put them in the back of Jessica's small SUV in the garage. His truck wouldn't hold the kids for a long drive.

John walked out of the house and up the street to the stop sign where Ridgewood and Beechwood met. He heard the diesel engine of the bus in the distance and then it appeared beneath the canopy of trees on Beechwood and rolled to a stop. A few kids John vaguely recognized got off and made their way up the street, backpacks sagging from their shoulders. Caitlin and James jumped from the bottom step, ran up and hugged him and said, "What are you doing here?" and he told them he got off work early and that they were going on a special vacation.

"What about school?"

"School will be fine. Don't worry. This is a special trip. Just you guys and me."

"What about Mama?"

"Mama is spending time with a friend, but don't worry, we're going to have a great time. I've got all your bags packed and we're going to leave real soon."

"Where are we going? Will it have a pool?"

"I'll make sure it has a pool," he said.

"What's on your clothes?"

John looked down. The right leg of his jeans was soaked through with blood and it had turned a deep shade of brown, nearly black. And there were spatters of blood on his shirt. He hadn't even noticed.

"I was just working on my truck. It has an oil leak," he said and then they walked toward the house.

Mark from across the street, wearing his typical brown camouflage hunting jacket, walked across his yard to meet them in the road.

"Hey, John," he said. "Everything all right over there? Trooper's car has been there a while."

"Of course," John said. "He's just in there talking to Jessica."

"Mind if I ask about what?"

"Just follow-up for the investigation into Tommy," John said. "Say, is Maryanne home?"

Mark looked at him funny.

"Well, yes, she is. She thought she heard screaming and gunshots. She actually called the police, thought something was wrong. Could you ask the officer to come out and speak with me, please?"

"Sure thing, Mark," John said. "Let me just get the little guys here inside and I'll let him know you're looking to talk to him."

John took his son and daughter to the garage door, opened it and then closed it behind them. He opened the door to the car and sat them in the back seat and had them put on their seatbelts.

"Now listen to me very carefully," he said. "I want you to sit here and listen to the radio and do not, for any reason at all, come out of the garage until I come get you. I have to do a couple things and it will ruin the surprise, okay?"

"Okay, Daddy."

"Good," he said and reached in the driver's side, put the keys in the ignition, started the car and then turned up the radio. "I'll be right back," he said. "Remember, stay put, no matter what and listen to the music."

He walked inside the house and locked the door to the garage behind him. He went over to Trooper Badgely, unwrapped him, took his pistol and a couple magazines from his holster, and then wrapped him back up again. He put the pistol in his waistband beneath his shirt and then walked outside to meet Mark in the street.

Mark stood beside the police cruiser, looking in the windows. John walked up the yard and said, "He said he'll be out in just a minute," and Mark said, "Yeah, okay, I don't know if you saw the Neighborhood Watch texts but it really sounded like—"

"Have you seen this car parked in my driveway before?" John said.

Mark looked at him for a moment. He was uncomfortable. He shrugged. "Well.... Yeah. A few times, but...."

John took the pistol from his belt and shot him through the head. Mark's body dropped, crumpled at the side of the cruiser.

He heard a scream from across the street and John saw movement at the window. He walked across the street and kicked through the front door and Maryanne was screaming and crying and trying to dial her phone but she was shaking too badly. John smacked the phone from her hand and knocked her to the floor. He shot her twice through the chest. He stopped for a moment, breathed in the smoke and looked around at this sad little place, taking in all the furniture and pictures and decorations, suddenly puzzled by all of it.

He walked back out to the police cruiser, hefted Mark up off the ground and over his shoulder. The deadweight was surprisingly heavy, and he brought Mark back inside his house and dropped him next to Maryanne and then walked out and locked the door behind him. He walked back to the cruiser. He could hear the faint sound of sirens coming over the hills. *These fucking people,* he thought, *always calling the cops when they haven't done shit to protect us.*

John picked up a rock and smashed it through the driver's-side window of the police cruiser and looked inside. He popped the trunk and saw a case with a black military rifle and magazines loaded with rounds. It was the same type of black rifle he'd shot at Roy's house and he remembered its intricate workings, how to load it, how to chamber a round, how to flip the safety off. He remembered the thrill of pulling the trigger as fast as he could like an action movie hero. He took the rifle out of its case, loaded a magazine and grabbed a couple more. He thought of taking the kids and running now but the sirens were too close, coming in hot and fast, and he needed as much time as possible to get away. This was his chance to take it to all of them, to let them know that everything was not okay, that there would be hell to pay, and he was a man who would not be disrespected.

If they had just listened to him from the beginning, none of this would be happening. They would have actually searched for Lucas, rather than just waiting for him to turn up; that bitch Meredith Skye would have told the truth, and little Tommy Locke would still be alive. Maybe he and Jessica could have worked things out.

They lied, people died.

He'd heard that somewhere before, seen it during his swirling, drunken late-night internet searches. Once you choose a path, it's hard to stop or switch in the middle. They chose their path, now he chose his.

He waited, rifle in hand, crouched behind the cruiser. He thought of Roy and the other men at Roy's house. They probably would've never expected this from him. But that was fine. He would live eternally in their memories. He thought of firing round after round into the fake boar on Roy's property. He remembered the tears in Roy's eyes when he talked of losing his family.

A state police cruiser appeared on Ridgewood. He waited until it passed the abandoned house and opened fire.

★   ★   ★

The house was spotless again, but for a slight smell of vomit that lingered beneath the Pine-Sol. It had been such a busy day, an active day. A housewife's job was never done, it was an all-encompassing lifestyle and required dedication. She made herself a cup of coffee and, for a moment, took in the silence. Finally, it was quiet and clean and she was fully and truly alone with her thoughts.

After having thought it through a little more, she had placed another call to Vinnie's school to let them know he was ill and would not be attending class for several days, and another to Joe's job to let the scheduler know that Joe would be out for a couple days as well, indicating the illness was worse than previously thought and would require more time off. No one questioned a thing. The family had already suffered so much, who would they be to question her? Frankly, as soon as she gave her name on the phone there was a brief pause as the school nurse or the scheduler recognized who she was and realized that this was the woman whose son was murdered, the woman who hadn't spoken since it happened, the woman who was forever scarred. And then they said something along the lines of, "Of course, we'll take care of everything and I hope your family gets well soon," and so she would have the next couple days to herself and, after that, she wasn't sure. It didn't matter at the moment. This was her time and she wouldn't sully it by wasting her mind on what others thought. What did it truly matter to them where Joe and Vinnie were? They were her family and she was the only one to whom it mattered and she was fine. The rest of the world could go about its day, its life. No need to worry for her household.

She sat at the kitchen table and sipped her coffee and took in the stillness of her home. She looked at the floor where Joe and Vinnie had finally lain and gasped and stopped making such a racket. The hardwood floor shined with her careful disinfecting and polishing. The memory of their bodies intertwined in a last-minute embrace as they stared into eternal nothingness seemed only a dream that had lingered into daylight.

The rest of the day stretched out ahead of her. Amber was unsure what to do with herself. Freedom, it appeared, could be a bit confusing. The schedule of life she previously lived by was gone, but there remained an anxious feeling that she was on the clock, that jobs and tasks needed to be completed. She imagined it would take some time to reset her life, to remake it without concern for when Joe and Vinnie and Tommy had to get up for school or work, what they needed to eat and where they needed to be at specific times; she no longer had to worry about massive loads of laundry or cooking for four or dishes to be washed. She no longer had to worry about putting the dogs out or taking them back in when their barking was sure to irritate the neighbors. She decided that she would return to work this week. She would call her boss and tell him that she'd like to be put back on the schedule. It would be good for her, to have some place to go and something to do and she could use the money.

There were also some logistical issues: she would unenroll Vinnie from school later this week, tell them that the loss of his brother was too much (when clearly he seemed to be reveling in the attention) and she would compose a resignation email for Joe to send to his boss. Few questions would be asked. People would understand. The loss of a child was too much to bear and everyone needed a fresh start.

She sat on the back porch and let the cool autumn air touch her skin and the sun warm her insides and she laid her head against the back of the patio chair, felt herself melting into the plastic. She shut her eyes and watched sun spots.

She winced when she heard another loud crack and then listened as the familiar sound of the school bus rumbled through the neighborhood a short while later. Then two smaller pops that made her think of Joe and Vinnie. John had two young, beautiful children. Little James had often played with Tommy. He was a sweet young boy. And John's daughter, Caitlin, was a smart, responsible girl who always seemed to want to help with everything. A little worker, that one.

Then there were sirens in the air, wailing, echoing all over town, and then came bursts of gunfire like she'd never heard before, fast and sharp and popping over and over again. A seemingly endless cacophony of sound that threatened to beat in her eardrums. She went back inside and walked to the front window and looked toward John's house. The road was blocked off by fire engines and police cars. She could see police officers, state troopers, firemen crouched, hiding behind the protection of their vehicles. She could hear more shots. They sounded so close.

A heavy hand banged at her door, a deep and desperate voice yelling it was the state troopers. She opened the door and the trooper, decked out in a black, bulky bulletproof vest, was crouched on the ground, gun in hand. He pulled her into the house and told her, "Get down! Get your head down!" and now he was inside her house, crouched on the ground with her.

"Is there anyone else in the house?" His voice was loud, trying to reach her over the chaos of sound outside. His eyes wide and bright blue, intense and glassy. He gripped her arm to keep her from moving or standing up.

"No one else is here," she said.

"Do you have a basement?"

"Yes."

"Where?"

She pointed to the door in the hallway leading to their unfinished concrete basement.

"Get into the basement and lock the door. Stay down there until we come for you. We can't evacuate, it's too hot. This is an active shooter situation!"

He motioned for her to go to the basement door and stay low. He watched as she crawled on hands and knees to the door and opened it and slipped inside into the dark. The trooper girded himself, took his handgun in both hands and crept quickly and quietly back out the front door, shutting it behind him.

She stood at the top of the basement stairs and looked into the darkness below. The scent of Pine-Sol was gone and there was a fog of illness and death. She flipped the light switch for the basement. Joe and Vinnie were crumpled together at the bottom of the stairs.

Vinnie had fallen on top of his father, back and head against the basement wall, cloudy eyes open, staring at her, watching her. She walked down the steps to join them.

★　　★　　★

The funny thing with life-changing events is they seem to begin on perfectly normal days and then nothing is normal again, but when

Elizabeth looked back on those events – the end of her marriage, the murder of Tommy Locke, the scandal of Antwone Diller's death – she saw that nothing had really been normal leading up to them. It had all been brewing beneath the surface until finally a crack in the Earth's crust allowed it to swallow you whole. Or maybe that's the definition of normal: the silencing of tectonic forces until one day the Earth shakes. Elizabeth had felt earthquakes before. Nothing like the big ones that destroy buildings and roads and leave a city in rubble, but the minor East Coast quakes that sound like distant explosions. She recalled one morning being woken from sleep as if someone had just jostled her, only to find the room empty and a deep echo fading in her mind. She had stood out of bed confused, wondering what happened, whether a car had somehow driven into the side of her house or perhaps a massive tree had fallen in the backyard, but there was nothing. She was left with only a confused, deep feeling of insecurity that something big had happened and her four walls were not enough to protect her. It wasn't until several hours later that she and the rest of the world learned it was an earthquake.

The first thing she heard, just around noon, was what sounded like two fireworks going off nearby. Not the small, fun bottle rockets kids light off during the summer months but rather these big, fast cracks of explosion that made her think somebody's mailbox had just been detonated with cherry bombs. The text messages started coming from the Neighborhood Watch, questions, speculation, explanation – *Did hunting season start yet? That sounded really close! Sounded like Ridgewood Drive.* The mention of her street in particular gave her pause.

She went to the front door and looked outside, up and down the street, but saw nothing out of the ordinary. It was a bright, sunny day. The air was cool and still. There was nothing but the fading sound in her mind. She looked down the street and all looked normal, save for John Ballard's truck parked behind a red car she did not recognize in his driveway. But then, maybe he was home from work early, maybe he'd taken the day off, maybe they had company in from out of town. She wasn't even sure what she was looking for. One would think if it were gunshots, people would be running or screaming or there would be police sirens, but there was nothing but peace and silence.

Elizabeth returned to her computer, where she'd been composing more press statements lambasting Andrew Whitcomb as a fear-mongering opportunist capitalizing on tragedy. October was quickly approaching, the final month before the election, and she was scrambling to pull ahead. She had lost her substantive lead, the polls had them nearly even. That could be changed. She was out there now, she was fighting back, she would prevail as she had done her entire life. Now was not the time for cowardice. She would not run from this fight.

Elizabeth was sequestered in her office, monitoring her campaign's social media feed, when she heard another loud explosion muffled by distance. The text messages started coming through again and now she felt nervous, wondering what in the hell was going on out there. She walked again to the front door and peered down the street. There was a state police cruiser parked outside the Ballards' home. She walked back inside and sat down on the couch near the bay window where she could see down the street. She saw John Ballard walk out from the garage looking dirty as ever in stained clothes and go to the bus stop. She watched the children get off the bus and walk, hand-in-hand, with their father. The school bus passed by her house and she watched it go and heard the heavy diesel engine fade into the distance. She saw Maryanne's husband from across the street talk to John. It all seemed pleasant and fine, the mysterious explosions would remain just that. Although the police cruiser was still there, she had yet to see the trooper, but the presence of the police reassured her that all was being handled by the proper authorities.

She saw Mark standing near the trooper's car, seemingly waiting for something. John walked out of the house and said a few words to him. Then she saw John pull something black from his waistband and there was a small crack and Mark fell to the road. For a moment, Elizabeth had no idea what was happening. She saw Mark lying on the pavement, she saw John walk across the street and out of view. She heard two more cracks and it was only then she realized she had just witnessed the murder of someone she knew by another person she knew and somehow it seemed so ordinary. It was so instantaneous, so undramatic, that she kept running it through her mind to be sure it was real and then, when she was sure, she began trembling and ran from the window and called the police.

She could hear them coming now, closer through the trees, winding through the back roads. She was crying, but wasn't aware of it. It was just tears streaming down her cheeks absent any real thoughts. She wasn't sad or angry. She felt nothing, but there they were. She heard the first police car roar past her house, sirens blazing, and then it sounded like the world exploded. She heard more gunfire. So fast this time that she fell to the floor to protect herself. She heard the sound of a collision, metal slamming into an immovable object, and all the electricity in her house was suddenly gone. There were more sirens coming over the hills, more shots ringing out. The whole neighborhood was a war zone.

Somewhere in her house glass shattered and drywall turned to dust and she screamed.

The shots kept coming, pieces of her walls were falling apart and it dawned on her that he was shooting into her house. He was trying to kill her. He was trying to kill everyone. And the shots felt closer and the bullets were so fast, there and gone, before she even heard the shot.

Elizabeth waited, huddled on the floor, heart pounding. There were more shots, but this time they sounded far off and nothing pierced her house and she thought he must have changed directions. She felt a moment of opportunity to run and before she could fully think it through she ran for her keys and then to the garage. She started the car, and waited an agonizing ten seconds while the garage door shuddered to life and opened to daylight. She heard more shots, closer now. The sirens were gone and she felt abandoned. She put her car in gear and sped out of the garage, spinning the wheel out of her driveway toward Leadmine Brook, ducking her head so that she could just barely see the road. She heard shots again, a sound like rocks pelting the back of her car and the rear window shattered.

She let out a scream no one but herself could hear and cut the wheel left onto Leadmine, her car bouncing over the curb and tearing through her own lawn until she was back on the road and speeding, driving faster than she had ever driven before.

It wasn't fast enough; it would never be fast enough to outrun the bullets. She glanced in the rearview mirror for a moment and saw him walking up the street, rifle leveled directly at her before he disappeared from view behind the trees.

She looked from the rearview mirror down to the road ahead, and she could see the lights, a veritable wall of police cars and fire engines in front of her.

More guns, pointed directly at her head.

CHAPTER TWENTY-EIGHT

John couldn't hear the shots coming at him. There was no more ringing in his ears. It was like there was a wall between himself and the world. He had only his sight and the knowledge they were all out to kill him. He didn't even feel the first bullet, didn't notice it until he saw the blood on his hand and on the street. There was a wall of fire trucks and police cars at the corner of Ridgewood and Beechwood and he would occasionally see movement in the trees or behind the vehicles and he would open up with more fire and they would stop moving. He wasn't sure where the bullet came from. He turned the rifle back toward Leadmine but saw nothing there, no cops, no fire engines. It was strangely silent on that end of the street. He crouched behind his truck and took aim again. There was no other choice but to fight now. It had all come down to this. This would be his stand, this would be where he showed the world what it meant to laugh him off, to ignore him, to tell him he didn't know the truth. He reloaded the rifle with the last magazine. John rose and fired five more rounds. He wasn't even aiming. The rifle was his voice, the shots his primal scream. He'd get them to back off, then rush into the house, get into Jessica's SUV with the kids and drive as fast as he could out of there. He didn't know where he would go, but it didn't matter. He just needed that time with his children, time to tell them he loved them and he was trying to protect them as they drove into an unknown future. He pictured it in his mind: blue skies, the quiet of the road, passing by trees and houses as they ducked away from the chaos and danger of this life and barreled toward a new one. Things would be better in the end.

His side was bleeding and starting to cramp. It was like a pressure bulging out from his insides, a fire creeping toward his heart. He couldn't feel the fiery pain of infection in his leg anymore. His head felt hot, his vision blurry like a fever. He let off a few more rounds and then felt something slam into his back and white sparks flashed before his eyes. He spun against the side of his truck and fell to the ground.

He could see them now: movement up the street toward Leadmine. They were trying to pull a fast one, distracting him on one side while quietly creeping up from the other. He reached his hand to his back and felt a hole, warm and wet. He saw a black-garbed figure move behind a tree on the Lovetts' front yard. He raised the rifle and sent off a volley of shots, watched as the figure ducked back behind the tree and froze. In that moment it felt like a game, something he and his friends played in the summer when he was a child, ducking behind trees, pretending to shoot at each other with plastic toy guns and then arguing over who was dead and who was alive. It occurred to him for a moment that they were all like kids on the playground, children in oversized bodies, playing cops and robbers, cowboys and Indians.

"I got you!" he shouted, but he couldn't hear his own voice. "You're dead! I got you!" He fired off another three shots toward the Lovett house and then felt something punch his chest. He didn't know where it came from. He didn't see anything or hear anything. It was just fire now creeping throughout his whole body.

John tried to move but it was hard. He was breathing heavy like he'd just made a hundred-yard dash. Sweat poured down his face and his vision was strange; everything was so far away. He looked to the front door of his house. His arms had fallen to his sides and the rifle was on the ground. His head rolled to the side and he stared down at it. There was a voice coming from somewhere far away, as if over a microphone, telling him to stay down, to not move. In the distance he saw figures creeping toward him, a small army of kids pointing toy guns in his direction.

But he was bigger than them, bigger than their tiny bullets and their pathetic orders. He could win this game still. John rolled to his hands and knees and began to crawl between his truck and the red car of Jessica's lover. He dragged the rifle with him and there was the sound of rocks striking the side of his truck and then he was safe between the two vehicles. He willed his arms to work and he picked up the rifle and fired more shots down the street. He didn't even look when he fired, couldn't bring his body to twist that way, but they all scattered and started firing back and glass shattered and fell on him in tiny pebbles of blue and white.

From where he sat he could see the husk of the abandoned Widner house. He stared at it for a time. He used to tell Caitlin and James it was haunted. He told them of ghosts that wandered its halls, not alive, but not yet dead, either. The past still haunted that place and then it haunted Lucas Lovett and then it haunted him. It hung like a specter over the whole neighborhood. It piled bodies in white sheets beneath the pale yellow streetlight.

He waited for a long time, for what felt like forever. He wasn't sure if it was forever or just a few seconds. Time had lost all meaning. He just kept breathing in and out. He held his gun tight to his chest. He stared at the front door to his house and thought he could make it the twenty feet or so inside, but every time he decided to make the run his body would not move, so he waited.

It was growing dark outside, which he found odd. How much time had passed? Where was he, exactly? Where were Caitlin and James? He couldn't remember anymore. It was an odd thing to forget, but it seemed to matter less and less as the sky turned dim and the air became cold. He slid onto his back and stared at the darkening sky and it was huge and deep. It was all he could see and he felt himself pulled upward toward it, into it, and beyond into space.

It became cold, very cold, and he shivered, but he kept watching. He wanted to watch it all, to see it unfold, to finally see the truth, this thing he had feared for so long.

The voice over the microphone spoke again, but it was so far away. He was in the stars now, traveling through dimensions to another place, somewhere far away.

He looked down from the sky and could see them all simultaneously, the living and the dead, strangers and neighbors, all the people watching this game play out till the end, streaming across airwaves and cable lines and wifi signals into computers and phones and televisions across the country.

Their eyes were wide. They were all watching him and, in these final moments, they did not look away.

★   ★   ★

Amber sat alone in the dark, dripping basement with the dead, and she could hear the shooting outside. Time disappeared and it seemed to last forever.

Beneath it all, she could hear the sound of whispering, two people locked in a heated conversation meant to be kept from her. She sat against the cold wall of a corner and could see them there, bodies intertwined and fused together, a monstrous stillbirth of conjoined twins. But she could still hear them talking down here. She could still hear their pleas and demands; she could hear them crying out in pain, choking on their own bile.

You betrayed us, murdered us, and for what?

They would never understand. There was no way to explain it to the dead.

She stared hard at them, looking to see their lips move, looking for a slight rise and fall of their chests to show they were still alive and breathing. Vinnie's pretty head stared up at the basement door; Joe's head lay beneath him, staring to the side, neck twisted at an impossible angle.

There were more gunshots outside, rapid fire now.

The whispers, the accusations, came louder and she tried to cover her ears but it did not block the sound of their voices. They grew louder and her head ached with it and she could no longer listen to their cries.

We loved you, they said. *We loved you and look what you've done to us.*

"You never loved me," she said.

You took everything from us.

"You took everything from me," she said. "We're all better off now."

Murderer, they whispered.

"You brought the murderer into this house and left me all alone!"

You will be with us here forever, they told her. *You can never escape us now.*

"I'll chop you up and bury you both!" she screamed.

Gunfire sounded through the walls.

Vinnie's head rolled to the side and his dead, blank eyes stared straight into her.

We can see so much from here, they said. *There is no past or present or future. We can see all. We are watching. We are God now.*

Your fate is sealed, they said. *It always has been.*

She heard footsteps across the living room floor upstairs, weight creaking the floorboards, pressing down, and the long, baleful sound of dogs howling in the night.

We are not alone in this place, they said. *There are so many just like us.*

She stared into Vinnie's eyes and, for a moment, she thought she saw him smile.

CHAPTER TWENTY-NINE

Elizabeth just kept driving. She didn't know what else to do. She had escaped the neighborhood, the place that had bred within her feelings of comfort and safety at one point and then fear and foreboding in the next. A place like so many others, where she wanted acceptance but found the process political and grueling and ultimately futile. Now it was littered with gunfire and death and horror. The whole block was a haunted house of sorts now, a place that when she thought of it – and she tried not to – stirred a deep, emotional uneasiness and fear. She would never return, but she had nowhere else to go.

The police had stopped her as she fled Ridgewood Drive and then moved her to safety behind the blockade of fire engines and ambulances and black, tank-like personnel carriers purchased from the military that could withstand a roadside bomb in Iraq. They didn't even question what she had seen or heard or done. They just told her to get out of the area as quickly as possible and find somewhere safe to stay for the night, but she couldn't think of anywhere to go and she had left her purse and wallet behind when she fled the house so she couldn't pay for a hotel room or even food, although she was not hungry. She had been under a hail of gunfire yet still felt stupid for forgetting such necessities.

Instead, she just drove. She had a full tank of gas. It was enough to get by, she supposed. But she was now adrift, homeless and aimless. She had her cell phone but couldn't think of whom to call and she suddenly realized just how alone in the world she really was. Even when she thought of someone she could call, it all seemed such an enormous burden to lay at their feet; the burden of telling the story, of explaining what had happened from beginning to end, the burden of Elizabeth Tutt, political pariah, a woman without a home.

The sky had turned from deep blue to green in the fading sun, and an unfathomable darkness grew out from the ridge of hills at the eastern horizon of the city and threatened to extinguish every light. She didn't listen to the radio. She could still hear the shattering of glass, the falling of sheetrock, the whine of bullets piercing her home. She didn't know what to make of it all and now wondered if she really knew anything at all. Her whole life had been nothing but posturing, posing, repeating things said by men and women for decades, if not centuries, but now done through the lens of a callous era of digital media where everyone was connected but no one was really connected at all. Nothing she had done was original or authentic, and she had done it through platforms that were, by their very nature, distortions of reality, phony and superficial to the point of pure fiction.

Somehow, seeing her neighbor gunned down in broad daylight and her being shot at was the most real, authentic thing she'd ever experienced. It left her in a daze, unable to speak her truth and with no one left who would listen anyway.

Then she thought about the faraway look in the eyes of children she would see when she door-knocked in the city, the ones who helped their mothers create wreaths and little memorials of candles, crosses and construction-paper posters placed at the sites where fathers, sons, brothers, cousins had been murdered. Her own constituents, bathed in reality – true reality – knew so much more than she, and yet she'd always wondered why they were so soft spoken, so quiet and hesitant. There was nothing to say in the face of it. There was nothing to do that would make it any better. Real life is nothing but a rampage killing, but we try to make little happy lives amidst the gunfire. Hope springs eternal in those moments between deaths.

Not knowing where to go, Elizabeth instead drove to places she knew. She drove to her old condominium where she and Alan had lived as a married couple for so many years. It was a quiet city street, lined with expensive brick buildings within walking distance of downtown and city hall, awash in streetlights and nice cars and security cameras. It all looked right out of a Hallmark movie. She stopped in front of her old condo and stared up at it. There was a light on in the living room and she could make out the shadow of people moving behind a curtain. She thought of Alan, of their life together. It hadn't been a Hallmark movie, but it was close enough. It was a happy little life and yet she had run from it as if it were burning her. Happy little lives grow boring. We desire strife and drama and life-or-death situations. When they don't come naturally, we make them up and find the perfect excuse to do so. And so she had. She'd had her affair knowing it would eventually come out and wreck her little life and send her on an emotional roller coaster that would, for all its ups and downs, create a thrill. And she went into politics where the high drama, the fame and admiration and hate would feed her, enthrall her, and yet, even in those moments, she had run away.

She thought of that last day door-knocking with Meghan when she'd fled the home of that man who was so angry at the things he had seen, at reality as she now knew it. She thought of when she ran from reporters when news broke that Antwone Diller had died in police custody. More reality – just not hers at the time. For so long, she'd been unable to face it in its entirety.

She drove to the community college where she'd worked and sat outside her old building to stare up at the classroom where she used to teach some of those very same kids who'd seen reality head-on from a young age and then wondered why she wasn't getting through to them, wondering why they weren't more interested in politics and history and getting an A for writing an essay about thoughts they'd never had from people they'd never met and none of which would matter one iota to their day-to-day survival.

She finally drove to the Democrats' campaign office. The lights were out and doors locked and she sat in the car in silence staring at the ridiculous posters in the windows, the marquee across the top, and she marveled at the charade of it all. The parking lot was empty and it was dark but for a distant streetlight. She rolled down the window and sat for a time breathing in the night air. This was the last place she could think to go and yet it seemed like she was staring at her own grave. Her life was divided into sections, each warring against the other to maintain its illusion, and this was the final resting place. She tried to bring the illusion back. She tried to tell herself that her life was meaningful, that she had accomplished things and influenced people, but reality kept creeping in. Had she died this day, had one of those bullets pierced her window and caught her in the head, she would be a flash in the news, a statistic, an easily replaceable, cheap political sign in the window of a strip mall.

'Let's Kick Tutt!' Yes, indeed.

A clinking of bells and whistles came from her phone, a call coming in from a number she did not recognize, and suddenly she felt compelled to answer, to hear another human voice. At this point, she could talk for hours on end with a telemarketer insistent that she switch cable companies.

"It's on fire!" the voice screamed when Elizabeth answered. "The Tree of Life! It's on fire! Someone lit it on fire!"

And there it was. The one thing she had brought to life, the real tangible thing that she had helped bring to the world was now burning.

"Who is this?" she said.

"This is Amy. Amy Salgado from the museum!"

"How is it on fire?"

"Someone's burning it!" she screamed again.

Elizabeth hung up the phone and started her car. The museum was on the other side of the city and she drove her Volvo with the same speed and intensity out from the strip mall parking lot as she had when she fled her own home earlier in the day. She took a left onto Pearl Street, gunned it down to the light, looking for oncoming traffic before taking the right and speeding toward the Interstate to get across town. She took the on-ramp at sixty and then onto the Interstate, which crossed above the depressed city in an elevated marvel of engineering where the tops of buildings lined the highway. She drove fast, her poor old car's engine straining, wind whistling through the bullet holes in the rear window. She wasn't sure why she drove so fast, why she needed to get there so badly. She knew there was nothing she could do, she knew the fire department would be there trying to put out the blaze, but she felt she needed to be there, the same as she needed to be at the Tree of Life's opening.

And she was angry. Furious, in fact, when it finally occurred to her. All of it, her whole life for the past three months, seemed to bleed into this moment, to turn it for her into a moment of truth and reckoning. She couldn't help but feel it was a personal attack. As if the universe hadn't given her enough, there was this one last insult, this last kick to the ribs when she was already beaten and on the ground. She would not just wait for the news to report it, she had to be there, she had to see for herself. The list of possible suspects and motives poured through her mind.

It was two miles to the exit and she sped past other cars in a frenzy. Her mind and body seemed to work as one with no conscious thought. Rather, she seemed to move on air, the same way she felt when she finally realized she had to flee her home or risk being killed.

The exit was upon her before she realized and she cut across three lanes of traffic to reach it, cars blaring their horns, slamming on brakes to avoid collision, the off-ramp with its blind curve sharply twisted into nearly a full circle that emptied out onto South Main Street, the museum just a mile up on the right, and she took it at high speed, the little station wagon leaning heavily to one side, threatening to tip over. And, as the off-ramp twisted toward South Main, there were suddenly people. People everywhere in the street, overflowing the intersection, hundreds of them, seemingly thousands, carrying signs and shouting at her and jumping from the road onto the median and screaming, and there were bodies thrown up over the hood of her car breaking her windshield or falling beneath, her tires kicking up, the car bouncing and rocking and her head and neck and spine jolting and something snapping beneath the wheels and she screamed and stomped on the brake and the car skidded into the intersection and stopped.

For a moment she sat in pure stillness. She didn't know what had happened and the image of a man being thrown over the hood of her car blared in her mind. She had the feeling of falling off a cliff, knowing there was nothing she could do now to turn back. She was at the mercy of something bigger, more powerful than her. Elizabeth stared at the lights on her dashboard for a moment, catching her breath. Somewhere down the street she could see an orange glow clouded in smoke rising up from the ground as if a portal to Hell had been opened. Red, white and blue lights flashed in strobe. She looked at her windshield, now with a crack in the shape of a star, and beyond it she could see throngs of people, closer and closer. She felt a million eyes on her, watching.

She saw a sign made from cardboard and a piece of lumber: *Justice for Antwone.*

For a moment, she took a breath and whispered to herself, "Oh, my God."

Elizabeth's door was open and she felt a rush of air and hands grabbing at her and then a fist across her face and another and another and she saw more stars and flashes of light. She didn't know where she was anymore or what was happening. She felt herself pulled from her car and she fell to the pavement and it was cold and slightly damp and there were more blows. She felt bones in her body breaking. She felt warmth dripping down over her face. She tried to get up and there was a boot to her face and she fell back again onto the hard ground. There were so many blows from every direction, a crowd of people all eager to punish her. She could feel the pressure of them but not the pain. Behind watering, closing eyes she could see their fists, but not their faces. She heard their screams and shouts but couldn't understand them.

She felt a boot hit her in the ribs and she was forced onto her side. Someone stomped on her hip and she felt part of her body go slack. Through a break in all the legs and bodies she could see a clear line cut through the crowd to the highway off-ramp littered with bodies, crumpled like bags of laundry on the street. She could see people standing over them, crying, shouting, cell phones in hand, trying to revive them, frantic jerky motions of a man pumping on a woman's chest, screaming at her to breathe. Somewhere a child was crying, screaming for his mother, as another woman huddled him in her arms and whisked him away.

It was an accident.

She couldn't tell if she said it out loud or just in her mind. There seemed little distinction. It all blurred together; mind and body, thought and reality. *I didn't mean to,* she said to no one and nothing. Then she felt something hard and metal strike her forehead, and she felt something collapse into mush and suddenly nothing seemed to matter at all.

She gazed upon the numbing truth; existence shed its veneer and revealed a monstrous, thronging body of violence. It was hers and hers alone to experience now. The crowd now left her, giving her body a wide berth. She lay on her back and it felt as if she were melting into the ground, the world growing farther away, and she stared up into the night sky.

She saw the Tree of Life burning, the black glass of its maze rippling like a stone tossed into a pond at night. She felt the heat scorch her skin and saw herself reach through the melting glass into an infinitude of worlds, of disembodied voices, of circuits like synapses that gave way to the great beyond, an abyss that crawled over her skin, moved up her arm and shoulder, enveloping her.

She saw the world as it truly was, hazy in smoke and fire, suffused with anger and fists and a billion open mouths screaming with a billion voices from all over the world calling for blood and sacrifice.

She heard the voices now.

We are God.

We are the one true world.

Aren't we glorious?

And then she was back in her home on Ridgewood Drive. It was late and dark outside, and she was alone, and she heard something knocking, quietly at first, and then louder, more insistent.

She rose from her chair and approached the front door.

She reached out a hand to open it.

CHAPTER THIRTY

Dorothy Trimble sat in her chair at the window and watched their bushy tails twitch and shake as they scrambled up and down the trees. *Such wonderful little creatures*, she thought. They chattered and chased, jumped and climbed, harvested and hoarded. She loved watching them from her little perch in her rocking chair.

Dotty. They used to call me Dotty when I was a little girl, she thought. She wasn't sure how she got here or where she was exactly, but she had a vague sense of it. It didn't matter, really, because she could watch these little creatures running about and that was all that mattered.

She called for Vernon, but he did not answer. She called again but this place was empty and hollow and so she merely sighed and continued to stare out the window. There was such a mess in the living room and Vernon had been asleep for days. But she shrugged it off. It would all take care of itself eventually. The poor boy could be lazy and forgetful at times but he would get to it. Sometimes she wondered what his life would look like after she was gone. He seemed so lonely. If only he would sit with her and watch the antics of these frenetic, chattering little creatures. He would see there was a whole world out there to enjoy and so many goings-on.

It wasn't just the squirrels she could see. At times, she would see a car or two go down the road. She would see men and women walking. Sometimes she would see a policeman milling about, their patrol car driving through. Other times she saw pretty young women holding microphones and standing in front of cameras.

It was all such a busy place, everyone chattering and chasing and harvesting and hoarding. They were fascinating creatures, really. Their tails twitched and they moved about with such a sense of purpose that it made her smile and laugh.

She caught sight of a black squirrel, skinny and small, running down the trunk of a tree in the front yard and skittering about, searching the yard, the grass, the driveway before running at full tilt back up the tree from where it came, something in its tiny little mouth.

The day was bright and warm and the late morning sun streamed through the trees, which were just now showing signs of turning color. It was a beautiful day and she thought about taking a walk, but thought again and remained in her chair. She had nothing to put on for such a walk and she couldn't remember where her nice clothes were, nor her sneakers.

Dorothy found a box of crackers while rummaging through the kitchen and she ate them slowly, one at a time, letting the salt and grain melt in her mouth slowly before finally swallowing. It all seemed so perfect now, watching the little creatures, savoring something simple in the light of a beautiful morning.

She saw a periwinkle-colored car pull up the driveway and Dorothy sat more upright in her chair, adjusting her glasses. The car stopped and a young, pretty woman stepped out and Dorothy hoped beyond hope that she was here to see Vernon, that maybe he had found himself a new girlfriend and could begin his life all over again. She loved the poor boy and she hoped that one day he would find someone to love him in the way every young man needs.

She watched as the girl walked to the front door. She heard the doorbell ring and then knocking.

She heard the girl's voice. It sounded so serious.

"Mr. Trimble? Vernon? Are you home? Mrs. Trimble, are you there?"

Vernon could sleep through a hurricane, she thought, and this young woman sounded so insistent, so serious.

The knocking came harder now, more doorbell ringing.

Dorothy Trimble thought she should get up and answer the door, but then something caught her eye: a bushy tail twitched in the trees above and one big, fat squirrel chased another through the branches. They jumped from branch to branch and then onto a completely different tree.

She watched them run and scurry and flirt and twitch.

It was like they were flying.

The doorbell rang again. The girl was on her cell phone now. She could wait. The young had all the time in the world and yet were always in such a rush. They would learn eventually. Besides, Dorothy wanted to see what these fascinating, wonderful little creatures did next.

EPILOGUE

I warned Brett about John Ballard. We would lie in bed together some mornings and I would show him the increasingly erratic and nonsensical emails, sometimes dozens, Ballard had sent to me over the course of his sleepless nights and I would tell Brett, "This guy is going to explode at some point. I think he's getting dangerous." But Brett, oddly enough, was sympathetic to the big lug. He recounted the way John cried the night Brett arrested him, the way Ballard told him, "My wife is going to leave me over this," when Brett was booking him. Ballard was totally beaten that night, head hung low, big shoulders stooped, his mouth working nonstop saying, "This is the end. This is the end of everything. What am I going to do?"

"Sometimes, you can't help but feel sorry for people," Brett told me. "He made a mistake and now he's gonna pay more at home than he will in the court. He's not a bad guy, I don't think."

"He's losing it," I said. "He's going down a dark road."

"He's just lashing out. Not the brightest bulb in the pack," he said.

When my news station's police banner exploded with calls of shots fired on Ridgewood Drive, I knew almost immediately what had happened. I knew Brett was on shift that day; I knew he was the on-duty resident trooper that day in that tiny town which has now become the focal point of countless news articles, think pieces and public broadcasts. In that moment, I did the best I could to block out whatever morbid thoughts and worries I had to jump into the news van and race down there to cover the story. The police had blocked off the entrances in and out of the neighborhood and no matter who I pleaded with, who I called from the state troopers, no one could give me a straight answer if Brett was okay. I just got the official non-answer of, "This is a developing active shooter situation, we don't have any additional information at this time." So, I continued on, buried my fears and worries.

I tried not to cry on camera, but I teared up anyway during my coverage. Half a year later, they gave me an award for my on-the-ground coverage.

The official story: John Ballard, thirty-eight years old, had caught his wife and her lover in their home and killed them both in a crime of passion. He then opened fire on police responding to calls of gunshots, murdered two neighbors who were witnesses to the shooting and then began a rampage, shooting at nearly everything and everyone in his small, quiet hamlet while his two children sat in a running vehicle inside a closed garage. The children were found dead of carbon monoxide inhalation after officers finally shot and killed Ballard and broke through the front door to find Jessica Ballard, her boyfriend Lawrence Peterson, and State Trooper Brett Badgely dead of gunshot wounds inside. The death of the children was particularly tragic, as it appeared Ballard had planned to escape with them.

That was the biggest headline grabber, naturally. Mass shootings always get the big headlines, the clicks, the shares, the sociopolitical think pieces. But, my God, when everything else that happened on that block began to emerge from the rubble – no one had ever seen anything like it before.

From time to time, in small towns across America, there will be occasions of violent outbursts that suddenly drive the murder rate in one of those idyllic, small white towns sky high, the kinds of towns featured constantly on true crime shows that supply suburbanites with both fear that their lives are at imminent risk and the satisfaction of knowing the authorities are on the case with the tools to find and put away these psychopaths. Generally, those outbursts of violent crime in these small, forgotten places are the work of a lone serial killer or a mass shooter, but in all my research for my upcoming *New Yorker* feature, I couldn't find a comparable example to what happened on Ridgewood Drive that day. This was different; there seemed to be something else at work – there were too many coincidences, too many moving parts, too many intersecting individual paths of violence to just chalk it up to chance.

That night, after John Ballard had been stopped and his home raided with the concomitant horror, officers found Amber Locke, who lived just up the street, in her basement babbling incoherently with the bodies of her eldest son and husband, both of whom she had poisoned with incomprehensible amounts of antifreeze and rat poison. She even poisoned the dogs, which social media users found even more unforgivable than the fact that she'd killed her son and husband shortly after attending the funeral of her youngest son. Her attorneys are trying to raise the argument of temporary insanity, but prosecutors aren't buying it. She was investigated heavily for the death of Thomas as well, but all the evidence in that case led back to Lucas Lovett, the troubled, runaway teen who neighbors all believed had set fire to an abandoned house, the spark that started this entire, cascading series of events.

Just a couple houses away from Amber Locke, down Beechwood Avenue, authorities were alerted by a visiting nurse that she couldn't make contact with Vernon Trimble, nor his mother, who was stricken with Alzheimer's. In fact, no one had heard from Vernon for days. Police were able to break through the door after repeated attempts to make contact and found Mrs. Trimble dirty and disheveled and covered in blood, sitting in her rocking chair at the window. They found Vernon stabbed to death in the living room. Mrs. Trimble had to be subdued by medical personnel and kept screaming about "the boy in the trees", after they had strapped her to a gurney and took her to the hospital for evaluation and medical care. I had interviewed Vernon outside Rep. Elizabeth Tutt's house as he sought to quell public perception that Elizabeth had called the cops on some Black kids from the city who were raising money for their football team. One of those kids, Antwone Diller, died in police custody after being tased and suffering an asthma attack that sent him into a rare cardiac event. That case is still ongoing.

I have to say, I feel especially bad about Elizabeth Tutt. Elizabeth was part of my beat. We knew each other well, to say the least. We had a good relationship in which I gave her generally good press coverage and she gave me access. The Fake News crews love to rant about this online, but that's just how the world works. How else am I supposed to get stories? Publish or perish isn't just for academics, it's worldwide now if you want to be somebody. But when Brett tipped me off about Antwone Diller's death and the rumors circulating the trooper barracks about who had called 911, I couldn't let it slide. It was too big, it was too worthy. Was it a hit piece? No. I reached out for comment, but no one, including Elizabeth, responded in time and my editor said we had to move before anyone scooped us. It was all business, but still, I feel bad about it. Diller's death wasn't her fault. She had called the police several times about someone harassing her, knocking at her door night after night only to disappear into the darkness. I'd have been scared, too. Talk to anyone on the street and they pointed the finger directly at Lucas Lovett.

The poor thing; Ballard had never liked her to begin with (most of the neighborhood didn't) and he had opened fire on her house as well. Fifteen shots had gone into her house and four more into her car as she escaped a veritable war zone. Later that night she plowed her car into a group of protesters who'd gathered just down the street from the Amherst Museum where Shondra Waite's Tree of Life exhibit had been lit on fire. Two protesters died, one is still recovering from a broken hip and leg. Elizabeth was killed when she was dragged out of her car and beaten by protesters who had just seen friends and family run down in the night. Manslaughter charges are still winding their way through court. I covered Elizabeth Tutt's funeral. Hardly anyone showed but her ex-husband. Frankly, I didn't feel I was the best person to cover this event, but the newsroom had experienced a mass exodus of reporters and it fell on me. Still, in hindsight I wish I could have apologized to her. She wasn't a bad person. She had managed to escape John Ballard's shooting spree only to get caught in the crossfire of something much bigger. Collateral damage doesn't care who or what you are.

It has taken so much time, so many tears and feelings of guilt and remorse, to get my head around all this and still sometimes I feel like I'm spinning. Everything comes so fast. I pitched the New Yorker so I could sort it all out in a public way. I told the editors my story, my involvement, my inside knowledge and they jumped on it, a way of holding up a mirror to the insanity working its way through American society, but, really, this piece is more for myself, a way for me to understand what happened, to reconcile my own involvement, to process my own grief at losing Brett, to exorcise the demons.

Hindsight is twenty-twenty, as they say, and in working my way backward from what happened to why it happened, I come to Lucas Lovett and the abandoned property on Ridgewood Drive that caught fire on August 3, the spark, as it were, to the eventual forest fire that burned so many.

Lucas Lovett's body was recovered from the Tree of Life exhibit that he set fire to outside the Amherst Museum. One of the glass panels in the interior of the exhibit fell on him and melted, essentially encasing his horribly burned body in melted glass. The coroner described it as "a nightmare", but added the boy was already dead when it happened. "Still, it was one of the worst autopsies I've had to perform," he said. Why Lucas chose the museum exhibit to target with his pyromania is anyone's guess. The boy was deeply disturbed, mentally unwell and harbored godlike delusions, likely a combination of his zealously religious upbringing and his growing mental illness. Lucas had been flagged by school administrators from a young age as being potentially harmful to others, and as he grew and matured his antisocial behavior became more pronounced: fights at school, selling marijuana, auditory hallucinations, delusions of grandeur and a fascination with the abandoned house across the street, where neighbors said he would occasionally sit on the roof and watch the neighborhood until his mother would scream at him to come down. His social media posts were plagued by strange, nonsensical ramblings and he had few friends, save for Vinnie Locke up the street.

John Ballard, for all his faults, was right about some things.

Lucas did set fire to that house from the inside. It wasn't fireworks. Before he died, Brett told me the fire marshal who was on the case, Ron Kleese, was two weeks from retirement and hadn't done a thorough inspection of the house owned by Charles Widner. Kleese was just trying to get through his last weeks before saying goodbye to it all and collecting his pension with as little trouble as possible. Following the shooting and press coverage, the Fire Department ordered a second review by the newly appointed fire marshal, who determined, in fact, the fire was an act of arson started inside the house.

Police had an easier time tracing the murder of little Thomas Locke to Lucas Lovett. Despite their investigation into Amber Locke's possible involvement, the kitchen knife recovered at the crime scene had Lucas's fingerprints on it and he'd taken it from the home of Nancy Willis, an elderly woman suffering from COPD who rarely left the house and required an oxygen tank to help her breathe. Nancy had been found dead in her home by Ballard, who immediately suspected Lucas's involvement. Police have yet to know what exactly caused her death, but I'll give that one to John Ballard, too.

Of course, no one believed Ballard at the time, myself included. He was an unstable drunk, prone to bouts of mania. Why would anyone believe him? According to neighbors (the Carter family has been instrumental in my understanding the dynamics of the neighborhood), his own wife thought he was losing his mind, a combination of alcohol, lack of sleep and conspiracy theories. His supervisor at work thought Ballard was becoming unstable and, based on the countless emails he sent me, I agree. But that doesn't mean he was wrong about everything. The fire marshal said the house fire was caused by kids playing with fireworks at the time, the police believed Nancy Willis died of natural causes; who was I to disagree and write about unfounded theories espoused by a guy who'd been banned from his daughter's dance class for staring at underage girls and muttering to himself?

Still, I can't help but feel guilty, in some way, for all of this. My therapist says it's a form of survivor's guilt, but I think it's worse than that. I try not to delude myself, to think that I could have prevented all this in some way, but at night after a couple glasses of wine as I lie in bed alone, missing Brett, I wonder if I had just listened, dug a little deeper, maybe Brett would still be here with me today.

I scrolled through the brief Neighborhood Watch Facebook page, documenting the posts, their calls for investigations, their comments that no one would protect them from these threats, both real and imagined. Calls for arms, for lookouts, for security camera footage; alerts to say something when you saw something. The Neighborhood Watch page started just after the Thomas Locke killing and was absolutely paranoid. Maybe justifiably so. But when the head of it was none other than John Ballard himself, you can't understate the irony.

Shamelessly, I tried to interview the Lovetts outside their son's funeral. Naturally, they declined, but it was necessary to try. That may have been shitty journalistic practice, but I was angry. They have since disappeared, moved to another part of the country. I finally secured an interview with Meghan Brooke, Elizabeth Tutt's former campaign manager, who resigned right after I called her about the Antwone Diller case. Meghan is now a staffer for another Democratic representative, but she confirmed that Elizabeth was being harassed with late-night knockings at her door. "She was scared," Meghan told me. "But still, after that news broke, I knew there was nothing I could do for her; and frankly, at that point in politics, it's every man and woman for themselves. You jump ship so you don't go down with it."

I spoke with the nurse tending to Dorothy Trimble. She said that Vernon had increasing difficulty keeping his mother safe from herself, and had even taken to tying her down in her bed to prevent her from wandering the house on her injured feet. Vernon had insisted on taking care of her, worried that sending his mother to a nursing home would suck up any money and home he had. "People get put into impossible positions sometimes," she said. "Unfortunately, that's the state of healthcare in this country. He wanted to keep trying, and it ended badly."

I even managed to talk with Dorothy Trimble. She spoke as if Vernon were still alive. She waited for him to visit while she sat near the window of the nursing home watching squirrels run up and down the trees outside. She spoke briefly of the boy who visited her in the night, the boy in the trees, she called him. I showed her a picture of Lucas Lovett and she said, "Oh, that's him! Isn't he lovely! Where is he?"

I told her I didn't know.

But I did try to find out who Lucas Lovett was. I was able to view a copy of his birth certificate, which listed his mother as Tonya Seaver and the father as one Charles Widner, owner of the house Lucas had burned.

The Carters and the Atkinses were the only people I could find who had ever interacted with Charles when he lived on Ridgewood and they both described him as a drug-addled eccentric who would warn people away from his property by saying it was laced with booby traps and had a brief and intense relationship with Tonya. Tonya, herself, went down a difficult road in her relationship with Charles, eventually culminating in an arrest for possession of heroin and psychedelic drugs, for which she received a slap on the wrist and mandated inpatient substance abuse therapy. Based on the dates of her court case and Lucas's birth certificate, she was pregnant with Lucas while in rehab.

I found Charles Widner. He lived about an hour away and I reached him by phone. It took a while but after repeated calls he finally agreed to an interview. I can't attest to his state of mind when he agreed.

Indeed, he didn't remember speaking to me after I showed up at his door, having traveled an hour across state, getting lost on some back roads and eventually winding my little car down a dirt road between two mountains that bathed everything in permanent shadow. Charles Widner's home wasn't much different from the house he'd left abandoned on Ridgewood Drive: tall, uncut weeds in the front, the forest closing in on him; the house itself appeared in a state of near collapse, and maybe that was next for Charles. He was gaunt with starvation, his skin an unhealthy gray and mottled with track marks, a wild look in his eye when he ripped the door open wearing nothing but dirty boxer shorts and stained undershirt. He screamed at me, demanding to know who I was and why I was there, and I nearly ran away but I felt frozen. I stuttered that I was a reporter, we had spoken on the phone a few days ago and he'd invited me out to speak with him about his house on Ridgewood Drive and his son, Lucas.

"I have no son!" he yelled. "She never said it was mine!"

"I just want to find out about your life, Mr. Widner," I told him.

"You're not from social services?"

"No," I said.

"Do you have any money?"

"I don't," I said.

He turned and walked back into the darkness of his house but left the door open so I quietly, gingerly stepped inside. The smell was overpowering at first, a combination of mold, rot and, somewhere, spoiled meat. The floors seemed to crawl; black flies the size of hummingbirds bounced off the ceiling with an audible tick and the patterned wallpaper seemed to shift and change. There was an illusion of movement all throughout this place, like the vibration of living cells beneath a powerful microscope. I immediately felt disoriented, dizzy, even high. There was little light, a gray, shadowed pallor hung in the air. Hypodermic needles, half-smoked joints and cheap beer cans littered the tables. He lay on the couch like a forgotten god and I was afraid to sit on the old cushioned chair across from him, worried I would be jabbed in the ass by a forgotten needle, but I sat anyway.

Charles lit a joint and offered it to me, but I declined. I took out my digital recorder and asked if I could record our conversation and he waved it off as if he didn't care, holding his breath until he exhaled a contrail of blue smoke into the room.

"I remember you now," he said with a graveled voice, hoarse with dry throat. "Sometimes, it seems like every new day is the beginning of life all over again, one without history. So I forget sometimes, ya know."

"That's okay, everybody is busy," I said, although I doubted he was busy with much. "But it was the history of your house I wanted to talk to you about."

"I told them to stay away from that place. I told them all it was haunted, but they didn't listen. They just wanted me to tear it down or fix it up and sell it. Guess there's no use talking about it now that it's burned down."

"Haunted by what?" I asked.

"By the same thing that haunts anyone or anywhere, the past. You can't see it, it doesn't actually exist because it's gone, but there it is, guiding us through the present, weighing on us, brutalizing us with its burden. What is a ghost, but something from the past, am I right?"

"I suppose you are."

"Nothing to suppose in all this. That house was a repository of the past. We all have things in our history best left alone."

"So maybe the house held some bad memories, shall we say, for you, but why didn't you sell it to let some other family possibly make some good memories there?"

"Nah...wouldn't work. You sully something enough, you invite enough darkness into a place and you're not just going to be able to whitewash over it. I've had my history. I've had my troubled times, as I'm sure you can tell. I don't deny it. I embrace it. It's everyone else who wants to deny it and pretend it's not there. I got into some things when I was living there and they were things best left in the confines of those walls."

"Why not tear it down then?"

"Everyone needs a reminder. Every neighborhood needs a haunted house. There always needs to be a place they can point to and say, that is a problem, that place is not okay. A place for kids to wonder about at night and dare each other to walk past alone. Every place needs a little ugliness. People need to be reminded of the burden of the past, even if they hate it."

"So what was so terrible about that place? What history was it – to use your words – haunted by, then? What in your past would make the place so unbearable?"

Charles took another long draw from his joint and sat forward on the ratty sofa and he looked at me with gray eyes that, perhaps, used to be blue.

"I communed with the ugliness in that place. I invited it in. The way a library has books, I brought in everything I could to it, all those dark corners of history – slavery, Nazism, Manson, Helter Skelter, the Illuminati, the occult – I brought it all in there and communed with it. I altered my mind so I could feel it, understand it, embrace it. And then my consciousness sunk into the walls, sunk into the floorboards, the very foundation of that house was soaked with it. And then I could feel it all watching me. I could feel it every day, the eyes of the past, the eyes of fear and resentment and atrocity and sacrifice and death. It all lived there with me. I painted the walls with eyes and the eyes would blink. I would see them blink, and then I would turn to face it and it was just as it was before. It was a living, breathing, watchful thing. And it watched me. After a time, it began to speak to me. And the voice became so overwhelming that I finally one day, up and left. I couldn't take it anymore. It was enough to drive you mad."

He smiled when he said that. He was raving.

"And so rather than just tear it down, you let it sit and fester?"

"I told them to stay away. They just thought I was crazy. They didn't listen. Look where it got them."

"You think the house, or whatever it was haunted with, somehow contributed to what happened in that neighborhood?"

"Clearly, I'm not the only one who thinks so," he said.

"What makes you say that?"

"Well, you're here, aren't you? You're here asking about the house for this big story you're working on, right?"

"Well, I don't necessarily subscribe to the idea that—"

"But you're here! You're here asking me why I abandoned the house, why I wouldn't sell it off or tear it down. You're here to understand what happened and clearly you think that house was a part of it. You want something that ties it all together. You want a reason."

"The house burning down was certainly a catalyst for some of what happened. I can attest to that," I said. "But certainly it didn't have anything to do with some of the other tragedies that occurred."

"Are you sure about that?" he said. "Fear, loathing, paranoia, the feeling that you're being watched, hunted. It can drive people to do things. It can drive them to insanity."

"Let's talk about what it drove Lucas Lovett to do—"

"I'm telling you, he's not my son. I hold no responsibility for whatever he did."

"He was strangely drawn to your house. He burned it down and then killed a little boy in the ashes. How do you feel about that?"

"Unsurprised," he said.

"Why?"

"I told you, the house could speak. It was filled with the insanity of the past. If that boy was drawn to it, maybe he heard that voice speaking to him, urging him to do things."

I could see this conversation was getting me nowhere in terms of answers, although I knew from the outset of this project that there would be no real answer. For something like this, there never can be. I looked at my digital recorder as it ticked away the minutes and seconds. My visit to Charles Widner would certainly cast some color on the piece. Perhaps his fascination with the occult and Nazism and Charles Manson and the Helter Skelter race war would serve as background, to portray what happened in this small, quiet neighborhood through a frame of American political upheaval, populism, paranoia and race-consciousness. Maybe it all kind of fit together in that way. There had already been several think pieces about Elizabeth Tutt's tragically ironic demise. There were so many ways to paint each individual story: the paranoid, alcoholic, jilted husband; the beleaguered housewife; the go-nowhere son beset by financial worries tied to medical costs; a disturbed teenager failed by our mental health system. It was all right there in each story. Individually, you understood, but taken all together, the story became inexplicable, a mystery to be pondered. I was trying to connect dots and form a picture, but more and more it seemed a picture drawn by the likes of Charles Widner.

I looked up for a moment and he was eyeing me and I suddenly felt more uncomfortable. It wasn't his place or what he was saying necessarily, but it was the way he looked at me in that moment. Something suddenly coursed throughout my body, a fight-or-flight response.

"I should probably be going," I said. "I've taken enough of your time."

"You're trying to make sense of it," he said. "I get it. But you'll never be able to understand it. I could help you understand it, if you're willing."

"I don't know, Mr. Widner. I do have to be going...."

"It'll only take a moment. I told you, that house was a repository of the past, of the insanity of the past. Things we can never really escape, that haunt us to this very day. If you understand that, you understand the whole thing and then you can write your article and know what you are talking about."

"But the house is gone, now," I said. "And everything with it. That repository is burned to the ground."

"Nothing is ever really gone," he said. "I can still hear the voices at times. You can, too."

"Not to my knowledge," I said.

"Log on to your computer sometime and think about it. Eyes watching all over the world, documenting everything, uploading it to this new dimension where we, in turn, become the watching eyes. Disembodied voices lamenting history, gnashing their teeth with rage, fighting over the past. Ghosts in the machine, watching us, haunting us with their rage."

"It's just the internet," I said.

"And yet it's guiding all the world at the moment," he said.

"Fair enough," I said. "So you say you can help me understand? Because, frankly, I understand what you're saying about the past. Maybe I don't believe there's some kind of supernatural element to it, but I understand it on a metaphorical level."

"Metaphorical level. You're stuck up here," he said, pointing to his head. "You're trying to think through something you can't think through. It's too big. It's too mean. It isn't about logic. You have to feel it for yourself."

"I'd rather not," I said. "I should really go."

"Suit yourself. I think if I showed you, you would understand, though."

"What could you possibly show me? A life-sized rendering of Charles Manson? A swastika? Sorry, I've seen it all before."

"You're thinking too small," he said. "You're still stuck in your head."

"Where is this thing you want to show me?"

"Just upstairs," he said.

I looked at the staircase, broken and crooked. It disappeared into the ceiling, a darkness above. I looked at it and then I looked at Charles Widner and sized him up. He had a few screws loose, for sure. He was bigger than me, naturally, but was he dangerous? I wasn't sure. He was old and in poor shape. He was high on marijuana and God knows what else. In my pocketbook was a small can of mace. I took my digital recorder and put it in my purse, transferred the mace to my hand and then moved it to my jacket pocket.

I smiled. "Fine," I said. "I'll take a look but then I'm leaving. My boss is expecting me at a meeting shortly and it will be Hell to pay if I'm not there."

"We all have Hell to pay eventually," he said. He stood up and wavered toward the staircase. It creaked with each step he took. I followed in his steps, the smell of him wafting back onto me, choking me. I would shower when I got home.

The ceiling of the second floor was low, very low. He practically had to duck his head and it was clear that this house had never been meant for two floors, the second having been squeezed in by an overzealous carpenter. It was dark, but he pulled the chain on a single lightbulb and turned left down a short hallway toward a room with a closed door.

I hesitated and he turned to look at me. "You want to understand that old house? You want to understand what drew Lucas to it? You want to understand what happened to all those nice people? Why they went crazy and killed each other off?"

He stepped aside and held his arm toward the door, ushering me forward. It was stupid, but then, this was what could really make my article; this could be the part that no one knew about, the insanity of a single man that had somehow been loosed upon a neighborhood. The cornerstone of what I was building professionally, personally.

Maybe it could help me understand what happened to Brett; why I kissed him goodbye that morning and never saw him alive again. I had to try to understand. I owed him that much.

I stepped forward and turned the handle and walked into the room. It was tiny and completely empty, with a lone window streaming sunlight through the dust, and in front of the window a small desk with a lone laptop computer sitting in the middle of it. On the screen were faces, men and women, and I could see that they were talking incessantly, waving their hands in unheard expressions, but there was no sound, just their faces twisted with rage.

And the walls....

The walls were covered in eyes, painted in deep, dark red. I stood for a moment in that place and I heard a voice whispering behind me.

I turned and said, "What was that?" but Charles wasn't there. The doorway and the hall beyond it were empty. I turned back around and, for a moment, I could have sworn one of the eyes blinked.

"Is this it?" I called out to him.

And then, he was in the room behind me. I turned around, startled. He was so close to me. A metal blade in his hand caught the sunlight from the window and flashed across my eyes.

"No," he said. "This is only the beginning."

I fumbled in my pocket for the mace, but there was already something inside me, and I could feel it moving about. Charles Widner held me there in that room full of eyes in an embrace as I finally felt everything let go, and it felt strange, so very strange.

He whispered in my ear and all around me, the eyes blinked in and out of existence.

"There is so much to see from here," he said. "We are God now."